Praise for the novels of *New York Times*
bestselling author Stephen Frey

THE INNER SANCTUM

"Bank executive Frey knows finance . . . [a] convincing portrayal of the lure of easy money." —*Publishers Weekly*

"A fast-paced financial thriller . . . entertaining."
—*Library Journal*

"The key word for this novel is thriller . . . if you go along for the ride, you can certainly enjoy." —*Mystery News*

". . . Frey ventures into the world of government and politics, with murder, betrayal, and romance to spice the brew."
—*Florida Times-Union*

THE VULTURE FUND

"A fast-paced thriller—action, adventure, romance, even a little morality tale." —*Newark Star-Ledger*

"A gripping thriller . . . secretive velvet-gloved villainy . . . unstoppable excitement." —*Richmond Times Dispatch*

"Stakes so high, no one can be trusted." —*Poisoned Pen*

"A Wall Street and Washington shocker from the author of
The Takeover." —*Kirkus Reviews*

"Frey, dubbed the Grisham of financial thrillers, follows his
Takeover debut with another hot story." —*Daily Variety*

"The action gets hotter and hotter and finishes with a stunning conclusion . . . mesmerizes readers." —*Booklist*

continued on next page . . .

THE TAKEOVER

"Gets your blood racing . . . fast-paced and convincing."
—*Chicago Tribune*

"Captivating . . . thrilling conspiracy and intrigue."
—*New York Daily News*

"Better than *The Firm* . . . resembles Robert Ludlum when Ludlum was fresh and young . . . a grand first novel."
—*St. Petersburg Times*

"Offers insiders' knowledge of the high-stakes world of investment banking." —*Wall Street Journal*

"Entertaining and energetic . . . superbly taut. . . . Frey keeps up the suspense right to the end."—*Financial Times*

"Fast action . . . the author's worst-case scenario of scary political ramifications could easily become tomorrow's news." —*Pittsburgh Post-Gazette*

"Enormous wealth, murder, dirty tricks, political intrigue, colorful villains, relentless pacing . . . enjoy!"
—*Publishers Weekly*

"Money, sex, secrecy, conspiracy, killings . . . exciting."
—*Mystery News*

"Grishamesque skullduggery and intrigue."
—*Library Journal*

THE LEGACY

STEPHEN FREY

AN ONYX BOOK

ONYX
Published by New American Library, a division of
Penguin Putnam Inc., 375 Hudson Street,
New York, New York 10014, U.S.A.
Penguin Books Ltd, 27 Wrights Lane,
London W8 5TZ, England
Penguin Books Australia Ltd, Ringwood,
Victoria, Australia
Penguin Books Canada Ltd, 10 Alcorn Avenue,
Toronto, Ontario, Canada M4V 3B2
Penguin Books (N.Z.) Ltd, 182–190 Wairau Road,
Auckland 10, New Zealand

Penguin Books Ltd, Registered Offices:
Harmondsworth, Middlesex, England

Published by Onyx, an imprint of New American Library,
a division of Penguin Putnam Inc.
Previously published in a Dutton hardcover edition.

First Onyx Printing, June 1999
10 9 8 7 6 5 4 3 2 1

  REGISTERED TRADEMARK—MARCA REGISTRADA

Printed in the United States of America

PUBLISHER'S NOTE
This is a work of fiction. Names, characters, places, and incidents either are
the product of the author's imagination or are used fictitiously, and any resemblance to actual persons, living or dead, events, or locales is entirely
coincidental.

For Stephen Fertig, Eugenia Stalfort
and Joan McDonald.
Never forgotten

ACKNOWLEDGMENTS

Lil, Christy and Ashley.

Cynthia Manson, Stephen and Julie Watson, Michael Pocalyko, Dr. Teo Dagi, Walter Frey III, Chris and Christine Tesoriero, Barbara Fertig, Lori Lipsky, Kimberly Perdue, Barbara Hall, Judy Hansen, Gordon Eadon, Lee Thompson, Jeff Faville, Arthur Manson, Kevin and Nancy Erdman, Jim and Anmarie Galowski, Brooke McDonald, Betty Saif, Jim McPartlan, Gerry Barton, Pat and Terry Lynch, Mike Lynch, Dr. Tom Lynch, Nita Mathur and Dileep Bhattacharya, Bob Geist, Mark Randles, Robert Wieczorek, Jr., John Paul Garber, Rachel Simon, Jim O'Connor, Brian LaLonde and David Tashjian.

PROLOGUE

November 1963

HER REAL NAME WAS MARY THOMAS, WHICH SHE KNEW wasn't a tag likely to attract the eye of a fast-track Hollywood producer with time in his day for only a cursory scan of a casting sheet. So now she went by Andrea Sage.

A Manhattan native, Andrea had fled the city after completing her studies at N.Y.U., intent upon escaping a tyrannical father obsessed with the idea of her following his footsteps onto Wall Street. She had no desire to commit herself to a lifetime of dealing stocks and bonds. So, the morning after graduation, she slipped out of her parents' Upper East Side penthouse, emptied the trust account her grandparents had set up for her on her tenth birthday, caught a taxi to La Guardia Airport and flew to Los Angeles in search of stardom on the silver screen. Andrea was young and beautiful and, at the tender age of twenty-one, ready to conquer the world.

Six months had elapsed since her freedom ride to the West Coast aboard the Pan Am jet, and things hadn't progressed as quickly as she had anticipated. Her beauty had landed her a few bit parts in low-budget films. However, the roles were nothing to write home about—and she still hadn't. Her mother had no idea where her only child had gone, and Andrea was beginning to feel guilty about not at least calling to say she was safe.

An unusually cool and rainy autumn had transformed Los Angeles from a sunny sanctuary into a depressing land of exile. So on a whim, to try to forget about the looming inevitability of crawling back to Manhattan to face her triumphant father, Andrea took a few days off from her waitressing job at the Beverly Hills Bistro and bought a plane ticket to Texas. She wanted a respite from her cramped studio apartment overlooking the back of a Chinese restaurant, a chance to explore another area of the country—and to see this man who had so captivated the public.

Andrea squinted through the lens of the Bell & Howell movie camera she had purchased the day before, practicing with it before the event began. She stood near a small tree, a few feet from a reflecting pool's retaining wall, and aimed to her right, where a crowd was milling about in front of a tall building on the other side of the intersection. Then she panned left and followed the pavement as it snaked away toward the triple underpass at the far end of the plaza. This would be the motorcade's route.

As she gazed at the underpass, Andrea heard a buzz ripple through the onlookers. She glanced back to her right and saw flashes of the motorcade approaching. Once more she aimed up Elm Street at the people standing in front of the building across the intersection. This time the movie camera shook slightly. She took a deep breath to calm an inexplicable uneasiness, then began filming as the sleek black open-top limousine made a slow sweeping turn to the left off Houston Street and cruised into her field of vision. She focused on the man in the back of the vehicle, marveling at his overpowering charisma, obvious even through the lens. As the limousine coasted past her, she began to move alongside it, able to shoot the man almost in close-up as he waved to the crowd. For some reason the Secret Service had been lax about security along the route that day.

Moments later Andrea heard a loud pop—like a firecracker exploding somewhere in the plaza—followed quickly by a second one. With the second pop, the man in the back of the limousine hunched forward, his elbows up and out, his hands to his neck. Still filming, Andrea continued to half walk, half run along Elm Street. She was vaguely aware of moving past a little girl wearing a red skirt and white sweater who had run past her only moments before. She also sensed a sudden panic in the crowd, as the understanding that something terrible was happening began to sink in. At the sound of the third shot, people began to take cover, and Andrea stopped moving.

Then the fourth shot came. More of a blast this time, it was definitely louder and closer. Instantly the man's head snapped back toward Andrea and a fine red mist sprayed the air, forming a crimson halo around him. The man's body slumped to the left, his brain exposed and bloody.

At once people were screaming and running in all directions, but Andrea wasn't sucked into the flood of panic. She calmly kept filming, detached from the horrible events rapidly unfolding around her, as if the lens somehow protected her. As Andrea watched, the man's wife climbed out onto the limousine's trunk and reached for a piece of her husband's head that had been torn away by the killing shot, but she was quickly pushed back into her seat by a Secret Service agent and the vehicle sped away toward Parkland Hospital. Andrea followed the limousine until it was gone, then refocused on the spot where it had been at the moment the red mist sprayed the air. Behind that spot, people were sprinting toward a grassy area and a fence beyond.

Suddenly everything went dark. Andrea panned up, and for a moment the entire lens was consumed by an angry face. Then two large hands tore the camera from her grasp and pushed her to the ground roughly.

A sharp pain shot up her back. "You have no right to treat me that way!" she screamed.

"I have every right," the man snarled. "Now get out of here."

"Give me my camera!" she insisted.

"I said, get out of here!"

Andrea jumped to her feet and made a grab for the camera, but the man easily repelled her with a thick forearm to the chest, and she tumbled to the ground once more.

"I'll give you one last chance," he said through clenched teeth. "Leave or I'll arrest you."

One look directly into the man's steely gray eyes and Andrea's confident sense of surreal detachment evaporated, replaced by the get-the-hell-out-of-here sensation that she had stumbled upon a hornet's nest. She realized it would be pointless to protest any longer, so she turned and scrambled over the grass on her hands and knees, then staggered to her feet and sprinted wildly away through the chaos. When she finally dared to look back over her shoulder, the man who had brutally confiscated her movie camera and the film of President Kennedy's assassination was gone.

1

TRADING FLOORS AT NEW YORK CITY'S LARGEST AND most powerful brokerage houses can be intimidating places. The cavernous rooms are often raucous, typically devoid of warm and nurturing decor, and always staffed by aggressive, impatient opportunists buying and selling massive amounts of stocks and bonds and other financial securities with house money. These opportunists sit side by side at long narrow desks resembling lunch counters. In front of them are the two primary tools of their business—phone banks and computer screens constantly relaying market information. Traders base their split-second investment decisions on this information, as well as on the tips they receive over their many phone lines. Sometimes they remain within their capital limits—predetermined, management-imposed dollar amounts they may commit to transactions—and sometimes they don't. Caffeine is a trader's only dependable ally, while ulcers and the fortieth birthday are mortal enemies. On these floors tempers flare regularly, physical confrontations occur more often than most would admit, stress is constant, and privacy is nonexistent. It is a god-awful career, except for one thing. Traders can make more money in a year than many people can in a lifetime.

Cole Egan scrutinized his three computer screens for any hint of what was going on at the Federal Reserve's Open Market Committee meeting in Washington, but the markets were dead calm. That would change in a heartbeat and all hell would break loose if the Fed officials suddenly exited the meeting and made what—up until yesterday—Cole had considered an unexpected announcement. An announcement that could send his huge government securities portfolio plummeting into a death spiral.

Every six to eight weeks, the chairman and district governors of the world's most powerful central bank convened behind the tightly shut doors of an ornate Washington conference room to determine the general course of interest rates in the United States. At the conclusion of most meetings the Fed took no action, and interest rates continued to fluctuate with supply and demand as traders bought and sold bonds and money-market instruments for their clients and firms. But if the Fed announced new targets, interest rates spiked or fell to those levels almost instantly. The Fed was that powerful.

In front of Cole lay two keyboards. With them he could access Reuters, Bloomberg and the Internet—all the real-time information services a nineties trader required. But nothing in those databases could give him what he really needed right now, which was a listening device planted inside the Federal Reserve conference room. As far as he knew, no one had that.

Cole gazed out the window at the skyscraper across Fifth Avenue. He didn't allow others to see it, but the waiting was killing him. Yesterday, lower-level Fed officials had sent subtle signals to the market that the committee might raise interest rates to head off a sudden spurt of inflation. For the last month Cole had been betting that the Fed wouldn't raise interest rates at this meeting and had structured his portfolio accordingly. If the Fed raised rates even slightly, his portfolio could lose millions of dollars in seconds, because he would be stuck holding securities earning a rate of return that was less than what the market was offering. And there was no chance to get out at this point, because the market had already moved against him in anticipation of the Fed announcement. If he sold now, he'd be selling at a huge loss.

Cole took a deep breath. If the announcement he was dreading came and his portfolio tanked badly, senior executives sitting in plush offices on the top floor of Gilchrist's world headquarters building would hit the roof—right before they sprinted down to the trading floor to rip his heart out. There would be no compassion from them, only punishment. Cole shut his eyes tightly. Even with the chaos constantly swirling around him, trading could be a lonely business.

Gilchrist & Company was a powerful brokerage house, rivaling such preeminent firms as Goldman Sachs, Morgan Stanley and Merrill Lynch in its ability to raise capital for corporations and governments around the world. It also rivaled those firms in its ability to trade stocks and bonds for its own account and earn billions of dollars each year in profits. To ensure its proprietary trading success, Gilchrist hired only the best and brightest individuals, constantly snatching top-performing people away from other Wall Street firms or cherry-picking the cream of the crop from the nation's most revered business schools.

Compensation packages for those lucky few were lucrative—millions each year if you were successful—but there was a catch. You had to consistently make money for the firm, and lots of it. One losing year was tolerable—barely. Two in a row and you consumed your morning coffee and bagel at the unemployment office.

During his first few years on Gilchrist's trading floor, Cole had enjoyed reasonable success buying and selling government securities with the firm's capital. He had hit no home runs during that time, but he had smacked plenty of singles and doubles—trading floors are rife with sports analogies—and as a result, he'd been paid solid, though not earth-shattering, year-end bonuses. Cole's January bonus checks were made out for several hundred thousand dollars. Not close to the tens of millions the home run hitters earned, but he was happy nonetheless. After all, six-figure checks were nothing to sneeze at. Particularly for a guy from the blue-collar side of a small upper Midwest town on a lake.

Unfortunately, Cole's performance had taken a turn for the worse. Last year he hadn't been able to buy a hit, and he had lost twenty million dollars of the firm's money. Now he was approaching the end of an even worse year. He was on the bubble, and everyone on the trading floor knew it.

"How you doing there, sport?" Lewis Gebauer asked smugly, ogling a young woman in a short, tight skirt who was walking past them.

"Fine, Lewis," Cole replied curtly, glancing quickly at Gebauer and then back at the computer screens.

Gebauer was grossly overweight and almost bald, with pallid skin that hadn't seen the sun in years; and he sported ties and shirts permanently stained by the fat-laden foods he consumed in huge quantities. Despite his offensive physical appearance, he had deluded himself into believing that he was quite a ladies' man, and he kept a close eye on any woman who visited the trading floor. He was insufferably obnoxious and universally disliked, but he traded government bonds with startling success. In the last five years he had earned more than three hundred million dollars for Gilchrist & Company, buying and selling the U.S. government's thirty-year debt obligation. As thanks for his performance and to make certain he wasn't lured away by a competitor, Gilchrist senior executives had bonused him sixty of those three hundred million. Gebauer lived in an opulent stone mansion in Connecticut with his third wife, a twenty-six-year-old platinum blonde he'd met at a bar in Manhattan and married two days later.

"I'm doing fine, Lewis," Cole repeated.

"Really?" Gebauer gummed an unlit Cuban cigar from a box he had smuggled into New York through Kennedy Airport after a trip to Paris. "That's not what I hear." Gebauer enjoyed kicking people when they were down. It was entertainment for him, it made the day go faster.

Cole had been forced to sit next to Gebauer since his first day on the trading floor, and he had grown to detest the man just as everyone else did. Now he recognized that Gebauer was bored with the afternoon lull and was simply trying to start an argument in order to make the time pass more quickly. In these situations it was sometimes effective to launch a preemptive strike. "I'm surprised you can hear anything, with all of that protein sprouting from your ears."

Two traders on the other side of the desk snickered

loudly at the ear-hair crack. Cole was fast with a comeback, not someone you dueled with carelessly.

"I hear you've got a big fat mortgage on that Upper West Side penthouse condominium you bought two years ago," Gebauer sneered, adding specifics to his verbal attack. He had no intention of backing down. "And I hear you haven't gotten a bonus since George Bush was president," he exaggerated. "Thanks to that, you're way behind on your Mount Everest-size mortgage." Gebauer's pulse quickened as he recounted the information recently conveyed to him by the man with an ugly scar cutting through his left cheek.

Cole tried hard to focus on the computer screens and ignore Gebauer, but the numbers in front of him blurred as the question raced through his mind. How the hell did Gebauer know about the bonus and the mortgage? Only Gilchrist's top executives knew he'd been shut out of the bonus pool last year, and he hadn't told anyone on the trading floor he even owned an apartment, much less a penthouse with a huge mortgage. He stole another glance at Gebauer. Several times over the last few days, papers on Cole's desk seemed to have been rearranged when he returned to the trading floor after procuring one of the six Diet Cokes he drank daily. Surely, he realized, Gebauer must be responsible.

"Young blood with the sabre tongue isn't talking much now," Gebauer crowed.

One of the traders on the other side of the desk stood up and stretched casually, using the opportunity to glance over the computer monitors and phone banks at Cole to judge for himself whether Gebauer's mortgage missile was on target—trading floors thrive on gossip—but there was no way to tell for certain. Cole's face remained impassive.

"And I hear your honey has the same problem I do, lover boy," Gebauer continued, full of confidence now that Cole had gone silent. "I hear she likes girls, if you get my drift," he said, smiling lewdly.

Cole's right hand slowly contracted into a fist. He could send Gebauer into next week with one right to the jaw and probably earn a standing ovation from everyone on the floor. He swiveled in his seat, as if to take a swing, just as one of his ten phone lines began blinking. He stared at the blinking light for a few moments before finally unclasping his hand. Forget Gebauer, he told himself. The guy isn't worth it.

Cole punched the blinking line instead of Gebauer and grabbed the receiver. "Hello."

"Who is this?" The voice was cold.

"Cole Egan," he answered, forcing himself to be cordial. Gilchrist senior executives sometimes buzzed the trading floor just to see how quickly calls were being answered.

"What is your middle name, Mr. Egan?"

Cole was instantly annoyed. "Who the hell wants to know?" In the background he heard someone shout a warning about an imminent announcement by the Federal Reserve and pressed his palm over the ear not covered by the phone to drown out the growing din. "Who are you?"

"Tell me your middle name," the voice insisted.

The noise level on the floor rose to a dull roar as a senior Fed official appeared on the many television monitors positioned around the Gilchrist trading floor. Cole hesitated, torn between the chaos erupting around him and something in the voice at the other end of the line.

"Your middle name," the voice demanded.

"Sage," Cole snapped, impatient to cut off the

caller. Like any good trader, he sensed a tempest bearing down on his portfolio and knew he should be directing his full attention to that right now, not the call. "What's it to you?"

"I'm an acquaintance of your father."

The Fed announcement burst like water through a cracking dam, and bedlam exploded as traders shouted orders simultaneously over multiple phones, desperately attempting to take advantage of, or protect themselves from, the interest rate increase suddenly imposed by the central bank. But Cole heard none of it. He had blocked out everything except the icy voice that spoke of his father.

"I have bad news for you," the voice continued. There was no sympathy in the tone. "Your father is dead."

The news hit Cole like an avalanche, but he gave no indication to the individual at the other end of the line. "I can't say I'm overcome with grief," he offered defiantly. He had seen his father only a few times in his life, having been raised by an aunt and uncle after his mother's death. He had believed all his life that his father never wanted him.

"I don't care whether you grieve or not," the voice said indifferently. "My job was to deliver this message for the agency, and to deliver an envelope to you which is now out front at the reception desk. Goodbye, Mr. Egan." The line went dead.

"Hey, Egan!" one of the traders on the other side of the desk yelled. "I've got a guy from Merrill Lynch on the line. He says he wants to buy some of your five-year paper. He says you're probably ready to sell it at this point."

"And Nicki's on line three!" another trader hollered.

Cole knew he shouldn't leave the desk right now, not seconds after the Fed announcement, but he had to. The envelope out front involved his father, and anything having to do with his father took precedence over everything else. "Tell both of them I'll call back!" Cole yelled over his shoulder as he dropped the receiver on the desk and sprinted through the chaos toward the reception area outside the wooden doors at the far end of the room. He dodged a young assistant bringing coffee to the junk bond traders, raced the last few yards to the doors, burst into the reception area and stopped short. There were always visitors milling about here, and he scanned every face carefully, trying to memorize distinctive features of each one. Finally he moved toward the reception desk, and the noise from the trading floor subsided as the door swung shut behind him.

"Hi, Cole." Anita Petrocelli smiled cheerfully at him from behind the large desk. She was a young Queens native whose infatuation with Cole was almost as pronounced as the dark mole above her upper lip.

Cole always looked great, Anita thought, but today a special intensity in his gaze made him look even better. He was tall and broad with rugged features— a strong nose, strong chin and sculpted cheeks. His wavy jet-black hair contrasted starkly with his neatly pressed white cotton dress shirt and matched his onyx cuff links perfectly. His hair was long on top but short on the sides and in the back—not the more conservative style worn by most of the men who prowled Gilchrist's trading floor. His dimpled smile was alluring and mysterious, as if he were hiding something. The three holes in his left earlobe provided a tiny window into a rebellious adolescence. And his large steel-gray eyes, surrounded by long thick lashes, were the sexiest she had ever seen.

He had taken her to lunch several times—probably just to be friendly—and through their conversations in the more relaxed atmosphere away from work she had come to know his total abhorrence of conformity simply for conformity's sake, and his love of being different simply to be different. She had also come to know his considerable appetite for risk. He was constantly wagering on something. The stakes didn't really matter, and he never took her money if he won the bet. He simply loved to take risks. She found this devil-may-care attitude electrifying. So did other women at Gilchrist, she knew. He was quite a package.

For Anita, the best thing about Cole was that he had made it to his twenty-ninth birthday single. There were rumors that he had a steady girlfriend, but no proof, and without a gold band on his left-hand ring finger she considered him her primary target. Maybe even with one on, she admitted, slightly ashamed of herself. She had made no secret of her attraction to him. He had always told her she was too good for him. She understood this was his way of letting her down gently, but she continued to flirt with him anyway. After all, if she kept hammering long enough, the wall might finally crumble.

"What can I do for you, Cole?" she asked, batting her eyes playfully.

"Is there anything out here with my name on it?"

"Yeah, me." She placed her elbows on the desktop, rested her chin on the back of her hands and batted her eyes again. "I went down to Greenwich Village and had your initials tattooed on a very private part of my anatomy last—"

"I'm not kidding around, Anita," Cole interrupted.

"Boy, you're grouchy this afternoon." Her smile disappeared as she scanned the desk quickly. Most days he gave her that dimpled smile she adored and a compliment on her hair or her outfit. "Oh, yeah, here's something." She handed him a large brown envelope with his name neatly typed across the front.

"Who gave this to you?" Cole wanted to know.

Anita shrugged. "I don't know. A messenger must have left it here while I was away. I didn't notice it was here until you said something."

Cole turned abruptly and headed toward a small conference room off the reception area before she had finished speaking. She pushed out her lower lip, pouting. Usually he was so polite.

Cole moved into the conference room, closed the door, ripped open the envelope and poured out its contents—a typed note, an official-looking document and a small key that clattered onto the tabletop. He picked up the key and shoved it into his pocket, then read the note. It made two requests. First, he was to place an obituary notice in the *New York Times* marking his father's death. Second, he was to proceed immediately to the Chase Bank branch a few blocks down Fifth Avenue from the Gilchrist Building and retrieve the contents of a safe-deposit box the key would open.

Cole picked up the official-looking document that had been inside the envelope. It was a death certificate with his father's name on it. Jim Egan had appeared at Gilchrist's main reception desk six months ago, unannounced. It was the first time Cole had seen his father since high school graduation. The elder Egan had taken Cole to lunch—a sandwich, chips and a Coke at a delicatessen on Forty-seventh Street. The conversation at the deli had been full of uncomfortable pauses, and there were no great revelations as to the elder Egan's near-lifelong absence. After lunch the encounter had ended with a strange, forced handshake in front of the Gilchrist Building. Cole had offered a tour of the trading floor, but his father had adamantly refused, then taken off down Fifth Avenue without another word, disappearing into the lunch crowd hurrying along the sidewalk.

Cole stared at the death certificate. Christ, if he had just known that would be the last time they would ever see each other. He might have pushed harder for answers to the questions plaguing him for so long. And he might have said something to his father that mattered.

2

COLE SHOVED THE TAPE INTO THE VCR. THE MACHINE clicked several times and the tape began to roll as he sat down in one of the comfortable chairs positioned in a semicircle before the wide-screen television. He was on eight, two stories below the Gilchrist trading floor, in a screening room the institutional salespeople used for impressing investors with flashy presentations describing companies Gilchrist was about to take public. It was after five o'clock and the floor was deserted, but Cole had locked the door to the screening room anyway.

The tape had been the only item inside the Chase safe-deposit box. There was no will bequeathing millions, no sheaf of bearer bonds, not even a piece of fine jewelry. Not that Cole really expected any of those things. According to Cole's aunt, his father's only sibling, Jim Egan had never been concerned with material possessions. Cole glanced at the rows of videocassettes of old presentations lining the shelves on the far wall, then looked out the window into the darkness of the late autumn evening. Perhaps this tape was a message from the grave explaining why a father had neglected his son for so many years, or a pathetic attempt to evoke pity from someone who no longer cared.

The tape began with a bright day in a park. Cole watched as a motorcade moved in front of a building and toward the camera. The images seemed eerily familiar, yet he couldn't quite place them. His eyes narrowed as he gazed at the crowd, the motorcycles and the limousine. The motorcade inched closer, and suddenly Cole snapped his fingers, recognizing the Kennedys and the Connallys inside the open limousine. There was President Kennedy in the backseat waving, Mrs. Kennedy in her pink outfit and matching pillbox hat beside the president, and Governor Connally sitting in the seat directly in front of Kennedy. Of course. It was a copy of the Zapruder film. The film constantly used as part of Kennedy assassination documentaries.

Cole watched for a few moments longer, then shook his head, confused by what he saw on the tape. In the Zapruder film President Kennedy was on the side of the limousine closer to the camera. Here he was on the side away from the camera. Governor Connally should have been on the camera side as well. Everything was reversed. Abraham Zapruder had filmed from the other side of Dealey Plaza. Cole's pulse jumped as the realization struck him: this wasn't the Zapruder film.

The limousine continued rolling and the picture began to move slightly up and down, as if the person shooting the footage was running alongside the vehicle. Suddenly President Kennedy lurched forward as a bullet smashed into his upper back. The impact jerked

Kennedy's elbows up and out and pulled his hands toward his neck, an involuntary neurological reaction to the inch-and-a-quarter copper-jacketed bullet damaging his spinal cord. Still the picture moved with the vehicle as Kennedy's body stiffened and Connally began to react to his own wounds. Suddenly the picture stopped its subtle up-and-down motion, and Cole realized that the person making the film had ceased trying to keep up with the limousine. Then the killing shot came, tearing the president's head apart with appalling force.

"God," Cole murmured. It was shocking footage, so shocking he almost forgot the seven-million-dollar hit his portfolio had taken in the aftermath of the Fed announcement this afternoon.

On the screen there was instant pandemonium with people racing everywhere. The camera followed the limousine as it sped away, then panned back to the spot at which the killing shot had struck the president. People were sprinting across the street toward the grassy knoll, then the screen went dark.

"The end," Cole said aloud.

But it wasn't the end. A face suddenly appeared on the screen. "Jesus Christ," Cole whispered, moving forward to the edge of his seat. The face on the screen was his father's, much younger than the face he had sat across from at lunch six months ago, but obviously Jim Egan's. Then darkness enveloped the screen once more.

Cole knelt down in front of the television, rewound the tape and played it again. As the limousine drifted slowly ahead, he noticed something he hadn't seen before—a rifle barrel protruding over the fence behind the grassy knoll. There could be no mistaking what it was, so clear were the images. Almost instantly a tiny puff of white smoke burst from the end of the gun, and the crimson halo appeared immediately as the president's head snapped back toward the camera. "Damn." Cole recoiled as blood and skull fragments and brain matter spattered the air, and pandemonium broke loose once more.

He stopped the tape, rewound it and played it again—this time in slow motion—watching intently as he knelt on the floor, his eyes only inches from the screen. He pressed the button time after time, moving the tape ahead inch by inch. There was the rifle protruding over the fence, the puff of smoke, the president's head snapping back toward the camera and exploding, the rifle disappearing behind the five-foot-high fence and the president slumping down toward Mrs. Kennedy. Everything coming within a few cataclysmic seconds. Then the limousine moved away, people panicked, momentary darkness shrouded the screen, his father's angry face appeared and finally there was permanent darkness.

Cole tried to swallow but couldn't. His mouth was bone dry.

He rewound the tape to the puff of smoke and froze it there, mesmerized, his eyes riveted to the rifle. Was this Badge Man? That was the name attributed to a blurry figure apparently clad in a Dallas police uniform standing behind the fence and visible in certain photographs taken of the grassy knoll just before the killing shot—a blurry figure seen by conspiracy fanatics so anxious for subterfuge to exist that they were willing to see anything in a picture as long as it tilted the assassination answer toward something darker than one madman firing a Mannlicher-Carcano out the sixth-floor window of the Texas School Book Depository.

Cole touched the screen where the rifle lay over the fence. He had never put much stock in conspiracy speculation about the assassination. It was irrational to think that, if in fact a conspiracy had really existed, after all these years nothing of substance would have come to light. People couldn't keep secrets, that was human nature. But here was proof of the conspiracy. Absolute proof of suspicions that had tormented people for decades. Confirmation beyond all doubt that John F. Kennedy had indeed ridden the open limousine into a killing zone that November day in Dealey Plaza. Confirmation that Lee Harvey Oswald hadn't acted alone, if at all.

The VCR whined as the tape moved forward. When his father appeared on the screen, Cole stopped the tape. For thirty seconds he studied Jim Egan's face, unaware of anything except the man on the screen in front of him. Finally he shook his head and pressed the rewind button. When the tape was fully rewound, Cole removed it from the VCR and replaced it in its unmarked black plastic case.

In 1964 *Life* had paid Abraham Zapruder $250,000 for his film of the assassination. What would the media pay today for something that provided not only another graphic view of the assassination but, more important, proof that the killing shot had come from the grassy knoll? What would they pay for proof that a conspiracy had existed? At least a few million, Cole was willing to wager. Maybe more. Maybe much more.

Suddenly his hands began to shake. This was the answer to his problems—and his prayers.

As Cole reached to shut off the television, out of the corner of his eye he noticed the doorknob silently rotating. The tiny hairs on the back of his neck rose straight up and his head snapped toward the door. It sounded strange, but on the way back from Chase, he had felt as if he were being followed.

The knob turned all the way to the right, then the latch rattled against the metal frame of the lock as the person outside pushed. But the door didn't open because it was secured from the inside.

"Hello," Cole called out hoarsely. He suddenly realized how many people would want to see this tape played publicly—and, more important, that a few might not. That those few might take extreme measures to suppress what he now possessed. "I'm working on a presentation. Could you come back later?"

"It's the cleaning service," a woman replied in a thick Eastern European accent.

Cole checked his watch. It was only five-twenty. Typically the cleaning people didn't make their rounds until much later, at least not on the trading floor.

"It will only take a short while to vacuum the carpet," the woman persisted. "That's all I need to do in there."

Cole hesitated. "All right, just a second."

A moment later he moved silently across the carpet to the door. Holding his breath, he pressed his ear to it and listened intently. Then he stepped back, unlocked the door and swung it open.

Just outside, a dark-haired woman stood beside a large plastic trash container. It coasted atop tiny rollers so she could easily move it with her on her rounds. As Cole stepped through the doorway, she plunged her hand under the top few sheets of wastepaper in the trash container, then looked behind her toward sounds coming from down the hallway. Then she whipped back around to face Cole.

He saw her eyes fix on the black videocassette case in his hand—and saw, too, the glint of what might have been a pistol barrel barely protruding from beneath the wastepaper.

Four young men, chuckling loudly, rounded a corner thirty feet from the screening room. They were traders from the corporate bond desk. Cole raised a hand to them. "Hello, gentlemen," he said calmly.

"Hey, Egan," the man at the front of the pack answered. He was carrying a videocassette case as well. Cole nodded at it. "What's that?"

The man held up the cassette case. "There's a bachelor party for one of the guys on the desk this Friday night, and we need to prescreen some of the entertainment." He seemed unabashed, though the others milling behind him smiled sheepishly at the admission that they were about to view a porn flick. "Want to watch?"

"No, thanks." Cole brushed past them and headed for the stairwell.

The trader holding the flick turned to the cleaning woman. "How about you, honey? Want to see it with us?"

The woman didn't respond as she watched Cole yank the stairwell door open.

Instead of climbing the stairs back up to the trading floor, Cole headed down, taking the steps two and three at a time. He had to get out of here right now. He leaped four steps onto a landing and slammed into the cinderblock wall. Hardly noticing the pain shooting through his left shoulder, he pushed off and kept going. Maybe he was just being paranoid. Maybe that hadn't been a gun in the trash container beside the cleaning woman. But at this moment it seemed far better to let his imagination run wild—and survive.

At the ground floor Cole stopped as he was about to shove open the fire door leading from the stairwell into the main lobby of the Gilchrist Building. He reached forward, then pulled his hand away, as if the metal handle were electrically charged. The woman upstairs might be working with people who were right outside this door, people she could have alerted by now. He took a step back and wiped his forehead, uncertain of his next move. The stairs went down no farther. There was no basement access through which he could slip out of the building unnoticed. He glanced up. He could return to one of the upper floors and try to call the police, surrounding himself with coworkers to keep enemies at bay. There would certainly still be people around.

But who was he kidding? The tape he had watched in the screening room would ignite a national firestorm and probably a new investigation into the Kennedy assassination. If someone wanted to suppress the tape badly enough, she might not care about killing a few people in the process. That was why he had darted away from the traders outside the screening room upstairs. The cleaning woman might not have hesitated at taking them all out if it meant getting her hands on the tape. And what was he going to tell the police anyway? That a cleaning woman with a thick accent and a gun was chasing him? New York City cops would laugh at him.

A door banged open several floors up and he heard footsteps descending the stairs rapidly. There was only one choice. Cole slammed open the door and burst into the high-ceilinged lobby.

Teeming with commuters headed toward taxis, trains and buses, the lobby was a swirling mass of mostly indistinguishable humanity rushing home after a long day. However, Cole managed to pick one face out of the crowd immediately. The man was dodging clusters of people, fifty feet away at most, heading directly toward him, his gaze locked on Cole even as he avoided the human obstacles. Cole recognized the man as one of the people seated in the reception area this afternoon as he had rushed out to claim the envelope containing the note and his father's death certificate and the key to the safe-deposit box. A man who had seemed engrossed in the *Wall Street Journal* while Anita joked about having initials tattooed on a very private part of her anatomy. A big man, easily six-four and broad, with fair skin, rosy cheeks, a young-looking face—except for the deep crow's feet around his eyes and the corners of his mouth—and a wispy shock of curly blond, almost yellow, hair.

Cole turned and bolted through the lobby, plowing into and knocking over a young woman as he glanced back at the blond man, who was gaining ground. The contents of the woman's bag spilled onto the marble floor and she screamed angrily, but Cole kept going. As he squeezed through the door to the outside on the heels of another man, cold November night air rushed at his face and inside his shirt. Without a coat, it was freezing. He glanced left and right, vapor pouring from his mouth and nose, then sprinted south on Fifth Avenue past the Chase branch from which he had collected the tape earlier, dodging people as he ran. At Forty-second Street he pushed through the crowd waiting for the light to change and threw himself blindly into six lanes of rush-hour traffic.

A bus driver spotted Cole at the last second. He yanked the bus's huge steering wheel to the right and slammed on its brakes. The bus skidded over several traffic signs and a fire hydrant as the crowd on the corner tumbled out of the way.

Cole dove to the pavement and rolled across the

blacktop to the double yellow line in the middle of the wide street. He heard the roar made by the water surging out of the hydrant against the undercarriage of the bus, and the screams of pedestrians as they were hit by the torrent forced violently out from beneath the vehicle, but he didn't look back. He didn't have time. The shrill sound of a car horn bore down on him, and he scrambled to his feet and jumped instinctively, clutching the cassette against his chest as he bounced off a taxi's hood and windshield and slammed heavily to the pavement again. Another oncoming car veered away and smashed into a truck to avoid hitting him. He struggled to his knees, dazed, and looked back across the intersection. The blond man had vanished.

Cole shook off the effects of the impact and headed down Fifth Avenue once more. As people scattered from his path, he searched frantically for policemen, but there were none. Though he hadn't seen the blond man across the intersection, he still sensed the pursuer's presence. Cole glanced left, right—and suddenly had a plan.

He swerved sharp right and sprinted up the steps of the main branch of the New York Public Library. It was an impressive structure, two blocks long and several stories high, its wide front steps flanked by a pair of imposing stone lions. He bolted between them and past several people lugging bags of books, then slowed as he moved through the revolving door. The guard to the left of the door eyed him suspiciously, but Cole didn't hesitate. He swerved right again and climbed the steps to the second floor two at a time. At the spot where the wide stairway turned ninety degrees left, he glanced back down at the door, but there was still no sign of the blond man.

Cole trotted across the second-floor hallway to the stairs leading to the third story and began to climb again. At the top of the steps he walked quickly ahead, turned right into the Bill Blass Public Catalogue Room, then proceeded directly through it and into the library's main reading room. It was the size of a basketball court, filled with hundreds of people seated at long wooden tables and immersed in resource material.

A musty smell from thousands of ancient volumes crowding the walls reached Cole's nostrils. He hesitated for a second to scan the mammoth space, but didn't linger long in the entrance. He moved quickly to the west wall, knelt down, pulled several atlases from the bottom shelf, placed the cassette case against the back of the bookcase, replaced the atlases and walked calmly away. He found an open seat near the middle of the room and sat down in the spindly wooden chair. He hadn't taken his eyes from the entrance for more than a few seconds since entering the large room, not even as he had hidden the tape behind the atlases, and the blond man hadn't appeared.

A young woman studying a faded *New York Times* glanced up, went back to her paper, and then looked up again. Cole was acutely aware of the perspiration pouring down his face and the thin streak of blood staining one arm of his white shirt.

"Are you okay?" she asked.

"I'm fine," he said without taking his eyes from the door. "I recently graduated from law school, and the bar exam is coming up. I'm just a little tense."

The young woman smiled nervously, as if unsure what to make of the out-of-breath young man with the sweat-streaked face and the bloodstained shirt. Finally she picked up the archive copy of the *Times* as well as her book bag and walked away. She was new to the city and had been warned that it was full of lunatics.

Cole gazed at the door. There was still no sign of the blond man. His eyes flashed to the spot in the stacks where he had hidden the tape, then back to the door. Still no blond man.

Cole leaned over, hiding his arm beneath the table, removed the onyx cuff link, pulled the torn shirt sleeve up above the gash and inspected the wound quickly. It was nothing serious. He rolled the shirt sleeve back down and, wrapping his fingers firmly around the shredded material, applied direct pressure. Two to three minutes of this and the blood should coagulate.

Cole allowed his head to fall back against the chair but still didn't remove his gaze from the entrance. Maybe his imagination was indeed playing games with him. A cleaning woman with a gun. A blond man chasing him down Fifth Avenue. The notion that they were after him seemed almost silly, now that he thought about it. He laughed and shook his head, then groaned as he felt a sudden stiffness in his neck. He'd suffered a good deal of pain and probably cost New York City several hundred thousand dollars in damages as a result of that imagination, but the hell with it. He had in his possession a tape of President Kennedy's assassination—one proving conspiracy—and he controlled history. That justified at least a trace of paranoia. He'd make up the damages to the city after he'd sold his piece of history to the highest bidder. Right after he had taken care of his in-arrears mortgage that Lewis Gebauer had somehow found out about, as well as a few gambling debts he had recently accumulated. There should still be millions left over.

Millions of dollars others would love to get their hands on, too, Cole suddenly realized.

He sat up in the chair. Maybe others had known about this tape and had been waiting years for that Chase safe-deposit box to be opened because they couldn't access the box themselves. The people at Chase had been very careful and had required a picture identification and a signature from Cole before they would allow him to inspect the contents of the box. Even if others had known about the tape, they wouldn't have been able to retrieve it if they weren't named in bank records as individuals with access to the box.

Cole laughed once more. There he went, letting his imagination get the better of him again.

He checked the entrance one last time. Fifteen minutes had elapsed since he'd hidden the tape behind the row of atlases, and still he'd seen nothing suspicious. He took a final look around. Then he rose unsteadily and, without retrieving the tape from its hiding place, limped toward the door. His right ankle had begun to swell as a result of his collision with the taxi at the corner of Fifth and Forty-second.

Five minutes later he had ridden the elevator to the first floor, staggered down the library steps past the lions and hailed a cab.

3

NICKI ANDERSON WAS TALL AND SLEEK, WITH SILKY gold hair that cascaded down her back. Her face was perfect—thin yet sensuous—highlighted by wide emerald eyes, a delicate nose and bee-stung lips. Her skin was fair and unblemished, her body toned but full of soft curves. She was an exquisite product of her Scandinavian bloodlines. Still, in New York City exquisite women were like restaurants or taxis or pigeons—they were everywhere.

Six months ago Nicki had left Duluth, Minnesota, and moved to New York to follow her dream—a modeling career on the fashion runways of Manhattan. It was costing her middle-class parents most of their retirement cache, but they were convinced that Nicki would take the industry by storm and that the resulting cover-girl fame would earn Nicki and them much more than stocks and bonds ever could.

Nicki had presented her portfolio to all the top agencies but had been unceremoniously rejected. She didn't tell her parents, because even one rejection would have crushed them. Two months ago she had caught on with a smaller agency that was finally beginning to find her work. It had been a difficult road, but through it all she hadn't lost her smile.

Cole eased onto the bench seat at Emilio's, a casual, out-of-the-way Upper West Side cafe where he and Nicki could relax. "Hey there," he said as he sat down. His senses were on alert, eyes constantly scanning the place for anyone who might have followed him from the library.

"Hello, Cole." Nicki leaned across the small, scratched table, took Cole's face in her soft palms and kissed him gently on the cheek. She had always greeted Cole this way, even as a child back in Duluth, and he liked it, especially because she wasn't this way with others. Even with friends, she was reserved.

"You look great," Cole said approvingly. She wore an oversized sweater and faded jeans. It was an all-American country-girl look he thoroughly enjoyed.

"Thanks." Her expression turned curious as she sat back in the seat. "What in the world happened to you?"

He glanced down, worried that blood from the cut on his forearm had seeped through the bandage and the dark blue sweater he had purchased on his way from the library. But nothing was visible on the sweater. "What do you mean, 'what happened?' "

"You look like you've been through a war. Your hair's all messed up, you're perspiring and your hands are shaking. I've never seen you like this. Are you okay?"

"I'm fine," he assured her. He wasn't going to tell her anything about his sprint to the library or the cut on his forearm. There was no reason to alarm her simply because he had allowed his imagination to run wild. Once he had sold the tape, then he'd explain what had happened.

"Just a tough day on Wall Street, huh?" she teased.

"Yeah," he answered quickly, not really concentrating on what she was saying.

"Oh, come on, Cole," Nicki pressed. "I know how stressful it can get on the Gilchrist trading floor, but you handle that every day. What happened?"

"A couple of guys tried to mug me on Broadway while I was walking over here. I didn't want to say anything because I know everybody back in Duluth told you how dangerous New York City is, but it wasn't a big deal, really."

"Did they take your suit jacket?" She pointed at his sweater, grinning. Cole always wore suits.

"What? Oh, the sweater." He forced back a wince as he shifted in the seat. "The heat in the Gilchrist Building went out today for a while. That's why I'm wearing it," he lied. "I just forgot to change back to my suit coat when I left."

"Do you always keep a spare sweater at work?"

"As a matter of fact I do, Agatha Christie." She was like a pit bull sometimes. Once her curiosity was aroused, she didn't let things go without a satisfactory explanation. He tried to change the subject. "How was your day?"

"Great." She tossed her hair back over her shoulders. "I waited tables at lunch, worked out for a few hours at the gym this afternoon and when I got home there were a couple of guys waiting in the lobby of our building. A couple of really big guys."

"Oh?"

A white-aproned waiter with a long ponytail interrupted their conversation. "Good evening, my name's Jimmy. Can I get you two something to drink?"

"I'll have a glass of merlot," Nicki said, smiling up at the short thin man with hair as long as hers.

"Coke, please." Cole didn't bother looking up.

"I'll be right back with your drinks." Jimmy darted off.

"Coke?" Nicki laughed. "Since when do you drink pop after work? I don't think I've ever seen you order anything but alcohol after a tough day on the Gilchrist trading floor."

"I don't feel like drinking tonight." He shouldn't indulge in anything that would make him vulnerable, even though a good stiff scotch would go a long way toward taking the edge off his nerves and deadening his physical pain. "Tell me about these two big guys waiting for you in the lobby."

"They weren't waiting for me, they were waiting for *you*."

"What did they look like?" Cole asked, trying to seem unconcerned.

"Like mobsters."

He rolled his eyes. "Oh, come on."

"I'm not kidding, Cole. They wore flashy suits and lots of gold, and sunglasses even though it was almost dark outside. They wanted to talk to you. I told them you wouldn't be back for a while, but they said they'd wait anyway. That was around five o'clock. They weren't in the lobby when I came back down to walk over here. They were polite, but they still gave me a bad feeling. Somehow they knew I lived with you."

"Did one of them have curly blond hair?" Cole realized that asking in detail about the men's physical characteristics might set off a warning bell in Nicki's head, but he had to know. "Almost yellow in color?"

"No, both of them had dark hair."

Jimmy returned and placed the wine and the Coke

down on the table. "Are you two ready to order?" he asked.

"We haven't even looked at the menu yet," Cole answered. "Could you give us a few more minutes?"

"Sure." Jimmy turned and moved off to take an order from a couple at another table.

"Were you expecting a visit from someone with curly blond hair?" Nicki's voice wavered slightly, as if she were suddenly uneasy.

"No." Cole picked up his glass, touched it to hers and guzzled half the soft drink in one gulp. He was thirsty as hell.

"Then why were you so specific about one of the men having curly blond hair?" she wanted to know.

"Why are you so full of questions tonight?" Cole spiced his tone with a hint of irritation, hoping she would drop the subject.

"Because I care about you," she answered gently. "Did the men in the lobby of our building have anything to do with that incident a couple of weeks ago?"

Cole let out a long, slow breath. One night after a brutal day on the floor a few months ago, he and a trader on the corporate bond desk had gone out for a few drinks. The evening had culminated at an underground casino in Brooklyn called the Blue Moon. Cole had always heard rumors that these kinds of gambling establishments existed in New York, but had never been to one. The very private club offered craps, poker and blackjack as well as tuxedo-clad dealers and scantily dressed women who brought free drinks to the gamblers. It resembled an exclusive high-roller room in Las Vegas or Atlantic City, except that it was overtly controlled by the Mafia—controlled by people who would extend credit while you sat at their gaming table, then suddenly cut it off. And if you didn't repay them as required, they might cut off something other than your credit.

Over the past few months Cole had become a regular at the Blue Moon's craps tables. Two, sometimes three nights a week he would take a cab across the East River to roll the dice and relieve the stress of a trading floor day full of losses he couldn't seem to shake. After just one knock the decrepit basement door would creak slowly open and he would step from a seedy Brooklyn street into a world of tacky opulence. Surveillance cameras had tracked his progress down the trash-strewn stairway, and the men at the door were given approval by other men watching screens in the control room to allow Cole immediate entry into the establishment. He was a good customer building up quite a tab.

Two weeks ago the men at the Blue Moon had finally demanded a five-thousand-dollar payment on his hundred-thousand-dollar gambling debt. It was late, and by that hour he had just enough money left in his wallet to pay for a cab ride back to Manhattan. He couldn't tap an automated teller machine because he had already maxed out his limit for the twenty-four-hour period. And there were only a few dollars left in his lone account anyway. He was living paycheck to paycheck these days.

However, the three large men crowding around him in the back room of the Blue Moon didn't want to hear excuses. They wanted money, and Nicki was Cole's only option. He was aware that she frequently kept a good deal of cash in the apartment and could withdraw more from an ATM if she needed it. An hour later she had put together a thousand dollars and made it to Brooklyn. The men in the back room agreed to accept just the thousand dollars, but they made certain Cole understood that he needed to come up with the other four thousand quickly.

Cole had repaid Nicki during the cab ride back to Manhattan by offering to forgo her next month's rent—exactly one thousand dollars. She had accepted the offer and up until now hadn't mentioned the incident again. He had been hoping the issue was dead, but obviously he'd been wrong.

"I apologize for all that," he mumbled, shaking his head. "I really do."

"It's okay. I just worry about you." Her voice was soft and caring. "I always have."

"I'm fine."

Nicki heard the code word right away: Cole always said that when the world seemed to be closing in around him. " 'Fine'?" She tilted her head subtly forward, as if paying homage to him. "All hail the Wall Builder." It was her nickname for Cole when he was putting up emotional barriers. "It's that I-don't-need-anybody-else Cole Egan showing his face again."

"Don't start with me," he warned good-naturedly. She knew him so well, he suddenly realized. "Today I—" But he interrupted himself before he finished the sentence.

"You what?" She sensed that he had been about to tell her something important. "What were you going to say?"

"Nothing." For a moment he had considered telling her of his father's death, but he needed more time alone with it before he could say anything.

"You just won't accept help. It's that manly thing, I guess."

"I took your thousand dollars two weeks ago," Cole pointed out.

"I'm not talking about financial help," she said.

"I'm talking about something more important, like someone to lean on emotionally when you've had a bad day."

"Mmm." Cole glanced away.

Nicki took a sip of wine. "Cole, I hate to be the bearer of bad news, but you got a Federal Express package today from your mortgage company. It was marked 'Urgent' on the outside, so I opened it. I wasn't prying, I just thought you might want to know what was in it right away."

"What do they want?"

"They want to be paid immediately or they claim they'll take legal action."

Cole scratched his head, grinned, then waved at the waiter. "Now I will accept a little help." A little liquid support, he thought to himself. "Scotch on the rocks, Jimmy," he yelled across the restaurant.

Jimmy moved to the bar and returned quickly with the drink. "Here you are."

"Thanks." Cole took the glass from the waiter. This wasn't a good idea, but the hell with it. He nodded in Nicki's direction, said, "Here's to rewriting history," then took a long swallow.

"What was that?" she asked.

"Oh, nothing."

Nicki shook her head. "I don't know how you do it."

"How I do what?" he asked, setting the glass down on the table after another long and welcome swallow.

"You've got some pretty serious money problems and you don't seem worried. I don't know how you can be so calm."

Cole had been as honest with Nicki about his financial troubles—the gambling debt, the in-arrears mortgage, almost no money in his bank account and

minimal bonus prospects from Gilchrist in January—
as she had been about her modeling agency rejections.
"Nicki, a hundred years from now no one will even
know we were here," he answered, winking.

"At Emilio's?" A curious expression came to her
face. "What's that got to do with anything?"

"Not the restaurant."

"What, then?"

"*Here*-here." Two dimples and the character lines
in his cheeks appeared as he smiled broadly. "No one
will know we existed. You know, on earth."

It was Nicki's turn to roll her eyes in exasperation.
"I know something's wrong, now that I hear the Cole
Egan what-the-hell attitude toward life."

"What do you mean?"

"You always get existential when something really
bad happens. It's your escape hatch."

"You're wrong," he protested, taking another gulp
of the stiff drink.

"Wager it all every day and never look back," Nicki
said, ignoring him. "You can't win if you don't take
risks, and you never know if today is your last day,
so risk it all because no one will care about you when
you're gone. It's that bet-the-ranch, screw-the-world,
make-it-big-or-bust attitude that's tainted your brain
ever since I can remember." She toyed with her napkin. "At some point that attitude is going to catch up
with you."

"Nah." Cole gazed at her as he took another sip of
the drink. God, she was beautiful. "It'll all work out."
As long as the videotape was still in its hiding place,
he thought to himself.

Nicki shook her head. "You just love putting yourself in precarious situations and somehow finding a
way out, don't you, Cole? Beating the odds makes

winning sweeter. That's what you told me that Fourth
of July before you moved to New York, while we
were watching the fireworks over Lake Superior." She
smiled at him. "You know you're crazy."

"Not really."

"Oh, yeah, and self-destructive."

"I think you enrolled in at least one too many psy-
chology courses in college."

Nicki took another sip of wine. "It's your darn father's fault," she said, ignoring Cole's curriculum
crack. "If he hadn't shipped you off to live with your
aunt and uncle after your mother died, you'd be a normal well-adjusted male." She hesitated and gave him a
playful look. "As well adjusted as that can ever be." She
laughed, leaned over the table and kissed him on the
cheek again. "But if your father hadn't sent you to
Duluth, I would never have met you." She pulled back
slowly. "And you probably wouldn't have that devil-
may-care streak all the women you date seem to find
so irresistible."

Cole watched her intently as she settled back onto
the seat. She was beautiful and smart and he was terribly attracted to her. He always had been. And there
seemed to be a spark on her side as well. But nothing
had ever happened between them, even since she had
come to live in New York. They were just roommates.
Nicki's parents were neighbors of his aunt and uncle
back in Duluth, and he was acting as a big brother—as
he always had—while she embarked on her modeling
career. He was protecting a naive Midwestern woman
from the dangers of the big city in exchange for the
thousand-dollar-a-month rent payment he so desperately needed to keep his penthouse creditor at bay.

Cole sipped his scotch. Maybe that was it. Maybe
they were both afraid of starting anything because of

the connection back home. Or because they'd known each other for so long and they were worried they might destroy a wonderful friendship if they became lovers and the relationship didn't work out. Or because she was five years his junior. He had always been too old for her as they were growing up. She was still a child when he was in high school and starting college, but perhaps they had reached a point now where the age difference no longer mattered. Cole laughed to himself quietly. Maybe he was just deluding himself about the spark on her side.

He took one more swallow of scotch. "Let's go out on a date tonight," he suggested boldly. They had gone out before in the city, but always in a group or with the understanding that it wasn't really a date. "Just you and me."

Nicki was watching someone at the bar. As she turned back toward Cole, a nervous smile played across her lips. "What?"

"Let's go out on a date," he repeated. "A real date. None of this friend stuff."

"Would I still have to pay you rent?" she asked slyly. Then she glanced around to see if anyone had heard her questions, as if she were surprised at herself for saying the words.

"Of course," he said, raising one eyebrow and grinning. "Agreeing to one date doesn't absolve you of your financial obligations."

"Oh, thanks a lot!" She laughed, reached across the table and grabbed his forearm.

The pain shot up his arm all the way to his shoulder. Instantly he groaned and pulled back. The hit to the cut had been too direct to hide the hurt.

"Are you okay?" She had heard the pain in his voice. "I'm sorry."

"I'm fine, Nicki," he said, using a paternal tone. "So what about our date? I've got an errand to run first, but we could go out after that." The fire in his arm slowly subsided.

She glanced down at the table. "I'm supposed to see Maria later on."

Cole reached again for his drink. Maria was another model, almost as pretty as Nicki. Together they made a striking pair. Since coming to New York, Maria was the only real friend Nicki had made, and when Nicki wasn't out with Cole, she was out with Maria. The two women had become almost inseparable over the past few months. It was strange, now that he thought about it. When the three of them were in the apartment together, Maria was cold to him, almost protective about Nicki.

He frowned. That bastard Lewis Gebauer had made a stupid crack this afternoon on the trading floor about Cole's honey liking girls. He must have been talking about Nicki liking Maria. Cole shook his head. That couldn't be. But then, Gebauer had known about his bonus freeze-out and his in-arrears mortgage. And Cole had run into Maria coming out of Nicki's bedroom early one morning last week as he was headed to the shower. Maria claimed to have slept on the couch and quickly volunteered that she had simply gone into Nicki's room to say goodbye before she left. But she had seemed nervous.

Suddenly Cole caught a fleeting glimpse of curly blond, almost yellow, hair moving past the bottom of the restaurant's elevated front window. He rose quickly from his seat and bolted to the door, but by the time he reached the sidewalk there was no sign of a man with curly blond hair.

"What is your problem tonight? You're like a cat on a hot tin roof."

Cole turned around quickly. Nicki had followed him out of the restaurant.

"Are you okay?" She smiled up at him sweetly.

"I'm fine," he said. How the hell was he going to explain this?

"What were you doing?"

"I thought I saw Mick Jagger walk past the window," he stammered. "I was going to get his autograph for you, but it turned out not to be him."

"I'm not really into the Rolling Stones, Cole. They're a little old for me, so I'm not very disappointed." She wasn't completely convinced by Cole's explanation, but it didn't matter. "But thanks anyway."

"Sure."

"Cole?"

"Yes?" He glanced into her eyes. She was so young and innocent and nice. The cutthroat modeling world hadn't poisoned her, not yet anyway. She was still the same lovely girl he had known growing up in Duluth.

"I'm really glad you asked me out," she said softly. "I didn't think you ever would."

"So you'll go?"

She nodded. "Of course. I had a crush on you when I was ten years old, for crying out loud, and it's only gotten stronger since. I care very much about you, Cole. It's half the reason I came to New York."

"Well, why didn't you say something before this? You could have saved me a lot of stress." He laughed loudly out of relief. "I've been wondering whether or not to bring this up for months, ever since you got here."

"I guess I'm just shy." She hesitated. "And I couldn't bear the thought of you saying no."

"As if I would." Not in a million years, he thought to himself. "What about Maria?"

"No problem. I'll call her and cancel. She was going to meet me at the apartment after our dinner." Nicki checked her watch. "I can probably catch her before she leaves her place in the Village."

"Couldn't you call her on her cell phone?" Cole asked.

Nicki shook her head. "She doesn't carry one. Maria agrees with my attitude toward cell phones. She doesn't like people being able to reach her all the time. And we think people walking down the sidewalk or sitting on the subway with phones stuck to their ears are obnoxious."

Cole nodded to himself. Of course. Nicki had no need to make herself feel important by carrying a phone with her everywhere she went. In her own quiet way, she had complete confidence in herself and didn't need status symbols to bolster her self-image.

Nicki took Cole's hands in hers. "I want a kiss."

"Right here?"

"Yes. I guess I'm not as shy—"

But Cole didn't allow her to finish. He wrapped his arms around her slender waist, pulled her to him and kissed her deeply. And their intense mutual attraction, which had lingered beneath the surface for so long, erupted suddenly and passionately on the New York City sidewalk, far away from the quiet Duluth neighborhood where it had begun.

Finally he pulled back, thinking he had never enjoyed a kiss more in his life. "Nicki, I have to run that errand, but I won't be gone for long. While I'm away,

I want you to stay here at the restaurant. You can sit at the bar and have a drink until I get back."

"I'll wait for you at the apartment."

"No!"

She looked at him strangely. His reaction had been so strong. "Why not?"

"I want you to stay here at Emilio's." He made certain his voice was calmer. "The restaurant is closer to where I need to go, so I won't be away from you as long."

"But I want to put on something nice before we go out."

Cole ran his fingers through her long blond hair, then pulled her close again. "You look stunning as you are," he whispered into her ear. "Do me a favor and stay here."

"Okay," she murmured.

At 7:25, five minutes before the library was to close for the evening, the young man who had seemed to be taking copious notes from a *World Book Encyclopedia* volume rose from the long table, replaced his note-book in his backpack, slung the pack over his shoulder and moved casually toward the west wall. He was short and wore a New York Yankees baseball cap pulled low over his eyes.

When he reached the location, he knelt down, pulled the atlases from the shelves, placed them gently on the floor and extracted the cassette case from its cave. He slid the tape into his backpack, secured the pack's buckle, took a quick look around, then rose and sauntered away. He didn't ride the elevator to the first floor as Cole had. He preferred to walk down the wide open stairway instead. On the stairway he could see everything around him from a distance.

He moved his head and whistled softly as if enjoying a song playing on his Walkman, but a discerning eye would have noticed that the machine's PLAY button wasn't depressed. There was no music blaring through the earphones because that would have been stupid. Music would have blocked out other sounds, and the young man needed all his senses in perfect working order right now because he was running a gauntlet.

The guard at the library's front door motioned to the young man to open the backpack for inspection. The young man cheerfully complied, placing the pack on the counter and continuing to move to the imagined song. The guard peered inside the pack, then removed the cassette case and checked inside it carefully.

The young man grimaced. He wasn't concerned that the guard was going to appropriate the tape. Library videocassettes were clearly marked and this one wasn't. But now anyone watching would have seen the guard take the case out of the pack. The young man glanced around. He noticed nothing out of the ordinary.

The guard closed the cassette case and shoved it back into the young man's pack. The young man smiled beneath the brim of his Yankees cap, zipped up his green down jacket, grabbed the pack and moved out of the building. Once past the stone lions, he turned right onto Fifth Avenue, turned right again at Fortieth Street and continued walking until he reached Bryant Park—a large rectangle of meticulously manicured grass surrounded by tall elm trees stretching from the back of the library all the way to Sixth Avenue. On a summer evening the park would have been crowded with people enjoying comedians or musicians performing on the stage erected at the west end, but in the darkness of the cold fall evening it was deserted. The young man jogged across the grass through the gloom as a raw drizzle began to fall. He was almost home.

As he reached the other side of the park, he took a shortcut over a patch of ivy and through a grove of trees. It was a terrible mistake. The solid metal pipe smashed into the back of his skull collapsing fragments of hair and skin and bone into his brain. He fell forward onto his chest, hands above his head grasping at the ivy. He managed to pull himself forward only a few inches before he moaned pitifully and his eyes rolled back in his head. Then Agent Graham lay motionless, his fingers still clutching wet leaves.

The blond man didn't bother removing the backpack from the young man's corpse. He simply bent down, ripped open the buckle, shoved his meaty hand inside the pack, extracted the cassette case and opened it. From his leather coat he took out a small flashlight, cavalierly unconcerned about the possibility of being caught standing over a fresh kill. He switched on the flashlight and inspected the tape in the dim light. He pushed his tongue into the opening made by his missing lower front tooth and a tight smile crossed his thin lips. Then he extinguished the flashlight, shoved it back in his coat, closed the cassette case, pulled it tightly against his chest, turned and disappeared into the mist.

4

AVERY ZAHN, TWO-STAR ARMY GENERAL AND DEPUTY director of the Defense Intelligence Agency, sat outside the Oval Office door in what was for him an undersized chair. He was six-seven—a former basketball pine-rider at the United States Military Academy—and at fifty-one he still retained the rail-slender build of his playing days. He was gangly, with large ears that stuck almost straight out from the sides of his head. During his life he'd endured an abundant amount of teasing about his ears, and as much as anything this mocking of his physical appearance was the basis for his stoic demeanor and the huge chips sitting squarely on each narrow shoulder.

The Oval Office door opened suddenly and Eric Walsh, the president's chief of staff, poked his head out into the waiting area. "We're ready for you," he said self-importantly.

Zahn nodded stiffly as he rose from the seat. Walsh was the yuppie type, a type Zahn detested. Walsh wore expensive suits and flashy ties and in the morn-

ing parked his BMW in the closest space to the door
of the West Wing of the White House. He was short
and slight, with perfectly combed dark hair, tortoise-
shell glasses and a universe-size ego. As Zahn entered
the Oval Office, he ducked, an automatic reaction
after years of head bumps. He didn't care for Walsh
at all, but no one saw the president without also seeing
Walsh. They had been inseparable since the president's days as governor of North Carolina.

Richard Jamison, president of the United States,
was doing his best to terminate a telephone conversation and motioned for Zahn to sit in the chair positioned to the left side of the great desk. It was a black
captain's chair—Duke University's motto etched into
the back in gold lettering—and was larger, though
only slightly more comfortable, than the chair in which
Zahn had been sitting outside the Oval Office.

Zahn eased into the chair while Walsh sat in the
one on the right side of the president's desk. Jamison
stood behind the desk, gazing out through the large
window into the night, charming someone at the other
end of the phone. As much as Zahn disliked Walsh,
he liked Jamison. Not because he wanted to, but because he had to. Jamison was personally responsible
for Zahn's appointment as deputy director of the DIA.
It was an appointment that had revived a foundering
military career. Zahn knew why Jamison had selected
him over several more deserving candidates, but that
was all right. You took what you could get in this
world, any way you could get it.

Jamison was tall, tanned and graying slightly at the
temples. He possessed movie-star good looks and a
silver tongue Zahn knew was also forked. Zahn
shrugged to himself. Maybe that was just something

politicians were born with, and something they needed to possess in order to succeed.

"We thank you for your support, Senator," Jamison said politely. "My love to Alice and the girls." He nodded several times, smiling into the phone's mouthpiece, trying to disengage. "Right, goodbye." His smile evaporating, he replaced the receiver on its cradle and glanced at Walsh as he sat in the chair behind the huge desk. "Eric, the good senator from Michigan is a pompous asshole."

Walsh put a hand to his face to hide a grin. Jamison used profanity liberally when he was conducting small meetings in the Oval Office. The habit amused Walsh because Jamison had managed to craft such a virtuous public image.

"And his wife's as fucking ugly as the south end of a northbound wolverine." Jamison winked at Walsh. "Quite a little slut in her college days, too, if our information is correct."

This time Walsh chuckled out loud.

Zahn had been absentmindedly fiddling with his military hat, which lay on his lap. At the sound of Walsh's laughter, Zahn glanced up and saw the president staring at him.

"Hello, General Zahn," Jamison said cordially.

"Hello, Mr. President." Zahn could only imagine how Walsh and the president would joke about his ears after he left. When Walsh had leaned into the waiting area outside the Oval Office, Zahn had caught the young man looking at them. But if Walsh and Jamison wanted to have a little fun at his expense, that would have to be acceptable. After all, Jamison had caused his military stock to rise after a long slide. And there was that other matter as well.

"How are you this evening, General?" the president asked.

"Fine."

"And as talkative as ever, I see."

Walsh chuckled again.

Zahn shifted uncomfortably in his chair without saying anything. He felt the perspiration building beneath his uniform. He was too self-conscious to easily endure any kind of attention.

"Right." Jamison folded his hands together atop the desk and cleared his throat. Zahn was as stiff as a board, and it was silly to think that he might all of a sudden become an interesting conversationalist. It was better to get down to the matter at hand than to try and drag any shred of personality out of the general.

In his peripheral vision Zahn noticed Walsh's posture subtly stiffen as the president's demeanor became serious.

"Update me on Operation Snowfall," Jamison demanded abruptly. He was all business now. "Specifically, what we talked about last week."

"Yes, Mr. President." Zahn was happy. The idle chitchat, something for which he had never possessed an affinity, was over. Now they could get to work. "We should acquire what we seek this evening, if we haven't already," Zahn said, checking his watch. "I have a report, from the man I told you about, that Cole Egan took something out of a safe-deposit box at the Chase Bank branch at Fifth Avenue and Forty-third Street in Manhattan this afternoon. We believe what he retrieved from the box is what we're looking for."

The president reclined in the chair and chewed thoughtfully on the end of his gold Cross pen for a moment. "Really?" He was surprised that it could be over so quickly, but then Zahn was efficient. He wasn't someone you'd spend more than a few seconds conversing with at an Embassy Row cocktail party or a state dinner, but he was coldly efficient, and therefore the perfect man to head this mission.

"Yes, Mr. President."

The president leaned forward over the desk. "You know how goddamn important this mission is to me."

"Yes, Mr. President." Zahn was like a puppy dog in Jamison's presence.

A minute of silence ensued as the president took in this unexpectedly positive piece of information.

Zahn began rocking slightly in his chair. It was what he always did when he was about to address someone of superior rank without being prompted, and when he thought what he was about to say was humorous. "Kind of ironic." Zahn cackled through his nose when he laughed. "Isn't it, Mr. President? This whole thing, I mean." It was a feeble attempt at something other than his typically stoic demeanor, and it failed miserably.

The president's eyes narrowed. "It sure as shit is," he hissed. He had no desire to be reminded of the irony.

Walsh shook his head. What an idiot Zahn was.

Zahn nodded nervously, wishing he could have taken back his comment.

"General Zahn, I hope for your sake everything works out well this evening. I informed my associate that you would acquire what we seek very soon. He was delighted to hear that." Jamison pointed a finger at Zahn. "I don't want him to be disappointed," he said ominously. "I can't have that."

"I understand, Mr. President." It was all Zahn could do to speak.

"Good. When you have procured the damn thing, I want to be informed immediately. You may call Mr. Walsh at any hour tonight." Jamison gestured in his chief of staff's direction. "That will be all, General Zahn."

"Yes, sir." Zahn rose and walked out the door, which clicked shut behind him.

"What do you have on Zahn?" Walsh asked, an impish grin tugging at the corners of his mouth. "Why is he so petrified of you?"

The president stood up, turned and gazed out through the window into the darkness beyond. "General Zahn comes from a very old, very high-profile Southern family. A family that has called Charleston, South Carolina, home for two hundred years." Jamison loosened his bright red tie. "A very traditional Southern family from a very traditional Southern town, where gentlemen are gentlemen and ladies are ladies," he said in his smooth North Carolina accent.

"What's your point?" Walsh asked impatiently. He was the only one in Washington who could get away with so impertinent a tone.

"My point is that General Zahn leaves his wife and children one night a month for his lover, which wouldn't be so bad in and of itself. Hell, we've all strayed at one time or another. But I doubt Zahn's mother, father, sister and the rest of his extended family would want to hear that the general's lover is a nineteen-year-old male cadet enrolled at the Citadel. That might be cause for some explaining on the Charleston social circuit."

Walsh's grin grew wider. "Having that kind of information seems to make General Zahn fairly malleable."

"Very malleable." Jamison turned away from the window.

"So that's why you had no hesitation about informing Zahn of the circumstances." Jamison could be secretive about his motives sometimes, even with his chief of staff. Now Walsh was finally being shown the light on this issue.

"Hell, that's why I promoted him to deputy director of the DIA, and why I gave him responsibility for the mission. Our associate will be monitoring our progress carefully. Whoever was leading the mission would have asked questions. I can be open with Zahn and answer any of his questions because I know he'll take whatever I tell him to his grave without telling anyone else. Closet homosexuals are good that way, especially ones with wives and children."

"Mmm." Walsh wanted to go over the bigger picture one more time. He had counseled the president against all of this many times over the last few days, and it seemed to him worth one more review. "Do you really feel this whole thing is necessary?"

"Absolutely," the president answered forcefully. "You know how much I want a second term, and I don't have the financial war chest for the campaign, not like the one you tell me my opponent will have, anyway. I don't have time for thousands of coffee meetings and dinners, either. And there's so much scrutiny on campaign finance these days, I don't want to have to count on a substantial amount of fundraising to win reelection." Jamison sat back down in his chair. "I need votes, Eric, and what we are doing will ensure that I get them. As it did the first time around. As it did in 1960." Jamison thought back to Zahn's comment about irony. The general had been right on the button in more ways than one.

"But you're the incumbent," Walsh argued. "Stay the course and you're a lock to be reelected next year."

"Tell Jimmy Carter and George Bush that," Jamison said quietly, gazing down at his desktop. "I can't change my mind now anyway. My associate wouldn't take kindly to that."

Walsh nodded in resignation.

"We're already in bed together," Jamison pointed out. "We might as well make the sex good."

"I suppose," Walsh agreed.

The president glanced up, forcing a positive tone into his voice. "How did the attorney general hearings go today?"

Walsh waved his hand as if swatting at a fly. "Ah, the senators on the committee are all chiding her on her lax record monitoring the casinos while she was attorney general for New Jersey, but ultimately they'll approve her. We've got the votes. It'll only be another couple of days before we can break out the champagne and toast her appointment."

The president smiled. "Good." Things were progressing on schedule. His associate would be happy.

5

THE LONE GUARD SEATED BEHIND THE MAIN LOBBY'S long front desk wore a plain light gray business suit, as all Gilchrist & Company security personnel did when they were on duty. He also packed a snub-nosed .38 in a leather shoulder holster beneath the suit coat. Most of the guards were former New York City policemen. They never smiled, rarely engaged in conversation with nonsecurity personnel and were coldly efficient in protecting the Gilchrist premises.

Cole held up his plastic photo identification card as he signed the after-hours register. The guard nodded stiffly, and Cole moved to the elevator banks. As the car ascended, he checked his wristwatch. It was pushing eight o'clock. He had kissed Nicki goodbye after leading her back inside Emilio's, then caught a cab to the Gilchrist Building. After he finished here, he would return to Emilio's and pick her up. Cole smiled. He couldn't wait to be with her again. They would tell each other many things tonight. Things they had always wanted to say, but never had.

The elevator stopped on eight, and the doors slid open to a dimly lit floor. As Cole stepped into the hallway and the elevator doors closed behind him, he suddenly realized how quiet it was here. The only sound was the hum from the few fluorescent bulbs still lighted. He moved through the glass doors leading to the inner offices, turned right, and walked down a long dark corridor toward the screening room he had used this afternoon to view the tape.

Halfway there Cole stopped suddenly. A shadow at the end of the corridor seemed to be moving. He squinted. There it was again. He swallowed hard as he realized the moving shadow was only being made by a bulb about to die. Stay calm, he told himself. Control your fear.

He moved forward once more, checking back over his shoulder every so often. Finally he reached the screening room and moved inside, flipping on the light as he entered. He walked directly to the rows of video-cassette cases lining the shelves and pulled one out. As he gazed at it, he laughed to himself. This was the tape he had retrieved from the Chase safe-deposit box earlier in the day. The one he had hidden in the stacks of the New York Public Library was a decoy, an old presentation a Gilchrist investment banker had produced for a buy-side client. If anyone had followed him into the library and watched him hide that tape behind the atlases, then retrieved it thinking it was the tape of the Kennedy assassination, they would be sorely disappointed.

Cole flipped on the television and the VCR, then pulled the tape from its case and inserted it into the slot. He wanted to make certain no one had pulled a switch. Almost instantly the limousine was turning left in front of the building, and a wave of relief coursed through his body. The idea of hiding the real tape here and taking another one away had occurred to him as the cleaning woman had pushed for immediate access to the screening room. When he had opened the door, he'd seen her glance down at what she thought was the Dealey Tape—as he was going to call the cassette when he began his auction tomorrow with the media. He was fairly certain that the woman would never have thought to check the tapes in the screening room, but you never knew.

His shoulders sagged and he leaned back against the wall for a moment. The last few hours had seemed interminable without the Dealey Tape actually in his possession, and he suddenly realized how drained he was, physically and mentally. But he would probably improve when Fox offered ten million dollars for the Dealey Tape—and feel even better when ABC offered more.

When the tape had ejected from the VCR, Cole replaced it in its black plastic case, turned off the television and the VCR, and headed toward the screening room door. In the event that someone had followed him to the library and taken the tape from behind the atlases and now realized he had been fooled, Cole was going to be careful. He was going to stay at the Marriott Marquis tonight and would get a room for Nicki as well. There was no reason to take a foolhardy chance by returning to the apartment. The blond man who had chased him down Fifth Avenue could easily find out where he lived—after all, two "mobsters" in sunglasses had—and it wasn't as if one scrawny doorman was going to stop someone looking for this piece of history. By this time tomorrow a megadeal for the Dealey Tape would be struck. It would be too late for those who might want to keep it from the public, or to acquire it for themselves so that they could make the deal and get the money.

Cole flipped off the screening room light, stepped into the hallway—and nearly ran into a short dark man with a scar slicing from the bridge of his nose down his left cheek all the way to his jaw.

Before the man could react, Cole slammed his scarred cheek with a hard right fist. It was instinct, and it saved his life. As the man toppled backward, Cole stumbled over him and toward the same stairway door he had slipped through several hours before to avoid the cleaning woman. The man grabbed for Cole's legs, but Cole was quickly past him and into the stairwell, taking the steps even faster than he had this afternoon, leaping from landing to landing, the cassette case tucked like a football in the crook of his right arm. He heard the door slam open above him and several sharp reports as the man with the scar aimed his gun down the stairwell and began firing.

In seconds Cole had descended several stories. He hadn't imagined a damn thing. They were after him, whoever "they" were. The cleaning woman, the blond man, now this man with a scar. All of them after the Dealey Tape. A bullet zipped past him, pinging the metal handrail, and Cole ducked as he jumped onto the second-floor landing. One more set of steps and he was back in the deserted lobby.

The guard lay facedown behind the desk in a pool of blood. Cole caught only a fleeting glimpse of the prone body as he tore across the lobby. Christ, these people weren't screwing around. What the hell had he stumbled into?

Rage erupted as Cole thought of his father. Jim Egan must have known this would happen. He must have known there would be people willing to go to any lengths to obtain the Dealey Tape. Why else would he have arranged for it to be conveyed so covertly?

As Cole burst through the outside door onto Fifth Avenue, the stairwell door slammed open behind him. The man with the scar fired from across the lobby and glass shattered. Cole ducked again and started left, but he noticed a woman coming at him down Fifth Avenue. It was the same woman who had been outside the screening room beside the trash container as the bond traders had sauntered down the hallway. But she wasn't wearing the robin's egg blue uniform of the cleaning staff anymore. Now she was wearing black from head to toe.

Cole whirled and took off in the opposite direction. He sprinted south on Fifth Avenue all the way to Thirty-eighth Street, then crossed Fifth and headed east down the shadowy cross street to Madison Avenue before turning up Madison and finally running west on Thirty-ninth for a short distance. During the day the streets would have been jammed with people, but now they were deserted. He stumbled into a recessed doorway, smashed the dim bulb above the door with the cassette case and stood perfectly still in the darkness, his back against the inside wall, gasping for breath as quietly as he could.

For ten minutes he stood in the dark doorway, slowly regaining his breath. He was certain he had put a fair amount of distance between himself and the woman. He had played wide receiver for the University of Minnesota football team. That was seven years ago, but he was still in excellent physical condition, still very fast. There was no way she could have kept up with him.

Finally he peered out of the doorway into the

gloom. He saw nothing unusual and stepped out of the doorway, crossed the street and began jogging back toward Madison Avenue. There he would catch a cab, pick up Nicki at Emilio's, anonymously call 911 to alert the police to the Gilchrist security guard's plight and get to the safety of a hotel that would take cash up front without requiring a credit card imprint. That was where he and Nicki would stay tonight, not the Marriott Marquis. The crazies chasing him might be able to track them down if he used a credit card, but not if he used cash. Hotels that would accept cash without the guest having to produce a credit card weren't the nicest places in the world, but he'd take safety over style for this one night. He clutched the Dealey Tape tightly. It was more valuable than gold.

The woman stood directly in front of Cole on the sidewalk, clutching a pistol. He stopped abruptly a few feet away from her, unable to believe what he was seeing. He hadn't noticed her until he was practically on top of her. He glanced around frantically, but there was nothing he could do now.

The man with the scar on his left cheek raced up behind the woman, breathing heavily. He patted her on the shoulder, pointed at the tape in Cole's hand and mumbled something unintelligible into her ear. Then he moved to where Cole stood and grabbed the tape. Cole didn't release his grip on the tape right away, but the man yanked harder and finally tore it loose.

"You thought you'd made it, didn't you?" The man remained in front of Cole for a moment, smiling smugly.

Cole didn't respond.

"Sure you did," the man answered himself. "But even if you had given us the slip, we would have gotten you when you went back to your apartment. It's all set to explode," he said, still smiling. Then he turned and walked to where the woman stood. "Shoot him," the man ordered loudly.

Instinctively Cole put his arms up and ducked, then dropped to the ground and rolled. He heard the crack of a gun, but felt no pain. Maybe you don't feel a gunshot wound right away, he thought as he scrambled behind a parked car.

Suddenly Cole saw the man with curly blond hair sprinting up the street, pistol in hand, aiming at the man with the scar, who had taken off toward Madison Avenue. And he saw the woman lying on the side-walk, blood oozing from a neat hole in her forehead, her gun at the end of her outstretched fingers. Then the street became quiet as the two men disappeared around the corner.

Cole bolted from his hiding spot behind the car and ran west, away from the corner around which the two men had disappeared. Within seconds he had reached Fifth Avenue and flagged down a cab.

Minutes later the cab screeched to a halt in front of Emilio's. Cole jammed a ten-dollar bill into the slot in the Plexiglas between the front and back seats, then moved quickly into the restaurant.

"Where's the woman I left sitting right here forty-five minutes ago?" Cole shouted at the bartender, who was busy fixing a round of drinks.

"Huh?" The bartender didn't look up.

"The woman I left sitting right here." Cole repeated himself as he pointed down at the stool beside which he was standing. "You and I talked briefly before I left. I told you to make certain she didn't leave."

The bartender finally glanced up as he finished mixing the last drink. "What did she look like?"

"Tall, blond, beautiful, with a face you couldn't possibly forg—"

"Oh, right." The bartender snapped his fingers and pointed at Cole. "Sure, I remember now."

"Well, where the hell is she?"

"She just took off." The bartender waved at Jimmy to let him know that his round of drinks was ready.

"What?"

"Yeah. She was trying to call some friend of hers but couldn't reach her. She said the woman was supposed to be meeting her at her apartment." The bartender gestured at the door. "So she left to meet the woman. She said to tell you she'd see you back at the—"

"Give me that phone!" Cole interrupted.

"What?"

"Right there!" he yelled, pointing at the cordless phone standing next to the cash register on the counter behind the bar.

"Sure." The bartender picked up the phone and tossed it to Cole.

Seconds later the information operator had given Cole the main number for his apartment building and he had punched it into the phone's keypad. The line rang ten times before a recording finally answered. "Dammit!" He tossed the phone back at the bartender, then turned and raced out of Emilio's.

Emergency lights flashed red and orange across Cole's face as he stood on the sidewalk gazing at the two ambulances and three pale blue-and-white police cruisers parked at odd angles in front of his apartment building. There were several hundred residents in the forty-story building—many of them elderly and likely candidates for emergency service—but he still had a terrible feeling about what was going on. Slowly he limped forward, putting one foot in front of the other as if in a daze. He was exhausted and his ankle was swollen, but he barely noticed the pain. His gaze was now fixed on the building's front door.

"Hey, buddy, you gotta stay here while we bring the victim out." A large police officer stepped in Cole's way.

Cole glanced at him. "Victim?"

"Yeah." The policeman gestured toward the night sky with his flashlight. "There was some kind of explosion up in one of the penthouses and a young woman was hurt pretty bad. We need to keep the entrance clear so the paramedics can bring her out."

"A young woman?" Cole's voice was barely audible.

"Yeah."

"Do you know which apartment it was?"

"Huh?"

"In which apartment was the explosion?" Cole asked again, his voice shaking.

"I don't know," the policeman said impatiently. "Look, you're gonna have to step back." The policeman spotted another resident moving toward the front door and moved away to intercept him.

As the policeman moved away, Cole saw two uniformed paramedics rolling a white-sheeted stretcher out through the lobby and broke past the small crowd that had gathered.

"Hey, buddy!" the policeman yelled. "Stop!"

But Cole kept running. As he neared the stretcher, his heart sank. Bandages and gauze covered most of a young woman's face, but he thought he recognized the ring on her limp hand. He stopped and grabbed his hair with both hands. "Jesus, is she all right?"

The paramedics shook their heads somberly as they lifted the stretcher into the back of the ambulance.

"Cole!"

Cole pivoted toward the voice, and relief flooded through him at the sight of Nicki sprinting toward him. She too had broken through the thin line of policemen.

As Nicki neared the ambulance, she pointed at the hand of the woman on the stretcher with its distinctive ring. "Maria!" she screamed, lunging for the back of the ambulance.

But Cole caught her as the paramedics closed the door and the emergency vehicle moved away, siren screaming. He wrapped his arms tightly around her as she sobbed into his chest. "It's okay, sweetheart," he said comfortingly, the feeling of relief that the victim hadn't been Nicki still pulsing through him.

"No, it isn't," she cried.

He nodded. It really wasn't okay, but there was nothing either one of them could do about it. "Come on," he urged gently, guiding her away from the apartment building.

"Where are we going?" she asked through her tears.

"I'm taking you home."

6

FOR THE BETTER PART OF FOUR DECADES WILLIAM Seward had been a history professor at the University of Virginia. Now that he was seventy-two years old, Seward taught just one class and that was in the spring semester. It was an upper-level course covering the Civil War, or the War of Northern Aggression, as Seward preferred to call it. The class was his only commitment at this point, at least to Mr. Jefferson's university.

This late in November the leaves had fallen, and as Seward watched from his living room window, he could make out a silver government-issue sedan moving slowly through the bare-branched trees and over the crushed-stone lane leading down into the small valley which his cabin overlooked. The cabin lay secluded in a thick grove of oaks halfway up a small mountain. The site was only a few miles west of the university's hometown of Charlottesville, but it was remote. The closest house was more than a half mile away. Here Seward could do research in solitude—

and direct one of the most clandestine operations ever initiated by the United States government. Operation Snowfall.

Seward moved from the window to the stereo and turned on gentle symphonic music. It helped soothe his nerves. He enjoyed little-known composers others didn't appreciate, but he could listen to whatever he wanted because he lived alone. He wasn't married and had few living relatives.

Seward was tall and angular with thinning hair the color of cotton. His face was kindly, and traces of a slight smile were permanently etched into the corners of his pale lips. With age, his salt-and-pepper eyebrows had become bushy and his lower teeth crooked—the result of refusing to have his wisdom teeth removed because he couldn't risk the potential truth-serum effects of anesthesia. Both of his knees were stiff from arthritis and he needed a cane to walk. He spoke in a soft voice tinged with a pleasant Virginia accent, and lately he seemed to forget a word now and then or address one of his students by the wrong name. In private, some faculty members speculated that he was on the precipice of senility, but they were gravely mistaken. Behind wire-framed glasses, Seward's dark eyes burned brightly, and behind the dark eyes was the mind of a twenty-year-old. His senility was simply an act. People expected a man in his eighth decade to forget a name every once in a while, so he gave them what they expected. He couldn't risk stepping out of character.

The silver sedan pulled up outside the cabin door. Seward heard the driver cut the car's engine as he relaxed into a large leather chair positioned on one side of the stone fireplace. Seconds later there were two sharp raps on the cabin's thick wooden door.

"Come in," Seward called sternly as he rested his cane against the arm of the chair.

Commander John Magee entered the cabin, nodded formally, closed the door and sat down in the chair opposite Seward's.

"Good afternoon, Commander," Seward said.

"Good afternoon," Magee responded tersely.

The thirty-nine-year-old Magee was five feet seven inches tall, had dark hair and dark eyes and maintained a wiry, steel-strong build with a constant and rigorous exercise program. Acne scars covered his ruddy face, and through this pocked visage ran a long scar extending from the bridge of his nose all the way down his left cheek to his jaw. He was an ex-Navy SEAL, having attained the rank of full commander at the youthful age of thirty-six, and was now on loan to William Seward from an elite special-forces unit of the CIA. In that unit Magee had been extensively trained in everything from high-tech explosives to germ warfare. He was coldly efficient at whatever task was at hand and possessed an intelligence quotient of 164, an IQ he was not shy about marketing.

"How are you, sir?" Magee asked.

Seward noticed subtle derision in the way Magee articulated the word sir. "Fine, Commander Magee," Seward answered calmly, exhibiting none of the irritation gnawing at him. Seward knew that the young commander considered him long overdue for an appointment with a Florida continuing-care facility. Seward knew this through his extensive Pentagon grapevine, of which Magee was not aware. However, it wasn't the lack of respect that so angered Seward today. It was something far more important.

Through four decades Seward had made it a point not to initiate friendships with any of the six men who had previously held Magee's position. Becoming friendly with those men wasn't a good idea, because it made the "unfortunate accidents" at the end of their tours of duty with him all the more difficult. Still, in most cases Seward hadn't been able to resist developing a sense of companionship with the men.

Magee was different. Magee's attitude was so overwhelmingly offensive that Seward was actually looking forward to the day Magee would suffer his inevitable accident. The attitude was highlighted by an abrasive aura of invincibility and utter confidence, combined with an all-knowing, all-seeing demeanor. Given the slightest opportunity, Magee would launch into a self-serving oration, trumpeting his unparalleled knowledge of everything from aviation combat tactics and incendiary devices to predicting human behavior. Seward had worried over the last two years that this supreme self-possession might ultimately lead to trouble, but his direct superior, General Avery Zahn, had steadfastly maintained that Magee was the best man for the job.

Now, however, Seward's instincts had proved correct. Magee's behavior last night in Manhattan had almost precipitated disaster. He should have listened to his instincts, Seward now realized. General Zahn should have as well.

"How was the drive down Route 29?" Seward asked hesitantly. He hoped this would be a benign enough question not to spark one of Magee's self-promotion speeches.

"It took me two hours and twenty-two minutes to get here from downtown Washington," Magee replied. "I've obviously done this trip a number of times, but I've never actually timed it before, so today before I left Washington I wrote down on a piece of paper how long I thought it would take. I wrote down two hours and twenty-three minutes. I was off by only one minute."

"Oh?" Seward rolled his eyes. Magee was off and running on another ego trip.

"Yes. You see, I have an incredible innate ability to judge time. Christ, it works even if I'm asleep. I never have to request wakeup calls when I stay in hotels, or set the alarm at home. I wake up exactly when I need to, always. It's subconscious, my mind working at several different levels simultaneously. I think that's always been a key to my incredible success at such a young age. Knowing things without even having to—"

"Thank you, Commander Magee," Seward interrupted. He could tell from Magee's expression that the commander wasn't happy about being cut off, but the hell with him. "Let's get started. Do you have the tape?" Seward asked impatiently.

Magee opened his briefcase sullenly, withdrew the videocassette case and placed it on the maple coffee table between them. "Last night I acquired this tape on Thirty-ninth Street between Fifth and Madison Avenues."

Seward let out a long slow breath as he saw the tape physically in front of him. He tried not to allow his emotion to show, but that was impossible. He had been studying and shadowing Jim Egan for too long. If Magee hadn't acquired this damning piece of evidence last night, thirty-five years of work would have washed down the drain like so much dirty bathwater.

Suddenly Seward could no longer contain his anger. "What the hell were you thinking about last night?"

Magee's posture stiffened. He had never heard this tone in Seward's voice and was unprepared for the rebuke. After all, he had successfully completed the mission. "What did you say?"

Seward gritted his teeth. "I told you to acquire the tape as benignly as possible. Under no circumstances were you to jeopardize Cole Egan's life. You completely disobeyed my orders."

"I got you the damn tape," Magee snapped. Christ, he was tired of reporting to this doddering old fool. It was time to get back to the CIA. "And how would you know I jeopardized Cole Egan's life?"

"A Gilchrist window was shot out last night, and there was an explosion in Mr. Egan's Manhattan apartment, killing an unlucky young woman named Maria Cooper." Seward gritted his teeth more tightly. "I believe that explosion was meant for Cole Egan. It's quite a trail of violence, too closely timed with your Manhattan visit to be coincidence. That's how I know you jeopardized his life."

Magee shifted uncomfortably in his chair but said nothing.

"You *had* to use your power, didn't you?" Seward asked disdainfully. Magee was one of those psychopathic military zealots Seward had run into before. "You had to kill, now that you're insulated." Magee could commit murder and suffer no consequences. The government had bestowed that privilege upon him, and it sickened Seward that Magee would take advantage of this newly acquired carte blanche. "You fired on Cole Egan as you chased him out of the Gilchrist Building last night, and you wired his apartment for the explosion, didn't you?" Seward demanded.

Still Magee said nothing. But Seward thought he noticed a tiny smile move Magee's scar. "What about the people under your command?" he asked curtly.

"Catherine is dead," Magee answered without emotion. "Some idiot came running at us immediately after I took the tape from Cole Egan."

"What?" Seward caught his breath as his heart rate jumped.

"Yes. The man shot Catherine. Fortunately, I eluded him."

This was bad news. "Did you get a good look at this man?" Seward asked quickly, his pulse racing.

"All I can tell you for certain is that he had curly yellow hair."

"You mean blond hair."

"If I had meant blond, I would have said it. Blond is a generic term covering many different shades. This man's hair was yellow."

"Is everyone else accounted for?" Seward asked, trying to ignore Magee's arrogance.

Magee shook his head. "Agent Graham is missing. I presume he is dead as well."

"Dammit!" Seward slammed his fist on the table. "You really screwed this up, Magee."

So fire me and let me go back to the CIA, Magee wanted to say. But he held back. Something told him that discretion might be the better part of valor right now.

"Do you realize what kind of trouble you might have caused us by harming Cole Egan," Seward raged, "if our investigation into the Colombian affair turns up answers we don't anticipate?" It was improbable that the investigation would turn up those answers, but then Jim Egan was an improbable man. Seward had learned that a long time ago. "Cole Egan must stay alive."

"Look, I'm sorry." It took the only ounce of humility Magee possessed to say the words. "You told me it was absolutely imperative that we acquire that tape." He gestured at the cassette case sitting on the table.

"Cole Egan turned out to be a resourceful man, so as a precaution, in the event I couldn't catch up with him, I wired the apartment for an explosion. That way, if we couldn't get the tape, nobody else could either. It's too bad about the woman in Cole Egan's apartment."

"Uh-huh." Seward was seething. He knew Magee didn't give a rat's ass about the young woman. "Fortunately, using our powers of persuasion, we were able to convince the New York City Fire Department that the explosion was an accident."

"Good." Magee was suddenly impressed with Seward's abilities to manipulate. Perhaps he had underestimated the man after all.

"What about the fat man on the Gilchrist trading floor?" Seward asked. "I believe his name is Lewis Gebauer."

"What about him?"

"Is he suspicious of what's going on? Did you screw that up too?"

Magee shook his head. "No, he's positive I'm a private investigator working for the company holding Cole Egan's mortgage. Gebauer is an idiot. He's got no idea what's really going on. He just wants to screw up Egan's life. For some reason they hate each other. Of course, Gebauer would be an easy man to hate."

As are you, Seward thought to himself. "Is Gebauer still useful?"

Magee knew what that meant. "Yes, if you want to maintain close surveillance on Cole Egan." It meant that Gebauer's days were numbered.

"All right," Seward said, more to himself than Magee. He was beginning to calm down. "You leave for Colombia tonight, Commander," Seward reminded Magee, holding up his left hand and studying the nail of his index finger as he spoke.

"I'm ready," Magee answered confidently.

"I hope you don't find anything alarming down there."

"I hope not too, sir."

Seward heard the derisive tone again as he picked up his cane and the tape, rose stiffly from the chair and limped out of the living room. At the doorway he hesitated momentarily. "Have a pleasant trip, Commander," he said, then closed the door behind him and limped down the hallway toward his study.

Magee shook his head and rose from the chair. What a bastard Seward was. And he had to endure a five-hour round trip just to put up with that crock of shit. Magee picked up his leather briefcase and headed toward the cabin door.

Seward watched through the study's tinted window as Magee strode to the silver government sedan, slid behind the steering wheel, gunned the motor and guided the car back down the driveway. He kept watching until the car had disappeared into the forest, then turned to face General Avery Zahn, who was sitting in a chair across the room.

"Did you get all that?" Seward asked. He was still angry.

Zahn gestured at the television in one corner of the study. He had observed the conversation between Seward and Magee via a tiny camera and microphone concealed in the stones of the living room fireplace. "Yes," he said calmly. "I got it."

"Commander Magee went over the line in New York. I told you he would. He could have screwed up everything. He still might."

"He got the tape," Zahn observed.

"Yes," Seward agreed. "But Commander Magee

was specifically ordered not to harm Cole Egan. If he had, we might have had real trouble on our hands."

"Relax," Zahn urged. "Commander Magee did what he had to do."

"Why would we have had real trouble?" The short man dressed in a charcoal suit spoke up for the first time from his seat on the couch. His voice was gruff, as if he were suffering from laryngitis.

Seward glanced at the man. Though short, he exuded natural power. Not political power, but a cruder, rawer power. He wasn't military, and Zahn wouldn't explain his presence. Zahn even seemed slightly intimidated by him.

"There is always the possibility that a second tape exists," Seward said without awaiting Zahn's approval to offer the information. There was more than a possibility, Seward judged. Even though Seward had never met Jim Egan, he felt as if he knew him very well after studying him for so many years. "Jim Egan was an intelligent man. He could have easily made another tape. Cole Egan is our link. Without him we'd be blind again."

The short man pursed his lips twice as he processed this new, disturbing possibility.

"Jim Egan could have given someone the original film, too," Zahn snapped, obviously irritated at Seward's unauthorized editorial. "But he didn't."

Seward's eyes narrowed as he studied General Zahn. So the president hadn't told Zahn everything. "Yes, he did give someone the original film," Seward corrected Zahn quietly.

"Huh?" Zahn lurched forward in his chair, and the short man's eyes flashed to Seward's.

"Eight years ago a woman delivered the original film of the assassination to a civilian CIA employee who lived in the woman's apartment building," Seward explained. "The woman claimed to have come upon the film while she was clearing out her father's attic after he had died."

"So we have possession of it?" Zahn asked. So the president was holding back on him.

Seward nodded.

"Why did the woman give it to a CIA employee?" the short man wanted to know. "Why didn't she sell it for a great deal of money?"

Seward smiled. "Those are excellent questions, and ones I might have asked if I'd had a chance. Unfortunately, the woman died in a terrible car accident on the Capital Beltway only a few hours after giving away the film."

"And you think the woman got the film from Jim Egan?" Zahn asked.

Seward nodded again.

"Why do you think that?" the short man asked.

"I checked the woman out. Her father wasn't dead at all. He was still alive and had no connection whatsoever to President Kennedy's assassination."

"That doesn't mean anything," Zahn argued. "Maybe she found the film some other way and was being patriotic. Maybe Jim Egan never really had it at all."

"Jim was throwing me a curveball," Seward said softly. "He wanted me to think he no longer had the film so I'd stop watching him. I'm certain he gave the film to the woman with instructions to give it to that specific CIA employee, because in fact that CIA employee wasn't really a civilian at all. That was just his cover. That CIA employee was my direct assistant for Operation Snowfall at the time. He is now dead." Seward hung his head for a moment. The man had died in one of those unfortunate accidents at the end of his tour of duty. "Jim must have somehow found out who I was and who my assistant was. He was a clever man." Seward paused. "I'm also certain that the woman who delivered the film to my assistant didn't die in an accident. I'm certain Jim killed her."

"What?" This was too much for Zahn. "Why in the hell would he do that?"

"Because he didn't want her telling anyone else what she had delivered," Seward responded. "He wanted the existence of that film to remain secret until now."

The short man nodded subtly. "So you think he might have made one or more videocassette copies?" the man asked in his gruff voice.

"Yes," Seward answered definitively. "He was a careful man. He knew he was being monitored."

"Is that our only potential problem?" the short man asked. Seward was obviously much better informed than Zahn, and while he had the chance he was going to ask questions.

"There's Colombia," Seward offered.

"Enough, Mr. Seward," Zahn interrupted. "We'll deal with that if we have to." He was annoyed. "I think you're being paranoid."

Seward nodded stiffly. "All right," he said. If that was the way Zahn wanted to play, so be it. He was the general.

"Play the tape," Zahn ordered.

Obediently, Seward moved to the VCR positioned beneath the television and inserted the tape. He had seen the images many times while watching the original film, so this would be nothing new for him. But he was interested in seeing the reactions of the other two men to the shocking footage.

7

THE LASSITER RIVER BEGINS IN THE REMOTE FOREST OF northern Wisconsin and flows through deep gorges and towering pine trees until it empties into Lake Superior forty miles east of Duluth, Minnesota. The river is fast-flowing, rocky-bottomed, relatively short—just thirty miles point to point—and accessible only after an arduous trek through the dense pines or at two small bridges maintained by Oswego County. The property on either side of the river is owned by a small group of monied individuals as well as the federal and state governments.

Except at the tiny town of Hubbard, through which the Lassiter runs, only an occasional home is visible among the trees as one travels downstream, because there are only twelve estates along the entire length of the river. During the late spring and summer months these estates are occupied by members and guests of wealthy Minneapolis and St. Paul families, but the mansions are rarely inhabited from October to March. During these months the homes can be buried beneath mountains of snow dropped by a constant barrage of Alberta clippers and lake-effect storms.

The town of Hubbard, ten miles south of Lake Superior, is little more than an outpost in the middle of the forbidding pine forest. The town consists of a gas station still displaying a rusted Esso sign, a diner, a motel, a few modest clapboard homes and a drinking establishment known as the Kro Bar. The townspeople, mostly farmers and loggers, are not overly friendly to strangers—not even to sportsmen who journey to the Lassiter in the summer to enjoy some of the best rainbow trout fishing in the country and to spend money on rooms at the motel, food at the diner and alcohol at the Kro Bar. It is an isolated land, and most of the natives, including a few Chippewa Indians, seem to prefer it that way.

The sleek green-hulled canoe gathered speed as it cruised into the top of Devil's Run just above a half-mile stretch of the river called Big Lake where the Lassiter expands to several hundred feet across and slows considerably. The few canoeists who find their way to the Lassiter are usually nervous at this point. Devil's Run is a wild stretch of white water, and the odds of losing control and capsizing in these rapids are high. But Cole paddled confidently toward the first drop. He knew the Lassiter like the back of his hand and after years of experience had learned to identify submerged objects by reading surface swirls and shadows. He had grown up on this river fly-fishing, hunting and canoeing with the friends of his youth, most of whom he had lost contact with after moving to New York City. They couldn't understand why he would abandon the pristine woodlands of Minnesota and northern Wisconsin to live in a place where crime was a way of life and the real outdoors was hours away.

To them, no amount of money was worth that sacrifice. Maybe he should have listened to them, Cole thought to himself as he maneuvered the craft into the top of the rapids.

Cole guided the bow of the canoe through the boiling water, deftly avoiding sharp rocks and submerged logs as he bounced downstream. Finally he steered to the right of a huge boulder at the bottom of Devil's Run and slipped into the calm headwaters of Big Lake. He pulled the dripping paddle from the water, placed it across the gunwales and allowed the canoe to drift freely with the current as he relaxed and enjoyed the serenity of the fall afternoon. The only sounds on the river were the fading roar of the rapids behind him and the shrill screech of a territorial bald eagle overhead as it vacated its perch atop a dead birch tree, irritated at the uncommon human intrusion into its domain. The sky was a cloudless deep blue, and the scent of a far-off fire drifted through the air as the sun sank toward the horizon.

The temperature turned chilly over the calmer water, and Cole zipped up his wool jacket, then took a tired breath as he gazed into the dark pine forest rising from both banks of the river. The New York City Fire Department had officially ruled the explosion that had killed Maria Cooper an accident, but Cole knew the truth. "Dammit!" Cole's voice echoed through the pines. Maria was dead and it was his fault.

He had comforted Nicki all the way out on the flight from New York to Minnesota. But she was inconsolable, believing that Maria's death was *her* fault because she had left the key for Maria at the front desk. Cole had assured her over and over that there was no reason for her to feel guilty, that nothing she could have done would have prevented the accident. He hadn't yet told Nicki of the Dealey Tape and the frantic chase through Manhattan two nights ago—let alone how the man with the scar, as he stood in front of Cole with a smug smile on his face and the Dealey Tape in his hand, had boasted about the apartment being set to explode. Cole didn't want to scare Nicki any more than she already was. More to the point, he realized that Nicki might want nothing to do with him if he told her the whole story. If she found out that he had been withholding information from her before he left Emilio's to retrieve the Dealey Tape from the Gilchrist screening room, she would blame him for Maria's death. And rightly so.

Cole shook his head. He should have contacted someone at the apartment building and ordered the doorman not to allow anyone into his place *before* leaving Emilio's. He slammed the side of the fiberglass canoe with his fist, and noise reverberated through the trees again, this time frightening a flock of sparrows from a branch hanging over the quiet water. He watched the birds fly away, wishing he could turn back time.

As the birds disappeared into the distance, Cole picked up the paddle and headed slowly toward shore. He and Nicki had rented a car at the airport yesterday after the morning flight from New York to Minneapolis, then driven four hours north up Interstate 35 to Duluth. He wanted to get Nicki out of Manhattan for a while, and he needed time for himself too. He needed time to deal with the death of his father, the loss of the Dealey Tape, and his guilt about Maria's death. He couldn't do that on a crowded trading floor with Lewis Gebauer hassling him and the trading losses hanging over his head. He was fairly certain he would have been safe in New York now that he no longer possessed the Dealey Tape, but he wanted to leave all that behind for a few days and convalesce on a river he adored rather than in a city he endured.

The canoe slid into a small cove and he guided the bow between two large rocks protruding from shore. Fifty feet into the forest was a campsite consisting of a crude stone grill and an old picnic table constructed by the family who owned this stretch of the Lassiter. The uninitiated would have paddled past the campsite without seeing it, but Cole had used this place many times on previous trips.

He jumped from the small craft onto the shore and looped the bow line around a low branch, then knelt down, picked up a stone, tossed it into the calm water and watched the waves move outward in growing concentric circles. Last night Nicki and her parents had eaten a somber dinner at his aunt and uncle's house. Afterward he and Nicki had taken a short and mostly silent walk through the neighborhood. She was still too grief-stricken about Maria to say much. Then he had seen her home and given her a quick kiss on the cheek as her mother, who had come straight home after dinner, spied on them from the living room window. For several minutes he had stood outside the door after she disappeared inside, staring at it, wondering if he would ever be able to tell her what had really happened in Manhattan.

At six o'clock this morning he had secured the canoe to the top of an old corroded Suburban his uncle kept behind the garage and driven from Duluth to the Lassiter's headwaters. He wanted to be alone, as he had sometimes in his youth when the realization that his father had abandoned him became too much. The Lassiter would be the perfect refuge from the world, as it had been years ago.

He had navigated the upper half of the river today and would paddle the lower half tomorrow after camping in this spot overnight. In a few days, when the solace of the Lassiter had helped him gather his strength, he would return to Duluth and tell Nicki the truth—if he could bring himself to do so—then fly back to Manhattan to face his gambling debts and trading losses. But for now he simply wanted to be alone.

He gazed into the dark forest. This was his only reliable sanctuary, yet he couldn't shake the eerie feeling that something was out there and that it was closing in on him.

He turned toward the canoe, bent down and pulled out a nylon bag containing a tent, then slung the bag over his shoulder and headed for the clearing where he would make camp for the night.

The .44 lay on the wooden picnic table in front of the blond man, pointed directly at the tent. Gray morning light was just seeping down through the pine branches as the sun climbed above the eastern horizon. The man looked up through the pine trees at the lightening sky. God, it was desolate out here. There probably wasn't another human being within ten miles. He rubbed his hands together to warm them, then ran them through his curly blond hair and smiled. Cole Egan was in for quite a surprise.

"Don't move."

The blond man froze as he heard the calm voice and felt cold steel pressed against the back of his neck.

"Raise your arms." Cole cocked the .22-caliber pistol. "Get them up, I said." He had carried the gun with him on these trips since he was a teenager, but this was the first time he had ever actually aimed it at anyone. "Now!"

"Easy, son." The man raised his arms slowly. "Don't do anything stupid."

"I think you're the one who better not do anything stupid. You're the one with a gun pointed directly at the back of his head. Make a move and I'll have no problem painting those trees across the way a bright red, believe me. Shoot first and ask questions later is my attitude right now."

"All well and good," the blond man replied evenly, "but the only gun with ammunition in it is lying on the table in front of me. I took all the bullets out of your little popgun last night. While you were visiting the sandman."

Cole moved the end of the .22's barrel slowly down until it came to rest between the blond man's shoulder blades. "Is that so?"

"Yes. Now put away your toy before you get hurt, and we'll have ourselves a nice friendly chat. All I want to do is chat."

"Three nights ago you were chasing a man with a scar on his face down Thirty-ninth Street in Manhattan. That was right after you had shot a woman in the head. Before that you were chasing *me* down Fifth Avenue. You'll understand if I don't just give up my weapon, shake your hand and introduce myself."

"There's no need to introduce yourself. I know more about you than anyone else on earth except yourself, Coleman Sage Egan." The blond man glanced over his shoulder. "Throwing yourself in front of that bus on Forty-second Street was unnecessary. Dramatic, I'll grant you, but totally unnecessary. You would have saved yourself a lot of pain and anguish if you had let me talk to you." He rubbed his chin for a moment. "And you might have saved a few other people some of the same."

Cole closed his eyes and allowed the barrel of his gun to drop. Maria was dead and Nicki might never forgive him if she knew the truth.

The blond man felt the gun fall away from his back. It was a tiny lapse in concentration on the part of his adversary, but that was all he needed. In one swift motion he grabbed his .44 from atop the picnic table, spun around and pressed the end of its barrel roughly against Cole's cheek. "Son, I'm a professional. I kill people for a living. Don't fuck with me," he hissed through clenched teeth. "Now drop your gun."

Cole swallowed hard. The man was cobra-quick. "You may be a professional," he said quietly, "but you aren't very good at following a person through the woods. I knew someone was behind me yesterday when all the birds kept getting agitated. You should learn a little river etiquette. Paddle in the middle of the river, then you won't bother them so much. And you won't give yourself away." Cole glanced down at the man's .44. "There aren't any bullets in your clip and you know it. You can feel the difference between a loaded and an unloaded gun, at least you ought to be able to. My gun is the one that's loaded." He brought the barrel of his .22 up against the blond man's chest, then pointed it skyward and fired to prove his point.

"Holy Jesus!" The blond man fell back onto the picnic table bench, taken completely off guard.

"You bedded down last night above Devil's Run in that little clearing on the west side of the river," Cole continued as the sound of the shot echoed through the trees. "You couldn't have been more obvious. *I'm* the one who removed ammunition last night. I took all yours while you were snoring away, and not just what was in your gun." Cole laughed as he reached down, pulled the .44 from the blond man's grasp and tossed it toward his tent. "But I don't think you're here to kill me. If you were, you would have tried to shoot me last night while you thought I was in my tent. But you never made a move downriver to my camp."

"Very good." The blond man clapped several times. "A chip off the old block. I like your style, son."

"Thanks, but who the hell are you?"

"Bennett Smith." Smith extended his right hand.

Cole didn't take the man's hand. Instead he moved to the other side of the picnic table and sat down

"I remember you," Cole said as he stared at the man. "You were sitting in reception three days ago reading the *Wall Street Journal* when I came through the trading room door. You delivered the envelope to the receptionist, didn't you?"

"Yes."

Cole noticed that Smith was missing a lower front tooth, which caused him to lisp slightly. It was a lisp Cole hadn't heard over the trading room line when Smith called demanding to know his middle name. "Did you deliver it for my father?"

"Yes, for your father." Smith talked quickly, in a low voice.

Cole also noticed that Smith stared straight at him whether Smith was listening or speaking. It was Cole's experience that most people locked eyes as they listened, but constantly looked away as they spoke, a certain indication that they were accustomed to bending the truth, whether or not they actually were at that moment. Smith always stared directly into the eyes, except that every few moments he would casually glance first to the left, then to the right, whether he was speaking or listening, performing a continual reconnaissance of the immediate area. It was always the same. First left, then right, as if he expected to see an enemy out there in the trees.

"How do you know my father?" Cole asked.

"I worked with him. Over the last thirty-six years we saw each other almost every day of our lives."

Cole felt a sudden rush of excitement. Bennett Smith would be able to answer all those plaguing questions he had about his father. "You just told me you delivered the envelope to the Gilchrist receptionist desk for my father, but when you called me on the Gilchrist line, you said you were delivering the message and the envelope for 'the agency.' What did that mean?"

Smith smiled. "You have your father's memory for detail, in your eye and your ear."

"Answer the question."

"And his patience." Smith shook his head. "Or lack thereof. Christ, if you aren't one for the genetic scientists, I don't know who is."

"What do you mean by that?"

"You probably remember meeting your father only a few times in your life, correct?"

"Yes."

"Yet you're his spitting image—demeanorwise, I mean. You're better-looking than he was, but I feel like I'm staring at his personality twin." Smith paused as he performed his reconnaissance ritual again. "You never really knew him, yet you're just like him. It's eerie." Smith turned his head slightly to the side. "Do you like to gamble?" He was grinning. "Ever feel the urge to bet on things?"

Cole said nothing.

"I knew it." Smith slammed the picnic table with a huge fist as he saw the answer in Cole's expression. "Your father was the same way. It was his only weakness. Like I said, you're one for the genetic scientists."

Cole placed his pistol down on the picnic table bench. "Mr. Smith, you keep alluding to my father in the past tense. Is he really dead?"

"Yes, he is, son," Smith answered matter-of-factly.

Cole felt a pang of sorrow in his chest, and heat rushed to his eyes. "When?" he asked hoarsely.

"Forty-seven days ago. Back in the beginning of October." Smith could see the pain in Cole's face.

"Where did he die?"

"In the mountains outside Zaraza, Colombia. It's a small town in the southern part of the country."

"Are you absolutely certain he's dead?"

"Absolutely."

Cole winced. He'd just have to accept the fact that Jim Egan really was dead. Still, he wanted answers. "Tell me about my father. Who was he? What did he do?"

For the first time Smith looked away without performing his reconnaissance. He simply stared down at the table. "That's classified."

"Did he work for the government?"

"Yes."

"But you aren't going to tell me about him."

"I really can't."

"Then why the hell did you follow me here?" Cole asked, suddenly furious.

Smith grimaced, and the crow's feet at the corners of his eyes and mouth became more obvious. "I wanted to know what was in that Chase safe-deposit box."

"Why didn't you take the key and go to Chase yourself?" Cole asked angrily. "You probably put the death certificate inside the envelope. You must have read the note. Maybe you even wrote it. The key was right there."

"I might have done that, except Chase would have required identification and a signature. Your father appointed you as the only person allowed access to that box other than himself. He got your picture and your signature from your aunt."

"You seem like the type who could overcome a little detail like that fairly easily," Cole shot back.

"Maybe, but—Cole, I respected and admired your father a great deal. Despite what you have reason to believe, he was a man of character, a man of courage and conviction. We went to hell and back together and he saved my ass more than a few times along the way. He was my best friend. He wanted you to go to that Chase box, not me. I promised him I would deliver the envelope to you in case he died, and I kept my promise."

Cole heard emotion in Smith's voice for the first time. "Why didn't you just hand the envelope to me in reception? Why all the intrigue?"

"Again, because it was your father's request." Smith looked to the left and right twice this time. "He asked me to deliver the envelope to you with as little noise as possible. I knew what that meant."

"But then you stuck around."

"Yes."

"Why?"

"Your father guessed you might need help after you took possession of whatever was in the safe-deposit box."

A right-on-the-money guess, Cole thought to himself. "He never told you what was in the box?" he asked skeptically.

"No." Smith pushed out his chin defiantly. But Cole thought he saw the man flinch.

"Why did he want you to deliver the envelope *after* he died?"

"I don't know. As I said, I have no clue what was in the box."

"Who were those other two people back in New York? The woman you shot and the guy with the scar on his face."

"I don't know," Smith said again. But it seemed to Cole that Smith's rosy cheeks flushed a brighter red as he answered.

"I don't believe you! What kind of game is this?"

Smith held his hands up, palms out. "Easy, son. It's no game. I have an idea who those people were, but I really don't know for certain." He stared into Cole's eyes. "If my guess is correct, it would confirm what your father and I believed all these years. Now, what was in the box?"

Cole was becoming exasperated. "Tell me about my father."

"Even though I shouldn't, I will. But first tell me what was in the box."

For several moments Cole said nothing. He had every reason not to trust this man, but Bennett Smith might be the only person in the world who could shed light on the mysterious life of Jim Egan. A life Cole wanted to know about very badly. "A videotape," he finally admitted.

"Of what?"

Cole hesitated again. "President Kennedy's assassination."

"Are you familiar with something called the Zapruder film?" Smith asked.

"Yes, I've seen that recording of the assassination and this wasn't it, I promise you."

Smith raised one eyebrow. "Did the tape in the safe-deposit box shed any new light on the assassination?"

"Yes," Cole responded quietly.

"There was another gunman." Smith was stating, not asking.

"Yes," Cole confirmed.

"Behind the fence on the grassy knoll?" This time it was a question.

"Yes."

"Jesus H. Christ," Smith whispered. "No wonder they came after you with everything they had. You're lucky to be alive, son. Lucky they got the tape without killing you. Lucky I got there when I did. I assume that's what the man took from you on Thirty-ninth Street—the tape, I mean. You don't have it anymore, do you?" he asked.

"No," Cole admitted dejectedly. "So who were they?"

Smith pushed his tongue into the gap formed by the missing lower front tooth. "God, it all makes so much sense now."

"What makes sense? Dammit, I want answers."

"I know, and you deserve them." Smith looked to his left as the eagle Cole had disturbed yesterday screeched from across Big Lake. "I'm going to tell you a story. I probably shouldn't, but I will." He shook his head. "Bastards," he muttered.

"Come on," Cole urged.

Smith rubbed his mouth with the back of his hand. "Your father and I were Dallas police officers and roommates in 1963. We were twenty years old and had only been on the force about a year at the time. On November twenty-second we went to Dealey Plaza to see the president on his way from Love Field to his Trade Mart luncheon. We had both worked late the night before, until around four in the morning, I believe. We were tired, but we wanted to see Kennedy. Christ, everyone did.

"We parked in the lot behind the grassy knoll well before the motorcade was to pass by, then walked up the railroad tracks to the triple underpass and stood on top of the bridge, on the west side of the plaza. That vantage point provided a perfect view." Smith swallowed hard, as if this was bringing back unpleasant memories. "The motorcade came up Main Street, turned right onto Houston, then left on Elm in front of the Depository. The limousine was just beginning to accelerate after making the sharp turn onto Elm when everything went nuts." Smith cleared his throat. "Your father and I heard the first shot very distinctly, but from our position there wasn't any way to pinpoint where it had come from. There were buildings all around the plaza and the echo was tremendous." A faraway expression came to Smith's face. "I still remember your father yelling, 'Did you hear that?' I answered affirmatively. I also remember that we didn't look at each other while we were talking. We were too busy searching the plaza for gunmen. Our training kicked in automatically."

"What happened after that?" Cole was riveted to Smith's words, visually aware of nothing but the man's face.

"The second shot came, louder than the first."

"The magic bullet," Cole prompted.

"I think of it as the pristine bullet," Smith said.

"After supposedly being fired from the Depository's sixth floor, traveling through Kennedy, smashing Governor Connally's rib and his wrist, then lodging in his thigh, the bullet they found on Connally's stretcher at Parkland Hospital looked as if it had never been fired. It had lost less than three percent of its original weight, less than three grains. I've fired a lot of bullets from a lot of different guns in my time, and I can tell you that doesn't happen, not after smashing through two bones, anyway. That bullet should have looked like a piece of chewed gum." Smith paused.

"Go on," Cole urged.

"Mmm." Smith rubbed his chin again. "Well, then the killing shot came. It tore the top of President Kennedy's head right off, at least that's what it looked like from where we were. It was really more to the side, but it was awful, regardless."

Cole felt his stomach churn. The Dealey Tape had graphically illustrated how awful that moment was. "And then?"

"Your father and I decided immediately to assist. We weren't on duty, so we were dressed in street clothes. We realized that not being in uniform could create a problem because the in-uniform people wouldn't recognize us as law officers, but we didn't care. We had to help. It was instinct.

"Your father ran south on the tracks, then down onto Commerce Street and into the plaza. I went north back toward the train yard. As I got to the other side of the bridge, I saw a man running away from the fence behind the grassy knoll. He was carrying what looked like a tool box. I chased him, but I couldn't catch him. He had too much of a lead." Smith shook his head. "I guess I was that damn close to making history."

"Me too," Cole murmured, remembering the man with the scar smiling smugly as he snatched the Dealey Tape. "Then my father must have taken the film away from someone as he ran across Dealey Plaza."

Smith nodded. "Not just someone, son, he took it away from your mother." Smith saw shock register on Cole's face. "A young woman named Andrea Sage."

Here was the answer to another of those long-unanswered questions. Cole's aunt and uncle had claimed all these years not to know his mother's name or anything about her except that, according to his father, she had died when Cole was a year old. They said they had never met her, and explained that his father had fallen out of touch with everyone in the family after a secret wedding to a mysterious woman. Then he had brought one-year-old Cole to live with them, and disappeared again.

"So my mother's maiden name was Sage," Cole said quietly.

"Yes," Smith confirmed. "That's why I asked you to identify yourself with your middle name on the phone. Your middle name was her maiden name. Your father said he never told anyone that except me. I wanted to make certain the person who picked up the phone on the trading floor was the person I was looking for. I couldn't take a chance that the wrong person got hold of that envelope. I waited in the reception area until I saw that you had it."

So his aunt and uncle hadn't been lying all these years. They really hadn't known anything about his parents. He had always suspected that they might be withholding information because his parents were criminals and his aunt and uncle didn't want him to know the truth.

"Why wasn't Andrea Sage up with the two of you on the railroad overpass?"

"She wasn't Jim's wife at that point. In fact, he had no idea who she was. They met for the first time in Dealey Plaza seconds after President Kennedy was shot, though they didn't really have much of a chance to introduce themselves properly." Smith smiled. "God, it really all fits together now."

"What fits together?" Cole asked impatiently.

Smith pried a splinter from the tabletop, inspected it briefly, then flicked it away. "One morning a few days after the killing a very pretty young woman walked into the Dallas police headquarters and announced that she had recorded the Kennedy assassination on a Bell & Howell spring-wound movie camera. Andrea Sage was that pretty young woman, and she said she was certain the film could shed light on what had happened, except for one small problem. Someone had forcibly ripped the movie camera away from her only moments after the shooting. Then she dropped the real bombshell. The person who had confiscated the camera and the film was a Dallas policeman. An officer named Jim Egan."

"What?" That made no sense to Cole. "She wouldn't have known he was a cop. You said my father wasn't in uniform that day."

"That's right, I did."

"Did he identify himself when he took the film away from her?"

"No, he didn't. Andrea identified him later on her own. She watched Jack Ruby shoot Lee Harvey Oswald on television and saw your father in the background. He was in uniform when they were bringing Oswald out. Andrea recognized his face after she had seen the killing replayed a few times on television.

She said she waited after recognizing him before she came forward because she was certain he must have passed the film on to the proper people. However, when nothing came out about the film in the press, she decided to follow up."

"But in all the books and accounts of that day you never hear about this," Cole pointed out. "I mean, there's the airman on leave from Alaska who claimed to have a camera confiscated and—"

"And several others," Smith interrupted. "I know. But this story remained under wraps, primarily because no one believed Andrea, not even the few reporters who heard about it. Your father adamantly denied her accusation about taking the camera, and she was acting mysterious. She gave her permanent address as a Dallas hotel, and she wasn't willing to produce any identification proving who she was. It was a simple case of believing a man who had a good, though brief, reputation as a law officer over a woman who seemed to be trying to generate her fifteen minutes of fame."

"But she wasn't lying," Cole said defiantly.

Smith pressed his tongue in the gap between his teeth again, then smacked his lips. "Apparently not." A strange expression came over his face. "But how did you know your father confiscated the film from someone? He could have gotten it any number of ways."

Cole was hesitant to reveal too much. But Bennett Smith was providing answers to questions he had wondered about for many years and he didn't want the information flow to stop. "At the end of the Dealey Tape—"

"That's what you call it?" Smith interrupted again.

Cole nodded.

"Incredible." Smith shook his head, reached across the table and slapped Cole on the shoulder.

Cole grinned. "What?"

"Your father was always naming things too. He named his gun, his badge, his boots. It didn't matter what it was. He named everything." Smith sat back down on the bench seat still chuckling. "Go ahead, I interrupted you. I apologize."

Suddenly Cole liked Bennett Smith even though the man was a self-described professional assassin—a claim Cole did not doubt for a moment. While he took actions many would not approve of, the man gave the impression he could convince anyone that honorable men had to commit unsavory acts to ensure the security of a republic. Smith indeed had killed the woman on Thirty-ninth Street in cold blood, but she had been about to pull a trigger herself. Smith had saved his life and that was reason enough to like him.

"It's okay," Cole said. "At the end of the Dealey Tape, after the limousine takes off and my mother—" Cole swallowed the words. "*My mother.*" It sounded strange now that he was beginning to get to know her, even if she was dead and the familiarity was coming through a conduit. "Sorry." He glanced at Smith.

"It's all right." Smith wasn't a sentimental man, but he could understand what Cole was going through.

Cole coughed, then continued. "As I was saying, the tape goes black for a second, then my father's face appears. It's fuzzy, but it's obviously him. Then the tape goes black again. I guess his face appears because he's about to take the camera from my mother."

Smith whistled through his missing tooth. "Jim really had the tape all these years. You know, that was another one of his traits. He could keep information to himself and tell no one, not even his best friend." Smith performed his reconnaissance once more, then looked back at Cole. "But you said what was in the safe-deposit box was a tape, not a film."

"Yes. I played it on a VCR at Gilchrist right after I picked it up from the Chase branch."

"Then at some point your father must have made a copy, film to tape, and probably enhanced it in the process."

"He must have," Cole agreed.

Smith's eyes narrowed. "That means the original film could still be out there."

"I guess." Cole wasn't interested in a film he had zero likelihood of recovering, and he didn't want Smith distracted from the revelations he was yielding. "What happened to my mother after that?"

Smith seemed to be still pondering the fate of the original film.

"Hey." Cole banged the table with his hand.

"Huh? Oh, sorry." Smith rubbed his eyes for a moment. "It was the strangest thing. She went to a few reporters to try to stir up interest in her story, but they had already written her off as a fraud, as someone trying to cash in on what had happened. She kind of faded from the picture pretty quickly. And initially your father claimed to hate her. He said she was a rumormonger and a liar. I actually believed him, and why wouldn't I?" Smith laughed. "Then about two weeks later I found out that Jim and Andrea were dating. A week after that they were married. The first I knew was when he left our apartment and explained that he was moving in with Andrea. I thought I was going to have to pay the rent myself, but even though he moved out, he kept paying it. Of course, that was your father. If he made a deal, he kept his side of the bargain no matter what. He always said that all you really had in life was your reputation. And he was right."

"My father married Andrea Sage even after she had gone to the police and said he had taken the film from her?" Cole asked.

"Yes."

"That's bizarre."

"It is, and it gets even stranger."

"How?"

"I really shouldn't tell you this."

"Come on," Cole urged.

Still Smith hesitated.

"Please, Bennett." It was the first time Cole had addressed Smith by his first name. "I need to know."

"I know you do," he said, glancing toward the Lassiter. The sun was well above the horizon and its bright rays were setting the river's surface ablaze. "What say we get going? I'd appreciate the chance to paddle downstream with you. We can keep talking on the river."

Cole nodded slowly. "Okay."

The Colombian boy was only twelve years old. He was thin, with a thick mop of straight blue-black hair, and wore nothing but a filthy pair of ragged shorts and muddy Nike basketball shoes. But his skin was a deep brown, so the strong tropical sun didn't burn his chest or back.

Commander Magee broke into a slow trot as the boy darted ahead of him on the narrow jungle path. They had been hiking for more than two hours and Magee was beginning to wonder if the thirty dollars he had pressed into the boy's grimy palm were going to bear fruit. "How much farther?" Magee yelled in

Spanish to his young guide. Magee was fluent in Spanish, French, German and Russian.

"No too long way to there," the boy replied in broken English. He smiled back at the gringo. It was the first time he had used the man's native tongue.

A short time later they reached a clearing next to a muddy river. As they neared the water's edge, Magee saw a large crocodile slither along the opposite bank where it had been sunning itself and plunge into the river with a loud splash. For several minutes Magee took in the sight, memorizing every detail about it. This was where the gun battle was supposed to have taken place.

Finally he turned to the boy. "You said there was a grave."

"Yes." The boy gestured downriver and took off again.

Magee followed, lugging the shovel on his shoulder. A few minutes later he hustled around a bend and found the boy squatting down, pointing at a mound of dirt in the shadow of a crude cross made of tree limbs. "Move back!" he ordered, dropping the shovel. The boy obeyed as Magee knelt down and touched the bare earth.

"You happy?" the boy asked. "Maybe give me more dollars?"

Magee looked up. "Maybe." His eyes narrowed. "The man who made this hole and buried the body, what did he look like?"

"He was a big man." The boy spread his arms wide, then pointed at his head. "His hair was the color of the sun."

That had to be the man who had chased him in Manhattan, Magee thought to himself. "Let's go back to your village."

"You no dig?" the boy asked curiously.

"No."

The boy found it strange to have trekked so far through the jungle simply to turn back around again. But he had heard that Americans were odd, and this one with the scar running through his cheek certainly fit that description. He shrugged his shoulders. "Okay."

As the boy turned to go, Magee stood up, slid a long serrated hunting knife from his combat belt, grabbed the boy around the face and plunged the blade deep into the boy's throat, slicing it wide open. The boy dropped to the ground, grabbing at his neck, gasping for air. He writhed on the ground for a short time but soon lay still. Magee smiled. He could have simply snapped the boy's thin neck, but he liked the sight of blood. Seward was right. He enjoyed killing. And the more painful the death, the better.

Magee removed the thirty dollars from a pocket of the boy's grimy shorts, then picked up the body and hurled it into the water. It splashed loudly as it hit the surface. Within seconds Magee saw the sinister eyes of crocodiles gliding just above the surface as the reptiles torpedoed toward the boy. Magee glanced up. High clouds bringing the afternoon rainstorm were beginning to form over the mountain crests off to the west. Between the crocodiles gorging themselves on the flesh and the rain washing away the blood, there would be no trace left of the boy in a very short time.

Magee picked up the shovel and began to dig.

8

THE CANOE BOBBED AND TURNED AS COLE MOVED INTO the rapids, using deft strokes of his paddle as well as raw power to maintain perfect balance through the white water. At the bottom of the rapids, Cole steered into an eddy near the bank and looked back upriver. He laughed aloud as he watched Bennett struggling to maintain control of his craft. He was in no real danger because the river was relatively shallow here, but his pride was suffering a severe blow.

Cole dropped the anchor on shore, moved to the front of his canoe, leaned out and snagged the bow line of Bennett's canoe as it floated swiftly past. All he had to do was hold on, and the canoe drifted out of the fast water and into the shallows with the current.

"Thanks," Bennett yelled gratefully.

Cole smiled. "No problem."

Ten minutes later they were feasting on a shore lunch of turkey sandwiches and potato salad, food Cole had brought with him from his aunt's kitchen.

"This is good," Bennett announced through a huge mouthful, glancing around. "Boy, it's nice out here."

"Yes, it is," Cole agreed. It was another beautiful day. There were no clouds in the sky and the temperature had risen into the fifties, which was warm for northern Wisconsin at this time of year. "Now earn your lunch, Bennett."

"Huh?" Bennett had just taken another bite of the sandwich.

"When we were back at the camp you told me that my father married Andrea Sage," Cole reminded him. "That it was bizarre, but that the situation became even stranger." Maybe Bennett had hoped Cole wouldn't press for further information, but there wasn't any chance of that.

"Right." Bennett finished chewing and swallowed. "About a week after your father married Andrea in front of a justice of the peace, he and I were approached by members of something called the Defense Intelligence Agency. They wanted us to join the agency immediately."

"What is the Defense Intelligence Agency?" Cole asked.

"Exactly what it sounds like. An intelligence group contained within the Department of Defense and established in 1961 to serve the Joint Chiefs of Staff and coordinate intelligence operations of the different service branches. The DIA employs mostly civilians and is rarely operational, meaning that it isn't involved in anything clandestine or covert. It operates primarily as an analytical group, although the DIA director, who is always a three-star general or admiral, also has reporting responsibilities to the director of Central Intelligence."

"Does the DIA still exist?"

"Oh yes."

"I've never heard of it."

"Surprisingly, not many civilians have. It doesn't grab the headlines the way the CIA does."

Cole started to take another bite of his sandwich, then hesitated. Suddenly Jim Egan's lifetime absence might be somewhat justifiable. He could feel the weight of the bitterness and resentment lift slightly. "My father was with the DIA?"

"Yes. He and I joined a month after being approached by DIA officials. Our superiors on the Dallas police force recommended strongly that we agree to join. It was almost as if we wouldn't have had a job with the police force anyway if we had refused. We always found that a little odd."

"What happened after that?"

"We went through thirty-six months of intensive training, then went on our first mission. Ten of us slipped into Cambodia to rescue four Navy A-6 pilots. Our information was that they were being held in a jungle prison just across the border from North Vietnam. It was a top secret mission. We were never officially there. If we hadn't come back out, no one would have come looking for us."

"But, Bennett, you just told me the DIA isn't involved in covert operations."

"Officially not, which makes it a wonderful platform from which to conduct those kinds of missions."

"My father was an intelligence agent for the federal government," Cole said aloud. He liked the sound of that.

"Yes, and a damn fine one." Bennett wanted Cole to be proud of his father and to understand. "So fine he didn't have time to raise a child when his wife died. Son, they sent your father and me on some very important and dangerous missions. He and I went into Cuba, East Germany, even the Soviet Union. A lot of people are safe today because of things your father accomplished. You really were better off having your aunt and uncle, and the country was better off having him."

"Did my father kill people?" Cole's voice was calm as he asked a difficult question.

"Intelligence can be a nasty occupation," Bennett said.

Cole had his answer and didn't want to dwell on it. "My mother. How did she die?" His aunt and uncle had known she was dead, but had no idea from what or how.

This would hurt, Bennett realized, but Cole had asked and he would get his answer. "She and your father were living near Fort Dix, New Jersey, in 1970. Your father and I were away on a top secret mission. One night while we were gone, some hippies hopped up on drugs broke into the house to rob it. They must have thought the house was empty. Your mother surprised them and they killed her. Fortunately, they didn't harm you."

Cole closed his eyes and shook his head. He'd never get to know either of his parents.

"They didn't inform your father of Andrea's death until he arrived home a month later," Bennett continued. "You were only a year old, and one of the army wives on the base took care of you until your father returned. When he did, he took you to your aunt and uncle." Bennett saw the bitterness on Cole's face. "You shouldn't blame your father for what happened to you, Cole. He was in a tough situation. They were difficult circumstances for both of you. His sister was the only option he had. He knew it wouldn't be like having your real parents, and he felt very guilty about that. He blamed himself enough for both of you."

"I never blamed him," Cole said halfheartedly.

"I'm glad to hear that."

Cole glanced up at Bennett. "You said taking me to my aunt and uncle's was the only option my father had."

"Uh-huh."

"Why didn't he take me to my mother's parents?"

Bennett bit his lower lip for a moment before answering. "He told me that your mother and her father didn't get along very well. He never met the man, but he didn't like what Andrea had told him. On the other hand, he trusted his sister completely. He said she was a wonderful woman, so the choice was pretty easy for him. I think it seemed more natural for him to take you to his side of the family."

Cole nodded and glanced at the river rushing past. His aunt *was* a wonderful woman. "Thanks for telling me all this, Bennett. And thanks for saving my life the other night, too. I should have said that before."

Bennett waved. "I just wish I had gotten there sooner. Then you'd still have your Dealey Tape." He smiled as if he was still amused that Cole named things the same way his father had.

Cole sighed. "I guess that tape was my inheritance."

"Yes, and a very valuable one."

"Do you think so?"

"Does it really show a shooter behind the fence on the grassy knoll?"

"Absolutely. It's very clear. The picture bounces around a bit at first, as if my mother was running alongside the limousine as she was filming. But the picture becomes still well before the killing shot. It's obvious where the bullet comes from. You can see the rifle over the fence and the puff of smoke from the barrel. Then the president's head explodes."

"You have no doubt that the footage is authentic?" Bennett asked.

"None at all. There's no way anyone could have recreated what was on that tape."

"Then I'd say it's worth millions."

For a few moments they sat in silence, pondering what might have been. Finally Cole spoke up. "Do you think my father ever told my mother he had the Dealey Tape?"

Bennett wiped crumbs from his lips with the back of his hand. "That's a good question. I don't know. I doubt it, now that I think about it. He never told me, and I spent more time with him than anyone, including your mother. Of course, she probably always suspected."

"I still don't understand why my father would marry Andrea Sage so quickly after she had accused him of confiscating the movie camera and lying about it. Bennett, he doesn't sound like a man who did things rashly."

"He wasn't," Bennett agreed. "And why would the DIA come looking for your father and me so specifically?"

Cole looked up. He had heard an ominous tone in Bennett's voice. "Are you saying—"

"I'm not saying anything." Bennett took another bite of his sandwich but kept talking. "A little while ago you asked me who those other people in Manhattan were, the woman and the man who took the Dealey Tape from you, and I said I didn't know."

"But you said you had an idea."

"Yeah." Bennett gazed at Cole, as if trying to decide whether or not to provide any more information.

After almost a minute he pushed a piece of bread from the gap between his lower teeth using his tongue, then began. "There were rumors about an ultrasecret operation buried deep within the DIA. Supposedly members of the operation could be identified by a brand beneath the fingernail of their left index finger, but that was probably just a crock of shit. Anyway, the objective of the operation was to make absolutely certain no one ever proved that a conspiracy had existed in the assassination of President John F. Kennedy."

Cole's eyes narrowed. "So people in the operation knew that in fact a conspiracy had existed?"

Bennett shook his head. "No, listen carefully to what I'm saying. They were to make certain no one ever proved a conspiracy existed."

"How did you set out to prove something didn't exist if you didn't know whether it actually did?" This was crazy.

"You assume it did, then create so much noise around the events that in time all facts become bogged down or lost in a haze of half-truths and outright lies. Actively disseminate so much disinformation and propaganda that no one can make sense of anything. It's classic political strategy. Also make certain that anything that *is* absolute proof of a conspiracy and could pierce the haze of half-truths and lies you have created never makes it to the public's attention. Something like your Dealey Tape."

Cole saw where Bennett's explanation was leading. "People in the operation concocted phony stories and fabricated evidence with respect to the assassination. Is that right?"

"That was the rumor." Bennett's eyes were burning. "Think how easy it would have been to implicate the

Mafia by paying a few people to swear they saw Lee Harvey Oswald with David Ferrie and other known associates of organized crime. Or implicate the FBI by claiming they saw Oswald take a package from an agent in a parked FBI car in New Orleans a few months before the assassination. Or throw suspicion on your own defense establishment by aggressively reminding everyone through the press that one of Lyndon Johnson's first official directives as president was to reverse JFK's order to bring the troops home from Vietnam." Bennett was becoming animated, waving his arms in the air as he talked. "Their objective was supposedly to create so many conspiracy theories that no one could really put credence in any single theory, and to quietly make certain everyone understood the motivations of each of the entities implicated in the assassination. Why each one would want JFK dead."

"But why, Bennett? Why go to all that trouble?"

Bennett laughed. "You're too young, aren't you?"

"What do you mean?" Cole was too fascinated to be insulted by Bennett's condescending tone.

"The term Iron Curtain never scared you, did it?" Bennett didn't wait for Cole's answer. "You were born after the Cuban Missile Crisis and the Bay of Pigs. You may have read about them, but you didn't live through them. You never practiced the duck-and-cover maneuver beneath your desk at school in the asinine hope that it would save you from an all-out atomic war. None of that rings a bell, does it?"

"No," Cole admitted. "President Reagan was calling the Soviet Union the evil empire when I was in school, but none of us really paid attention to him. In fact, we thought it sounded pretty silly."

"Exactly." Bennett nodded. "But you must understand that the communist specter was a constant con-

cern in 1963, a damn huge preoccupation with the
public at that time. In fact, it was a potential time
bomb. After President Kennedy's assassination, senior
government officials knew that if enough sentiment
was whipped up by conservatives against the Russians
or the Cubans, all hell might break loose. They realized that if Russia or Cuba could be linked directly to
the assassination, we might have a full-scale atomic
war on our hands. Communists were red devils at that
point. People in this country were absolutely convinced that the Soviet Union really was an evil empire
trying to destroy the American way of life at any cost.
By using Cuba as their base ninety miles from the
U.S. border. And by using Lee Harvey Oswald and
others to assassinate the president. Remember, Oswald had spent time in Minsk and was the only mem-
ber of the Dallas Fair Play for Cuba Club." Bennett
articulated the word "club." "He had corresponded
and conspired with many known communists. That
was truth." Bennett paused. "When President Johnson
approached Chief Justice Earl Warren about heading
the commission to review the Kennedy assassination,
he warned Warren that if a hurricane of public sentiment whipped up against Khrushchev and Castro,
there could be war. Johnson actually called the
Atomic Energy Commission to obtain an estimate of
how many people could be killed in an atomic attack
launched by the Soviets. The AEC told him forty million Americans an hour would die. That blew him
away. It scared the shit out of him." Bennett's eyes
narrowed. "The Warren Commission was the official
response to the assassination. The DIA propaganda
operation was the unofficial one, and the more important one."

"People in this DIA operation found individuals

who would make up stories about the assassination and then tell . . . who?" Cole asked hesitantly.

"Newspaper reporters and writers." Bennett smiled wanly. "This country loves conspiracy theories It always has and always will. The members of the operation would have known this and would have taken advantage of it. Supposedly, they actively promoted the Mafia theory immediately to divert attention from Cuba and Russia as fast as they could. It would have been the easiest one to play up, because Bobby Kennedy was going after organized crime very hard at his brother's urging. Oswald and Ruby were known to have ties to the Mafia. This theory effectively took the spotlight away from Cuba and the Soviets. As the weeks and months passed, the operation then promoted other theories as well. By the time the House Select Committee met in 1978 to study both the John Kennedy and Martin Luther King assassinations, there were more theories going around than anyone could possibly get a handle on. If you look at the witnesses who came before that committee to testify with respect to the Kennedy killing, many of them had never testified to the Warren Commission. But, poof, all of a sudden they can remember minute details fourteen years later. And many of the ones who had originally testified changed their stories drastically the second time around. The reporters and writers really picked up on the whole conspiracy phenomenon. Look how many books have been written over the years implicating everyone from the Joint Chiefs to J. Edgar Hoover. Christ, some of them accuse space aliens of the assassination—and some people believe it. One of the best breaks anyone trying to create propaganda got was Jim Garrison, that New Orleans district attorney who tried to frame a local businessman in the conspiracy. Garrison was a certifiable nut case, and he muddied the waters forever."

"I thought from what I've read that Garrison actually unearthed a lot of useful information."

Bennett shook his head violently. "His allegations were all trash."

"Maybe he worked for the operation," Cole speculated.

"I think that's unlikely."

"How the hell do you know so much about the operation?" Cole asked suspiciously, glancing at Bennett's left index finger.

Bennett folded his arms across his chest, suddenly aware of how agitated he had become over the last few minutes. "I don't *know* anything. I told you, I'm just guessing about all of this. Your father and I worked for the DIA, but not in that operation. We just heard rumors from others at the agency. What I'm telling you is our own speculation, nothing else."

"Were you and my father part of that operation?" Cole looked directly into Bennett's eyes. He wanted to see the other man's reaction to the question.

"No, I told you," Bennett answered firmly. He stared straight back at Cole as he gave his answer.

"Is that why my father confiscated Andrea Sage's movie camera?" Cole asked. "Because he knew the film inside might prove conspiracy?"

"Think, Cole."

"What do you mean?" Cole was instantly irritated with himself because Bennett seemed disappointed, as if Cole had somehow let him down. Suddenly Cole didn't want to disappoint Bennett Smith.

"If your father had taken the camera from your mother because he was part of the operation, that would imply that the operation was in place before the assassination, and that there was prior knowledge of it," Bennett pointed out. "That in fact the operation was part of the assassination. In my heart I've always believed there was more than one gunman in Dealey Plaza that day, and that a conspiracy did exist. But I never have, and still don't, believe the federal government or any law enforcement agency was involved in the actual killing. I could be convinced that the government was involved in an operation to cover up what happened, but not in the assassination itself."

"But—"

Bennett held up a large hand. "I know what you're going to say, that I'm naive to think our government couldn't have been involved. I assure you, son, I'm not naive. But if you don't agree with me, consider this. Why would your father give you that tape if he had dedicated the last thirty-five years of his life to suppressing what that tape showed? If in fact he was involved with the operation to disseminate propaganda, and therefore the assassination?"

"Because we aren't worried so much about Russia anymore," Cole answered. "The tape no longer carries that provocative power. And for obvious reasons, he couldn't be alive when the tape became public. The senior people at the DIA wouldn't have taken kindly to that, so he waited until he died."

Bennett smiled. "Maybe you aren't worried about Russia anymore, but plenty of people within the Department of Defense and the CIA still are, including me. You're naive if you think Russia is no longer a legitimate threat."

"That's not the point," Cole argued. "The point is that the Dealey Tape wouldn't cause a world war anymore, even in the unlikely event it led to proving Russia was involved with Kennedy's assassination."

"You aren't understanding my point, son. You don't work for thirty-five years to suppress something, then suddenly go against your training."

Cole was unconvinced. "Then why did my father take the movie camera from Andrea Sage, and why didn't he turn the film over to his superiors on the Dallas police force immediately?"

Bennett shook his head. "I honestly don't know. Until this afternoon I wasn't certain he had actually taken the film from her. I thought Andrea might have made the whole thing up, as everyone else thought she had." Bennett shrugged. "Maybe your father realized the dire implications of that film instantly and felt it was better held in his hands than anyone else's. Maybe in the hours immediately following the assassination he viewed it and realized how valuable it could become and wanted to profit from it. Or—and this is what I really think—he fell in love with your mother the second he saw her, and he was trying to protect her, knowing that she could be in danger if people thought she really *had* made the film. Remember how many people connected with the assassination met with mysterious and violent deaths afterward. There was the hooker who was babbling in a hospital about someone wanting to kill the president a few days before the assassination. They found her dead on a lonely road. And there was Bowers, the guy who was up in the train tower overlooking the area behind the grassy knoll the day of the assassination. He died in a suspicious car accident. Maybe your father anticipated the danger. His ability to instantly grasp a situation and understand its long-term implications was incredible. He was a very intelligent man."

Cole felt a lump rising in his throat. "Did he really love . . ." He hesitated. "Andrea Sage?" He couldn't decide whether to refer to her as Andrea or his mother. The emotional disconnect from her was still strong.

"More than anything, son. He told me it was love at first sight many times. Andrea was a real stunner, I'll tell you. That's where you get your looks, not from your father." Bennett chuckled. "She was an intelligent woman, too. She was all he talked about when we were away on missions. I told you before that he didn't usually do irrational things, but in Andrea's case he did, and he never regretted it." Bennett took a deep breath. "Half of him died the day he found out she'd been murdered. I was there with him. But he realized he had to get on with his life. One way he did that was to start taking a big interest in you, through your aunt."

Cole gazed toward the Lassiter. "Really?"

"Yes. He knew everything about you. About how you were such a good fly fisherman, how you loved this river, how you were a star football player at the University of Minnesota and a hotshot Wall Street trader after college. He talked to your aunt every few weeks to get an update on you no matter where in the world he was. But he always told her not to let you know he called. I don't know why he was like that. Maybe he thought it would be easier that way. Maybe he figured he'd been away from you for so long, you would resent him if he tried to speak to you directly. Anyway, I heard every damned detail of those phone conversations. He probably made up a few things, too." Bennett smiled warmly. "But I enjoyed it. I never had children of my own, so I sort of adopted you from a distance."

The two men glanced at each other, then quickly looked away.

"How much longer until we reach the mouth of the river?" Bennett asked after several minutes of silence.

"A few more hours." Cole stood up from the rock on which he had been sitting. "We'd better get going."

9

BENNETT SMITH SIPPED HIS JACK DANIEL'S AND GES-
tured at an emblem mounted on the wall behind the
bar. It read KRO BAR. Beneath the letters was a large
black crow and in its talons was a long metal bar,
curved at one end. Bennett elbowed Cole, who sat on
an adjacent stool nursing a beer. "I like that," Bennett
remarked, pointing at the emblem again. "A *crow*
holding a *crowbar,* and the spelling is incorrect in either case just to add a little spice."

Cole smiled. Bennett was slurring his words.

"It's like life," Bennett continued. "There are always two sides to every story. It's always a guessing
game. This place could be named for the bird or the
hunk of metal it's holding. I bet if you asked the
owner what he named the place for, he'd give you a
different answer depending on the day."

Cole laughed loudly. The pearls of wisdom had continued all the way down the river that afternoon.
There was one every few minutes, and he had enjoyed
them all. He glanced at Bennett, an imposing man

with that tall, broad build and the unkempt shock of curly yellow hair. A man of above-average intelligence, Cole judged. No rocket scientist, but someone who seemed to possess more important qualities than a sky-high IQ. Qualities like sincerity, honesty and loyalty.

They had reached the mouth of the Lassiter at Lake Superior around five, as darkness was beginning to fall over the territory. Then they had hitchhiked back to the Lassiter headwaters to retrieve their vehicles, eaten at the Erdman Diner across State 7—the lonely road connecting the tiny town of Hubbard to the outside world—and afterward walked across the road to the Kro Bar for drinks. Bennett had turned out to be excellent company. In between the pearls of wisdom, he had continued to answer questions about Jim Egan and Andrea Sage. The more alcohol Bennett consumed, the more Cole learned, and everything was good. Cole's bitterness over being abandoned was dulling with each answer—and each beer.

"This place is starting to get crowded," Cole observed, raising his voice as someone fed quarters into the jukebox and the first selection began to play. It was after nine-fifteen. When they had first arrived after their meal of homemade stew across the road at the Erdman Diner, the place was almost deserted. Now it was packed with locals from all corners of Oswego County. Cole turned back toward Bennett. "Bennett, you have an interesting way of looking at life." Cole heard himself slurring a word or two as well.

"I'll take that as a compliment, son," he said, winking at Cole.

"As you should," Cole assured him.

Bennett finished his whiskey, caught the eye of the

scraggly-haired bartender and ordered another drink for himself and another beer for Cole. "I don't usually say things like this, but I really enjoyed coming down the river with you today, Cole. It was like being with your father again."

"Thanks." Those words meant a great deal to Cole.

"I've missed him."

"Me too."

"Hey, you're hell with that paddle." Bennett changed the subject quickly. The conversation was becoming too personal. "I couldn't follow you into some of those rapids. I never like to take the easy way out of anything, but a couple of times I had to bail out into the calmer side channels. I would have tipped over if I'd followed you through the white water. But I should have known you were good. Your father said you spent a lot of time on the Lassiter growing up. At least that's what his sister told him."

"I did spend a lot of time here. I was on the river almost every weekend in the summer when I was in high school and college."

The bartender returned with the drinks and without a word snatched the twenty-dollar bill Bennett had put down on the bar.

"People aren't too friendly around here," Bennett observed.

"Don't worry," Cole said. In all his years on the Lassiter he'd never had a problem with the locals. "They won't give you any trouble." He finished his beer, pushed the empty glass across the sticky bar and picked up the full one the man had just delivered. "You know, you still haven't answered one of the questions I asked you on the river today."

Bennett watched a young woman drag her partner out onto the empty dance floor. She wore a tight top, tight jeans and cowboy boots. Around her delicate neck hung a red bandanna, knotted at the front. "Oh?" he asked aimlessly. "What question was that?"

"When you called me on the trading floor you said you were delivering the envelope 'for the agency.' But it was really for my father. Why did you mention the agency?"

"There were no individuals at the DIA. We were trained to think as a team. When I mentioned the agency it was a slip of the tongue. It was what we always said."

"Mmm." Cole took a sip from the next beer as he too watched the young woman with the red bandanna move to the music. Other women had stepped onto the floor, but she was by far the prettiest, and the best dancer. "Bennett, you said you always believed there was more than one shooter in Dealey Plaza."

"Yes, I did."

"What do you base that on?"

"Three things. The pristine bullet, Houston Street, and Jack Ruby." He listed his reasons quickly. "As I said before, I don't believe the pristine bullet went through Kennedy and Connally. One bullet certainly could have done the damage—there was no 'magic' involved. With Connally turned in his seat, the two men were lined up perfectly if you really study the Zapruder film. But the bullet would have lost a lot more than three grains. Somebody was trying to manipulate something there."

"You mentioned Houston Street," Cole prompted.

"Yes. If the assassin in the Depository building had been the only shooter, he would have gone for Kennedy as the limousine was coming at him on Houston, not as it was moving away from him on Elm. He would have had an unobstructed shot when the limousine was on Houston. But with the limousine on Elm Street, someone in the sniper's nest on the sixth floor of the Depository building would have had to fire through the tree branches of a live oak. They waited until Kennedy was on Elm so that all the assassins would be able to fire at Kennedy simultaneously. So that they could trap him in a crossfire."

Bennett drew himself up on the barstool. "And the Jack Ruby thing is ridiculous. I don't care how distraught you are over the assassination, you don't kill the accused that way, on national television in front of millions of people. I was standing right next to your father as they brought Oswald out of the Dallas Police and Courts Building. Ruby jumped out and shot him before anyone could do anything. It was so public. That action doesn't make sense unless you owe someone big-time, which Ruby did, and you're dying of cancer, which he was. He was repaying a debt. I'm convinced of that." Bennett took another swallow of whiskey. "I know a lot of people say Jack Ruby had no idea when Oswald was coming out, which would indicate that the murder wasn't premeditated and that Ruby was simply being opportunistic. But I don't buy that argument. I think the murder was carefully planned and that Oswald was executed. Jack Ruby had lots of friends on the Dallas police force. I saw him around the station all the time myself. He could have easily found out when they were bringing Oswald out to transport him. There's no doubt about it."

"But Oswald requested a change of clothing right before he was transported," Cole pointed out. "If he hadn't asked for the change of clothes, he would have been gone long before Ruby ever got there, because Ruby had just made it to the scene."

Bennett lifted an eyebrow. The kid wasn't getting it. "You read that in a book, right?"

"Yes," Cole said hesitantly. Then it hit him.

"Try this on for size instead," Bennett said. "What if it was really the other way around? What if one of the deputies ordered Oswald to change clothes at the last minute?"

"To give Ruby time to get there," Cole finished the thought.

"Exactly. See, you have no idea where that author you read got his information. Even if the author had all the best intentions—which he might not have had, depending on who he was—he had no way of really knowing whether his source was telling him the truth or was leading him astray. Maybe the *author's* source was telling the truth, as far as the source knew, but the *source's* source was paid off. Maybe the trail goes back several iterations so no one can ever find the truth. It's beautiful."

It could so easily be the case, Cole thought to himself. "Why is there such fascination with President Kennedy's assassination, Bennett?" Cole asked.

Bennett gazed at the Kro Bar emblem on the wall behind the bar. "Because there's never been anything bigger than his assassination to hit this country. Almost everyone over the age of forty remembers exactly where they were the instant they heard Kennedy was shot, or at least they say they do. Some people can't remember proposing marriage, or being proposed to, but they can remember every detail about being told Kennedy had been shot. And everyone *under* forty has heard so much about the assassination that they naturally consider it to be one of the most important events ever." He took another sip of Jack Daniel's. "The assassination marked the end of innocence for us all. It was a watershed event in our history. The world went downhill from then on. Drug abuse became prevalent, Vietnam poisoned us, Martin Luther King was killed and a second Kennedy was too." Bennett ticked off the events on his thick fingers. "And the media didn't protect us after the assassination. They started reporting everything in graphic detail. The idyllic fifties were gone forever. After the killing shot tore through John Kennedy's head, we couldn't hide from the reality around us any longer. We had to accept it because it was right there every day on the front page of the morning paper and on the evening news. First Kennedy's murder, then Oswald's. The king was dead, and so was the patsy."

Cole had been waiting all day for the right moment to ask this question and he sensed the time was now. "Do you think my father was asked to join the DIA so they could watch him—that DIA operation you were talking about, I mean? I know you said you two weren't part of the operation, but if it did exist, having him in the DIA certainly would have made it easier to monitor him and control what he did. Do you think maybe the senior people thought there was truth to what Andrea Sage claimed and, by getting my father to join the DIA, they could keep a close eye on him?"

Bennett rubbed his lips as he stared down the whiskey glass. Slowly he began to nod. "Yes, your father and I always thought that. And we figured they wanted me to join as well because they knew your father and I were such close friends. They figured he might have said something to me about the film—although, as I've told you, he didn't."

"You said my father died in Colombia forty-seven days ago."

"That's right."

"How did he die?"

Bennett shook his head. "I told you before. I can't say anything about that, because it involves a covert operation that is ongoing. I would put people at risk if I gave you any details about his death. The other things I've told you are simply speculations about the past by your father and me. Still, if we were correct about those things, I wouldn't care if I did put those people at risk."

"You're certain my father died in Colombia?"

"Positive. I buried him next to a river in a grave I dug myself." Bennett could see that Cole was having a difficult time accepting his father's death. "I know it isn't easy to deal with, son, but you need to."

"But the death certificate was signed in Texas," Cole protested.

"Yeah," Bennett said softly. "As you pointed out before, I can usually overcome little details."

"I see."

"It's an awful thing, and ironic too."

"What are you talking about?" Cole asked.

"Colombia was our last mission. We were going to retire when it was over." Bennett stirred his drink with his finger. "So how is that girl you brought out here on the plane?"

Cole glanced up. He hadn't mentioned Nicki to Bennett.

Bennett saw Cole's surprise. "Intelligence. It's my business, son, remember? I know you lived with her. I know about the explosion in your apartment that killed her friend. It's always a shame when an innocent bystander dies."

Cole said nothing.

"You care about Nicki, don't you?"

Cole stared down at his beer. Yes, he cared. But no,

he'd never actually said so. Perhaps that Wall Builder nickname Nicki had tagged him with so long ago was accurate after all, much as he hated to admit it. He suddenly realized how hard he had been working all his life to erect emotional barriers to protect himself from being hurt again. It was better not to care so much, better not to let people get to you. Then if they abandoned you and left you with your aunt and uncle, the pain wouldn't be so bad.

"Yes, I do care about Nicki. She's a wonderful woman. She's beautiful, smart and sincere." He closed his eyes tightly. "And she's going to hate me if she finds out I'm responsible for her friend's death."

"You weren't responsible for the explosion, Cole."

"I should have anticipated the danger. I should have made certain no one went back to the apartment."

Bennett steered the conversation in a different direction. "You told me earlier you never blamed your father for leaving you with your aunt and uncle. But you did, didn't you?"

"Maybe." Cole started to say something more, then stopped.

"What is it, son?"

"Yeah, I felt abandoned, as if I wasn't wanted, but I dealt with that. But there's something else, too. There's the not knowing what you're supposed to be like. Other kids can look at their fathers and see how they react in certain situations and how they approach life. I never could."

"You had your uncle."

"It's different. That's why he's called an uncle."

"Maybe not having your father around was an advantage," Bennett offered. "You had no preconceived notions about what you were supposed to be or how you were supposed to act. Maybe that actually helped you achieve what you have achieved."

Cole laughed out loud.

"What?" Bennett asked.

"Like I've achieved so much, Bennett." He was becoming sardonic, which was a sure sign that the alcohol was taking effect. "I'm as good as bankrupt and I—"

"What are you talking about?" Bennett interrupted.

Cole took another large swallow of beer. Suddenly the combination of the alcohol and the stress of the last few days overwhelmed him, and he felt like unloading in a way he never had before. Maybe Nicki was right. Maybe it made sense to seek emotional support in certain situations.

"I enjoyed some success on the Gilchrist trading floor the first few years I was there. Nothing earthshattering, but enough for the senior people to take notice and throw me some pretty good cash at bonus time in January. I thought making money would always be that easy, so I went out and bought a big penthouse with a meager down payment and a big mortgage. I bought at the top of the Manhattan real estate boom. I was living large, living the dream. Then suddenly it wasn't so easy. The trades went away from me and I lost a ton of money. It happened that fast." Cole snapped his fingers. "I didn't get a bonus last year and I probably won't get one this year either. As anyone on Wall Street will tell you, a trader's salary is peanuts. You live and die by your bonus. Now I can't meet my mortgage payments, and I can't sell the place because the real estate market has tanked and the price I'd get wouldn't cover the mortgage. And my credit cards are just about maxed out." He didn't bother telling Bennett about his gambling debt at the

Blue Moon. "But it'll work out." His sarcastic tone became sharper.

"Some people would die for a chance to work on Wall Street or play college football. You never know how life would have turned out," Bennett lectured, "only how it *has* turned out. You can't look back, Cole."

Cole's expression became one of resolve. "I wanted to know my father, Bennett. It's as simple as that. But there's no chance of that now."

Bennett finished his drink. "How about a little pool, Cole Egan?" Bennett flashed a cheery smile, and held up the ten-dollar bill the bartender had given him as change for the twenty. "Ten bucks on a game of eight ball."

"I'm not very good," Cole said in a low voice, as if playing pool were the last thing he wanted to do right now.

"Sure," Bennett said cynically. "Come on."

"All right," Cole agreed. "But first I need to make a call. I want to see how Nicki is."

Bennett nodded and ambled toward one of the three pool tables at the back of the bar. He cut through the dance floor and almost ran into the young woman with the red bandanna around her neck. She smiled at him, then dipped below her partner's arm as he twirled her.

Bennett inserted two quarters in the pool table's slot and with a loud rumble the balls rolled down into a shelf under the end of the table. Bennett picked them out one by one, placing them in the triangular rack lying on the beer-stained green felt. By the time Cole had made it to the back of the bar, the table was ready for play.

"How is she?" Bennett asked.

"Okay," Cole answered. "She's still pretty upset about her friend."

"I can understand that," Bennett said. He pointed at the cues standing against the wall. "Choose your weapon. I need to warn you, though, when I was a teenager my career choices were law enforcement or the professional pool circuit. I could have made some good money with a cue."

"I guess it's going to be a long night for me."

Several drinks later Cole had hustled Bennett Smith out of a hundred dollars. Cole intentionally lost the first three games, driving the bet higher and higher, then quickly ran the table in the fourth.

"That's all for me," Bennett muttered under his breath as Cole dropped the eight ball in a corner pocket. He pulled out his wallet, counted the bills, then held them out.

"You don't have to pay me, Bennett." Cole laughed. "Really. I had a good time. It's been great just to talk to you." He put his hand on the older man's shoulder. "I can't tell you how much it's meant to me to learn about my father and mother."

But Bennett still held the wad of bills out.

"You don't have to pay me, Bennett," Cole repeated.

"Nonsense, I always pay my debts. I'd be offended if you didn't take the money." Finally Bennett stuffed the bills into Cole's shirt pocket. "Where the hell did you learn to play like that?"

"Around," Cole answered casually. "Hey, how about one more game?" He could see Bennett was going to leave and there were still questions he wanted to ask. "All you have to drop is the eight ball, and I'll give you a hundred to one odds."

"No way. You'd still beat me. I'm going to my cabin

and get some sleep." On the way into town this afternoon Bennett and Cole had each rented a small cabin
for the night at a campground a half mile from the
Kro Bar. "I'm tired." He held out his hand and
smiled. "It was a pleasure getting to know you
today, son."

Cole shook Bennett's hand firmly. "Likewise."

"I'll stop by your cabin in the morning before I
leave."

"I'd appreciate that, Bennett. You'll stay in touch
with me, won't you?"

"Yes, I will. Like I said, you can always leave a
message for me at that Washington phone number I
gave you. You won't get me immediately, but I check
my voice mail often, and I'll call you back as soon as
I can. Don't hesitate to call if you need me."

"I won't." Cole let go of Bennett's hand. "Bennett,
do you think I'm safe?" he asked. "Do you think that,
now that I don't have the Dealey Tape, the guy with
the scar will leave me alone?"

Bennett nodded slowly. "I think so." He paused.
"But watch your back for a while."

Cole laughed. "That's not too comforting."

"It isn't meant to be." Bennett quickly scanned the
place for the young woman with the red bandanna
but didn't see her. "Why don't you come back to the
campground with me?"

"Nah, I'm not ready to go to sleep yet. I'm going to
try and scare up another game. I need some legitimate
competition," Cole teased.

Bennett blinked slowly, pretending to be irritated.
"See you in the morning, Cole." He turned and
walked away, smiling to himself. He had known all
about Cole's prowess at pool.

"See you," Cole yelled over the music, watching

Bennett head for the door. When the older man was gone, Cole leaned back against the wall, pulled the wad of bills from his shirt pocket and counted the hundred dollars. He grinned. Maybe he could hustle enough pool to repay the people at the Blue Moon. He stuffed the wad of bills back in his pocket. He wouldn't put this money toward the Blue Moon debt, though. This money was going back to Bennett Smith tomorrow morning, even if he had to hide it in the man's car.

"Hi, cowboy."

Cole glanced up. Standing in front of him was the young woman with the red bandanna. "Hi yourself."

"Do you want to dance?"

Cole shrugged. "Sure."

The young woman grabbed his hand and pulled him out onto the floor. For twenty minutes Cole twirled her around like a rag doll. Finally, at the end of a fast song, she fell against him, breathing hard.

"I need to sit down," she screamed in Cole's ear over the start of a new song. "You're a heckuva dancer." She took his hand in hers. "Buy me a drink?"

Up close she wasn't as pretty as from a distance. She had beautiful blond hair, but her nose was too turned up and wide and her eyes too far apart. "Sure," Cole answered. "I'd be happy to. By the way, what's your name?"

"Debby. What's yours?"

"Cole," he answered as he guided her back toward the bar. "Do you live around here, Debby?"

"Yeah," she replied. "Outside of town a little ways."

Cole noticed several young men glaring at him. Obviously the local bucks weren't pleased that an out-oftowner had distracted her interest from them. "What'll you have, Debby?"

An hour later they were inside Cole's rented cabin. He had consumed several more beers after dancing and, despite his drunken state, had realized it wouldn't be a good idea for him to get behind the wheel of his uncle's Suburban, which was parked in front of the Erdman Diner. Debby had consumed only half of one drink all night and volunteered to give him a ride home.

He leaned back against the door as Debby pressed herself against him, kissing his chin and neck.

"You want me real bad, don't you, Cole?" she moaned.

"Debby, I—" But he couldn't finish the sentence. Suddenly he couldn't speak.

Debby brought her hands up to his chest and unbuttoned his shirt, kissing and biting his broad, hairless chest. "You're so hot for me, aren't you, sweetheart?"

Cole tried to stop her, but his hands felt as if they were tied to the wall as they hung at his sides. He couldn't remember ever having so strong a reaction to alcohol. Then the room started spinning wildly. He pushed past Debby and reached out for something to support himself, but his fingers met only air, and he toppled to the floor.

Debby bent forward at the waist, her long hair hanging down around her face, hands on her knees, giggling uncontrollably. Finally she fell to the floor herself, sprawled in front of the door.

This was going to make a hell of an impression on Bennett Smith when he knocked on the door in the morning, Cole thought to himself. A girl asleep on the floor next to him after he had told Bennett how much he cared about Nicki. Cole struggled to his knees.

"You've got to go home, Debby," he mumbled. He made it to his feet for a second, then began falling backward. It was the last thing he remembered.

"Did you find anything?"

"No." The woman shivered as she pulled the collar of her jacket up around her neck and over the red bandanna. It was freezing out here.

"Did you make a thorough search of the cabin?"

"Yes," she said, exasperated at the question. "He didn't have that much stuff. Just one bag and some camping equipment." She wanted to get home and crawl into her nice warm bed. "I looked for almost an hour but I didn't find anything unusual. He never moved, either. I popped those two tablets you gave me into his last beer and it was all I could do to get him back to the cabin and in the door. He never even moved when I took his wallet out of his back pocket, or when I put it back in."

The man smiled. The dosage the woman had given Cole would have brought down an elephant. "Okay."

"Can I go now?"

The man glanced up at the neon sign above the Kro Bar, still illuminated even though it was after three in the morning and the parking lot was deserted. It would be cleaner to kill her, but they might have been seen together, which could present a problem. And it wasn't as if she had any idea what this was about, or cared. She was just a local who was happy to have picked up some quick cash for her troubles. "Yeah, you can go. But remember, you never met me."

"Right, right." She trotted back to her old Ford pickup, jumped in, revved the engine and sped away, unaware of how close she had come to death.

* * *

"Cole. Cole!"

The voice was like a hot skewer searing through his brain. "Jesus," Cole groaned. He tried to raise his head, but the pain was too much, and he let it fall back to the cabin floor.

Bennett sat down in a large chair next to the unused bed and munched on an apple. "Looks like you tied one on last night after I left," he said, through mouthfuls of the fruit.

"Yeah." It wasn't just his head that hurt. His stomach felt awful too.

Bennett tossed the apple core into a trash can beside the dresser and smiled. "Seriously, are you okay?"

"I don't know," Cole mumbled. "I've had too much to drink before, but this is crazy." With a huge effort he made it to his knees and crawled onto the bed. "I've got this mineral taste in my mouth. It must have been bad beer or something."

Bennett's antennae were up immediately. "What happened after I left?"

"I met up with a girl."

"What did she look like?"

Cole rubbed his eyes. "Long blond hair, tight clothes. I don't know, I don't really remember." He pulled a pillow over his face. "Christ, I think I need to throw up."

Cole was describing the woman with the red bandanna, Bennett realized. He rose from the chair and pulled Cole off the bed. "Come on, son." He cased the room quickly, but he couldn't tell if someone had rifled through Cole's possessions.

"What the hell are you doing?" Cole tried to stay

on the bed, but he couldn't fight Bennett's overpowering strength.

"You said it yourself. You need to throw up. The faster what went into your stomach is no longer there, the faster you'll be feeling better. Come on."

"No, please, Bennett. I hate to throw up. Just let me suffer."

But Bennett ignored Cole's pleas. He guided the younger man into the cabin's tiny bathroom and pushed him down to his knees in front of the toilet. "What's gonna get things stirring down there?" Bennett asked evilly. "What do we need to think of?"

"Huh?" Cole's head felt as if it were going to split in half.

"Puking is as much mental as it is physical. What's your least favorite food, son?"

"Don't do this to me."

"Liver?"

"No, please."

"A couple of raw eggs? Maybe a little rotten chicken or a week-old roadkill carcass? Maybe you need to think of the last time you watched someone else get sick, and smelled that wonderful aroma."

"Damn you, Bennett!" With that, Cole hunched over the bowl and the poison came pouring out.

10

As Cole stood on the stone walkway leading to the Andersons' front door, wondering if coming here was a mistake, he saw that the modest two-bedroom house was in a sorry state of disrepair. He hadn't noticed this the day he and Nicki had driven up from Minneapolis, in the flurry of reunion. But in the long-shadowed light of the autumn afternoon the decay was evident. The front step was cracked and crumbling, the shutters were beginning to rot from water damage, and paint was peeling from the wooden siding in small curling patches. Nicki's father had labored on the Duluth docks for thirty years, loading taconite, wheat and lumber onto huge ships bound for ports around the world. It was a demanding job that unfortunately didn't pay well, and he hadn't been able to save a great deal of money over the years. Much of what he had saved had funded the start of Nicki's modeling career—her portfolio, expensive clothes and Manhattan living costs—and the house had suffered as a result.

Cole kicked at a pebble on the walkway. Nicki was going to be so angry when he explained to her what had happened back in New York. The fact that, when he knew of the danger, he had just ordered her to remain at Emilio's and hadn't told her what was going on. The fact that Maria's death might have been prevented if he had told her. He kicked another pebble, harder this time, and it skittered onto the brown grass. Why the hell hadn't he said anything? Why had he held back?

"Cole!"

He glanced up at the sound of Nicki's voice. She stood in the doorway dressed in a pair of jeans and a short sweater that didn't completely cover her flat stomach. "You sure can make a sweater look sharp."

"And you sure can make a woman feel good." Nicki smiled as she moved down the front step and slipped her arms around him. "I missed you over the past few days."

"I missed you too." He locked his hands at the small of her back. She felt so good against him.

"Come on," she whispered after a few moments. She reached for his wrist and led him toward the house. "Let's go inside."

Cole followed Nicki through the entrance hall to the living room, where she sat down on a floral-print couch that faced a dated Zenith console television. He hesitated for a moment in the living room doorway, feeling strangely guilty about being in the house alone with her.

"Come here, silly." Nicki patted the cushion next to her. "Why are you standing over there like that?"

"No reason." He glanced around. "Where are your parents?"

"In town doing some shopping. They won't be back

for a few hours." A sly smile turned the corners of her mouth. "Why?"

"I just wondered."

As Cole sat down, Nicki tucked her ankles beneath herself and rested her knees against his thigh. "You need a haircut," she said, brushing his bangs from his eyes.

Cole noticed a faint trace of perfume as her wrist moved past his face. It smelled wonderful. "So how are you?" he asked.

"I'm okay." She continued combing his hair. "Still sad," she murmured after a short time. "I got close to Maria over the last six months, which is unusual for me. I'm usually such a loner."

"I know." He and Nicki were very much alike in that way.

"Other than you and my parents, I was closer to Maria than anyone else in the world," Nicki continued. "She really kept my spirits up in New York when things weren't looking good in the modeling world. She would tell me that I didn't need to worry when I was receiving all those rejection letters from the agencies. She'd tell me that I had what it took and that if I kept at it, sooner or later I'd catch on, and she turned out to be right. I owe her a lot, and I miss her."

"Nicki, I—"

"And that's enough of that," Nicki said forcefully, interrupting Cole. "I don't want to think about sad things anymore. I've spent enough time being sad. Now I want to be happy." She kissed him on the cheek, her lips lingering too long for him to mistake the kiss as simply a friendly gesture. "Tell me about your trip to the Lassiter. Did you enjoy yourself?"

"Very much." He smiled. "I learned a lot."

A strange expression came to Nicki's face. "What does that mean?"

Cole gazed into her eyes. "My father died."

"Oh, God." She put her arm around his neck and hugged him gently. "I'm so sorry, Cole."

"Thanks." He could feel her heart beating against his chest. "It's okay, though." He had come to grips with the fact that his father was gone.

"How did you find out about his death?" she asked, pulling back slightly.

"I met an old friend of Dad's on the Lassiter. His name was Bennett Smith and he told me all about my father."

"That's kind of strange, isn't it? That you found this man up on the Lassiter, I mean."

"Bennett found me," Cole said softly.

"Oh. Well, did it turn out that your father lived in this area the whole time? You always told me that you didn't know where he was."

Cole didn't answer right away. Instead he kissed Nicki's soft cheek as she gazed at him, sadness at the news that he had lost his father filling her emerald eyes. Suddenly he wanted her very badly, physically and emotionally. Suddenly he wanted to find out how it would feel to become truly close to her and allow her inside the protective barriers he had built up around himself for so long. He wanted to learn to depend on her and let her depend on him. Perhaps this new attitude was born of the realization that beyond all doubt he was alone in the world—that both of his parents were dead. Or perhaps he had realized, after staring down the barrel of that woman's gun on Thirty-ninth Street, that there had to be more to life than keeping yourself from being hurt emotionally.

Whatever the reason, he wanted her more now than he ever had.

"It turns out that my father was an intelligence agent for the United States government," he said, caressing her cheek with the backs of his fingers. "Apparently he was involved in many top secret operations."

"You're kidding." Nicki's eyes opened wide. She slipped her fingers into his and pressed his palm against her lips. "That's wild."

"It is, isn't it?" The grin spread across Cole's face even as he attempted to control it. But why should he try to control it? he asked himself. Why shouldn't he let Nicki see how proud he was of his father? Why shouldn't he show her that he'd missed his father a great deal but was happy that he'd finally found out the truth about him? "Bennett Smith told me a lot about my father. My father was a brave man. He accomplished a great deal."

"That doesn't surprise me at all," Nicki said quickly.

"Why not?"

"Because I know his son," she whispered.

For several seconds they gazed into each other's eyes, then their lips locked and they kissed deeply. As their tongues came together, Cole pulled Nicki onto him so that her knees straddled his hips. While she struggled with the top few buttons of his shirt, he slid his hands beneath her sweater, running his fingers slowly up the velvet-soft skin of her belly until he reached her breasts. She wasn't wearing a bra, and as he cupped her breasts in his large hands, she moaned and pushed her tongue savagely into his mouth. He pulled the sweater up over her neck, then took one of her long pink nipples into his mouth, swirling his tongue around and around.

"Oh, God," she sighed, wrapping her arms around his head and kissing his jet-black hair as he took her nipple deeper. "That feels so good, Cole."

He eased her onto her back on the couch. He tore open the top button of her jeans, then pulled the jeans and her thong down to her knees. Instantly he was on top of her with her nipple in his mouth again, then he was past her breasts and licking his way downward.

"Cole!" She caught his face in her hands.

"What?" He glanced up, afraid that she was going to stop him, afraid she had suffered a sudden case of the guilts.

"There's a very comfortable full-size bed waiting for us upstairs in my room." She giggled nervously. "Why are we wasting time on the couch?"

He sat up as Nicki swung her feet to the floor, pulled off her jeans and thong, then stood in front of him. He swallowed hard. "You're incredible." He had seen her in a bikini, but never this way, and it was enough to take his breath away. Her breasts were full and firm, her waist almost nonexistent and her hips taut and shapely. "Really."

"Well, stop gawking and come with me," she said softly. She picked up her clothes, then took him by the hand and led him upstairs to her bedroom. Once inside, she dropped the clothes on the floor and moved to him, taking his tongue in her mouth again.

Cole picked her up, moved to the bed and placed her gently on top of it, then knelt on the mattress as they continued to kiss.

As he knelt above her, she finished undoing the buttons and pulled the shirt roughly out of his jeans, then moved her hands down, caressing him through the denim.

"Nicki." Her hands were like magic, even through

the jeans. He couldn't imagine how incredible it would feel when her fingers finally reached him.

"I've wanted you for so long, Cole," Nicki murmured.

She began to pull down the zipper of Cole's pants, but he stopped her and lay down beside her. "I need to tell you something first," he whispered. It was all he could do to stop her at this point, but he had to tell her. They had known each other too long and he cared about her too much to let her go any further without saying something.

"What, Cole? What is it?" Fear showed in her wide emerald eyes. "Are you—ill or something?"

"I'm fine," Cole assured her. "It's nothing like that."

"Thank God. What is it, then?"

"It's about the other night in New York," he began slowly.

"What about it?"

He hesitated. "Remember when you said how it looked like I'd been through a war when I first sat down at the table at Emilio's?"

"Yes." Her eyes were searching Cole's for the meaning of all this. "You told me you'd been mugged."

"Right." He closed his eyes for a second. This was even harder than he had thought it would be. "That wasn't what happened."

"What do you mean?" Nicki rose to one elbow. "What really happened?"

For the next five minutes Cole told Nicki about the Dealey Tape and what had happened in Manhattan before he met her at Emilio's that evening.

When he finished, she stared at him for a long time.

Finally she asked the obvious question. "Why didn't you tell me about this at Emilio's?"

Cole took a deep breath. "I didn't want to alarm you unnecessarily. I wasn't sure at that point that anyone was really after me. And I didn't see any reason to upset you if the whole thing was a figment of my imagination." He looked away from her eyes. "And I didn't want to confuse the Dealey Tape with what was going on between you and me. I can't tell you how good I felt after we kissed outside the restaurant. I didn't want the possibility that I was going to come into a lot of money to influence your feelings for me." The explanation had come to him at that instant and he had simply blurted it out without thinking it through.

"What do you mean by that?" She reached down to the end of the bed and pulled a blanket over herself.

Instantly he wished he could take back the words. "I mean, it's just that, well—"

"Are you saying that I might have told you I cared for you more than I did because you suddenly had a lot of money?" she asked, her voice cracking slightly.

"I didn't mean it that way, I swear." Cole backpedaled quickly, trying to think of some way out of this.

"But that's what you said." She rose from the bed, wrapping the blanket tightly around herself. "I can't believe you."

"I know that's what I said, but it came out wrong. It's not what I meant."

"Are you that insecure?"

"Nicki, I'm—"

"I've always loved you, Cole. I've never cared what you've had or haven't had. When I kissed you outside Emilio's, I thought you didn't have anything." She was talking quickly now, upset with him. "I didn't care. I was just happy that we were finally being honest with each other."

As Cole rose to a sitting position on the side of the bed, Nicki took a step back.

"Listen to me," he pleaded.

"And because of some stupid insecurity, Maria is dead!" Nicki cried, tears welling in her eyes. "If you had told me what was going on, I might have had time to stop her from going up to the apartment."

"I'm so sorry." Cole stood up and moved toward her.

But Nicki backed up against the wall, sobbing now. "Don't come any closer."

"Please, Nicki."

"Get out!"

For a few moments he gazed at her, then he turned and walked slowly out the door.

The other night the man had paid the blonde in Hubbard to drug Cole Egan and search his belongings. Now he sat in a car in Cole's blue-collar Duluth neighborhood, one eye on a newspaper and the other on the Andersons' front door. When the door burst open, the man hunched down behind the newspaper, then peered around it as Cole slammed the front door and stalked away. He watched Cole move down the street, then started the car and eased it forward.

11

NICKI HAD EVERY RIGHT TO HATE HIM, COLE THOUGHT
to himself as he studied the computer screens in front
of him. After a long flight back from Minnesota, Cole
had trudged into Gilchrist this morning from the hotel
where he was staying while his apartment was being
repaired. The repairs and the hotel bill would be paid
for with the insurance money that had come to his
mailbox in the apartment building lobby while he
was away.

He was back after just a week, but Nicki had remained in Minnesota. She had no desire to return to
Manhattan. She had perked up for a while, then suddenly and mysteriously become inconsolable again.
This information had come from Nicki's mother, who
seemed embarrassed that Nicki had refused to answer
any of Cole's phone messages. Cole pounded the desk
with his fist. Think of something else, he told himself.
Don't dwell on how close you came to having what
you really wanted.

Cole thought of Bennett Smith hauling him to the

bathroom of the cabin in Hubbard and managed a smile. Bennett was a character if there ever was one, a man Cole had enjoyed getting to know. Not only had Bennett made him feel a good deal better about his father, but he and Bennett had personally clicked. What had begun with a mutual thread—Jim Egan— had solidified on a more basic level as they found they shared a common approach to life: Don't let life control you, control it. And they had also found they shared many opinions and views on the world—political and otherwise. They were both fiscally conservative and socially liberal, believing that people should work for what they received but sometimes also needed a hand getting started. They found common ground on every major issue they discussed. And they shared an affinity for the game of pool, even though Bennett had exaggerated his proficiency at it, as Cole had understated his. Cole chuckled again, recalling Bennett's expression as he realized at the beginning of the fourth game he was being hustled. But Bennett had enjoyed the last and best laugh as he had watched Cole struggle with the cabin's porcelain princess for half an hour. And Cole had to admit he had felt much better after the struggle was over.

"What the hell are you smiling about?" Lewis Gebauer was in a foul mood. His portfolio had lost four million dollars during the morning trading session.

"Nothing, Lewis," Cole said. It was almost noon and the trading room had finally settled down after a chaotic few hours.

"Did you have a nice vacation?" Gebauer asked insincerely. "Where did you go? Wait, let me guess. You were traveling around the country visiting relatives to see if any of them would lend you money to help you out of your mortgage jam."

"How the hell did you find out about my mort-gage?" Cole asked quietly, leaning toward the fat man to make certain no one else heard.

A smile of satisfaction spread across Gebauer's puffy face. "I have my ways."

One of Cole's telephone lines began blinking. He considered pushing Gebauer harder on how he had come by his information, but it was obvious the man had no intention of revealing his sources. "Cole Egan," he barked into the receiver.

"Jeez, bite my head off, why don't you?"

"Sorry, Anita." Cole recognized the receptionist's nasal tone. "I'm not in a great mood." Despite the fact that his portfolio had gained in the morning session as interest rates had decreased unexpectedly, he was still unhappy. He had already tried calling Nicki twice this morning in Duluth, but the Andersons' answering machine had picked up both times. God, if he could just talk to her. "What's up?"

"There's someone out here to see you."

Cole's mood brightened. Maybe Nicki had taken an early flight back to New York this morning and was out front waiting for his apology, which he would be only too glad to give her. Or perhaps the people from the Blue Moon had decided to stop by. His spirits fell as quickly as they had risen. "Who is it?"

"Some woman who isn't your type."

That didn't sound like a representative from the Blue Moon—or Nicki. "How can you tell she isn't my type, Anita?"

"Because I'm the only type for you."

"I see." He could hear Anita laughing at the other end of the line. "I'll be right there."

"Why don't you let me tell her you're too busy?" Anita suggested. "Let me take care of her."

"If I let you take care of her, she'd probably end up in the East River, facedown." Cole suddenly realized that Gebauer was listening intently to the conversation. "I'll be right out," he said. "See you in a minute." He put down the receiver and headed for the doors at the far end of the trading floor.

Anita nodded toward a couch in a far corner of the reception area as Cole came through the door. He turned and was pleasantly surprised by what he saw. The woman sat at one end of the sofa, legs crossed at the knees, perusing a magazine. Shoulder-length sandy brown hair was swept back off her tanned face by a black velvet hairband. Her features were sharp—straight dark brows above turquoise cat eyes, a slim nose over thin lips and two perfect rows of teeth. She wore an attractive lace blouse and high-waisted pants that clung pleasingly to her slender figure.

"I'm Cole Egan." He stood a few feet in front of her. "Were you looking for me?"

Without urgency she closed the magazine, placed it on the glass-topped table beside the sofa, looked up at Cole and raised an eyebrow. "All my life," she said seductively. Her voice was gravelly and naturally tantalizing.

She was pretty, not breathtaking like Nicki, but she had an immediate and powerful sex appeal oozing from her cat eyes and her sinewy body. Nicki's allure lay not only in her beauty but also in her innocence. She was demure and quiet, and the possibility of unlocking that innocence had always fascinated Cole. This woman's allure came at him from the other end of the spectrum. She didn't appear to be that much older than Nicki, but something told Cole she knew what she wanted and would do anything to get it. Something Nicki wasn't capable of.

He grinned. "I don't know quite how to take that."

"Take it any way you want to," she said matter-of-factly. She stood up and offered her hand. "My name's Victoria Brown, but my friends call me Tori. I'd like you to do that."

It was almost as if her vocal cords had been damaged, but the effect was sexy as hell. "All right . . . Tori." Cole checked her hands quickly. Her fingers were long and her nails perfect, professionally glossed a subtle pink. And there was no wedding or engagement band on her left hand. "What can I do for you?" he asked.

"I'm with NBC News." She lowered her voice as she noticed Anita watching them carefully. "I saw your father's obituary in the *New York Times*. I'm very sorry."

"Thanks, but why did you bother coming here to give your condolences? Couldn't you have just called?"

"My office is in Rockefeller Center. It wasn't far to walk."

"It's freezing outside."

"And if I had just called, you might not have agreed to see me," she pointed out.

"You knew my father?" Cole asked.

"No."

"Then why are you here?"

"Let's go to lunch. My treat," Tori offered, avoiding the question. "A restaurant would be a much better place to talk. And it's about that time." She glanced at Anita again, then at Cole. "I'll explain at the restaurant," she assured him.

"I'm a government securities trader," Cole said. "Usually we eat lunch at the desk."

"I guess the market might fall apart if you weren't

around for even a little while. The way it could every night after you leave," Tori said, alluding to the fact that government securities traded actively in Tokyo and London while traders in New York were home asleep. "Unless of course the senior people only allow you to take intraday positions and you have to sell everything before your mother tucks you in at night," she teased.

"No, I'm a big boy." So Tori Brown knew her way around a trading floor. "I take overnight positions when the market's right."

"That sounds interesting. Maybe you'll show me some of those positions."

Cole smiled. Tori Brown was quite a pistol. "Mmm."

"So come on, let's go," she urged.

"I don't know." Cole was leery of people in the news business. They always wanted something and rarely had much to give in return. At least, that was his experience.

"You mean you'd rather hang around with a bunch of traders you see every day than me?" She smiled provocatively.

The image of Gebauer gnawing off a huge bite of his daily two-thousand-calorie chicken parmigiana hero flashed through Cole's mind. He could see the cheese and spaghetti sauce dripping out of either side of Gebauer's mouth and splattering onto the foil wrapper he used as a plate. "Okay, you convinced me. But how do you know so much about overnight positions?"

"I had a boyfriend who traded Eurobonds at Salomon Brothers."

"I see." It was obvious from her tone that the breakup hadn't been amicable.

"Where would you like to go?" Tori asked.

"How about La Reserve?" Cole suggested. "That's over your way, toward Rockefeller Center."

She shook her head. "I've got a better idea."

"Well, I'm glad you asked me."

"Welcome to my world." She smiled as she walked quickly toward the elevators.

Cole followed her, ignoring Anita, who was sticking her tongue out at him as he passed.

Fifteen minutes later Cole and Tori slipped into a booth at the Broadway Diner. It was loud and, instead of five-star French food, served hamburgers, sandwiches and malts.

"Interesting." Cole glanced around. The restaurant was decorated with fifties memorabilia.

"What's the matter?" she asked, grinning. "Not stylish enough for a Wall Street trader?"

"No, it's fine."

"Most of us can't afford La Reserve lunches, Cole. We don't make what you do."

"Don't be so sure," he muttered under his breath.

"What did you say?"

"Nothing." He smiled at her. "I assume NBC is picking up the tab for this."

"Yes," she agreed. "Of course it is. But our expense accounts are much smaller than Wall Street's."

"What do you do at NBC?" Cole asked, ignoring her pointed remark.

"I'm a producer."

"Do you have a card?"

She rummaged through her purse for a moment, then shook her head. "Sorry, I left them at the office, but I'll make certain you get one."

"Uh-huh." *Likely story,* he thought to himself.

A waiter with a bushy mustache sauntered toward

the table. "Are you two ready to order?" he asked as he was still walking toward them.

Cole reached for the menus propped between the paper napkin dispenser and the wall. "We haven't—"

"We're ready," Tori interrupted. "I'll have a chicken salad on wheat with lettuce and tomato and a Diet Coke." She pointed at Cole. "He'll have a cheeseburger, medium rare, with an order of french fries and a Pepsi. Give him the high-octane stuff. No diet for him."

"Be just a few minutes," the waiter said gruffly as he moved off.

"You're a woman who doesn't wait around." Cole replaced the menus behind the napkin dispenser.

"We don't have time to wait around in the news business."

"How did you know what to order me?"

"What American male doesn't like a cheeseburger? Oh, they might say they'd rather have a salad, that greens are healthier, but they don't really mean it."

Cole laughed, watching her closely as she constantly surveyed the restaurant. She was like Bennett that way, always searching the perimeter with her cat eyes. "How did you find me, Tori? I didn't mention myself in my father's obituary."

"I have a friend at the *Times*," she explained. "When I became aware of the obituary, I called her. She gave me your name as the person who placed it."

"I can't imagine that's standard practice at the *Times*—to give out names like that, I mean."

"My friends are very loyal to me, and I'm loyal to them. You'd never find out who my contact is," she said confidently.

"I'm sure I wouldn't." Tori Brown was tough and aggressive, and she didn't mind letting you know it.

"I'll get to the point." Without awaiting Cole's answer, Tori reached into her purse again and pulled out an old newspaper clipping stored inside a clear plastic envelope. She handed it to Cole. "Treat it carefully."

"Of course." He slid the yellowed paper from its sheath, carefully unfolded it and began to read.

"Let me give you the *Reader's Digest* version," she offered impatiently.

"Okay." But he kept reading as she talked.

"That is a back-page article from the November 26, 1963 edition of the *Dallas Morning News*. The story is about a young woman named Andrea Sage who claims she was in Dealey Plaza on November 22nd and filmed the assassination of President Kennedy with a Bell & Howell spring-wound movie camera she had purchased in Dallas the day before the shooting. Miss Sage was certain the film would be invaluable to the investigation. The trouble was, someone confiscated her camera and film just after the assassination occurred. The person she accused of taking her camera was—"

"—was Jim Egan," Cole interrupted. "My father."

"So I'm not telling you anything you don't know?"

"No." Thanks to Bennett Smith, Cole thought to himself.

"Good. Then you probably know why I'm here, too."

He shook his head. "Actually, I don't."

She lowered her head so that her chin was almost touching the formica tabletop. "I want to buy the film, of course," she said in a low voice. "And I have authorization to pay a great deal of money if we feel the footage is important."

"How much is a great deal?"

"Eight figures."

"But I thought the networks didn't pay for film footage."

Tori waved and shook her head. "That was in the old days. Now we have to compete with everyone else to survive. ABC paid a freelance photographer for footage of the Pol Pot trial last year. It happens all the time now." She picked up her straw and removed the paper wrapper. "Besides, all bets are off when it comes to a new recording of President Kennedy's assassination. The Kennedys are as big as the British royals in terms of public interest. It would be a windfall for NBC to have an exclusive on the recording, and my executives know that."

"What in the world makes you think I have it?" Cole asked.

"I figured that your father didn't want it to come to light while he was alive, for good reason. I assume he passed it on to you before he died."

Cole grimaced as he thought about the eight-figure authorization. And they would have gone higher if they'd seen it. "Well, he didn't pass it on to me." Cole nodded at the yellowed page. "It says right here my father denied taking the movie camera from Andrea Sage." He pointed to the third paragraph of the article. "Andrea Sage was making the whole thing up. He couldn't have passed it on to me because he never had it in the first place. The Sage woman was just trying to create her fifteen minutes of fame out of thin air," he said, quoting Bennett. Cole didn't want to give Tori the impression he had ever had it.

"I don't believe that for a second." Her strategy was to press him hard and watch his reaction carefully for signals. "Do you?"

"Yes, why wouldn't I?"

Tori shook her head. "You're quite an actor."

"What are you talking about?"

"There were over five hundred photographs taken of Dealey Plaza the day of the assassination. I know of at least two that appear to show a man taking a movie camera away from a young woman on the south side of Elm Street. The pictures are a little blurry, but it's obvious to me what's going on. You know he took that camera from Andrea Sage."

"I don't know anything of the sort." It was possible that such pictures existed, Cole realized. It was possible she was bluffing, too. "How did you just happen to see that obituary concerning my father?" he asked.

"I didn't just *happen* to see it. We run computer searches on old stories all the time at NBC. Thousands of them every day on all kinds of events. Unsolved murder cases, missing persons, historical events." She ticked them off. "We input tickler words into our computers and the computers scan new editions of all publications every day searching for the ticklers, from the *L.A. Times* to the *New York Times* as well as every paper and magazine in between. If the computers locate the tickler, they automatically pull and print the story in which it's contained. The JFK assassination is a perfect example. It's the same at the other networks, too. Every major news organization in this country is still trying to pry the top off that conspiracy can. Don't kid yourself. Your father is one of those tickler names in our computer. The network has been searching for him for years, ever since that story in the *Morning News.*" Tori pointed at the article lying on the table in front of Cole. "But we never found him. No one has, as far as I know, and I've been working on the JFK thing off and on for almost ten years." She spotted the waiter heading toward the table with their food and moved her silverware, making room for the plate. "After the assassination it's as if your father disappeared off the face of the earth, except for one thing. He married a woman named Mary Thomas in a justice-of-the-peace ceremony a few weeks after JFK was killed." Tori watched him carefully as she conveyed that fact.

His eyes shot to hers, then quickly back to the table. *Mary Thomas?*

"I found the marriage license for Jim Egan and Mary Thomas in Dallas about a year ago through a contact of mine down in Texas and traced Mary Thomas right here to New York City to her parents' Upper East Side apartment. I actually went to the apartment." Tori sighed in frustration. "It turned out to be a dead end, though. Mary ran away after graduating from college. Mr. and Mrs. Thomas claimed they hadn't heard from her since the spring of 1963." Tori paused as the waiter put the plates down and walked away without asking if they needed anything else. "But I'm sure you already knew all that. I assume Mary Thomas was your mother." Tori was watching Cole intently. "Right?" she asked.

"Yes," he murmured.

"It was strange, though."

"What was?" Cole asked quickly.

"I told your grandparents I had information about their daughter when I went to see them, but they didn't want to listen. I would think that if you hadn't heard from your daughter in thirty-five years, you'd jump at the chance to get information." Tori shrugged. "But they didn't, so I left. I felt like I was so close to something big, then the rug was yanked out from under me. And to think you were sitting just a few blocks away the whole time." She took a sip of Diet Coke, then picked up her sandwich. "It's odd how your mother and father disappeared after they were married. I talked to quite a few officers who were on the Dallas police force at the same time as your father. No one knew where he went. They didn't even know your father had gotten married, even men who said they thought they knew him pretty well. And Mary never called her parents to let them know about the wedding, or so your grandparents claim. It's all very strange." Tori took a small bite from her sandwich and continued talking. "The Andrea Sage woman falls off the map after Dallas, too. I can't find anything about her anywhere. Of course that happened to a lot of people involved with the Kennedy assassination. They just seemed to evaporate. It's mysterious, don't you think?"

"Yes," Cole answered automatically without really hearing her question. So Mary Thomas was his mother's real name, and she had been running away from her parents. No wonder she was less than forthright with the Dallas police about a permanent address and identification.

Cole shoved his plate away and stood. "I've got to make a phone call, Tori."

"Sure."

He was back in five minutes. As he slid into the seat across from her, Tori asked cheerfully, "Did my secretary give me a favorable report?"

Cole had indeed called NBC to confirm that Tori Brown was a producer with the news division. "Yes, she said you were a wonderful boss." Tori was sharp. He wouldn't underestimate her again.

"Good."

"She was expecting my call. Apparently you told her to stay nailed to her seat until she heard from me.

She sounded pretty hungry. I told her she could go to lunch now."

Tori laughed. "I figured you might want to check up on me."

Cole picked up the cheeseburger, then put it back down. "Tori, can you give me the address for the Thomases here in Manhattan?"

Tori glanced up from her plate. "What?"

Cole knew damn well she had heard the question. He had hoped she would make it easy for him and give up the address easily, but it was naive to think that, he now realized. "I want the address of those people you found in Manhattan. The Thomases. My grandparents."

Tori shook her head in disbelief. "You mean you didn't know about them?"

"No," he said quietly.

She shook her head again. "So they were telling me the truth. They really hadn't heard from Mary in all those years. I thought maybe they were just throwing me a curve to get rid of me."

She reached across the table and touched his hand gently. "I can't believe your mother and father didn't tell you who your grandparents were."

"Well, believe it." Cole glanced away. Growing up, he had always been jealous of those children who had a mother, a father and two sets of grandparents, especially at holiday times.

"I'm sorry." Tori squeezed his hand. "I shouldn't have spoken that way. It's just that—"

"It's okay," Cole interrupted. "But you could really help me if you'd give me their address."

Tori released his hand and straightened in the seat. "What about your mother? Where is she? Can I talk to her?" The questions came rapid-fire.

"I'd like to talk to my mother, too," Cole retorted, "but she's dead."

"Oh." Tori hesitated only a moment.

"When did she die?"

"I don't think that's any of your business."

"I guess not," she said. "What about the film, Cole?" She was pressing him, anxious to wrap him up before someone else got to him. "The one your father took from Andrea Sage."

"I told you, I don't know anything about a film! Now are you going to give me the Thomases' address?"

"No."

"You—" He stopped himself abruptly. "Fine, I'll call information and get their number myself."

"That won't help," she said quickly. "Their number is unlisted." Tori put a finger to her forehead. "But here's an idea. You could get the home address Mary Thomas gave the clerk in Dallas on the day of the marriage." She grimaced, as if her pain were real. "On second thought, that'll be hard to do. My friend in Dallas pulled those public records and destroyed them—for a small fee, of course." Tori smiled at Cole. "You look so angry, and I don't like that."

"I can't believe you won't give me the address." Cole slammed his fist down on the table. "They're my grandparents, for Christ's sake! I want to meet them before they die." Or I do, he thought to himself.

Tori's smile disappeared as she leaned over the table. "And I'd like to break a big story before *I* die," she hissed. "In case you haven't heard, that's how people get ahead in the news business. I've been struggling for years to get the suits at NBC to recognize me. 'Oh yeah, we like her work.' That's what they say. That's tantamount to 'She's a second-stringer.' Well, I

want more than that. I want to break a big story. I
want some respect and, dammit, yes I'll admit it, some
glory. This could be one of the biggest stories of the
decade, maybe ever." She paused. "I don't think
you're telling me everything, Cole. You come clean
with me, and I'll give you the Thomases' address.
Short of that, I'll give you a hint. They live on the East
Side between Fortieth and Ninetieth. That's about a
million people to cull your way through. That's assum-
ing I gave you the right name. Good luck."

Cole rose slowly from the table, pulled out his wallet, took a twenty from inside and dropped the bill on
the table. "Thanks for lunch," he said evenly, then
walked to the door and out onto Broadway.

12

POWERFUL GUSTS PICKED UP LOOSE PAPER AND DIS-
carded wrappers from the sidewalk and whipped them
into small cyclones—trash devils, as they were called
in Manhattan. Cole muttered to himself as he pulled
his overcoat up around his face, leaned forward
against the autumn wind and hurried down Broadway.
Tori Brown. How selfish could you be? Withholding
information about someone's family in the name of
breaking a news story. He turned onto Forty-Seventh
Street.

"Hello, Cole." A large man in a dark suit and sunglasses stepped away from a parked limousine and
moved directly into Cole's path.

Cole stopped, recognizing the man from the Blue
Moon, then turned around to sprint back to Broadway. But he ran directly into a second man who
grabbed him by the arm tightly.

"We're going to take a little ride," the second man
said in a thick Brooklyn accent, smiling as if this inter-
ruption were nothing Cole needed to worry about.

Cole forced a smile in return. "A little friendly outing, right? Maybe we'll take in a show and a nice dinner later, just the three of us."

"Maybe." The second man hustled Cole over the sidewalk to the limousine. The first man had already opened a back door, and Cole ducked as the second man pushed him in. The two men followed Cole inside and slammed the door shut, and the black Cadillac squealed away from the curb.

"Where have you been lately, Cole?" The first man sat on the seat opposite Cole. He removed his leather gloves and tossed them down. "We've been looking for you."

Cole spotted a pistol in the shoulder holster beneath the man's unbuttoned jacket. "I took a friend home to Minnesota. Her colleague was killed in an explosion at my apartment."

"We heard about that," the second man, who sat next to Cole, remarked indifferently. "We were glad it wasn't you. Then we couldn't have gotten our money back. And contrary to what you might think, we really do want it back. All of it." He grinned. "We're going to have some fun this afternoon making that point very clear."

"I know you want it back." Unless he came up with ninety-nine thousand dollars plus interest before the limousine reached its destination, it looked like he was in for a rough afternoon.

As they crossed the Brooklyn Bridge, the first man spoke up again. "You know, Frankie," he said to his companion as he gazed out the window at New York Harbor, "I read somewhere recently that this bridge first opened all the way back in 1883. And I think it was the first suspension bridge in the United States."

"Yeah?" Frankie, the man on the seat next to Cole,

obviously had no interest in the bridge's history or its construction.

"Yeah. And I read that on the day it opened, the city had a big parade. When the people at the front of the parade got halfway across the bridge, a rumor started that the cables were beginning to snap and, like, six people got killed in the stampede."

"I think you read too much, Sal." Frankie pulled two sticks of gum from his pocket, tore off the wrappers and shoved them in his mouth. "What do you think, Wall Street boy?"

Cole didn't answer. The partition between the driver and passenger compartments was open and he was staring through the windshield, concentrating intently on the road ahead.

"Hey!" Frankie kicked Cole in the ankle with the point of his sharp boot. "I asked you a question."

"Jesus Christ!" Cole bent over and grabbed his ankle. It was the same ankle he had sprained in his collision with the taxicab and it was still sore. "I didn't hear you," he groaned.

Frankie and Sal shared a harsh laugh.

"You better get used to that kind of thing, pal," Frankie warned. "Unless you've recently come into some cash."

The limousine coasted to a gentle stop. Two lanes of eastbound traffic were closed due to construction on the bridge, and the line of cars waiting to move into the single open lane was long.

Instantly Cole lunged for the door away from Frankie. He had seen the traffic tie-up ahead through the open partition and anticipated the opportunity. He hadn't heard any doors lock as they squealed away from the curb back in Manhattan, and he prayed that somehow the driver had overlooked that responsibility. Cole's prayers were answered as the handle gave way and the door sprang open. He pulled himself through the door, rolled onto the blacktop, scrambled to his feet, slammed the limousine door on Frankie's hand as the man tried to follow, then hobbled back toward Manhattan. As he ran past a plain-looking four-door sedan idling behind the limousine, the sedan's driver-side rear door opened suddenly, slamming into Cole's chest and legs. He fell to the blacktop, the breath knocked from his lungs by the impact. He lay for a moment in the fetal position, gasping for air, then was pulled roughly into the sedan. Suddenly there was metal pressed to the side of his neck. The sedan's driver jumped out from behind the wheel, slammed the back door shut, then slid back behind the wheel and followed the limousine as traffic began to move forward once more.

"I wouldn't try that again," a voice warned.

Cole opened his eyes.

The man beside Cole on the backseat smiled as he forced the barrel of a revolver against Cole's jaw.

"You guys are always smiling," Cole gasped. "You just hear a good joke or something? Or are you just happy people? Maybe they should call you happyguys instead of wiseguys."

The man said nothing as he brought the gun down from Cole's face.

"Well, I hope you're as much fun to be with as the guys in the other car were," Cole said, still trying to catch his breath.

The man shoved the gun into his coat. "I thought I saw you catch Frankie's hand in that door when you slammed it shut. Did you?" he asked.

Oxygen finally began to seep back into Cole's chest. "Maybe."

The man shook his head. "That should make things interesting. Frankie's got a helluva temper."

Minutes later the limousine and the sedan pulled up behind a warehouse deep in Brooklyn. Frankie stepped out of the limo and ambled casually to the sedan, then jerked the sedan door open and yanked Cole out by the wrist.

"Over there." Frankie pointed at a door Sal was holding open.

Cole noticed black-and-blue marks on Frankie's hands that had been made by the door slamming shut.

For several minutes Cole followed Sal through a labyrinth of hallways. Then Frankie's unhurt hand clamped down on Cole's shoulder, pivoted his body to the right and pushed him into a dimly lit smoke-filled office. Behind a decrepit wooden desk was another man Cole recognized from the Blue Moon—a man who was clearly senior to the ones who had ridden in the limousine and the sedan. The others nodded to this man deferentially as they crowded into the small room, but he didn't bother acknowledging them.

The man motioned for Cole to sit down in a ratty armchair in front of the desk. His crop of meticulously combed silver hair and his tiny brown eyes glinted in the light from a single bare bulb hanging from the ceiling. "You want anything to drink?" His voice was predictably tough but, unlike the others, he spoke with only a slight Brooklyn accent.

"No, thanks."

The man behind the desk lit a cigarette, then nodded at the others crowded in the doorway. "Frankie and Sal, go get things ready," he ordered. "Make sure the employees are out of there."

Cole felt perspiration beginning to build beneath his clothes as he watched Frankie and Sal disappear.

The man behind the desk took a long drag from the cigarette, then exhaled. "My name's Mad Dog."

Probably, Cole speculated, because of a very rotten disposition. "Hello, Mr. Dog," he answered.

Mad Dog snickered. "You're not going to be quite so cocky in a little while. You owe us a lot of money, Cole."

"Which I intend to pay you very soon."

"Almost a hundred and fifty thousand dollars, including interest," Mad Dog continued.

Cole performed several quick calculations. "I guess it wouldn't do any good to point out that the interest rate you're charging me violates every usury statute on the books."

Mad Dog smiled. "No, it wouldn't."

"I didn't think so." Cole cleared his throat. "Look, I can put together twenty-five thousand dollars by this time tomorrow."

"Don't lie to me."

Cole glanced up. "Huh?"

"You've got two hundred and twelve dollars in your only account at Citibank and your credit cards are all but maxed out," Mad Dog said. "The monthly after-tax amount of your salary wouldn't keep me in cigarettes for a week, and I don't believe anyone is going to lend you a dime."

"Well—"

"We need to work out a payment schedule," Mad Dog declared.

Frankie leaned into the office. "Everything's ready."

Mad Dog didn't take his eyes from Cole. "And we need to make you understand that we're serious."

"I know you're—"

Mad Dog held up his hand. "I want you to follow these gentlemen."

Cole glanced up at Frankie, then at Sal, who was looking over Frankie's shoulder, then back at Mad Dog. "Look, I—"

Before he could finish, Cole felt himself being lifted from the chair. Then he was in the hallway again, being hustled forward. He knew they had no intention of killing him, but he also knew that whatever Frankie and Sal had prepared was going to involve pain.

A left turn, a right, another right and the group moved into a large deserted shop area, its walls lined with tools. The men thrust Cole into a chair against the cinderblock wall, grabbed his right wrist, handcuffed it to a ring bolted to the wall a foot above his head, then locked his left wrist beneath a curved metal latch bolted onto a table next to the chair. The latch fit so snugly over his wrist that Cole could barely move his hand. He gazed down at his fingers. He had a good idea of what was coming, and the thought of it almost made him physically ill.

Mad Dog sat down in a chair facing Cole. He took another drag from the cigarette and smiled. "Now it gets real."

"I can get the money." Cole tried to remain calm, but perspiration was pouring down his face. "I get my bonus in January, only six weeks from now." He saw Frankie taking down a huge pair of bolt cutters from the wall. "I'm not kidding!" His heart was suddenly racing.

"I can't wait six weeks," Mad Dog replied.

Frankie moved to the table, took the little finger of Cole's left hand in his meaty paw and snapped it hard, straight away from the wrist. Pain shot up Cole's arm as the finger went numb, and he bit down on his lower lip to keep from screaming.

Mad Dog nodded at Cole's finger, now sticking out from his hand at a strange angle. "We do that for two reasons," he said, as if he were a professor of medicine guiding a group of interns through a tricky procedure. "It makes cutting it off easier, because now you can't move it around. And now it's numb, so you won't feel as much pain when it comes off."

"Thanks a lot."

Mad Dog nodded at Frankie. "Cole, the arrangement will be ten thousand dollars a month for the next three years. No more, no less. Do you understand?"

"Yes."

Frankie took Cole's finger and slipped it between the bolt cutter's sharp blades.

"Today we are going to remove the finger that Frankie has inserted in the bolt cutters. Miss a payment," Mad Dog warned, "and we'll take off the little finger on your right hand. Miss another one, you lose the thumb on your left hand. You get the picture, don't you?"

"Unfortunately."

Mad Dog took one last drag from the cigarette, dropped it to the floor and stamped it out. He smiled as he blew the smoke into Cole's face.

Cole stared at the mobster. This was one of those times in life where you just had to suck up your fear and get through a horrible situation the best you could. "What the hell are you waiting for?" he asked as he drew a deep breath and clenched his teeth.

"Tough guy, huh?" The man's smile disappeared. "Tell you what. We'll cut off two fingers today. Then we'll see how tough you are."

"Put down the bolt cutters."

The mobsters whipped around.

Bennett Smith stood in the shop doorway aiming his .44 directly at Mad Dog. "I'm a federal agent," he said calmly. "That man you have handcuffed to the wall is being sought by the Department of Justice as a potential witness with respect to a high-profile case which has absolutely nothing to do with any of you or any operations with which you may be involved. And I personally don't care what you're involved in. Do you understand what I've just said?"

Frankie reached for his gun. Bennett smoothly turned the .44 on the man, squeezed the trigger and nailed him through the wrist. Frankie dropped to his knees and his .38 flew through the air, clattering against the far wall.

"You stupid sonofabitch!" Mad Dog snarled at Frankie, who was writhing on the floor, clutching his wrist.

"Any more of that and I'll start shooting at everybody!" Bennett yelled. "And we'll see who's standing at the end." Sal backed up against the wall, hands raised, as Bennett aimed at him. "Then I'll rip this damn warehouse apart and take the temperature of the goods I find," Bennett yelled even louder. "My guess is, they'll all be hot."

"There's no reason for any of that," Mad Dog assured Bennett quickly. For all he knew, the guy with the blond hair had nothing to do with the federal government. But there could be an army of federal agents outside the warehouse, too, and he wasn't going to take that chance. "You can have him." Mad Dog snapped his fingers at Sal. "Unlock him."

Seconds later Cole was free from the latch and the handcuffs.

"Get over here!" Bennett ordered.

Cole moved quickly across the floor—stepping around Frankie, who was bleeding badly—until he was standing next to Bennett.

"Let me see the guns!" Bennett demanded.

The mobsters glanced at each other but didn't move.

"Come on! One at a time, and take them out slowly."

Reluctantly, they removed their pistols from their shoulder holsters.

"Throw them over here." Bennett pointed at the ground in front of his boots.

The men slid the guns across the smooth floor.

"Now your cell phones."

The men removed cell phones from their pockets and slid the phones across the floor as well.

"Get everything, Mr. Egan," Bennett instructed, acting as if they were not well acquainted. "Put it all in that bag." Bennett pointed at a bag hanging from the wall.

Obediently Cole gathered the guns and the phones and placed them in the bag.

"Put the bag outside the door."

Cole did as he was ordered, then returned to Bennett's side.

"Now what seems to be the problem?" Bennett asked.

"I owe them some money," Cole answered quietly.

"Gambling money?"

Cole hesitated. "Yes."

"Just like your damn father," Bennett muttered under his breath.

"Hey, I don't think that's—"

"Shut up," Bennett growled. "How much do you owe them?"

Bennett was talking to him as if he were an immature adolescent, and it made Cole furious, as it had when his uncle had admonished him as a teenager. His uncle had no right to talk to him that way and neither did Bennett. Only a father had that right. "I owe them plenty."

"How much?" Bennett yelled.

But for the second time in as many weeks Bennett was risking his own life to pry Cole out of a bad situation. Now was no time to be arrogant. "A hundred and fifty thousand dollars," he admitted.

"Jesus Christ," Bennett grumbled, shaking his head. Slowly he reached into his overcoat and produced a thick money clip. He tossed it at Mad Dog, who snagged it cleanly out of the air. "There's seven thousand dollars in that clip. I want your assurance that Mr. Egan will not be required to make another payment until the first of February. Not until he's had a chance to get that bonus I heard him telling you about. When he gets it, I want him to be able to pay off his entire debt in one lump sum. I don't want it stretching out. And there will be no more interest accrued between now and February. Do we have an understanding?"

"Yeah," Mad Dog agreed.

"If I find out that our understanding has been violated, I will bring the federal government down on you as hard as I can. And I'll put it out on the street that you're my personal informant." Bennett pointed directly at Mad Dog. "That you have been providing the government with information about your family's activities for several years."

"Hey!" The ploy worked perfectly. Mad Dog's fear was obvious and immediate. "Don't start that!"

"If he isn't hassled," Bennett gestured at Cole, "everything will be fine."

Mad Dog dropped the money clip in his shirt pocket. "Like I said. No problem."

"Good." Bennett glanced at Cole. "Get outside." Bennett stalked to the far wall, ripped the room's only phone off the wall, made certain it no longer worked and moved back to the doorway. He closed the door, locked it, jammed a thin piece of wood between the bottom of the door and the floor, picked up the bag full of guns and phones, then turned and began running. "Come on, Cole."

Cole needed no urging. He sprinted after Bennett, who raced down a long hallway—pausing only long enough to hurl the bag of guns and phones behind several boxes—then burst through a metal door on the far side of the building from where the men had brought Cole. They jumped into Bennett's rented Ford Taurus parked just outside the door and peeled away. Not until they had crossed the Brooklyn Bridge and were back in Manhattan did they begin to breathe normally.

Finally Bennett pulled the car to a stop in front of a deli and jammed the gearshift into park. "What the hell was that all about?" Bennett's face and neck were bloodred, still flushed from the confrontation at the warehouse.

"I told you," Cole said, rubbing his swollen little finger, "I owe them gambling money."

"Nothing else?" Bennett was seething.

For the first time Cole caught a glimpse of a mercurial temper simmering just beneath Bennett's fair skin. "No."

Bennett gazed at Cole, one eyebrow raised, as if he didn't believe what Cole had said.

"I swear to you." An odd expression crossed Cole's face. "Oh, wait a minute. You thought all that was about the Dealey Tape."

"Was it?" Bennett wanted to know.

"Christ, you thought they were trying to get it from me to keep it from becoming public." The realization set in.

"Were they?"

"No!"

"If that tape became public, the Mafia would come under intense scrutiny," Bennett pointed out. "You know as well as I do that the federal government would have to open up the investigation into the assassination all over again. The Mafia would certainly be one of the entities investigated. Federal agents would be crawling all over them again. The Mafia has done its best to maintain a low profile over the last few years."

That was true, Cole realized. Since John Gotti had been put away, the Mafia had gone quiet again.

"The last thing Mafia bosses want is federal investigators back in their boxer shorts."

Cole shook his head. "Look, I ran up a tab at one of their Brooklyn casinos. What happened back at the warehouse has nothing to do with the Dealey Tape."

"Don't bet on it." Bennett set his jaw.

"You're crazy. I went to the casino on my own. Nobody took me to—" He stopped short. He was about to say that no one had taken him to the casino, but that wasn't entirely true. The corporate bond trader had steered him to the casino that night. But it was insane to think the whole thing had been prearranged, to think that Mad Dog and his crew had any idea the Dealey Tape even existed.

"What were you going to say?" Bennett demanded.

"Nothing." There was no reason to bring up the fact that the trader had taken him to the Blue Moon. It would only arouse irrelevant suspicions. "What in the hell were you doing out there anyway? Not that I wasn't glad to see you."

Bennett relaxed into the car seat. "I told you. Your father was worried you might run into trouble after you went to that safe deposit box. I told him I'd make sure you remained unharmed."

"But I don't have the tape anymore. The guy with the scar got it. You know that."

"I do, but maybe some people don't."

Cole stared at Bennett for a few seconds. "What do you mean by that?"

"I think the woman you picked up at the Kro Bar drugged you. She probably went through your cabin after you passed out, searching your possessions."

"What?" That was a possibility he hadn't considered.

"I don't think you were hung over that morning. I think you were drugged."

Suddenly Cole remembered the nasty mineral taste that had stayed in his mouth for twenty-four hours. "Really?"

"Yes."

"What was she looking for?" Cole asked.

"I don't know. You tell me."

He saw Bennett's accusing look. "Who could she have been working for?" Cole asked.

Bennett shrugged. "Maybe those characters we just left locked in the warehouse. Maybe the DIA operation I told you about when we were on the river in Wisconsin."

"But the DIA got the tape," Cole argued.

"You don't know they were the ones," Bennett retorted angrily. "Neither do I. Like I told you, I'm not certain that operation inside the DIA ever really existed. All your father and I ever heard were rumors and innuendo. Like with anything compartmentalized, there was never anything definitive. We put two and two together and came up with ten."

They sat in silence for a few minutes. Finally Bennett checked his watch. "It's four o'clock and I need to get going. Do you mind catching a cab back to work? Do you have enough cash or are you going to have to knock over a bodega?"

"I think I can scrape the fare together somehow." Cole grinned. "And don't worry. I'm going to pay you back the seven thousand dollars."

"You're damn right you are," Bennett said quickly, chuckling. "Actually, it's expense money. Don't worry about it. I can convince my superiors I lost it."

"I pay my debts, too."

"I told you, don't worry. How's that finger?" Bennett asked, pointing at Cole's hand.

He held it up. "It'll be all right." Cole touched the skin, which was already turning black and blue.

"What about that girl of yours?"

"Same. Not great." Cole glanced out the car window at the deli. There was no need to tell Bennett that Nicki didn't seem to want to speak to him ever again. "It's good of you to ask, though," he said. Then he grabbed the handle, opened the door, turned back toward Bennett and held out his right hand. "Thanks for everything, Bennett."

Bennett shook Cole's hand. "I'm sorry about the way I talked to you back there at the warehouse. I saw that don't-talk-to-me-like-you're-my-father look on your face."

Instantly, Cole was embarrassed. "You had every right to say what you said. I was acting like a child."

Bennett released Cole's hand. "Make sure you call that Washington number if you need me."

Cole nodded. "I will. Thanks again." He patted Bennett's broad shoulder, stepped from the car, closed the door and waved as Bennett eased the car into traffic.

Cole puffed out his cheeks and exhaled as he watched the Ford disappear into the distance, then began walking. He was a long way from Gilchrist and needed to find the closest subway station. He didn't have enough cash to pay for a taxi.

Jamison paced back and forth behind the Oval Office desk. Zahn and Walsh sat in the chairs beside the desk, as they had the week before. "A second tape?" he asked

"Yes, Mr. President," Zahn answered hesitantly. "That is William Seward's concern."

"Did he voice this concern in front of my associate?"

"Yes."

"Dammit!" Jamison smashed his fist on the desk.

Zahn winced.

"Why the hell did you let him say that?" Jamison demanded, his eyes burning.

"I didn't," the general said. "Seward just blurted the whole thing out. Including a story about Jim Egan conveying the original film to him to throw him off the track." Zahn stared steadily at Jamison.

Finally Jamison folded his arms over his chest and glanced away. He knew Zahn was livid at not being told about the film.

"On what does Seward base his assumption that

there is a second tape?" Walsh asked. Like the president, Walsh was wearing a tuxedo. They were both about to head into a state dinner.

"I don't know," Zahn responded. "Just his analysis of Jim Egan's character, I think. He says Egan was too careful not to make a second tape."

"What are you doing about it, General?" Jamison asked. "I mean, is it possible that Seward could be right?" He was clearly shaken. He had already counted the mission in the "successfully closed" column.

"It's obviously possible," Walsh interrupted. "So what *are* you doing about it, General Zahn?"

"We have someone very close to Cole Egan who is monitoring the situation carefully."

Jamison stopped pacing for a second. He was already well aware of the person who was close to Cole Egan. "How did my associate react to the news?"

"Not well," Zahn answered.

Cole stepped from the hotel elevator. His apartment would be undergoing renovation work for at least a month. He whistled as he walked down the long corridor. During the afternoon—while he had eaten lunch with Tori Brown and been occupied with Mad Dog and his crew—interest rates had dropped a few ticks, increasing the value of his portfolio almost a million dollars. Suddenly the prediction was for additional rate drops in the next few weeks as a mass of weak economic data was being reported. Out of nowhere the possibility of receiving a bonus was looking better and better—and with it the possibility of paying off his debt at the Blue Moon. Life was funny. Just when things looked bleakest, they could turn on a dime.

Cole pulled the magnetic-strip hotel key from his

shirt pocket, inserted it into the slot, waited as the light on the pad turned green, then pushed. Just inside the door a note lay on the floor. He picked it up and in the light from the hall began to read. Finally, he shook his head and laughed softly. On a damn dime.

13

THERE WAS MAGEE'S FAMILIAR KNOCK—TWO HARD raps. "Come in," Seward called from the chair in front of the fireplace.

Magee pressed down the latch, shoved the door open with his shoulder and moved into Seward's Virginia cabin, briefcase in hand. "Good evening, sir." He nodded stiffly.

"Hello, Commander." Seward recognized that Magee was still annoyed from his last visit. "I hope the drive down from Washington wasn't too bad." As much as it annoyed him, Seward forced himself to use a conciliatory tone.

General Zahn had made it quite clear that he wanted everyone working well together at this point. No petty differences were going to "fuck up" anything. According to Zahn, those were President Jamison's exact words. The president wanted everyone involved to understand that nothing was going to get in the way of the operation's successful conclusion. If something did, heads would roll. Seward had realized that the threat was literal, and it had shaken him. He had been involved with Operation Snowfall from its beginning in 1963, and he knew by now that everyone was expendable. He was seventy-two years old and still in reasonably good health. There was no reason to die before his time.

"Why don't you get something to drink, Commander Magee?" Seward motioned toward the kitchen. "There's soda and coffee in there," he offered. "Make yourself at home."

"No, thank you," Magee said, tight-lipped.

"Then please sit down," Seward said politely.

Magee placed the briefcase on the floor next to the chair opposite Seward and sat without taking his eyes from the older man.

"Tell me about Colombia," Seward said. They never discussed matters as sensitive as this over the telephone, always face to face.

"Unfortunately, it was as we speculated," Magee answered tersely.

"I see." Seward frowned. "Come over to the table with me." Seward picked up his cane, rose with some effort and limped to a card table erected in a corner of the room. He pointed at six photographs spread out on the table. "Do you recognize any of these men?"

Magee perused the pictures. His eyes focused on one in particular. "Him," Magee said confidently. He tapped the picture of a fair-skinned man with a shock of yellow hair.

Seward cursed softly.

"He's the one who came out of nowhere in Manhattan after I took the tape from Cole Egan," Magee continued. "He shot Catherine. He probably killed Agent Graham as well."

"Graham was found?" Seward asked quickly.

Magee nodded. "He was found in Bryant Park with the back of his skull smashed in." Magee glanced at Seward suspiciously. "How the hell did you find this guy so fast?"

"When you told me last week that you had been chased in Manhattan, I did some digging. I spoke to a friend of mine in Washington and he sent me these." Seward pointed at the photographs. "These are pictures of the men Jim Egan worked closely with during his career as a DIA agent." Seward picked up the photograph Magee had identified and scrutinized it for a few seconds. "The man you have just identified is Bennett Smith. He was Jim Egan's primary partner on covert DIA operations over the last thirty-five years."

Magee nodded. "I see." So this operation involved the DIA. Seward hadn't told him that. Seward had simply told him to investigate the grave in Colombia and to inspect the body. There had been no particulars other than that. There hadn't been all along. "A young boy in Colombia informed me that a man fitting Smith's description was the one who dug the grave."

"That makes sense," Seward agreed. "Egan and Smith were on a mission together."

"What kind of mission?" Magee didn't expect to receive any specifics, but what the hell, he might as well ask.

Seward turned, limped back to the chair and sat down. He motioned for Magee to do the same. "Does the name Hector Gómez mean anything to you?"

Magee racked his brain for a moment. Almost, almost. There it was. "Yes, it does." He smiled, pleased with himself. "Gómez is the kingpin of a drug family out of Colombia." He had heard Gómez's name mentioned once at a Pentagon briefing.

"Jim Egan and Bennett Smith were in Colombia to

kill Gómez," Seward said matter-of-factly. "Commander, what I'm about to tell you is classified top secret and contained in a compartment into which you have just been admitted."

Magee nodded as he heard the official language. He loved this stuff. It was what he lived for.

"Iraq has experienced a huge influx of crack cocaine over the last two years." Seward could see Magee's resentment at being kept in the dark turning quickly to fascination.

Magee nodded again. He had performed SEAL team covert operations on Kuwait's beaches during the Persian Gulf War and had kept up with the political situation in the Middle East since. He was aware that drug abuse by Iraq's poor population had suddenly exploded despite hardline efforts by the government to stop the inflow. "I assume from what you are telling me that Gómez is supplying Iraq," Magee said.

"Yes," Seward answered.

"But why would we want to assassinate Gómez? It seems to me we'd be happy about what he's doing. More civil unrest in Iraq means their government has less time to focus on Kuwait or Saudi Arabia. It means they have less time to focus on moving the Republican Guard around and causing ulcers for our senior military officers. Our military spends billions every time the Republican Guard assembles at a border. Gómez is probably saving us a lot of money."

"Gómez doesn't sell directly to dealers in Iraq."

It took Magee only seconds to fully grasp the implication. "So from your tone of voice I'm guessing there must exist a covert operation in which we are the middlemen."

"That's correct." Magee might be arrogant and obnoxious, Seward thought, but he was also very intelligent. "It's an operation that perhaps ten people in the world are aware of." Seward knew that would impress Magee. "An operation which the Drug Enforcement Agency doesn't know about, which is where the problem arises." Seward paused as he switched gears. "A few months ago members of the Gómez cartel killed two Drug Enforcement Agency people in Bogotá and the DEA went ballistic. They wanted Gómez badly—"

"And the people who put the operation together were afraid that if the DEA got to Gómez, he would tell them what was going on in Iraq," Magee interrupted. "And the United States government would have a political nightmare on its hands."

"Right," Seward said stiffly. He hated the way Magee finished his sentences sometimes. "A nightmare of epic proportions. Jim Egan and Bennett Smith were sent down to Colombia to take out Hector Gómez before the DEA found him. Gómez was the only one who could identify the middlemen in the Iraq situation—in other words, identify the United States as funding those who delivered the cocaine. Egan and Smith led a small group of specially trained Army Rangers through the rain forests of Brazil and Colombia to Zaraza, where you went to recover the body. That was where Gómez's drug operation was based. Egan and Smith got Gómez, but Egan was lost in a gun battle when the Rangers attacked the Gómez compound."

"I haven't seen any news reports of Gómez's death."

"And you won't," Seward countered. "The Gómez family is the most secretive of any drug outfit operating south of the border."

"What does all that have to do with the tape I took from Cole Egan in Manhattan?" Magee asked.

"I believe that Jim Egan's disappearance in Colombia is linked to the tape surfacing at this time. Somehow Jim Egan arranged for the tape you recovered in Manhattan to be conveyed to his son, Cole. I've been trying to pry that thing out of him for thirty-five years. I knew he had it, but obviously I didn't know where it was. But I figured that when he died, the tape might appear. So I focused on anyone Jim was close to, including his son, his sister and the men he has worked closely with over the years, as people who might turn up with the tape. I had them all followed by teams. Your team was assigned to Cole Egan and you hit pay dirt." Seward paused. "I had a team after Bennett Smith, but they lost him about twenty-four hours before you followed Cole Egan to that Chase branch. Smith is a slick character."

"It seems coincidental that Bennett Smith just happened to be in Manhattan when Cole Egan got hold of the tape," Magee pointed out.

"Doesn't it?" Seward asked dryly.

"Do you think there is a connection?"

"I think we should assume so. I think we should assume that Smith delivered the tape to Cole Egan." Seward tapped the end of his cane on the floor. "Smith is a loose cannon at this point. He was very close to Jim Egan. There's no telling what he knows, or what he'll do." Seward paused. "He needs to be apprehended in light of his sudden appearance in Manhattan, and what you found in Colombia."

"Yes," Magee agreed. "But if he's AWOL, how will I find him?"

"That won't be hard," Seward replied. "Smith hasn't allowed Cole Egan out of his sight since that night in Manhattan."

"How do you know?"

Seward smiled. "Because *we* haven't let Cole Egan out of our sight either. We regained contact with him in Wisconsin. And by regaining contact, I'm not talking about Lewis Gebauer saying good morning to Cole on the Gilchrist trading floor. I'm talking about a professional following Cole's every move."

"Why did you continue following Cole? I got the tape."

"I've been shadowing Jim Egan for almost four decades. I thought it might be a good idea to stick with Cole a little longer, even after you got the tape, in case there was another copy." Seward raised a bushy salt-and-pepper eyebrow. "Which was why I ordered you not to harm Cole in Manhattan."

"And?" Magee didn't want to dwell on that issue.

Seward shrugged. "And we followed him from Wisconsin to Minnesota, then home to New York, but we didn't observe anything unusual. We even had someone in Wisconsin drug him and go through his possessions, but she found nothing suspicious. However, we're still watching him." Seward took a deep breath. "And Bennett Smith is still watching Cole too, although we aren't sure why." Seward pointed at Magee. "Which is where you come in. I need to know why Smith is sticking so close to Cole."

14

COLE GRABBED THE RECEIVER AND PUNCHED A BUTTON on his phone bank marked TUCKER TRAVIS. This line was a direct intercom to one of the largest government securities dealers on Wall Street. "Pick up Gilchrist!" he yelled, eyeing the six message slips cluttering his desk. It was only 8:30 A.M. but CNN and Fox had already each called three times this morning. Tori Brown had been just one day ahead of the pack. "Come on!" he shouted. "This is Gilchrist!"

"Yeah, Gilchrist!" someone shouted back over the line almost instantly this time. "It's Chris Tessorio at Tucker."

"Chris, this is Cole."

"Hey, Cole, baby. Sorry I took so long, but it's crazy out there this morning. Lots of securities are swapping hands." It had been all of ten seconds since Cole's first request for service, but that was aeons in the trading business. In those ten seconds Cole could have pushed a button for one of the other five dealers on his phone bank and Chris would have lost a large commission. "What can I do for you?" Chris asked.

Cole had met Chris's boss once, but never Chris. He wouldn't have been able to pick Chris out of a police lineup if his life depended on it, but they spoke at least five times a day and over the last few years had executed thousands of transactions together. But that was the trading side of Wall Street. It was strictly a phone business.

"Make me a market in the two-year." With the words "make me a market," Cole committed himself to a transaction. "A billion dollars' worth," he said calmly.

Chris whistled through the phone. "A billion, huh?"

"Yes," Cole replied evenly. If interest rates continued to decline the way they had over the past few days, a January bonus might still be a possibility with this trade. If rates rose back up to last week's levels, Gilchrist would lose millions on the trade and Cole wouldn't have to worry about a bonus because he'd be looking for another job.

"Do you know something the rest of the market doesn't?" Chris's curiosity was aroused.

"Maybe." Cole chuckled to himself. Nicki knew him so well. Bet the ranch, and why the hell not? In this city you could be shot to death minding your own business, doing your best to stay out of trouble. He was about to go looking for it.

"Talk to me, Cole." Chris was digging. "What's going on?"

Chris's questions annoyed Cole. Salesmen were supposed to take orders and give information, not try to pry it out of their clients. He had no intention of telling Chris that this trade was part of a scorched-earth, the-hell-with-it-all strategy that had nothing to do with some insider tip. Let him wonder. "Are you going to make me a market or what?"

"Yeah, yeah." Chris heard Cole's irritation. "Nine plus ten."

Cole checked his screen to make certain that Chris's price was fair. It was close and he didn't have time to bicker. "At ten I buy a billion dollars of the two-year." This trade was a bet that the market interest rate of the two-year U.S. Government issue would decrease and the price of the note would rise.

"Done at ten," Chris confirmed.

"Good." Cole hung up and reached for a stack of blank yellow order tickets sitting atop the bulkhead behind his row of computer screens. For an instant he gazed at the papers. They were almost the same color as Bennett's hair.

"What the hell was that?" Lewis Gebauer had overheard Cole place the buy order with Tucker Travis.

"None of your damn business, Lewis." Cole picked up the top ticket from the stack, filled it out quickly and tossed it into the out box.

"What's your problem this morning?" Gebauer asked through mouthfuls of a Bavarian cream donut.

Cole pushed his chair back and stood up. "Did you get that donut from Dino's, the little shop on the corner?" Cole gestured at the bag on Gebauer's desk. The deli's name was on the bag.

"Yeah," Gebauer responded hesitantly. "Why?"

"Somebody told me they closed that place down a half hour ago. One of the employees has hepatitis." As he turned and walked away, Cole could hear Gebauer spitting out the donut.

Cole threaded his way through the trading floor toward Barry Nelson's corner office. Nelson was the senior managing director in charge of all bond trading at Gilchrist. Through the office's glass wall, Cole saw that Nelson was deep in conversation with two other traders, but he knocked anyway. Nelson waved Cole off, but Cole yanked the door open.

"This better be important," Nelson snarled, glancing up from the desk over half-lens glasses.

"It is." Cole moved directly to Nelson's desk. "I'm taking a week off." Cole dropped a manila folder on Nelson's desk. Inside was a summary of all of his investments. He had penciled in the price of the Tucker Travis trade as he walked to Nelson's office. "Craig Leone will handle my portfolio while I'm gone." Leone was one of the traders who sat on the other side of the bulkhead from Cole. "I've already spoken to him about it."

"Leave us," Nelson barked at the man and woman seated in front of the desk, who were updating him on overnight losses in Gilchrist's London office. They were gone in a heartbeat, only too happy to be off the hot seat. Nelson removed his glasses and dropped them on the manila folder. "What's going on, Cole? You just took a week off."

"I have a family emergency."

"I don't give a crap. Tell whoever it is not to die yet, or hold off on the funeral if they're already in the morgue. The markets are going insane. A week after the Fed raises rates, suddenly they're coming down again. It's nuts out there." Nelson gestured toward the trading floor. "We're coming close to the end of the year, and the senior people are going ballistic. The firm's had a great year so far, and the execs are worried sick that we're going to give all our gains back now, just as we're all about to get bonuses." He pointed at Cole. "Listen, I want you on the desk every morning bright and early until December thirty-first."

"I can't," Cole snapped. "I've got to go."

"Cole, you're on the bubble here after last year.

You know that. I would think you'd want to be here to personally protect your trading positions, not trust them with Leone."

"I'll be back in a week," Cole said firmly.

"Christ!" Nelson picked up an autographed baseball from his desktop and flung it against the wall. The ball smashed into a picture of the 1927 Yankees, shattering the glass. "You are one stubborn son of a bitch sometimes, Cole."

Cole reached the office door.

"I need to talk to you about something else," Nelson yelled.

There was an edge to Nelson's voice that made Cole turn around. "What is it?"

Nelson's expression was grim. "About a week ago a Gilchrist security guard was stabbed down in the lobby. It was after hours, around eight o'clock at night. He died yesterday evening without ever regaining consciousness. We've kept this very quiet."

"That's terrible." Cole blinked slowly, trying hard to convince Nelson this was the first he'd heard of the incident. "But why are you telling me?"

"Your name was on the night register. You had signed in only a few minutes before the guard was found."

Cole had forgotten about that. He glanced out through the glass wall onto the floor and noticed Gebauer rifling through the message slips on his desk. "So?"

"So the police want to talk to you. They want to know if you saw anything suspicious."

"I came back that night to pick up some personal papers. I didn't see anything."

"One of the front doors in the lobby was smashed,"

Nelson pressed. "The police think it might have been shot out."

"I didn't see anything," Cole repeated. "If I had, I would have already told someone."

"Tell them that," Nelson urged.

"I don't have time."

"Make time."

Cole shook his head. He felt compassion for the guard, but the police would never solve the crime. If Bennett was correct, the investigation would pit the New York City Police Department against a covert operation buried so deep in the DIA no one was going to find it. "If the police want to arrest me, I guess I'll have to talk to them. But you better convey that to them soon, because I'm leaving." Cole turned and walked out of the office.

"Cole! Wait a minute!"

But he didn't. He moved quickly across the floor, which was breaking into chaos as the morning session started to heat up again, pausing only long enough to check an up-to-the-second two-year government interest rate quote on one of the Bloomberg terminals at the corporate bond desk. The rate was down five basis points, which meant that the long position he had put on only a few minutes ago with Tucker Travis was already up almost a million dollars.

Gebauer was still rummaging through papers on the desk as Cole made it back to his seat. "Can I help you?" Cole asked sarcastically, ripping the message slips out of Gebauer's hand.

"Why the hell are all these news people calling you?" Gebauer demanded.

"I won the lottery yesterday, Lewis, didn't you hear?" Cole stuffed the messages in his shirt pocket. "They want my story."

"Seriously!" Gebauer yelled.

"But I'm taking a week off to enjoy myself before I give any interviews. I'm going back to my room at the hotel, pack a few things and fly to Bermuda to enjoy some sand and sun." Cole watched Gebauer taking mental notes. So the bastard really was involved somehow. "Or am I flying to Hawaii?" He put a finger to his forehead as if he were thinking hard, then picked up his overcoat from the chair, slipped it on and headed for the door. "Maybe it's Rio," he called over his shoulder.

Gebauer cursed under his breath. Finally he headed for the door too. He needed to make a call quickly and couldn't do it on a trading room phone. All conversations over these lines were recorded.

At the reception desk, Anita smiled as she saw Cole coming toward her. "Hi, Cole."

He leaned over the desk, took her face gently in his hands and kissed her on the cheek. "See you in a week," he whispered in her ear. "I may need your help. Okay?"

She nodded, uncertain what that meant. "Okay."

"Thanks." He turned abruptly, moved across the reception area into an elevator and was gone.

For several moments she gazed at the silver metal doors that had closed behind Cole. Then Lewis Gebauer came puffing out of the trading floor. She watched the fat man move into one of the small conference rooms off the main reception room and slam the door. What a jerk he was. Not once since she had come to work at Gilchrist had he even so much as acknowledged her presence.

Cole stepped out of the elevator and moved quickly through the lobby. It was a sunny day in Manhattan and the air was crisp and cool. As Cole walked through the doors, he pulled sunglasses from his inside suit coat pocket and wrapped the curved stems behind his ears.

"Hey, stranger."

He'd recognize that gravelly voice anywhere, even after only one lunch. He glanced to the left. Tori Brown was leaning against the building wall, putting her cell phone back into a large black bag slung over her shoulder. Her brown hair was down today—there was no black velvet band—and she was wrapped in an ankle-length blue overcoat decorated with gold buttons.

"Hi, Cole."

Tori suddenly seemed to emit an aura of affluence he hadn't noticed at lunch yesterday, but maybe that was just because of what Cole had found out about her. "Hi," he said, making certain his voice was devoid of emotion.

She moved to where he stood and looked directly up into his eyes. "I know you're angry with me, and you have every right to be. What I did at lunch was inexcusable. I put my career goals in front of what was the right thing to do." She searched his face. "I want to make it up to you."

So Tori had a heart after all. Or perhaps she was trying to get closer to him for another reason. "What do you have in mind?"

"I want to take you to see your grandparents."

He had anticipated this offer, but his pulse jumped anyway. "As a matter of fact, I was about to get on a plane."

"Where are you going?" she asked quickly.

"You're a nosy person, you know that?"

"Sorry, it comes with the job." She smiled nervously. "If you can spare a few minutes, I'll take you to the Thomases' apartment."

"They might not be home," Cole pointed out.

"I know your grandmother is. I just called to make certain. I hung up when she answered, so she doesn't know we're coming."

Cole pressed his arm against his wallet, which was stashed safely in his suit coat pocket. Inside was the hand-scrawled note he had picked up off the hotel room floor last night. Nothing was going to happen until he made the first move. Until then, he could dictate the pace of the action. After that, everything would spin out of control and it would simply be a matter of trying to hold on for dear life. He made a snap decision. "Okay, let's go."

Tori turned and moved toward the curb, holding up her hand to hail a cab.

"Let's take the subway," Cole called out.

"I'm not going down into a hole," she mumbled to herself.

"What's the matter?" Cole asked as a taxi came to a halt in front of them. "Rich girls don't take subways?" He opened the door for her.

Tori ducked into the cab. "Park Avenue and Eighty-seventh Street," she directed.

"And you tried to tell me you couldn't afford lunch at an expensive restaurant." Cole slid onto the seat next to her and slammed the door as the cabbie punched the accelerator. "I guess you didn't hear me," he said loudly as the engine revved.

"I heard you," she said coolly. "Something about a poor little rich girl and five-star restaurants."

"You added a few adjectives."

Tori laughed. "Yes, I guess I did."

"You know, you have a nice smile, but it's as if you

have only so many you can use a day. It's as if someone rations you."

"You probably say that to all the women." But
Tori's smile widened. She grabbed the strap above the
door as the driver took a hard left onto Forty-second
Street and headed east. "How did you find out about
my family? I assume that's what you were referring
to. Do you have friends at the FBI or something?"

Cole shook his head. "No, I used Bloomberg and
the Internet. It's tough to hide yourself these days if
someone knows what they're looking for and has the
information systems available to do the research."

Tori gripped the strap even more tightly as the cabbie whipped left onto Madison Avenue, then began
weaving in and out of traffic. "Isn't that the truth?"

As the taxi raced north Cole put his head back on
the seat and stared up at the skyscrapers towering
over them. "Let's see if I can remember all this. Your
mother's name is Alicia Ferris Brown. She lives in Los
Angeles, California. Her occupation is chief executive
officer of Brown Communications, which owns outright, or controls a majority stake in, seven daily papers, four FM radio stations and an NBC television
affiliate. All of the properties are in midsize markets
where the competition isn't so tough, and they are all
very profitable." Cole removed his sunglasses and slid
them into his suit pocket. It wasn't so bright in the
cab and he hated people who wore sunglasses just for
effect. "Brown Communications is a private company,
so specific revenue and income figures are hard to
find, but reliable sources estimate that your mother's
net worth exceeds half a billion dollars." He hadn't
limited his research to Bloomberg and the Internet.
"I hope you don't mind, but I called the Gilchrist

media analyst this morning. Those equity people have a way of finding figures."

"You aren't telling me anything I don't know."

Cole kept going. "Alicia Brown's husband, Martin, died in 1985 of a massive stroke. Alicia has run the company since his death, turning it into one of the fastest-growing media concerns in this country. News articles report that even though she's closing in on seventy years of age, she's known as a dynamo in the industry. She has more energy than assistants half her age and expects them to keep up with her or else." Cole paused. "There's a footnote to the story. Alicia Brown has one child, a daughter, who is the only heir to the Brown fortune. The daughter's name is Victoria and she's thirty-seven." Tori was older than Cole had thought. "She's a producer at NBC News, and she goes by Tori."

Tori gave Cole a quick golf clap. "You should be a reporter," she said. "And you're right, I am a footnote."

"Do I detect a little bitterness?" he asked. "The Mom-never-had-time-for-me syndrome?"

"I've been trying to get my mother to notice me since I was five years old, but she was always on the road for a business meeting. My father's death was nothing but a very small bump in the road for her. The papers all play up the fact that she was able to take the reins after he died and turn the company into something really big, but she was always the driving force, even before he died. It was just that after his death she didn't have him in the way any longer." A wry smile crossed Tori's face. "I think in a way she was kind of glad when he passed away." The smile faded.

"At least you had parents."

"Yeah," she said softly, as if she was a million miles away. "The strange thing is, I never cared that much about my father's attention, even though he was always there for me. I wanted my mother to notice me. I wanted her to make time for me."

"It's like that a lot," Cole observed. "We don't usually care as much about the people who are always there for us. We take them for granted, which is terrible. It's the people who aren't around very much that we crave the attention of."

Tori turned on the seat so she was facing him. "How would you know about that? You've probably been in that latter category most of your life, one of those people others were always trying to get the attention of." It was her turn to tick off vital statistics. "If I'm remembering correctly, you were a high school all-American football player, received a full athletic scholarship to the University of Minnesota, were all-Big Ten your senior year and became a Wall Street trader after that—with Gilchrist and Company, no less, one of the most prestigious firms in New York." She saw that he was impressed. "As you said, Cole, it's tough to hide yourself these days from someone who knows what they're looking for and has the information systems available to do the research."

"I did say that, didn't I?"

"Yes, but you're ducking my question. How do you know about craving attention?"

Cole reached for his sunglasses.

"No." Tori pressed her hand over his.

"What?"

"There will be no hiding your eyes behind dark lenses." She took her hand away.

"That's stupid."

"No it isn't," she said firmly. "Tell me how you know."

He looked away. "My aunt and uncle raised me from the time I was a year old." He hesitated. This was close to home, perhaps too close.

"Come on," she urged gently.

Cole saw Seventieth Street flash by. In a few more minutes he would meet his maternal grandparents, and he was nervous for the first time in as long as he could remember. "You're a good interviewer. I should call you Barbara Walters." There it was, the instinct to name, as Bennett had noted. The same instinct his father had.

"Thanks a lot." Tori elbowed him gently.

"It's a compliment."

"So talk to me," she urged.

He hesitated a moment longer before continuing. "They did a great job raising me, even though I wasn't technically their child. My uncle showed me how to fly-fish and how to catch a football. My aunt constantly drove me down to the lake to fish or to Little League games. They were always there for me, and I never gave them much in return. In fact, I repaid their kindness by causing them a great deal of embarrassment when I was a teenager."

"How?"

"I was rebellious."

"All teenagers are rebellious."

"No other boy in the neighborhood had an earring." Cole pointed at the holes in his earlobe. "I had three."

"So what? That doesn't seem like a big deal."

"Our middle-class block in Duluth, Minnesota, was a long way from Los Angeles. I know earrings don't sound like much compared to what you probably saw in Beverly Hills—"

"Santa Monica," Tori corrected.

"Okay," Cole continued. "Earrings and cigarettes and wild hair at thirteen didn't go over well in a strait-laced, working-class, staunchly Lutheran neighborhood in the heartland. I'm sure I caused them more than a little humiliation and embarrassment at church socials. You can't hide in a small place like that. There is no anonymity."

"I guess you're right."

"One day when I was seventeen, after we won the regional football championship, I—" He swallowed the words.

"You what?"

Cole cleared his throat. "My uncle had just hugged me and told me what a great game I had played. He told me how proud he was of me in front of a bunch of other parents and I looked at him and said he had no right to be proud of me. I told him he had no right to take any credit for, or share in, what I had accomplished. Can you imagine that? Can you imagine a young man saying that to an uncle who had done nothing but take another man's child into his home and help him grow up the right way?" Cole gazed out the taxi window. "I couldn't have been more wrong, either. My uncle had every right to share in what I had accomplished, but I said it anyway. I was so damn mad at my father for missing that game, for missing my life."

"I told my mother the same thing," Tori said quietly. "She made certain I was accepted to the Columbia School of Journalism and arranged for my job at NBC. I resented her for doing those things."

The cab veered right onto Eighty-sixth Street, pitching Tori against Cole. "Why did you resent her?" he asked as the cab quickly turned left onto Park Avenue.

"Because I couldn't do it for myself. I didn't have

the grades to get into Columbia or the experience for the job at NBC. Everyone knew it, but I was accepted at Columbia and given the job at NBC anyway. My mother can accomplish anything. She's a powerful woman." Tori shook her head. "I didn't have the guts to turn down the charity, so I've been trying to prove to her I could do things on my own ever since. That's why I held back on your grandparents' address yesterday at lunch. I knew if I gave it to you, I wouldn't be of any use to you afterward. I wouldn't have had anything to hold over your head. I acted terribly and I knew it, but I want to break a big story on my own so badly." She paused as if gathering her strength. "I'm sorry. I don't say that very often. If it's any consolation, I didn't get much sleep last night."

"Here we are," the cabbie said gruffly. The taxi coasted to a stop.

Cole removed his wallet from his suit pocket, but Tori grabbed his hand. "Let me."

"Okay."

"It's the least I can do after being such a jerk." She placed several bills in the slot.

He gazed at her for a moment. Beneath that tough exterior she had a good heart, he decided. "It's all right. Hey, I'll never be able to thank you enough for today, really."

"That's a nice thing to say." She smiled, then glanced down. "My God. What happened?" she asked, pointing at the swollen finger Frankie had almost cut off yesterday in the Brooklyn warehouse.

"I caught it in a desk drawer," Cole explained quickly. "I'm fine." He opened the door, stepped from the cab, then turned to help her out.

A high-rise building towered over them as they emerged from the cab.

"They live in Apartment 5236," Tori said. "It's on the top floor." She brushed the hair out of her face. The wind had whipped up and the sunny day had turned cloudy during the ride from midtown. "You'll need a diversion to get in."

"Why?" Cole asked. "This isn't some kind of clandestine operation. We'll just call up to the apartment from the front desk and tell them who we are."

Tori shook her head. "They might not agree to see you. They didn't want to talk to me when I came here. Or they might not believe you when you tell them who you are. I think it's better to knock on their door unannounced." She gestured at the doorman. "And he isn't going to let you simply walk in."

Cole sensed that she had a plan. "So what are you suggesting?"

"I'll distract him, then you slip into the building."

"How are you going to distract him?"

Tori smiled provocatively. "Don't worry, that won't be a problem."

How could he have had to ask? Those blue eyes would do the trick. "Silly me."

Tori held out her hand and they shook. "It was nice meeting you, Cole Egan."

"Should I take that to mean you and I won't be seeing each other again?" he asked.

Tori laughed as their hands parted. "I assumed you wouldn't want much to do with me after my behavior at lunch yesterday."

"We all need to be a little forgiving in life sometimes." He gestured at the building. "And you did bring me up here."

"I did, at that."

Cole reached into his shirt pocket, pulled out the

message slips and handed them to Tori. "Do you know any of these people?"

Tori studied the names on the papers. "Yeah, they're competitors of mine."

"They must have seen my father's obituary too and had a contact at the *Times* who told them who paid for the space. Or maybe your contact makes a business out of telling everyone."

"Maybe I pay the contact a little better, and all that's worth is one day. But one day is usually enough in this business."

Cole glanced at the doorman, who was listlessly scanning a magazine. "Tori, what if I told you your instincts were right? That maybe there is a story here?"

Tori caught her breath. "Why would you do that?"

Because I need your help, he thought to himself. But he didn't say the words. He needed someone's help, but he hadn't decided yet if she should be the one. "After you distract the doorman, wait for me up at that coffee shop across the street." He pointed back over his shoulder.

"Okay."

"I might be a while."

"That's fine." She would stay in the coffee shop until Christmas if necessary. "I have plenty of time." She held out the message slips. "Here."

"You take those." Cole closed her fingers around the slips. "Do whatever you want with them." Cole was starting to trust her.

He had to trust someone, for Christ's sake. It would have been Nicki but she wasn't speaking to him. The only other person he could think of was Bennett— who must have pushed the anonymous note under the hotel room door last night. Cole had left a message on the answering machine at the Washington number after finding the note, but Bennett hadn't returned the call yet. He had called Bennett again from a Gilchrist conference room this morning and left another message, one that he hoped would keep them close.

"Wait for me at the coffee shop," he said again.

"I will. I hope it goes well with your grandparents." She waved and moved casually toward the apartment building's front door.

He watched her walk away. He was definitely starting to like her.

The distraction went quickly and smoothly. Tori explained to the doorman that her car doors wouldn't open—that every so often the doors jammed and she didn't have the strength to pry them open and would he mind trying? She smiled as she explained, then patted his forearm as she finished talking, and he was putty in her hands. She waved subtly at Cole as she led the doorman out of the building and down Eighty-seventh Street away from the front door, and Cole slipped into the now empty lobby and moved to the elevators.

The man sitting on the brick wall across the street who had followed Cole and Tori from Gilchrist's front door shook his head. Tori Brown was a smooth operator.

Cole felt perspiration covering his palms as he pressed the elevator button for the fifty-second floor. He wiped his palms on his suit pants, but his hands were damp again by the time he reached the top floor. The elevator doors opened and he followed the arrow indicating that apartments 5220 through 5240 were located to the right. He tried to concentrate on the wallpaper pattern to distract himself from the pounding in his chest, but it was no use. Thirty years and this meeting was finally going to happen.

He hesitated before the door for several moments, suddenly uncertain of whether he really wanted to go through with this, uncertain of whether it was worth making himself so vulnerable and allowing the walls to crumble slightly. Maybe these people wouldn't believe him when he told them who he was. Worse, maybe they would, but still wouldn't want to talk to him. That was something he hadn't considered. Maybe it was better not to know. Perhaps the best thing would be to leave the building, leave Tori at the coffee shop, leave New York and get to the business at hand. He glanced at his watch. There was still time to make the noon flight to Minneapolis out of La Guardia. He turned to go, then stopped. He didn't dodge difficult situations. He never had and he never would. This was something he needed to do. He took a deep breath, clenched his right hand, raised it and knocked.

Almost instantly, footsteps moved across the floor inside the apartment. "Who is it?" an elderly female voice called from behind the door.

"Maintenance."

The chain fell away, the knob turned and the door opened. For several moments grandmother and grandson stared at each other for the first time. Then the elderly woman put her hands to her mouth. So clearly were her daughter's features etched on the face of the handsome young man standing before her that she believed she was staring at an apparition. Then she fainted and fell to the Oriental rug.

15

THE PHOTOGRAPH SHOOK SLIGHTLY IN COLE'S HANDS. There was his mother, Mary Thomas—or Andrea Sage—smiling back at him. She was exactly as Bennett Smith had said, a "real stunner."

"I just can't get over it," Cole's grandmother murmured. "The resemblance is uncanny." She sat next to Cole on the sofa, clutching his arm tightly in her wrinkled hands. It had taken Cole and his grandfather almost five minutes to fully revive her after she had fainted to the floor. "Don't you think, Henry?" she asked the elderly man across the room.

Henry sat in a large armchair smoking his pipe. "Yes." His grandfather, Cole had already found, was a man of few words.

Cole smiled down at the diminutive woman sitting next to him. "Do you really think so?"

"Oh, Lord, yes. When I saw you standing outside our door, it was like seeing a ghost." She put her hands to her chest as if the feeling that had caused her to lose consciousness was coming back all over again.

"Easy, Margaret," Henry warned. "Cole and I don't want to have to revive you again." He winked at his grandson.

Henry was a man of few words, yes, but he was quickly warming to the idea of having a grandson. They had spent the last hour catching up. Cole learned that his grandfather had spent almost forty years at Lehman Brothers, one of Wall Street's most venerable firms, and that they had much common ground.

"No, we don't want—" Cole hesitated in the middle of repeating Henry's warning.

"What is it, dear?" Margaret asked, a concerned expression coming to her face.

A dimple appeared in Cole's left cheek. "I'm embarrassed to say this, but I don't know what to call you."

"Henry and Margaret," Henry interjected quickly. "None of this grandma and grandpa crap. God, then we really will feel our ages."

Margaret nodded in agreement.

Cole laughed. "Okay." He glanced back and forth at them, then shook his head. It was a strange thing, to have members of your family you hadn't known for your entire life, then suddenly meet them. It was like being in a time machine. "I want to ask you two a question. Well, actually," he interrupted himself, "I want to ask you lots of questions, but this one first. I ran into a young woman in the news business who claims she tried to speak to you one day a while back, but you didn't want to see her. Her name is Victoria Brown. She goes by Tori."

"I remember her," Margaret said.

"She was the one who led me here," Cole explained. "Why didn't you want to talk to her?"

"We didn't want to drag up old memories," Henry replied.

"But she might have been able to give you information about my mother. I would think you'd want to hear about her."

"We knew Mary had died." Henry inhaled from the pipe. "That was all we needed to know. We didn't tell the newswoman because we didn't think it was any of her business. Having you here is a different story."

"Wait a minute." Cole's eyes narrowed. "What do you mean, you knew she was dead?" Tori said they claimed they had never heard anything about Mary after she left in the spring of 1963.

Henry and Margaret exchanged uncomfortable glances.

"You didn't know she was dead, dear?" Margaret asked tentatively.

"Yes, I did, but I didn't think you would know."

"Why not?" Henry asked.

"I'm not sure." He didn't want to say that he had assumed his father just hadn't bothered ever to contact them.

"We found out in 1970." Henry's voice was barely audible. It had been a long time since his daughter's death, but he had never made it past the pain. "That was the year your father sent us a long letter telling us of Mary's demise, along with a box of her things and a death certificate I checked on in the New Jersey jurisdiction in which it was signed. At least, we assumed it was your father who sent us the letter. It was signed by a man claiming to be her husband, although we had never met him."

Cole was spellbound.

"Cole, do you want to see her room?" Margaret asked.

"Yes."

An eerie feeling overtook Cole as he moved into the bedroom. It was as if his mother were out running an errand and would return soon. A cotton nightgown hung from a hook on the back of the open closet door. Dresses dangled from hangers, one pulled out slightly as if she had considered wearing it that morning. Pairs of shoes lined the floor of the closet and another pair lay on the floor next to the bed. Stuffed animals were spread across the bed's quilt. College textbooks lined the desk beside the bed and a notebook lay open atop the desk, a ballpoint pen on the open page.

Margaret pulled an envelope from the top drawer of the desk and walked to where Cole stood in the doorway. "Here's your father's letter to us."

Cole took the faded envelope from her, extracted the handwritten letter and began to read. His eyes flashed across the pages. The letter said Mary had died at the hands of two drug-crazed intruders, exactly as Bennett had said.

He stared at the pages for a long time after he had finished reading the words. There was something else here, a connection of some sort that he couldn't quite make.

"It's such a shame." Margaret moved to her daughter's dressing table, picked up a silver hairbrush and touched it lovingly. "Not a day goes by that I don't come in here and think about her."

Cole replaced the letter in the envelope. "I'm sure you do," he said softly. "Margaret, you mentioned that my father sent a box of things along with the letter."

"Yes. It was full of personal items like jewelry and papers." She nodded at the hairbrush. "This was in the box. We gave this and a silver comb to Mary for

her sixteenth birthday. That's how we knew the letter
was authentic." Tears began to well in the elderly
woman's eyes. "I'm sorry."

Cole looked away from Margaret's eyes and down
to the hairbrush. Strands of his mother's hair were still
embedded in the bristles.

He let out a long slow breath. Perhaps it would
have been better if he hadn't come after all. This was
causing Margaret so much pain. And not just
Margaret.

"Are you ready?" Maybe he was wrong to come
around on her so quickly, but he had a good feeling
about Tori. More to the point, he needed her cash
and her willingness to use it. Trusting that airlines and
motels would simply accept his maxed-out credit cards
wasn't a viable plan.

Tori looked up from the paper she had been reading
for the last two hours. "Ready for what?"

"We're going on a trip," Cole replied.

"Where to?"

"I'll tell you when we get there."

16

IN A MATTER OF HOURS DEAD CALM WOULD AGAIN TURN
to absolute chaos. Cole was certain of that. However,
this time he was better prepared for it. This time he
knew exactly what he was looking for, where to find
it, and what to expect when he got there. And he
knew the terrain. This time the struggle would be
fought on his turf instead of New York City streets.

Cole glanced over at Tori, who sat next to him in
the plane's first-class cabin calmly perusing a magazine
and sipping a pre-takeoff glass of wine. He knew the
players, too.

Tori noticed him looking at her. "Why are you staring at me like that?"

"Do I need a reason?" Cole smiled and looked
away.

He knew the players, all right, but he didn't know
everyone's exact motivation. He was fairly certain he
had figured out who was friend and who was foe, but
there was always that seed of doubt, always that possibility he had misjudged someone. He glanced at Tori

again out of the corner of his eye. Motivation was the only variable in all of this now.

"Excuse me," a voice said loudly.

Cole was sitting in the aisle seat and had to lean toward Tori so a woman carrying two large bags could move past him and into the main cabin of the Continental Airlines Boeing 727. Following the woman was a young man who was in his early twenties, Cole guessed. He wore a golf shirt—BAY HILL G.C. embroidered above the pocket—and khakis. His only carry-on luggage was a small duffel bag. He was the same young man who had been watching them carefully in the waiting area at the gate. Cole nodded to him as he shuffled after the woman through first class and toward the rear of the plane. The young man nodded back politely, trying to act like any other passenger.

"Why are we flying to Los Angeles?" Tori asked, replacing the magazine in its pocket on the bulkhead in front of the first row. "You still haven't let me in on the big secret."

Cole turned to her as the young man moved past. "I told you, I'll let you know when we get there."

Tori rolled her eyes. She was tired of that explanation. "I think I have a right to know now. After all, I'm the one paying for three thousand dollars' worth of first-class tickets."

"You are, aren't you?" He grinned. "Well, you're rich. You can afford it."

"I'm not rich. My mother has the money."

"No offense." Cole touched her diamond bracelet. "But I doubt NBC pays you enough to splurge on things like that very often. And you were wearing a different bracelet when we went to lunch at the Broadway Diner that looked even more expensive than that one."

"I don't get an allowance from my mother," Tori said firmly. She knew what he was thinking. "The bracelets were presents."

"I don't know much about jewelry," Cole admitted. "But that present looks like it's at least ten thousand dollars' worth of allowance."

Tori was quickly becoming annoyed. Cole was very good at diverting conversations when he didn't want to answer a question. "And what's your problem?"

"No problem, I'm just making a point."

"I'm not rich," she said again.

"But you will be."

She waved her hand in disgust.

"You can afford the tickets," Cole said confidently. "That's the point."

"That's why I'm here, isn't it?" Tori asked.

"What are you talking about?" Cole's dimples appeared, as if he knew exactly what she was talking about.

"I'm here to fund this vacation, aren't I? Is Los Angeles just a stopover? Are we really headed to Hawaii?"

"Actually we're headed to a little-known island south of Hawaii," Cole teased. "An island that offers only one flight a week in and out of Colesville, the capital city. I wanted to get you alone and I figured if I took you there you'd have no choice except to stay. I knew you'd be mad at me, but I figured you'd get over it in a few days."

"You're impossible." But she couldn't keep from smiling.

Cole's expression turned serious. "I promise you, Tori, you will be very glad you came. And yes, one of the reasons I asked you to come with me was to fund this trip. I'm not doing well financially. You should understand that." He looked into her eyes. "But first of all, as we've established, you can afford it. And secondly, the amount of money you spend in the next few days will seem like peanuts in return for what you get. You won't be a second-stringer at NBC when this is over."

Tori nodded slowly. She could see the intensity in his eyes. "Okay."

The young man who had followed Cole and Tori to the Thomases' apartment building on Eighty-seventh Street and now to La Guardia Airport stowed his duffel bag in the overhead compartment and slid into his back-of-the-plane, economy-class window seat. Almost immediately a fat man in a cowboy hat and a pair of too-tight designer jeans settled into the middle seat next to him.

"Haddy," the fat man said loudly.

The young man crossed his arms over his chest, turned away and closed his eyes without answering. He had no desire to engage in meaningless conversation with this idiot for six hours. He shifted in the narrow seat, trying to get comfortable. William Seward was going to be happy. Cole Egan was on the move, and he was right on Egan's tail.

Through the plane's intercom a stewardess alerted passengers that boarding was almost completed and that the crew would be shutting the doors in just a few moments in preparation for takeoff. The young man could feel himself drifting off. He hadn't gotten much rest since the beginning of surveillance and here was a chance to catch five or six hours of sleep.

The plane pushed back from the gate and taxied toward the runway. It was early afternoon and there were only two flights ahead of them. Soon they would be winging their way to sunny Los Angeles, where the temperature was eighty-seven degrees. Passengers were reminded to set their watches back three hours. . . . The young man heard the pilot telling him all this useless information as his eyes fluttered shut.

Cole watched from behind the airport glass as the Continental 727 moved out onto the runway and began lumbering down the strip—the same 727 from which he and Tori had deplaned at the last minute, just as the flight crew was shutting the door. Seconds later he watched the aircraft lift off and head toward the overcast sky. A slight smile crossed Cole's face as the wheels folded up into the fuselage. He could only imagine the panic the young man in the golf shirt would endure when the realization that he and Tori weren't on board hit him. He was a young man Cole had noticed outside the Thomases' apartment on Eighty-seventh Street *and* for a moment in the Kro Bar as he was playing pool with Bennett.

Cole shook his head. His father had played this so perfectly. There were two tapes, and therefore two chances to get this thing right. Jim Egan must have realized that the first tape would cause a huge uproar, so not only had he sent Bennett to help but he had provided a second tape and a second opportunity. Cole was much better prepared this time, as the young man in the Bay Hill golf shirt would soon understand.

Cole passed a hand through his hair as he watched the plane climb toward the cloud cover. He could feel his father now—the way his father thought, how he had anticipated everything. It was an analytical mind at work, and Cole was simply executing a perfectly conceived plan. The note on the hotel room floor had stated that there was a tape hidden in the loft of the

Albion boathouse—a stone structure halfway down the Lassiter River—secured to the top of a beam in the boathouse's northeast corner. Few people knew about the Albion boathouse or where it was, and fewer still knew what it was called. Cole chuckled. The Albion family had no idea what was in their boathouse, which was doubtless just as well for them. He chuckled again. "Good going, Dad," he murmured.

"What did you say?" Tori was coming back from buying a Coke.

"Nothing."

"You know, you're really a fountain of information sometimes."

"Thanks."

"What now, Mr. Mysterious?" Tori asked.

"Now we go to La Guardia's east terminal and board Northwest flight 917 for Minneapolis." Cole was half expecting to see Bennett on that plane.

"I suppose I'll be paying for these tickets as well," she said.

"Absolutely," Cole confirmed.

They turned and walked back toward the main terminal to catch a cab over to the Northwest Airlines gates.

"So, do you?" Her eyes danced as she asked the question.

"Do I what?" Cole was still thinking about his father.

"Do you really want to get me alone?"

Cole put his head back and laughed. "Maybe."

17

THE DAMN AIRLINES. UNLESS YOUR DESTINATION WAS New York City or Los Angeles, you were pretty much locked into a specific carrier if you wanted a direct flight. Bennett studied the departure board. Other than Northwest Airlines, the only way to Minneapolis this afternoon was a United flight that connected through Chicago. The United flight didn't leave for another hour and a half and didn't arrive in Minneapolis until eight o'clock Central Time. But he didn't want to get on the Northwest direct flight because he didn't want Cole to see him on board.

Bennett shrugged. So be it. He walked to the United counter and fifteen minutes later had purchased a ticket after waiting in a long line. He would arrive in Minneapolis three hours behind Cole. But that was all right, because he knew where Cole was going. The message on the Washington answering machine had explained all of that.

Bennett moved through the metal detector and walked down the long corridor toward the gate. Cole would stay at his aunt and uncle's house in Duluth tonight, then head to the tiny town of Hubbard and on to the Lassiter River tomorrow. That was the message on the answering machine. Cole had even left his aunt and uncle's phone number. Bennett stopped at a newsstand to buy a paper. It wasn't that he was worried about finding Cole. That wouldn't be a problem. He was worried about what might happen to Cole while he wasn't around to protect him.

Why in hell, Bennett asked himself, had Cole come to this terminal if he was headed to Minneapolis on the Northwest flight? Northwest Airlines gates were in the east terminal. He shrugged. Maybe the cabbie who had brought Cole from Manhattan didn't realize that the Northwest gates weren't in La Guardia's main terminal. And who was that woman with Cole?

Bennett took a seat at the United gate marked "CHICAGO" and glanced at his watch. He had a lot of time to kill before boarding would begin. Maybe in the interim, with a few well-placed calls to Washington, he could find out who the woman with Cole was.

As Bennett relaxed in the seat a tiny dart struck him in the neck an inch below his left ear, spreading anesthetic through his bloodstream rapidly. He knew instantly what had happened and quickly flicked the sharp projectile from his skin, but it was too late. Already he was feeling the initial effects of the drug—a loss of motor control and blurred eyesight.

He stood up, searching for his attacker even as he tried to fight the effects of the anesthetic. His eyes fastened instantly on one figure standing ten feet away. The man wore a black homburg hat and a long black coat. Curly sideburns dangled from beneath both sides of the hat, and his face was covered by a mustache and beard. And there was a scar running down the left side of the man's nose and disappearing into his beard. It was the man who had taken the tape from Cole.

And then Bennett collapsed onto the floor. He could fight the drug no longer. With his last ounce of strength he pulled the airline ticket from his inside coat pocket and shoved it behind the ashtray stand beside him. Cole was on his own now. It was the last thing that raced through Bennett's mind. Then the darkness closed in around him.

"Help us here!" the man in the long black coat shouted. "This man has had a heart attack!" he yelled, pointing toward Bennett. Within seconds, a pair of paramedics were kneeling next to Bennett. After a few moments they lifted him onto a stretcher, then rolled him hurriedly away to an ambulance waiting outside the terminal.

Commander Magee smiled. William Seward had been correct. The young man following Cole knew exactly where Bennett Smith was—tailing Cole Egan as well. Magee glanced at the board behind the gate's ticket counter indicating that the flight's destination was Chicago. A puzzled expression came to his face. That couldn't be correct. Cole was on his way to Los Angeles. Bennett should have been, too. Magee watched as the paramedics hustled down the corridor, pushing the stretcher ahead of them. Bennett Smith must have simply been resting here while he waited to take a different flight to the West Coast than Cole.

Magee turned away. He needed to get to the restroom, lose the disguise and get out to the ambulance. Bennett Smith was in for a difficult afternoon.

*   *   *

Cole and Tori walked out of the airport terminal onto the sidewalk as the ambulance carrying Bennett passed by, lights flashing.

"I hate ambulances," Tori said quietly as a taxi pulled up in front of them. It reminded her of that Christmas Eve when paramedics had raced to their house to try to revive her father, who had never regained consciousness after his massive stroke.

The ambulance sped away from La Guardia Airport through Queens. As it crossed the bridge over the East River and into Manhattan, the driver extinguished the emergency lights. The ambulance cruised through Harlem and a few minutes later arrived at what appeared to be an unused warehouse. The warehouse door rose, then descended as the ambulance passed beneath it.

When the ambulance had come to a stop, Magee and the other two agents, dressed in paramedic uniforms, jumped out and lifted Bennett Smith from the back of the vehicle. Bennett was still strapped to the stretcher. They rolled him over the floor and into an office at the edge of the huge space, where they lifted his body from the stretcher and dropped him roughly into a large chair, then fastened his wrists and ankles to shackles bolted to the chair.

"Good," Magee said. "Now get out of here."

The other agents obeyed instantly.

From the office window Magee watched the ambulance taillights disappear behind the large metal door as it descended smoothly to the floor again.

"I see all went well," William Seward observed from a doorway at the rear of the office.

Magee turned away from the window. "Yes, it did."

"Did he have an airline ticket on him?" Seward

asked, hoping they would get a quick clue to Cole's destination.

Magee glanced up, giving away his embarrassment at not having checked. Quickly he searched Bennett's pockets. "There isn't one here."

Seward let out a frustrated breath. Somehow Bennett Smith had gotten rid of the ticket, knowing they would look for it. "I've checked with the airlines, but I couldn't find out anything. He probably purchased his ticket using an alias. I'm sure he has many."

"Who cares if he had a ticket anyway?" Magee asked. "We already have someone on Cole's ass."

"How long until he wakes up?" Seward asked without answering Magee's question.

"Not long. The guys in the ambulance administered a stimulant as we were coming in from Queens. It'll probably be less than five minutes before he's ready to talk."

"That's a good thing."

Magee heard concern in Seward's tone. "What's the matter?"

"Cole Egan has disappeared," Seward answered.

"What?"

"Yes." Seward limped to where Bennett sat shackled to the chair, his head leaning to one side, and poked Bennett's face with his cane. "It seems Cole gave our young professional the slip." Seward said the word "professional" sarcastically.

"But I was out at La Guardia not more than an hour ago and talked to the guy," Magee argued. "He put me onto Bennett Smith. Cole was waiting to board a flight to Los Angeles when I met up with our guy. We had been in constant contact for almost an hour by cell phone. When we met, he told me that Smith had followed Cole to the airport, then headed to the

United ticket counter. That's where I located Smith. He was just buying his ticket. Our guy had everything under control."

Bennett groaned as Seward poked him with the cane again, this time even harder. "He *thought* he had everything under control," Seward corrected Magee. "He called me from twenty-five thousand feet five minutes ago to tell me that Cole deplaned just before the flight backed away from the gate." Seward watched as Bennett's eyes fluttered open. "Our guy had to take a piss and decided to use the lavatory at the front of the plane where Cole was sitting so he could check on him. Imagine our guy's surprise when Cole wasn't in his seat, and the stewardess informed him that Cole had gotten off."

"What the hell's going on?" Bennett mumbled. He tried to stand up but the shackles kept him down.

"Good afternoon, Agent Smith," Seward began politely. "My name is William Seward. I am a senior official of the Defense Intelligence Agency."

Bennett tried to focus on the man's face but his vision was still blurred.

"I run something known as Operation Snowfall. I'll spare you the particulars," Seward continued, "but suffice it to say that I have a strong interest in a man named Cole Egan. It seems that you do too, and I want to know why."

Bennett's vision finally cleared enough that he could make out Seward's face.

"Why have you been following Cole Egan?" Seward persisted.

"How long have I been under?" Bennett tried to look at his watch, but it was against the arm of the chair, his wrist held there by a shackle.

"An hour at most."

"You don't have very long," Bennett offered. He didn't need to be told what Operation Snowfall was, or why Seward was interested in Cole Egan.

"Until what?" Seward asked calmly.

"Until Cole gets the second tape."

Seward processed the words for a moment. "Second tape?" It was what he had feared all along.

"Yeah, it's exactly like the one that cowardly little fucker over there took from Cole in Manhattan last week." Bennett nodded at Magee.

Instantly Magee started for Bennett from across the room.

"Commander!" Seward shouted, stepping in front of Magee. He couldn't have physically kept him away from Bennett, but the intrusion was enough.

"What tape are you referring to?" Seward asked.

"Don't give me that crap," Bennett said. "You know exactly what I'm talking about."

"How do you know there is a second tape?" Seward dropped his pretense immediately in the interest of saving time.

"Jim Egan and I spent thirty-six years together. I know." Bennett pulled at the shackles holding his wrists. "Eight years ago he made two tape copies of the film he took from Andrea Sage in Dealey Plaza, then had the film conveyed to people in Washington to throw them off track. He wanted to make them think that he really hadn't taken the film from Andrea Sage after the assassination. He wanted them to think that it had been hidden away in someone else's attic all these years so they would leave him alone." Bennett smiled as he thought how he had convinced Cole that he had no idea what was in the Chase safe-deposit box before Cole got to it. And how he had observed that the original film must still be out there somewhere. And Cole had bought the entire act. "But hell, you probably know all of that, Mr. Seward. You're probably the one who ended up with the original film eight years ago."

"Where is the second tape, Agent Smith?" Seward asked quickly, ignoring Bennett's accurate speculation.

"What makes you think I know where it is?"

"Come on, Smith!"

"If I did know, why the hell would I tell you?"

"Because you're a federal agent and I'm a superior officer and I'm giving you a direct order."

"So throw me in jail," Bennett said defiantly. "I'm retiring in a few months anyway. Jail can't be any worse than retirement for a man like me."

"Then tell me so you can save yourself some pain." Seward nodded at Magee. "As you can see, my friend over there would love an opportunity to get at you. And you aren't in much of a position to defend yourself."

Bennett gazed at Magee for a few moments. "I honestly don't know where the second tape is," he said quietly.

Seward glanced up. He thought he had detected a tone of sincerity in Bennett's voice.

"I didn't know where the first one was until Jim gave me an envelope to give Cole. Jim gave it to me just before we went on our last mission," Bennett continued. "He gave it to me in case he didn't come back. He had a premonition he wouldn't."

A premonition. What a bunch of crap, Seward thought to himself. "You are speaking of the mission to Colombia, correct?"

Bennett ignored what he knew was a remark intended to show him that Seward knew everything. "Like I said, Jim hid the tapes eight years ago, but he didn't tell me where. He told me he went to great lengths to hide them. He made certain he wasn't being followed before he even retrieved the tapes from their temporary hiding places. Before he put them where Cole could find them but no one else could."

And he had done an excellent job of being careful, Seward thought dejectedly. They had lost Jim Egan in Boston eight years ago after a wild trip around the country. "Why did he go to so much trouble to hide the tapes? Why didn't he sell them eight years ago if he wanted the world to see them?" Seward asked.

"He didn't want to be alive when they surfaced. He realized that would mean a death sentence, and he wanted to die on his own terms, or in the line of fire. But he also wanted to make certain that they did surface, that people knew the truth," Bennett explained. "And he wanted to give Cole something valuable as a way to make up for not being around for the kid's entire life. He felt very bad about that."

Seward sensed that Bennett wasn't yielding all of this information because of the oath to protect and defend he had taken so many years ago. "How do you know Cole Egan is going for a second tape right now?" Seward was trying to figure out Bennett Smith's angle in all of this.

Bennett smirked. "What the hell else would he be doing?"

What else indeed, Seward thought. "And you were following him?"

"Yes."

"Why?"

"Because Jim asked me to. He and I were very close."

Seward didn't believe Smith's motivations were so pure. "You directed Cole to that first tape at the

Chase branch." Seward pointed his cane at Bennett. "Is that correct?"

"Yes."

"Am I to believe that Cole had no idea where it was until you contacted him?"

Bennett nodded. "As far as I know, he had no idea it existed until I called him."

"Then how did he find out about the location of the second tape?" Seward asked. "You must have told him."

"No, I didn't."

Seward leaned forward until his face was directly in front of Smith's. "I can make this afternoon very uncomfortable for you, Agent Smith," he hissed.

"I didn't tell him anything about a second tape," Bennett snapped. "Someone else must have. It must have been that woman he's traveling with. Truth is, I figured she was one of your people anyway."

"You figured wrong." Seward pivoted and limped slowly away from where Bennett sat. When he reached the far wall he turned back around. For a long time he was quiet. Finally he spoke again. "Where is Jim Egan?" he asked casually.

Bennett tried not to let the surprise register on his face. "What?"

Seward smiled. If there was one thing he knew how to do, it was interrogate. "Where is Jim Egan?" he asked once more.

"He was killed on our last mission."

"In Colombia?"

"Yes," Bennett confirmed.

"You're lying," Seward responded calmly.

"No, I'm not."

"Yes, you are!" Seward yelled. "We found the

grave beside the river. There was a body in it, but it wasn't Jim Egan's."

Smith shook his head. "Jim Egan is dead, I swear to you."

"Where is Cole going?" Seward switched subjects again. He was like a boxer now, into his rhythm, keeping the other man off balance.

Tiny beads of perspiration broke out on Bennett's forehead, but he didn't answer.

"Where is Cole going?" Seward asked again.

Bennett stared at Seward for several moments. "What's in it for me?"

Seward managed to hold back his smile. People were so predictable. "What do you have in mind?"

"A retirement fund," Bennett answered. "Being a DIA agent doesn't pay very well, at least not as well as it should. I've been risking my life for this country for a long time, and I don't have much to show for it."

"What figure do you have in mind?"

"Ten million dollars."

"What you estimated you could sell the tape for if you got it, right?" Seward asked. The man was so transparent. "You were after the tape that night in Manhattan just like we were, weren't you, Agent Smith? That's why you killed our man in Bryant Park. You thought he had recovered the tape at the library."

Bennett stared at Seward but said nothing.

"Okay," Seward said softly. "I can arrange for ten million dollars. That's a small price to pay to suppress the tape. Now tell me where Cole Egan is going."

"I'll give you part of the information," Bennett said, glad he had instructed his secretary in Washington to destroy the answering machine tape. "Then you can give me part of the money. After I've received the partial payment, I'll give you further information. And so on."

"Very wise, Agent Smith, but I assure you there's nothing to worry about."

There was a great deal to worry about, Bennett knew. "Get someone to Atlanta right away."

"You would know better than to send me on a wild goose chase," Seward warned.

"Yes, I would."

"All right." Seward nodded at Smith, then limped from the room.

Bennett looked over at Magee when Seward was gone. "Hey, you piece of dogshit."

Magee sauntered toward Bennett until he was standing directly in front of him. "You aren't in much of a position to be calling anyone dogshit," Magee sneered.

"You wouldn't touch me," Bennett retorted. "Seward would have your ass. He needs me in a cooperative mood so I'll help you find Cole Egan."

Magee checked the doorway through which Seward had disappeared. "Personally, I think Seward is too willing to negotiate. The stick is a much more effective means of drawing information out of a prisoner than the carrot."

"Then take your best shot." Bennett stuck out his jaw. "Come on, asshole. I can't even move."

Magee chuckled. "You think I won't?" He'd go for the left eye, puncture it with one quick strike and blind Bennett permanently in that eye. It would be a very painful injury but one that wouldn't inhibit Bennett's ability to talk. When the bleeding had stopped, he'd probably be even more talkative. "You really think I won't?" Magee felt the adrenaline pumping through his system. God, he loved to deliver pain.

"I know you won't. You're too worried about what Seward might—"

With no warning Magee jabbed for Bennett's left eye.

And Bennett caught Magee's wrist with his powerful right hand as Magee's fingers were about to plunge into the socket. Bennett pulled Magee's wrist hard. Magee pitched forward and their foreheads smashed together. It was over instantly. Bennett had used the move before in real hand-to-hand combat, when his life was on the line. Magee had only practiced it half-speed in a gymnasium wearing protective headgear. Bennett knew where to aim. Magee had no idea what hit him, and went limp, collapsing onto Bennett.

Bennett laughed as he rifled through the other man's pockets, searching for the key that would unlock the shackles still holding his left wrist and ankles. He had been blessed with powerful, albeit small, hands in relation to his wrist size. If he was able to flex his wrist as the shackles were being applied, he could usually wriggle free if given enough time. It really wasn't as difficult as people thought.

He found the key in Magee's pants pocket. The agents in the ambulance should never have given him that stimulant before cuffing him to the chair. They shouldn't have given him the opportunity to pretend that he was still unconscious. He rolled Magee onto the floor, unlocked the ankle cuffs and stood up.

Thirty seconds later Bennett was jogging down a seedy street outside the warehouse. He spotted a young man standing beside a wreck of a black Cadillac. "Hey, I need a ride and I'm willing to pay," he yelled at the man. For some reason they hadn't taken his wallet or identification during the interrogation.

The man glanced at the blood trickling down Bennett's face but didn't hesitate. "Where to?" If the man had cash, that was all that mattered.

"Newark Airport. I'll give you a hundred bucks."

"Show me the cash."

Bennett pulled five twenties from his wallet and waved them at the man. "You get these when we get to Newark."

"Get in."

From a second-floor window, William Seward watched the Cadillac move away. Bennett had to think he had escaped on his own. They couldn't just let him go. Then he would have been suspicious and might not have gone after Cole. But now Bennett would lead them right to Cole—and to the second tape.

18

ERIC WALSH CHERISHED HIS JOB AT THE WHITE HOUSE almost as much as the president cherished his. Not because of any patriotic sense of duty to the country, nothing naive like that. Walsh's motivation was centered squarely on personal gain. After four years as the president's chief of staff, Walsh would have his pick of high-paying finance jobs on Wall Street.

The investment banks had already started calling. They coveted Walsh's global network of movers and shakers who could retain the investment banks to execute transactions and pay huge fees. In the investment banking world, access was everything, and Walsh had it. As chief of staff Walsh had developed strong ties to top government officials and corporate CEOs around the world. Walsh's job would simply be to introduce senior executives of the investment bank for whom he chose to work to his network of powerful people. Then he would step aside and let the dealmakers go to work, and earn millions for himself just for the handshakes.

Nine years ago Walsh had taken a sabbatical from his Charlotte law practice to run Richard Jamison's successful campaign for the governorship of North Carolina. Jamison was a real estate mogul and one of Walsh's clients. After the victory Walsh had left the law practice permanently and become Jamison's chief of staff in the governor's office. Five years later Walsh had directed another victorious Jamison campaign. This time the prize was the presidency. Again, Walsh had stayed on to be chief of staff. Now they were after one last victory so Jamison could spend four more years in the Oval Office.

But Walsh wouldn't stay on as chief of staff during the second term. After the election he would put his services up for bids. He had already informed Jamison of that decision. It was better to move into the private sector riding a wave of success. Walsh would be able to name his price at that point. The investment banks would offer him five, maybe even ten million dollars annually just to make the high-level introductions. He'd be able to retire a wealthy man after only a few years of work.

Jamison was understanding. He had made only one request: that Walsh remain with him through this last campaign. And Walsh understood why. Jamison needed him to remain the point person with the Bianco family until after the election. He couldn't risk letting anyone else in on the administration's dark secrets.

Walsh glanced around the empty office furtively, wondering if he was being watched. The Bianco family controlled the largest unions and thirty percent of the illegal drug trade in the United States. Over the last decade the Biancos had gained immense power in the underworld, and at the same time had maintained an extremely low profile. The FBI had nicknamed the Bianco family Crime Inc., and calculated that if the businesses they controlled were consolidated on paper by a Big Six accounting firm, the entity would rank well up in the Fortune 100.

Walsh checked his watch. It was after two in the morning and they were late, but that wasn't unusual. Unlike some Mafia families, the Biancos were fanatic about making certain that their Chairman, as they called him, was not being followed by the press, which was constantly trying to snap his picture. The Chairman had no interest in having his picture splashed all over the newspapers or being tagged with dapper nicknames, as John Gotti had. So Walsh would cool his heels patiently and accept the imposition. He would wait as long as it took, because the Chairman could destroy Jamison's administration with one phone call.

Ten minutes later the office door swung slowly open. The office was buried deep inside a building located on Interstate 95 halfway between Washington and Baltimore and owned by one of Jamison's real estate companies. Two large men dressed in conservative gray suits entered the room and nodded to Walsh. He stood up immediately, holding his arms straight out. One of the men frisked Walsh carefully while the other searched the office. Satisfied that Walsh and the office were clean, the man who had frisked Walsh returned to the office door and said something quietly to those waiting in the hall. Two more large men then entered the room, followed by a short man dressed in his traditional three-button charcoal suit.

Anthony Bianco a.k.a. the Chairman, was arguably one of the most powerful men in America, but few people in the country would recognize him as such.

Few would recognize him at all, which was exactly the way he wanted it.

Walsh shook Bianco's hand respectfully. He had known the man for nine years. They had first met shortly before Jamison's opponent for the governorship of North Carolina had met with an untimely death in a tragic plane crash only a few weeks before the election. Since that time, Walsh had been Jamison's messenger, transacting their business face to face with Bianco, because of course the president couldn't.

"Good evening, Mr. Bianco."

"Good evening, Mr. Walsh," Bianco replied in his gruff voice.

In nine years, Walsh couldn't ever remember them addressing each other by anything but their last names. "Please sit down." Walsh motioned toward the couch.

Bianco gestured toward his men, then followed Walsh to the couch. Three of the men exited the room while one took a chair just inside the door.

"How are the attorney general hearings going?" Bianco asked.

"Very well," Walsh replied. The woman President Jamison had nominated to head the Justice Department was Bianco's personal selection. The woman had allowed Bianco to run Atlantic City with little interference during her tenure as New Jersey attorney general, and now Bianco was elevating her to a much more important position through Jamison. "After some initial problems, we believe her approval is a lock at this point. We have polled the senators on the committee and we have the votes. They will recommend to Congress that she be confirmed," Walsh said confidently.

"Good." Bianco unbuttoned his suit coat. "What

about the tape?" he asked abruptly. "When I was at William Seward's cabin in Virginia with General Zahn, Seward said something about the possibility of a second one."

"We are following up on that possibility," Walsh assured Bianco. "We have someone very close to Cole Egan. If there is a second tape, we will find it."

Bianco stared at Walsh for several moments. "Perhaps it would help to have some of my people involved." He nodded at the man sitting in the chair across the room.

"Let us take care of this," Walsh urged gently. Jamison didn't want Bianco's people nosing around when the government was following Cole so closely. There was no reason to have the two organizations both on the scene in case things got nasty. That might create the possibility of a link between the Mafia and the Jamison administration, which was something both parties had to avoid at all costs. "Please let us handle it."

"For now," Bianco conceded. He was naturally uneasy about anything not under his direct control, but he also understood the need to keep the two organizations as far apart as possible.

"Why do you have such an interest in the tape, Mr. Bianco?" Walsh had never asked the question before, though he'd always been tempted to.

Bianco made a face, as if the answer should be obvious. "This country has been fascinated with President Kennedy's assassination for thirty-five years. People still want to know who killed him today as badly as they did in 1963. They don't believe it was Oswald, at least not acting alone. Lyndon Johnson didn't. Why should anyone else? If that tape became public, the investigation would be reopened immediately. I'd have federal agents crawling all over my fucking empire trying to get answers. I still have people around who knew Jack Ruby. People would have to start turning up dead. I don't want to have to go through that. Not after we've spent years toning down our profile."

"I—"

But Bianco wasn't finished. "That operation in the DIA blamed it on us thirty-five years ago. People would remember that. I don't need people fishing around." He smiled. "Nobody in the government needs it, either. Not with the suspicions most Americans already have about senior officials conspiring to keep sensitive information away from them."

"You're right," Walsh agreed.

Bianco tapped the arm of the sofa. "I have some information I want you to give to the president."

"What is that?"

"After careful analysis, I believe we can deliver New York, Illinois, Texas and Florida to him in the election next November. That's well over one hundred electoral votes. That ought to make him feel pretty good about his chances."

Walsh smiled, but not because he knew that would make Jamison feel very good. It was General Zahn's comment about the irony of it all that brought the smirk to Walsh's face. Kennedy had been accused of using the Mafia's help to win the 1960 presidential election, specifically of winning Illinois thanks to a few crime bosses and their influence over the unions. And here was Jamison, in deep with the Mafia himself, doing his best to keep the tape of Kennedy's assassination away from the public.

19

"GOD, IT'S DESOLATE OUT HERE." TORI GAZED THROUGH the windshield of the rented Jeep Cherokee at the dense northern Wisconsin pine forest, which seemed to be closing in around them at the edge of the headlights' glow. "We haven't passed a house for thirty miles, much less a town. And I can't remember seeing a car coming the other way. Are you sure we didn't take a detour to Siberia?"

Cole laughed. "It's not that bad."

"Yes, it is."

"What's the matter?" he asked. "Does all this isolation make you nervous?" He knew the forest did that to some people.

"You're darn right it does. I'm a city girl. I grew up in Los Angeles and now I live in New York. Those are places where people can get to you in the winter without needing a snowmobile or a team of huskies."

"You don't have much of that pioneer spirit, do you?"

"None at all. If it had been up to me to explore, we'd all still be back in Europe ruled by monarchs."

"Where's your sense of adventure, Tori?" Cole teased.

"I don't have one."

"Why not?"

"I don't like being alone," she admitted quietly, looking apprehensively into the pitch-black night outside.

Cole nodded. If you kept peeling away the layers long enough, you could always make it to the heart of the matter.

"Are there bears here?" she asked.

Cole shook his head. "No." He hesitated only long enough for her to feel a slight sense of relief. "Just wolves."

"Wolves?"

"Well, I've heard there are," Cole said. "I've never actually seen any wolf packs around here. But I have seen them in Minnesota, up on the Boundary Waters near Canada. People around here say those packs have migrated into Wisconsin over the last few years, but I don't know if that's true. Wolves won't hurt you," Cole assured her.

"Cole, I think it's time you tell me what this is all about." If she was going to deal with wolves, she was going to know why they were here.

Cole checked for stars, but they were hidden by an ominous cloud cover hanging low over the territory. The forecast was for heavy snow tonight and it wasn't even December. But that didn't matter here. He'd seen storms dump a foot of snow in a single November day in northern Wisconsin. "Not yet."

"What do you mean, 'not yet'?" She was irritated. "So far I've purchased airline tickets and rented a Jeep for who knows how long. I deserve answers."

When the plane landed in Minneapolis four hours

ago, Cole had decided to drive straight to the town of Hubbard and the Lassiter River instead of staying at his aunt and uncle's house in Duluth tonight. It would be too easy for his pursuers to stake out that house— maybe they already had—and he didn't want to endanger his aunt and uncle in any way. Plus, he didn't want the extra fifty-mile drive early tomorrow morning from Duluth if the snow turned out to be heavy tonight.

Cole reached in front of Tori and opened the glove compartment. "Here." He pulled out a Wisconsin map he had purchased when they stopped for gas an hour ago and handed it to her. "Turn on the map light and entertain yourself. I'll show you where we're headed."

"I don't really care."

"That's not a very good attitude."

Tori smiled for the first time in a while. "You're really good at that."

"At what?" He knew what she was about to say.

"At changing the subject."

"What are you talking about?" He continued to deflect.

"You want me to become interested in the map and forget that I've asked you what on God's green earth we're doing here." She too checked the sky for stars. "Or white earth, as the case may soon be." She had heard the weather forecast as well. "But I'm not going to be distracted this time. Now, what are we doing here? What is this all about?"

"I'll tell you later, promise."

"Now," she said firmly. "Or I'll stop paying for everything, Cole."

"Look, there's a couple of deer." He pointed at two does standing like statues on the side of the road, mesmerized by the Jeep's high beams.

"I'm not looking," she said defiantly.

"You're missing them."

"Cole!"

"Okay." The time to explain the situation had come. There was no getting around it now, but that was all right. He was convinced at this point that she was trustworthy. "Look, you were right on the button at lunch the other day," he began. "My father did take a film away from a woman named Andrea Sage in Dealey Plaza the day President Kennedy was shot."

"I knew it!" Tori slapped the dashboard.

Cole jerked the steering wheel left, taken off guard by her violent reaction to the news. "Easy," he warned.

"Sorry."

Cole smiled. "It's all right, but please, let's demonstrate a little control."

"I did get a little excited, didn't I?" she asked sheepishly. "But can you blame me?"

"No. Here's another interesting piece of information for you," Cole volunteered.

"What's that?"

"Andrea Sage and Mary Thomas were the same person."

"You're kidding!"

"No." Cole quickly explained how Jim Egan had ultimately married the woman from whom he'd taken the movie camera.

"That's incredible."

"It really is," Cole agreed. "Anyway, at some point my father made a tape copy of the film, then hid it in a safe-deposit box in New York City. A man named Bennett Smith gave me an envelope with a key to the safe-deposit box inside after I found out my father had died. In fact, Bennett was the one who informed

me of his death. Bennett was my father's best friend."
Cole shook his head. "I had my hands on that tape
last week in Manhattan, but someone took it away
from me at gunpoint after I retrieved it from the box."

"What?" Tori's eyes widened.

"Yes."

"Who took it from you? Do you know?"

"I'm not sure." He would tell her more about Bennett's conjecture later.

"It's too bad you lost it," she said, suddenly crestfallen.

"That's an understatement. But now I've found out
that there's one more tape," he said quietly.

"Really?"

"Yes. My father must have made two."

"That's fantastic." Her excitement returned instantly. "And it's stored somewhere up here?" she
asked.

"Yes."

"Did you have a chance to view the first tape before
the person took it away from you?" Her voice was
trembling slightly.

It was the first time Cole had heard that kind of
emotion in her gravelly voice. He nodded.

"And? Come on! Tell me what was on it."

"It showed that John Kennedy was killed by someone firing a rifle from behind the fence on the
grassy knoll."

"Oh my God!" She banged the dashboard once
more, then glanced at Cole apologetically. "Sorry
again."

"It's okay." He had been ready for her reaction
this time.

"Does the tape prove conspiracy?"

"Yes," he confirmed. "If you assume that someone

was up in the Book Depository, too, which I think
you can."

"That explains all your secrecy. Why we got on the
flight to Los Angeles, and why we sat in the first row.
It was so we could deplane without someone behind
us seeing us."

"That's correct." He paused. "If I told you half of
what happened to me in Manhattan last week, you'd
probably have me pull over so you could get out."

"Not in the middle of this Black Forest, I wouldn't,"
Tori assured him. "And what's the matter, don't you
think I can hold my own in a tough situation?"

"You didn't seem too happy about the prospect of
meeting up with wolves and bears."

"That's different." She turned on the map light,
then reached for the Wisconsin map Cole had placed
on the dashboard and spread it out across her lap.
"Show me where we're going," she demanded.

He leaned across the seat and pointed at a thin blue
line on the map snaking north toward Lake Superior.

She squinted. "The Lassiter?"

"Yes."

"What's so special about it?"

"I spent a lot of time on the Lassiter when I was
growing up."

"Does that have anything to do with why your father put the second tape here?"

"I think so."

"Where exactly is the tape?" Tori asked.

"I won't tell you that."

"You still don't trust me."

"I don't completely trust anyone at this point," Cole
said honestly.

"I want your word that NBC will get this tape," she
said quickly. "As I told you at lunch, I'm prepared to

pay a lot of money for it. And I've funded this entire trip," she reminded him, "and apparently put myself at some personal risk, though you didn't bother telling me that."

"Don't try to hang a guilt trip on me about that. You would have come anyway, even if I had told you."

"That's beside the point. And how do you know I would have come anyway?"

"You just said you could handle yourself in a tough situation. And you want this tape so badly it's eating you up inside. This tape is your Holy Grail. You want to be able to show your bosses at NBC you aren't a second-stringer. And there's one more reason you wouldn't have missed all this."

"And what's that, Mr. Know-me-so-well?"

"You want to show your mother you can do something pretty special all on your own."

Tori gazed at him for a few moments, then broke into a wide smile. "So you were listening in the cab on the way up to your grandparents' apartment." She was impressed. "A lot of men can convince you they're listening when they really aren't. Then you find out later they haven't heard a word." She hesitated. "I want the tape, Cole. You owe me that."

"For your troubles, I'll promise you the right of first refusal on the tape," Cole answered definitively. "I give you my word that I'll make certain you have a chance to match the highest offer of any other bidder."

"You're going to be a trader to the end, huh?" she asked, disappointment obvious in her tone. She knew someone might pay more than what she could offer. "Always looking for the best deal, always hungry for the money."

"It doesn't have anything to do with being a trader," Cole snapped. People outside the financial business always accused you of being money-hungry when they knew you were a trader. They always accused you of bringing everything in life down to the lowest common denominator—cash. As if they weren't trying their hardest to make as much money as they could, too. "You'd do the same thing if you were in my position."

"I suppose I would," she admitted.

"Besides, there's no reason to get excited," Cole warned. "I don't have the damn thing yet." He checked the rearview mirror, but there were no headlights. Maybe he really had eluded the pursuers. He glanced at Tori, who was staring off into the darkness again. Or maybe they already had someone very close to him and could follow from a distance.

Fifteen minutes later Cole slowed the Jeep as the road turned rough.

"What's going on?" Tori asked. She had been hypnotized by the unbroken line of trees flashing past the window.

"We crossed into Oswego County," Cole explained. "It's the county the Lassiter River runs through. We're almost home."

"Why is the road so bad?"

"Oswego County is responsible for the road now, and the county isn't what you'd call cash-rich."

"Why not?"

"There isn't a whole lot of industry up here. Not much of a tax base."

The line of trees moved suddenly away from the road and Cole guided the Jeep off the crumbling asphalt onto a gravel driveway leading steeply up into the dense pines.

"Where are we going?" Tori asked, grabbing the handle above the door as Cole guided the vehicle up the hill.

"To our lodgings for the evening."

This wasn't the same place Cole and Bennett Smith had stayed last week. The town of Hubbard and that campground were still twenty miles to the north.

Finally the driveway leveled off and a light appeared through the trees. Cole brought the Jeep to a stop and pulled the emergency brake. "We're here."

"Hey, Cole!" On the porch of the log home stood an older man in a checkered flannel shirt, jeans and suspenders. Straight black hair fell to his shoulders.

"Who is that?" Tori asked hesitantly, looking at the man in the Jeep's headlights.

"Billy Threefeathers." Cole smiled as he opened the driver-side door. "He's an old friend of mine. He's the one who taught me every rapid and every bend of the Lassiter River, and he's our host tonight." Cole hopped out of the Jeep, jogged across the driveway and shook Billy's hand warmly as the man stepped down off the porch.

Tori watched Billy Threefeathers and Cole shake hands. In the woods behind the log home she could barely make out a few tiny lights, probably coming from the guest cabins Cole had described to her on the way from Minneapolis. The smaller outer cabins would be their accommodations for the evening. She shivered at the prospect of a night alone in the North Woods. But if it meant getting her hands on that tape, it was a small price to pay.

A touch of the lighted match to the tinder and the fireplace burst into flames. Billy hunched over the hearth a few moments longer, fanning the fire until he was satisfied it would burn for some time. "You'll be warm all night now," he said.

"Thanks." Tori looked around the small cabin. Flames danced on the cedar walls, creating strange shapes that licked their way to the ceiling. "You sure you guys don't want to go back to the main house and tell a few more stories? All that fly-fishing stuff was so fascinating." After a late dinner, Cole and Billy had talked at length about flies, lines, rods and reels, as well as huge fish they had caught. The conversation had bored her to tears, but anything was better than being alone out in this small cabin. "It's only midnight, let's drink another bottle of wine."

"Sorry," Billy responded. He spoke in a solemn, gentle voice. "It's way past my bedtime."

"I'm tired too," Cole seconded.

"Is that fire really going to keep me warm all night?" Tori asked dubiously, wrapping her arms around her torso.

"The best heat is body heat." Billy laughed, showing two rows of crooked teeth. "I don't know why you two want to stay in separate cabins."

"It was Cole's idea," Tori answered quickly.

Cole shot Tori a curious look. That wasn't true. They hadn't discussed it. He had simply assumed that the sleeping arrangements would be this way.

"Tori, the thermostat is on the wall by the door." Cole gestured at it. "I came out here a while ago and turned it up. That's why it's warm in here now. The fire's a nice touch, but don't worry if it goes out."

Cole had come out to turn up the thermostat and to go through her luggage. He'd found nothing suspicious, but he'd taken her cell phone anyway. Now he wasn't worried about her calling any enemies in case he had misjudged her loyalties. There was only one phone in Billy's lodge. It was in his bedroom upstairs, and Tori hadn't left the first floor since arriving. She could call someone from a pay phone in Hubbard but the town was miles away and he had the only key to the Jeep.

"Well, I gotta go," Billy announced. "You can take care of yourself, Cole. You know where the wood is if you want a fire too. But remember to open the flue this time. It still smells of smoke in the cabin you stayed in last time, and that was two years ago."

Tori smiled. So Cole wasn't always as smooth as he thought he was.

"Good night, Miss Brown. It was nice meeting you." Billy tipped his ten-gallon hat and turned to go.

"Mr. Threefeathers," Tori called after him.

He hesitated at the door. "Yes?"

"Are there any wolves around here?"

Billy grinned. "No." He shook his head. "I guess Cole's been doing a little exaggerating about the dangers of the woods."

Tori gave Cole a withering gaze as he tried his best to look innocent.

"You don't have to worry about wolves," Billy assured her, pushing open the cabin door. "Just the children, and they won't really bother you." Without another word he was gone.

"What did he mean by that?" Tori asked.

"Nothing," Cole said calmly. "He's kidding."

"Tell me, Cole." An eerie feeling inched up her spine.

"Really—"

"Cole!"

"All right, all right. It's an old Indian myth. The Chippewas who lived around here considered the Lassiter life-giving. It was the center of activity for the tribe. It gave them fish and rice. They considered it important as far as the afterlife as well. They believed that the closer you were buried to it, the better your afterlife would be, so they buried their dead all along the Lassiter. Those who died young were buried at the headwaters, right down the hill, while the elderly were laid to rest at the mouth, down near Lake Superior. Everyone else was buried somewhere in the middle, according to their age. The older the individual, the farther downriver that person was buried." Cole pointed out the window into the darkness. "Some people claim to have seen Chippewa ghosts along the river. Up here at the headwaters they claim to see children. Billy swears he has seen them walking around the cabins at night, but I've been on the river for fifteen years and stayed in his cabins many times and I've never seen anything," he said earnestly.

Tori rolled her eyes. "Jesus."

"Don't worry."

"That's easy for you to say." She followed the shadows of the flames flickering up the walls.

"Well, good night. I've got to get some sleep." Cole walked to the door. "I'm in the next cabin if you need me." The door swung shut behind him.

Tori moved slowly to the door and gazed through the window, watching Cole walk to his cabin in the glow of the spotlight over the door. The first few snowflakes were beginning to fall.

The children were everywhere, all around her, leading her on, pointing the way toward a man at the edge of a field. He was beckoning silently for her to come to him. Then he faded and she was hanging by her hands from a rope, holding on for dear life, suspended thousands of feet above a city skyline she didn't recognize.

Suddenly Tori came out of the dream and sat bolt upright in the bed, perspiration covering her body. For several moments she stared at the dying embers in the fireplace, breathing hard as her heart raced. Finally she ran her hands through her hair and shook her head. The dream had been so vivid. It was the same dream she had had the night after her lunch with Cole at the Broadway Diner.

Then the howl came. It was a strange moan from the distance, and it made her flesh crawl.

Coyotes were plentiful in the area and harmless to humans, but she didn't know this. She threw the covers back, ran outside and raced barefoot through two inches of new-fallen snow to Cole's cabin, yanked open the door and yelled, "Cole!"

He came to consciousness quickly. "What the—"

"It's me!"

"Tori?" Cole reached for the lamp on the nightstand and flicked it on. "What's the matter?"

She stood just inside the door, shivering. She was wearing only a New York Knicks T-shirt that ended well above her knees.

"Hey, nice legs, Tori."

"Move over!" She ran for the bed, climbed in, pulled the covers over herself tightly and rolled so that her back was to him.

"What are you doing?" he asked. Instantly he felt intense warmth emanating from her, even though their bodies weren't actually touching.

"I heard something outside. I'm not staying out here in the woods by myself. You've got a roommate for the rest of the night."

"I could think of worse things."

"Turn the light off."

Cole reached for the lamp and flipped the switch. "Are you all right?" She was trembling.

"I'm fine," Tori said defiantly. She felt much better now that she was with him. "I had a nightmare. You know how those things are."

"Yes, I do." Cole put his head down on the pillow.

"I'm sorry to wake you," she murmured apologetically.

"It's all right."

For several minutes they lay in silence, then Tori reached slowly behind herself and found his hand. She pulled his arm around her, kissed his palm and held on tightly.

After a few minutes Cole ran his fingers through her hair and rubbed her head gently, then moved his hand down her side, reached for the bottom of her T-shirt and pulled it up. He hesitated for a second, then moved his fingers down onto her soft, bare buttocks. Then he heard her slow, steady breathing. She was asleep.

20

THE JEEP HEADLIGHTS CUT AN EERIE SWATH THROUGH the darkness and the falling snow, guiding Cole down the driveway and over six inches of new powder. He held his breath as the vehicle eased down a steep section of the driveway and into a sharp curve. The Jeep could slip off the driveway and become mired in the deep ditch on either side so easily. If it became stuck, he'd be forced to walk all the way back up the hill to Billy Threefeathers's lodge for help, which would cause a long delay in getting to the Albion estate. A delay that could cost him the prize.

Returning to the lodge might awaken Tori, as well— Cole had managed to rise from the bed and dress without disturbing her. She would demand to go with him this time, which might cost him the prize, too.

Suddenly the rear end of the Jeep swung to the left, then back to the right, and the vehicle began fishtailing down the slope. Cole took his foot off the brake and instantly the vehicle picked up speed. However, without the brake application the four wide tires regained traction and he was able to bring the Jeep back under control. As he came to a full stop at the end of Billy's driveway, he relaxed into the seat and took a few short breaths. Then he turned right, toward the town of Hubbard, and onto the virgin snow covering the county road.

The Albion estate was located halfway between Billy Threefeathers's lodge and Hubbard. The estate encompassed several thousand acres of pine trees and four miles of the Lassiter. On the entire property there were only two buildings—the main house and a boat-house. The main house was a massive eight-thousand-square-foot stone structure overlooking the Lassiter. It was built atop a ridge paralleling the river, and from it visitors to the mansion had an incredible view of the surrounding territory. From the back of the mansion a narrow path snaked its way down the slope in a series of hairpin turns until it reached the large stone boat-house. The boathouse was set on a slow-moving stretch of the Lassiter where the Albions' friends and children could swim and canoe safely without the threat of being pulled into fast water. This slow stretch offered some of the best brown trout fishing on the river. In the summer of his senior year in high school Cole had pulled a twelve-pound monster from this stretch with Billy Threefeathers in the back of the canoe, showing him precisely where to cast.

The snow was falling heavily, and Cole turned up the speed of the windshield wipers. He leaned forward over the steering wheel, searching the road ahead for deer, which might dart out from the trees into the Jeep's path. There were thousands of them up here, and they were drawn to the headlights instinctively. A collision with a big buck would end this excursion prematurely. Cole tried the high beams, but the reflection from the falling snow caused a terrible glare and he turned the lights down again.

The second tape was in the Albion boathouse. Cole could only guess that his father had decided to hide the second tape in the boathouse because of a telephone conversation with Cole's aunt long ago. Bennett Smith had mentioned that his father called his aunt every few weeks to check up on Cole. After catching the twelve-pound brown trout with Billy Threefeathers, Cole had related the story to his aunt and uncle at length over Sunday dinner back in Duluth, referring to the Albion boathouse several times. The note on the hotel room floor had specifically referred to the Albion boathouse as well. That must have been the connection and the reason for his father's decision to hide the second tape there.

Cole smiled as he guided the Jeep through the storm. No one else could have guessed what the note was referring to. It didn't identify a body of water or a town or even a state in which the boathouse was located. It had simply directed him to get to the Albion boathouse as quickly as possible. Then it had given him a specific location in the boathouse to look for the "package." If the note had fallen into the wrong hands, the person who found it wouldn't have had any idea what it meant anyway. The smile drained away from Cole's face. The note had also made clear that this was the last package.

The messenger had to have been Bennett, Cole reasoned. Jim Egan had trusted Bennett enough to deliver the first message. It seemed logical that Bennett would be responsible for the second one as well. Who the hell else could it have been?

Cole checked his watch as he guided the Jeep off the county right-of-way onto a snow-covered rutted dirt road used by loggers in the summer. It was almost five o'clock in the morning.

A hundred yards down the logging trail, Cole stopped and turned the vehicle around so that it was pointed back out toward the main road, then cut the engine. The entrance to the Albion estate was still a mile north of this location, but he preferred to park here and walk the rest of the way as a precaution. The entrance to the Albion estate was protected by a locked gate, and he didn't want to park the Jeep outside the gate right on the main road. It would be an advertisement to anyone passing by that someone was at the estate.

Cole walked back along the logging trail to the county road, hunched over against the driving snow, following the tracks made by the Jeep. Then it was a mile to the entrance of the Albion estate, another half mile along the Albions' long driveway to the mansion and a few hundred yards down the narrow path to the boathouse. He would retrieve the tape from the boathouse as quickly as possible and get the hell out of here. He pulled the parka's hood over his head and began jogging as the falling snow whipped past him. The tape was almost within his grasp.

Several hundred yards south of the entrance to the Albion estate, Cole crossed the main road. There were still no tire tracks on it. Usually the locals were up and moving by this time of the morning. But they knew better than to venture out in a storm this fierce.

Cole scaled the five-foot chain-link fence running along the Albions' property and moved into the trees on the other side of the fence. Darkness had yielded only slightly to a gray light, but the feeble rays were enough for him to make his way through the trees with relative ease. He wanted to stay off the driveway and hidden for as long as possible.

As Cole moved through the forest, a deer suddenly bolted away from behind a grove of trees. He jumped back, startled. "Jesus," he muttered. The snow had deadened the sound of his footsteps, and he was almost on top of the animal before it sensed his presence. Cole stood still, listening to the deer crash away through the underbrush. Finally the sounds faded and the woods were quiet again. Once more he began moving through the trees, roughly paralleling the Albion driveway. He squinted through the snow and the forest. Visibility was fifty feet at most.

When Cole was certain he had walked a half mile, he turned north toward the driveway. He would locate the mansion, then walk down the narrow lane behind it to the boathouse. He doubted anyone was in the huge house. In this area of the country people kept a close eye on the weather map, and the Albions would have known that forecasters were predicting several feet of snow for the territory. If the Albions had been up here recently, they were probably back at their estate in Minneapolis by now.

Cole broke out of the forest onto the edge of the driveway. Visibility had increased, but he still couldn't see objects more than a hundred yards away because of the driving snow. He glanced to his left toward the mansion, fifty yards away. There were no lights illuminated and no cars in the circular driveway in front of the main entrance. He glanced to his right, back up the long driveway toward the main road, but saw nothing suspicious.

Pine needles brushed against Cole's face as he turned back into the trees and began moving toward the river. He had decided not to use the lane to the boathouse after all. He would remain hidden for as long as possible. His paranoia was increasing with each step.

On the crest of the ridge overlooking the Lassiter, Cole paused for a few moments. From this spot he had an excellent view of the river and the boathouse below. The snow was still coming down hard, but it seemed to have abated slightly. Grasping tree trunks whenever he could, Cole made his way slowly down the steep slope. It was treacherous going, and he stopped every few feet to catch his breath, bracing himself against larger trees for support. During these short breaks he scanned the area for any unusual movements and listened for strange sounds. But as he drew nearer to the river, the wind whipped up, blowing snow into his eyes and obscuring all noises except the air whistling through the trees.

Finally Cole reached the riverbank. A thin film of ice had formed on the water's surface, and as he gazed across the ice he noticed the spot near the far bank where he had landed the huge brown trout many years before. Billy had pointed out the exact spot to cast, and Cole had hit the spot perfectly. He could use Billy's help now, Cole thought to himself as he turned and trudged through the snow toward the boathouse.

The Albion boathouse was constructed of the same stone as was the mansion. Sixty feet long and thirty feet wide, the boathouse was designed so that half the structure was over the water and half out. That way, with the river doors wide open in the summer, one could paddle or row a craft into the boathouse from the river, then step onto the docks inside protected from wind and weather. But now the structure was closed for the winter.

Cole stood in front of the boathouse's side door. It

was latched tightly with a small padlock, but he had anticipated this problem and pulled a small hammer from beneath his coat. He gave the padlock two powerful raps and it broke open. The door creaked on its hinges as he pushed it back and stepped inside. Dim light filtered through dusty windowpanes, but he still couldn't see much. As he turned on the flashlight he had brought from Billy's lodge, he smelled mildew and heard dripping water. He played the flashlight beam around the space. There were canoes, rowboats, life preservers, paddles, hoses and fishing gear hanging from, leaning against and covering the walls and floor. With the flashlight beam he followed the pipes that came down the walls and disappeared beneath the water. The pipes carried steam to keep the water inside the boathouse from freezing during the winter.

Cole moved quickly over the wooden slat walkway to a ladder leading to the loft. Wind whistling beneath the eaves, the faint trickling of water and his own labored breathing were the only sounds inside the boathouse as he climbed the wooden rungs.

The package was secured to the top of the beam in the northeast corner of the Albion boathouse. That was the simple message penned on the note Cole had picked up off the hotel room floor. He moved stealthily across the loft, carefully avoiding tarps, paddles and parts of old motors. When he reached the northeast corner, he took a breath and ran his hand slowly along the top of the wooden beam. At first he felt nothing but dust and dirt, then his hand hit something that felt like a canvas bag. His heart skipped a beat. It felt as if there was a case inside the bag. He ripped the bag away from the beam, brought it down, peered inside and saw a videocassette case. Fingers trembling, he pulled the case from the bag and opened it. It did indeed hold a tape. He closed his eyes, mumbled a quick prayer of thanks, then dropped the bag, turned and headed back down the ladder. He jumped the last few rungs to the boathouse floor, pivoted away from the ladder toward the door—and stopped dead in his tracks. The man with the scar running down his left cheek stood ten feet away.

"Hello, Cole," Magee said calmly. "What do you have there?" Magee gestured at the cassette case in Cole's hand with the pistol he was holding.

Cole felt no fear, just fury. He was going to lose the tape again. "Home movies," he answered.

"Home movies of you and your daddy playing ball in the backyard, I guess," Magee said sarcastically. "I understand you and he had so much quality time together while you were growing up."

"How did you find me, Scarface?"

"The name is Commander John Magee."

"Whatever," Cole answered insolently. "How did you get here?"

"Yeah, you probably thought you lost us for good when you ditched our man at La Guardia. That was a neat trick, I have to admit." Magee waved the gun at Cole. "But you forgot about your pal."

"What are you talking about?" Cole's eyes narrowed.

"Bennett Smith."

Cole turned his head slightly to the side. "What?"

"Somehow Bennett knew exactly where you were. We trailed him up here yesterday after he took a late flight from Newark to Minneapolis. He spent last night right here in the boathouse."

Of course, Cole thought. The message he had left on Bennett's answering machine in Washington had been specific about the Albion estate in Hubbard.

They had canoed past it last week and Cole had pointed it out. Bennett had gotten the message after all.

"He was sleeping like a baby," Magee continued, "until I smacked him on the head about an hour ago."

"Bennett's here?"

"Right over there." Magee pointed toward a mound in a far corner of the boathouse. "Beneath the tarp."

"Christ!" Cole kicked at a slat of wood.

Magee smiled. "It must be very frustrating to lose that tape to me twice."

Cole glanced up at Magee. "The public needs to see this thing."

"Maybe," Magee responded. "But they won't. National security, you know." He smiled wickedly. "Now give it to me."

"You don't know this is what you're looking for," Cole pointed out, stalling for time. "This tape could be footage of anything."

"I watched you go up to the loft and take it off the top of the beam in the corner," Magee answered confidently. "I'll take my chances. Now hand it over."

"Come and get it."

Magee laughed. "I don't have to. I'll just shoot you."

With a flick of his wrist, Cole sent the cassette case sailing past Magee's ear. It was a trick Cole had learned from his junior high school basketball coach. Whip the ball just past someone's ear and for a split second they're paralyzed. There was something about the eye following a projectile and freezing the rest of the body. As the ploy had worked on the basketball court many years before, it worked now. For one second Magee was paralyzed as the cassette case flew past him, and in that second Cole was on the smaller

man like a big cat. He smashed into Magee's chest
and they tumbled off the dock into the water together.
As they hit the surface, Cole grabbed onto Magee
and dragged the smaller man down. Even beneath the
surface, Cole could hear Magee sputtering as he
sucked water into his lungs. Cole had knocked the
wind from Magee, and Magee's body was running on
instinct, trying to resupply the lungs with air even as
he was under water. Magee struggled but Cole over-
powered him, pushing him further down into the black
water. Finally Magee's body went limp.

When Cole believed Magee was unconscious, he
brought the smaller man to the surface, pulled himself
up onto the dock, then turned and hoisted Magee up
as well. As Cole dragged him to safety, Magee swung
feebly at Cole, a pathetic attempt to turn the tables.
Cole swung back out of reflex with a hard right fist
that caught Magee flush on the scar, and he crumpled
to the wooden floor.

Cole rose to his feet, dripping wet, and stripped off
his down parka. The coat would do him more harm
than good now. It would freeze around him in the cold
air and weigh him down. He moved quickly across the
boathouse, retrieved the cassette case and Magee's
gun, then jogged to the tarp in the corner. He yanked
it back and found Bennett Smith, hands and feet
bound and a piece of duct tape covering his mouth.
Cole placed the cassette case and the gun on the floor,
ripped the tape away from Bennett's mouth and began
cutting the rope around his wrists with a switchblade
he had borrowed from Billy.

"I'm glad to see you, kid," Bennett gasped.

"I bet you are." Cole took several deep breaths. It
was cold as hell. He ran a hand through his hair. It

was already beginning to freeze. He had to get out of here fast.

Bennett shook his head. "What an asshole I am."

"You'll get no argument from me." Cole used a sawing motion and the sharp knife quickly sliced through the twine immobilizing Bennett's wrists. "You're losing your touch if you can be followed so easily by that idiot." Cole nodded at Magee lying on the dock.

"I know." Bennett held up his hands and squeezed them over and over, forcing blood back into the fingers. "I'm sorry, Cole," he apologized, rubbing his head where Magee had hit him.

"It's all right." Cole reached down and cut the ropes around Bennett's ankles.

"Thanks," Bennett said, struggling to his feet.

Cole was already back beside Magee. With a length of rope he had taken from a hook on the wall, Cole secured Magee's wrists and his ankles, then bound his ankles to his wrists. "That ought to hold him." Cole turned to Bennett, his expression grim. "Where is my father, Bennett?"

"What?"

But Cole saw Bennett look away. "Where's my father?" he asked again, more forcefully.

"Dead. I told you."

"Don't give me that," Cole snapped. "The note you slipped under the door of my hotel in New York was written by his hand. I matched the handwriting on the note to a letter my father wrote my grandparents telling them my mother had died. My father wrote the note that was slipped under my door. And you put it there after you got me out of that scrape in Brooklyn with the Mafia." Cole searched Bennett's face for a reaction but saw nothing. "You told me my father died in Colombia seven weeks ago," Cole continued. "You told me you buried him beside a river, but you couldn't have. The note slipped under my hotel door was written on a piece of a newspaper dated November first, which was well after the day you said he died."

"I don't know anything about a note slipped under any hotel room door," Bennett hissed.

"It was a note that directed me to this boathouse. Don't tell me you didn't look at the note."

"I told you, I don't know about any note."

"Why won't you be honest with me?" Cole asked. "After all this."

Bennett stared at Cole for a long time before speaking. "I kept the secret of the film all these years and your father never offered me one red cent from the pot of gold at the end of the rainbow," he said softly. "I never told anyone he had the thing, and I promised to deliver that envelope to you and to watch out for you after I did. I was his best friend, but he never offered me a penny. But I don't know anything about a note."

Cole swallowed hard as he saw Bennett bring a gun up from behind his back. "I'm sorry, son." It was Magee's gun. Bennett had picked it and the cassette case up from the floor where Cole had placed them before slashing the ropes binding his wrists and ankles. "I really am. I honestly liked you, and I can't say that about too many people."

"Don't do this, Bennett," Cole pleaded. "You're too good a man."

"I thought I'd lost you back in New York," Bennett said, ignoring Cole's entreaty. "I thought I'd lost my chance to retire happy." A faraway expression came to Bennett's face. "If your father had just offered me a little piece of the action, I would have been satisfied and none of this would have happened. But he wanted to keep everything for you. He was greedy."

"I'll split what I get for it with you," Cole offered, ready to negotiate if that would buy him time. "I mean it."

"You're not in much of a bargaining position right now. It's not as if you're the registered owner of this thing. Possession is ten-tenths of the law in this case." He held the tape up to prove his point. "I'm not sharing this with anyone. I guess it's true what they say. You can never have too much money. Besides, I'm going to need a lot of it to stay one step ahead of that guy's boss for the rest of my life." Bennett pointed at Magee, who was just beginning to regain consciousness.

Cole shook his head. "All that stuff about me being just like my father. Was that all crap?" he asked.

"Every word. I wanted you to feel you were like your father, and to hear it from me. I wanted you psychologically dependent on me. And it worked," Bennett said smugly. "I never saw your father gamble a day in his life. He was a hard man. He never gave in to those kinds of vices, but he heard you did. Your aunt told him during a phone call one night that you were betting on pro football games while you were in college. He was furious. He almost went to see you, but then he didn't. He figured it wasn't his place to discipline you after all those years."

"And the naming thing?" Cole asked, annoyed with himself for so easily falling for Bennett's line of bullshit. "My father naming his gun and his boots?" How stupid and gullible could one individual be in a single lifetime? "Was that a lie too?"

"I made that one up on the spur of the moment."

The crow's feet around Bennett's eyes and mouth appeared as he broke into a self-satisfied grin. "It's those little details that make people really believe your story. Of course, it was pretty easy to convince you, because you wanted to believe my story so badly. I could see that in your eyes right away that first day on the river, at the campsite. You wanted to connect with your father so badly."

"And you wanted me to trust you."

"One hundred percent."

"So I'd call you in Washington. So I'd keep you informed."

"Yes," Bennett confirmed.

"You were trying to get the tape that first night in Manhattan, weren't you? When you chased me down Fifth Avenue."

"Absolutely."

"But then he and his accomplice showed up." Cole gestured at Magee.

"Unfortunately."

"When you shot the woman and chased Magee, you were going after the tape, not protecting me."

"True."

"And when you didn't get it, when Magee eluded you in Manhattan, you decided to stick to me, because you knew there was a second tape. My father had told you that."

"Right on the money, Cole. You should have gone into intelligence."

Cole put his hand on a thick wooden timber supporting the boathouse's main beam. It was all so obvious now. "You stuck to me like glue. You figured if you followed me, sooner or later I'd lead you to the second tape. You saw the Mafia guys throw me in the limousine and you followed us to Brooklyn because at that point you were protecting an investment, not me."

"So to speak," Bennett agreed.

"But you really seemed worried that those guys were involved. That they were after the tape."

"I wasn't certain of anything at that point. It wouldn't have surprised me at all to find out that the Mafia was trying to get hold of it. The top Mafia people probably know this recording is around somewhere." He nodded down at the tape. "They have every reason to try and suppress it, just as the government does."

Cole spread the fingers of his left hand, then slowly contracted them into a fist as he moved his other hand higher up on the timber. "So honor and loyalty were never part of the equation," he said. "Your whole act was just part of a con designed to get to the tape. It was all for money."

"And what are you here for, son?" Bennett sneered. "To make certain history is rewritten, to make certain people know there was a conspiracy to kill President Kennedy? I don't think so," he answered himself. "If you still had the Dealey Tape and the highest bid came from people within the DIA when you ran your auction, you wouldn't care. You'd take their money in a heartbeat and let history stand. You're here for your piece of the pie too. You've got debts you want to get out from under. That's why you're willing to risk your life. There's nothing altruistic in your motivation, so don't try to lay anything like that on me."

"I wouldn't sell out a man I'd worked with for thirty-six years," Cole said tersely.

"Then you're a nicer guy than I am. But nice guys end up at the bottom of the trash pile." Bennett raised the gun. "The Q and A session is over, kid. This is the end of the line." He aimed the barrel at Cole's chest and squeezed the trigger.

Nicki's eyes fluttered open as the man clamped the rag down over her mouth and nose while two other men pinned her arms and legs to the bed, immobilizing her. The fumes surged into her lungs, and as she stared up into the man's eyes, his features blurred in front of her and she was unconscious quickly.

The man who had pushed the rag over her face pulled back, then signaled to the others to get Nicki out to the car parked in front of the Andersons' home as quickly as possible, while people in the neighborhood were still asleep. Then he turned and retraced his steps to the parents' room where they lay side by side, secured tightly to the bed. He knelt down and whispered his instructions to Nicki's mother one more time, then asked if she understood.

Wild-eyed, she nodded.

At the instant Bennett raised the gun, Cole loosened the end of a rope knotted to a brass cleat bolted to the timber beside him. The other end of the rope was attached to a ring at the bow of a rowboat suspended from the boathouse ceiling for winter storage. The rope whipped away from the cleat and through a hook screwed into the beam above Bennett's head, whining as it tore through the air. The bow of the rowboat dropped instantly and dealt Bennett a glancing blow to the side of his head just as he fired the gun. The bullet grazed Cole's arm and knocked him to the floor, but he was up again quickly. Bennett lay on his back, the gun at the end of his outstretched fingers. Cole leaped toward the weapon just as Bennett rolled and reached for it too. Their hands grabbed the gun at the same time, but Cole managed to get his finger on the trigger. He squeezed it over and over, spraying bullets into the boathouse ceiling. Finally the trigger simply clicked over and over. The gun was empty.

Blood was pouring down Bennett's face from the gash inflicted by the rowboat. He was groggy and dazed by the impact, but he was a horse of a man even with his faculties only partially intact. He slammed his body into Cole's, knocking Cole over, and was on him instantly, hands tightening around Cole's neck like a vise.

Cole grabbed Bennett's face with his left hand, digging his fingernails deep into Bennett's skin, but Bennett only squeezed harder. Cole felt himself beginning to black out. He dug his right hand into the wet pocket of his pants, pulled out Billy's switchblade, snapped it open and thrust it deeply into the back of Bennett's thigh.

Bennett screamed and lifted up, reaching behind his leg for the knife handle with both hands. As he did, Cole punched him and he tumbled away, still screaming madly.

Cole was on him again right away. With a huge effort he rolled Bennett across the dock and over the edge. Bennett splashed into the water and disappeared beneath the black surface. Cole scanned the dock quickly and saw the cassette case protruding from beneath the rowboat. He scrambled across the wooden floor, grabbed the tape, rose to his feet and darted for the door. Behind him he heard Bennett resurface, arms flailing.

The wind had risen to gale force now and the snow was blowing almost horizontally as Cole emerged from the boathouse, still dripping wet. He shielded his eyes for a moment, identified the path leading up the slope to the mansion and raced toward it, the Dealey Tape in the crook of his right arm. His boots were filled with water and felt like lead weights as he ran.

"Come back here, you bastard!" Bennett shouted. He had pulled himself from the water and was now moving forward through the snow in the same slow-motion gait as Cole.

The path up to the mansion was only a few feet wide and was now covered by almost eight inches of snow. Cole felt as if his lungs would burst as he labored through the snow, but he kept going. Suddenly he slipped and tumbled back down the hill, breaking his fall by grabbing onto the stump of a tree. He pulled himself up and loped back over his own footsteps, finally breaking into virgin snow again. Bennett was only thirty feet behind, and Cole could feel his strength failing. His clothes were almost frozen stiff and he could barely put one foot in front of the other.

At the top of the hill Cole stumbled toward the mansion. If he remained outside, Bennett would catch him. It was as simple as that. Bennett would simply follow his tracks even if he could make it to the woods, and he didn't have the strength to fight off another of Bennett's onslaughts.

Cole aimed for a first-floor window, ran as hard as he could over the snow-covered lawn toward it and dove over a hedge. He smashed through the glass and wood of the window and landed on a carpeted floor, then quickly staggered to his feet and headed for a stairway leading up from what appeared to be a large family room in a finished basement. He shivered as he raced up the steps. It was warmer in here, perhaps fifty degrees, enough heat to keep the pipes from freezing over the long winter. Only fifty degrees, but suddenly that felt tropical.

At the top of the steps, Cole lifted a ski jacket from one of the hooks lining the wood paneling of the stairway. As he did, he noticed the blood dripping from the wound where the bullet had grazed his arm. He heard a loud crash from the basement as he slipped into the jacket. That had to be Bennett coming through the window. Cole sprinted left down a hallway and into the kitchen, grabbed a long knife out of a butcher block on the counter and headed up the back stairs. At the top of the stairway he stopped and listened, but he heard nothing, only the whistle of the wind from outside.

He moved quietly down the second-floor central corridor, twisting and turning past doorways. Bennett could be anywhere along the corridor, behind any door or around any corner. Cole stopped as he saw the corridor open onto the main staircase ahead, then slid along the wall until he reached the steps. Checking back over his shoulder, he leaned around the corner. The main door was down there. If he could slip out without Bennett hearing him, maybe he'd be able to make it to the Jeep and get back to Billy's lodge. Even if Bennett realized he had left and followed his tracks to where the Jeep had been parked, it wouldn't matter, because at that point he'd be long gone. Cole began to move quietly out around the corner toward the top step.

Bennett stood behind the living room wall around the corner from the bottom of the main staircase. He licked his lip and tasted the blood trickling down his face from the gash in his forehead. He raised the knife he had taken from the kitchen. He had noticed one missing from the block and realized that Cole was armed as well, which was fine. Cole had no chance of winning a knife fight with him.

Bennett gripped the knife tightly. Cole was coming down these stairs right now. Coming down blind, unaware that the enemy was waiting at the bottom. He sensed Cole's presence. He sensed the kill, as he had in Bryant Park when he'd tailed Agent Graham, then smashed the young man's head with the pipe and recovered what he'd assumed was the first Dealey Tape. A tape that had turned out to be nothing more than a presentation about some company Gilchrist was going to take public.

Suddenly Bennett heard glass shatter upstairs.

"Dammit!" Instantly he broke from his hiding place. Cole must be trying to escape through an upstairs window by crawling out onto a porch roof, climbing down a support beam, then running into the woods. Bennett turned the corner and limped up the stairs. He reached the second-floor bathroom through which Cole had hurled the chair at the same time Cole reached the front door.

Having thrown the chair through the window, Cole had retraced his steps down the corridor and the back stairs. He waited only long enough to hear Bennett running down the second-floor corridor before he quietly opened the mansion's front door, then sprinted through the snow toward the woods.

21

"WHERE THE HELL HAVE YOU BEEN?" TORI WAS UP OFF the couch as soon as Cole burst through the front door and into the great room of Billy Threefeathers's lodge.

"Where haven't I been?" he muttered under his breath, heading straight toward the television located against the cedar wall directly in front of the couch.

"Cole, answer me!" She tossed her hair back and put her hands on her hips. "We were worried about you."

"I wasn't," Billy offered calmly from the kitchen adjoining the great room, where he was cooking an omelet. "You sure you two ain't married, Cole? You act like it."

"That'll be the day," Cole muttered again, kneeling down in front of the television and turning on the set and the VCR on the shelf below.

"What's that supposed to mean?" Tori asked curtly.

"Nothing." Cole withdrew the tape from the case and inserted it carefully into the VCR.

"What's that?" Tori suddenly forgot her irritation as she noticed the case.

"*Beauty and the Beast,*" Cole retorted. "With all this snow, I figured we'd need some entertainment today." He held his breath and prayed. In the time that the tape had been on the beam it would have been subjected to intense cold, heat and dampness. It might be blank and worthless by now. Finally, the tape began to play.

"Oh my God," Tori whispered as the black open-top limousine appeared. She sank back onto the sofa as the vehicle drifted down Elm Street away from the Texas School Book Depository.

Billy put down his spatula and moved to the counter separating the kitchen from the great room, his gaze riveted to the screen.

Cole smiled. It was the same footage he had watched in the Gilchrist screening room and the quality looked good. Just let there be a rifle, he thought to himself.

The limousine moved into view and out of nowhere the bullet tore into the president's back.

"He's shot!" Tori screamed as Kennedy hunched over. "My God!" She screamed again, gesturing at the television, her hands trembling.

"Sweet baby Jesus," Billy murmured quietly, mesmerized by the images.

Cole pointed to the place on the screen where the rifle lay over the fence. "There it is." His fingers were shaking, too.

"I see it, I see it," Tori yelled. She was down on her knees, crawling toward the television.

Suddenly the puff of smoke burst from the rifle barrel and the president's head snapped back toward the camera.

Tori put her hands to her mouth as Kennedy's head exploded. "Oh my God. That's horrible."

"How many VCRs do you have, Billy?" Cole asked over his shoulder as he stopped the tape and rewound it. "You saw the gun, right?" This time he directed his question at Tori.

"Yes, yes. There's no doubt where the killing shot came from," she answered. "It came from behind the fence."

"I just have one VCR, Cole." Billy could barely speak. He was awestruck by what he had just seen. He could still remember coming out of the woods that day in 1963 after shooting a big buck deer, heading to the Kro Bar for a posthunt drink and hearing that John Kennedy was dead.

"Are there any in the outer cabins?" Cole asked. The Dealey Tape in the VCR was almost certainly the last one, and there could still be plenty of land mines out there to avoid before the cassette was safe. It seemed like an excellent idea to make another copy while he could.

"No." Billy was still reliving that day in 1963.

"Cole, I'm prepared to offer you ten million dollars for that tape right now," Tori said, kneeling beside him, breathing hard.

Cole looked steadily at Tori. He knew what she was thinking: that this tape would be the centerpiece of one of the biggest television events in history. NBC would advertise the tape for weeks before broadcasting it on one of their prime-time newsmagazines, and make millions when they finally aired it. "See the Proof," the trailers would announce. Maybe the network would show a snippet of the tape during the trailer just to whet people's appetites. It would be a two-hour special, beginning at nine eastern, and NBC wouldn't actually show the tape for the first time until ten-thirty at the earliest. The network would keep a nation on the edge of its seats while it interviewed key players from both sides—those who had claimed conspiracy all these years, and those who had scoffed at the notion. Christ, the advertisers would pay through the nose, probably millions for a thirty-second spot, because the world would stand still for a night. It would be bigger than the Super Bowl or Princess Diana's funeral.

"Ten million, huh?" Cole made certain his tone projected ambivalence, even as the dimple appeared in his cheek.

"You're always negotiating, aren't you?" she asked.

"Always."

"I know my people will pay that much," Tori assured Cole. "But you have to make a commitment to me right now," she pushed.

He stared at her for several moments before responding. "You put that note under my door."

"What are you talking about?"

"Someone shoved a note under my hotel room door the day after I got back to New York." He had been absolutely convinced all along that it had been Bennett, but now he realized he'd been wrong. "It was you who put the note under the door," Cole murmured. "You're the only one it could have been."

"You're crazy."

But Cole saw the truth in her eyes. "No, I'm not."

"All right," she admitted softly. "You aren't."

"No—" Cole stopped short. He hadn't been prepared for her to admit to it so quickly. "How did you get the note?"

Tori glanced at Billy, then took Cole's hands in hers. "I've known your father for fifteen years." There was no telling how he was going to take this, but she had to let him know. "I love your father very much."

"What?" Cole laughed nervously. "Are you serious?"

"Yes."

"You and he are . . ." Cole's voice trailed off. He couldn't finish the sentence.

"Lovers," she finished the thought. "Yes." It was her turn to laugh. "What a relationship. I met him fifteen years ago in East Germany while I was covering a story, and I bet I haven't seen him more than thirty times in all those years. I sure know how to pick them." She smiled apologetically at Cole. "I didn't mean that the way it sounded."

"It's all right." Cole shook his head. Jim Egan certainly was a man of many surprises. But now, as he thought about it, Cole realized the relationship with Tori made a great deal of sense. His father wouldn't have had many people to trust, so he had spent fifteen years getting to know Tori. Making *certain* he could trust her. "My father gave you the note?" he asked.

"Yes, about three weeks ago—"

"Three weeks ago," Cole interrupted. "Then my father is alive."

"Yes."

He had been right after all. The exhilaration was incredible, like nothing he had ever experienced. "You're sure?" Cole asked.

"Absolutely."

"Keep going," Cole urged. "He gave you the note, and . . ."

"And he said to watch the *New York Times* for his obituary. When I saw it, I was to make contact with you and deliver the note. He told me he wasn't really going to be dead, that the obituary was just a signal."

Placed by a son who had no idea what was really going on. "Why didn't *he* just give me the note?" Cole asked.

"He was certain people were watching you and looking for him. He was in hiding. He couldn't risk leaving his 'lair,' as he called it."

"Where did he give you the note, in New York?"

"No, in a little town in Montana. That's where he was hiding. I flew out there and met him in a greasy diner. It was all prearranged six months ago, the time I saw him before Montana."

Cole snapped his fingers. Six months ago was about the same time his father had shown up at the Gilchrist trading floor.

Tori laughed. "You should have seen his disguise in Montana. He looked like the Unabomber or something with his long hair and beard and mustache. I would never have known it was him if he hadn't tapped me on the shoulder. He made me wait there an hour after the scheduled time. He told me it was because he was making certain I hadn't been followed. I thought maybe he was losing his mind at that point." She nodded at the VCR. "Now that I've seen the tape I can understand his paranoia."

Incredible, Cole thought to himself. His father had planned the whole thing for years. "Did he ever tell you about what he does for a living?"

"He told me he's an intelligence agent, but that's all. Of course, that's our entire relationship in a nutshell. There's always lots of mystery. I see him once every six months if I'm lucky. And we always arrange our next meeting on the last day we're together. I never hear from him in between. He's enigmatic, but I guess I kind of like that. It's wild. We meet in crazy places like Australia, the Swiss Alps, Rio." A smile crossed her lips. "It's so romantic. We have three or four days of incredible excitement, then he disappears and I have to wait until the next time. One time a few years ago he didn't show up at our prearranged meeting place in Tahiti. I was devastated. I was looking forward to seeing him so much. I stayed on the island for two days waiting at the hotel where he said he would meet me, but he never showed up. I thought he was dead. I cried all the way back to New York on the plane. A few days later a note showed up on my desk and gave me the next coordinates. That's what he calls our meeting places, coordinates. He's always naming things." She giggled like a schoolgirl. "He never apologized for not showing up in Tahiti, never even mentioned it again, but that's him. He never apologizes for anything."

Cole stared at her, unable to speak for a few seconds. "He's always naming things?" he finally whispered.

"Always," Tori confirmed. "He says he can never write anything down because of what he does, and naming things helps his memory."

So his father really was always naming things. Bennett hadn't been lying about that.

Tori sighed. "I didn't tell you all this, because he made me swear I wouldn't. He said he didn't want you distracted. He wanted you to get that tape and sell it."

"He told you that he had a tape of the Kennedy assassination?" Cole asked. "One that was different from the Zapruder film? He told you that was what he was sending me after?"

"Yes." She looked down at the floor.

"What is it?" Cole sensed Tori's mood changing.

She took his hands in hers again and looked back up at him. "Jim told me everything when I saw him six months ago. He told me that he had kept this film of Kennedy's assassination all these years, and that he couldn't release it because he felt he would be killed if he did, although he wouldn't tell me by whom." She hesitated.

"What's wrong, Tori?" Cole could see the pain in her eyes.

"I'm ashamed of myself."

"Why?"

"For the way I acted at lunch that day in New York, holding back on your grandparents' address the way I did. But you see, your father told me that you might already have the first tape at that point. I figured I would have heard something through the grapevine if you'd already made a deal with one of the other networks, but I hadn't heard anyone talking." She pursed her lips. "I really wanted to make certain that I got my hands on it. I really do want to impress my people at NBC, that's on the level. Your father told me the tapes existed, but he never told me where they were. I guess he trusted me to deliver a note to you, but not to hold the tape."

Just as he had trusted Bennett to deliver the envelope, but not to hold the tape, Cole thought to himself.

"But, Cole, I wasn't his lover just so I could get my hands on the assassination tape. You have to believe me about that," Tori pleaded.

"I do," Cole said gently.

"I didn't know anything until six months ago."

"I believe you. And don't worry about holding back on my grandparents' address. Ultimately you gave it to me." He smiled. "So all that stuff about finding the marriage certificate in Dallas and the ticklers in the NBC computers, that was all—"

"All made up."

"But you did visit my grandparents."

"It was the one way I could check out your father's

story. Remember, I *am* in the news business. I like to get confirmation when I can."

Cole was puzzled. "But those other news agencies called me at Gilchrist just a day after our lunch."

"People have been looking for your father for a long time, in exactly the way I described, with computers scanning periodicals and publications looking for tickler words. Even people at NBC. The ones who called you obviously saw the obituary and got your name from the *Times.*" She laughed. "I didn't need to do all that because I had inside information."

Cole smiled back. "You sure did." It was beautiful. His father had organized two completely separate methods by which to convey the Dealey Tape to his son, using his two most trusted confidants in the world—Tori and Bennett. He'd used two because he didn't completely trust either one. It wasn't in Jim Egan's nature to trust anyone unconditionally, as it wasn't in his own. Suddenly Cole felt the loneliness that came with never fully trusting anyone, but he quickly shook it off. After all, his father had been right. Bennett Smith, his lifelong friend, had betrayed the trust.

"I've got to get going," Cole said firmly. "I don't want to stick around here." He glanced out the window, half expecting to see Bennett coming up Billy's driveway.

"Huh?" Tori was instantly alarmed. She hadn't heard the word "we" in his sentence.

Cole stood up. "I'm going after my father. You said you met him in a small town in Montana. Which one was it?"

Tori stood up as well. "First let's get the tape to New York City. Let's get it someplace safe where NBC can have it guarded around the clock. Let's get you your ten million dollars, and *then* go after your father."

"No, it might be too late at that point," Cole countered. "I'm sure they're out there looking for him as we speak. I'd never forgive myself if I didn't get to him."

"Why would it be too late?" she wanted to know.

"It doesn't matter," Cole answered quickly.

"You Egans make me so mad sometimes. You don't tell anyone anything."

"Where in Montana did you meet him?" Cole demanded.

"I'm not telling you," she said defiantly.

"You're not going to pull this on me again." Cole grabbed her upper arms.

"It's for your own good, Cole. It's what your father wanted. He wanted you to sell that tape first and foremost."

"I don't care what my father wanted," Cole yelled, shaking Tori hard.

"You're hurting me!" she screamed.

"Easy, Cole!" Billy yelled, moving out from behind the island counter.

"Hey! Don't get in the way, Billy." Cole pointed a finger at his friend, then took Tori by her upper arm again and stared into her eyes. "My grandparents are one thing." His voice was trembling slightly. "My father is another. One way or another, you will tell me the town you met him in. Do you understand what I mean by that?"

She understood completely and wanted no part of what she saw in his eyes. "Powell. It's located halfway between Helena and Great Falls on the Missouri River," she said quietly.

"Okay. Is there anything else you can tell me?"

"He met me at a little diner in town. He didn't tell me where he was hiding."

That made sense. Tori might have given him away without even meaning to. He'd have to go to Powell blind and wing it when he got there. "All right." He released his grip on her, popped the tape from the VCR, replaced it in its case and headed toward the lodge door.

"Where are you going?" she shouted.

"To pack," he called back over his shoulder. "And then to Powell."

"Not without me, you aren't."

Cole stopped at the door. "Billy will give you a ride to the Duluth Airport. There are plenty of flights from Duluth to Minneapolis. From there you can make it back to New York easily."

"But—"

He held up a hand. "When I'm done in Montana, I'll call you. I told you I'd give you the right of first refusal on the Dealey Tape, and I won't renege on that. You can match any and all offers."

"And just how are you going to get to Montana?" A sly smile spread across her face. "Walk?"

Cole's shoulders sagged. He had completely forgotten about his money problem. He couldn't ask Billy for funds. The man had hardly any money. For a second he considered asking Tori for a loan, but he knew that wasn't even worth the effort.

"All right, pack your bags. I guess you're coming with me to Montana."

"Good. And maybe when we get there you'll give me my cell phone back."

22

THE MISSOURI RIVER IS FORMED BY THE CONFLUENCE of the Jefferson, Madison and Gallatin Rivers at a lonely spot called Three Forks, Montana, located sixty miles northwest of Yellowstone National Park. From Three Forks the Missouri flows north past Helena through the Big Belt Mountains to the tiny town of Powell. At Powell the river turns east toward Great Falls, then finally southeast through the Dakotas toward its St. Louis rendezvous with the mighty Mississippi.

Powell turns the Missouri east, and in return for this guidance, it clings to the wide river for protection like a storm-weary barnacle to a harbor piling, as if the Rocky Mountain peaks towering high above the tiny town might bend down to swallow it and its four hundred residents like the dinosaurs that roamed the region millions of years before. Powell consists of a small trailer park, a few clapboard homes, a diner that doubles as the local watering hole, several outfitter stores for fishermen and hunters, Miller's General

Store and a rundown seven-room motel also owned by Jack Miller and his wife. The interstate, a half mile west of town, shadows the Missouri's every move and connects Powell to the outside world—Helena, thirty miles to the south, and Great Falls, forty miles to the northeast. Between Powell and these two small cities is little else but the river, the mountains, the interstate and the single-track main line of the Burlington Northern Railroad, which shadows the river's course even more closely than the interstate does.

Cole eased the Jeep Cherokee off the interstate and down the gently sloping exit ramp. At the bottom of the ramp he turned left onto a lonely, uneven gravel road and headed toward Powell as morning light worked its way past high clouds and craggy peaks. It was just after nine o'clock. He and Tori had driven all night, twenty hours straight from Hubbard, alternating shifts at the wheel, stopping only twice for gasoline and food. It had been a marathon drive, but in a way he had enjoyed it. The drive had served as an opportunity to reflect on the incredible events of the last few days, and to figure out what he was going to say to his father—if they could find him.

"Where are we?" Tori groaned, rubbing her eyes.

"Paradise," Cole answered cheerfully. He meant it, too. He had never traveled in the Northwest before, but after only a few hours of the incredible scenery, he was already taken with it. "The place I'm going to live someday." Northern Wisconsin was beautiful, but Montana was something else. It was more majestic, more impressive and even more remote, which was the best thing of all.

"Oh!" She groaned again as she stretched, working a kink out of her neck. "Cole, why do you like these backwoods, off-the-beaten-track places? No, wait a minute," she interrupted herself. "Let me correct that. These off-the-*no*-track places."

"There are fewer people," he answered, braking as the road dropped down along the railroad. "And there's a track for you." Cole pointed at the two silver rails.

"Ha, ha."

Cole barely noticed her laugh as he continued gazing out the window. On the other side of the track was the river—two hundred feet wide at this point—swirling slowly east now that it was downstream from town. Rising a thousand feet straight up out of the far bank was a sheer rock face.

"Don't you like people?" Tori asked.

"Do you?" he asked, watching the sun gleam against the top of the peak.

"Mostly."

"Well, it's a free country. You're entitled to your opinion. And I'm entitled to try to change it, but I don't feel like trying right now because I don't have the energy." Suddenly he was exhausted. The rusting sign ahead indicated that Powell was just around the bend, and now that they were here, the adrenaline that had kept him awake through the gray hours of dawn was beginning to dissipate quickly.

Tori shook her head. Cole was a loner, just like his father. "At least there isn't any snow here," she observed, looking past Cole at the river.

"No, there isn't. It's supposed to stay warm. The temperature is supposed to get into the upper fifties today. At least that's what the weatherman on the radio said." Cole checked the sky. It was still clear. "They are calling for rain in the afternoon."

"So what's the plan?" she asked. She had tried to change Cole's mind yesterday afternoon as they had driven down from northern Wisconsin through Minneapolis to pick up Interstate 90. She had tried to convince him again to deal with the tape first, then go after his father, but he wouldn't listen. As Minneapolis faded in the rearview mirror, she had changed tactics, grilling him as to how he expected to find Jim Egan. She pointed out that it would be like finding a needle in a haystack the size of—well, Montana. Cole had grumbled back that he had a plan all right, but would provide no details. Now that they were finally here, she wanted to know how he was going to justify the ordeal they had just endured. "Come on," she urged. "I want to know."

Cole reached for his sunglasses sitting on the dashboard and put them on as the sun burst through a break in the peaks. "I have a picture of my father in my wallet. It's old, but he can't have changed that much since it was taken. We'll show it to people around town. Hopefully someone will recognize him. There aren't that many people here." The tiny town came into view as they rounded a bend. "Heck, you could probably fit all of Powell into one block of New York City."

Tori's mouth fell open. "That's the extent of your plan? An old picture you're going to show to a bunch of total strangers? With just that, you're willing to jump in a Jeep and drive almost a thousand miles?"

"Actually it's more than a thousand miles from here to Hubbard."

She hated it when he did that. She realized that deflecting the conversation was his way of saying he didn't want to talk about the important point, but she hated it anyway. She put her head in her hands as Cole steered the Jeep into the general store's rutted parking lot. She could feel a headache coming on.

"Your father was wearing a disguise the day I met him here in Powell." She pointed at the diner across the dirt road from the store. "He didn't want anyone to recognize him. I'm pretty sure he still won't. I'm willing to bet he hasn't been running down Main Street, if that's really what one would call this cow path, whooping it up and telling everyone who he is. Call me crazy," she said acidly, "but I've got this feeling."

"Do you have a better idea?" Cole was trying hard to control his temper, but it had been a long night and he was running thin on patience.

"Yes," she snapped. "Let's drive to the nearest airport and get on a plane to New York."

"Again with New York." Cole groaned as he reached into the backseat for the backpack. Inside it was the Dealey Tape. He wasn't letting it out of his sight even for a moment now. He pulled on the door handle and hopped out of the Jeep.

"Yes, again with New York!" Tori slid out her side and met him in front of the vehicle. "Wake up, Cole! Use your head. You've got one of the most important moments of history recorded on the tape inside that backpack." She grabbed him by the collar of his jacket. "We'll come back for your father, I promise."

"I thought you and he were involved." Cole still couldn't bring himself to say "lovers."

"Yes, so?"

"So I would think you'd be more concerned about his welfare."

"I am, but I don't know what in the world we're going to do out here except put ourselves at risk. He'll be found when he wants to be found. If there are two things I have learned about your father over fifteen years, they are that he can take care of himself and that if he doesn't want to be found, he won't be."

Cole tried to pull away from Tori, but she wouldn't let him go.

"Cole, you won't even tell me who's after him, or who chased you in Manhattan when you got the first tape." She paused, giving him a chance to explain, but he said nothing. "I don't mean to seem so insensitive." Her voice softened. "I know you think I'm just looking out for myself and my career. I am, I'll admit, but I'm also looking out for you. It's what Jim wanted, I swear to you. He wanted you to have the money and me to take the tape to my people. He wanted me to have a chance at some success too. I haven't told you that yet, but it's true. He had the whole thing figured out." Still Cole said nothing. "After we get the tape to New York, we'll go to the police. Or better still, the FBI. We'll find him, Cole. We won't stop until we do."

"We can't go to the FBI," Cole said quietly, "or the police."

"Why not?"

"Because it's the government that's after him—and me," he added.

A quizzical expression came to Tori's face.

"I didn't want to scare you," Cole continued. "It's people in the federal government who are after what I have in the backpack. People very high up in the government, if my information is correct. People who probably have every law enforcement official in this country looking for me right now. I can't show myself to the FBI or the police. They'd arrest me immediately, slap me with some phony charge, confiscate the tape and I'd never see it again."

Tori let go of Cole's collar and banged the hood of

the Jeep with both hands. "Exactly!" she said loudly. "Which is why I want to get that tape to a safe place right away!"

Cole leaned down until his face was just inches from hers. "We don't have time," he said, gritting his teeth. "Yesterday morning I went to a boathouse on the Lassiter and retrieved the tape I now have in my backpack, thanks to directions on that note you slipped under the hotel door. I barely got away with the tape, and my life." He pulled the jacket down and pointed to his upper arm. The shirt was caked with dried blood. "*That's* thanks to a bullet from a gun fired by one very pissed-off intelligence agent."

Tori's upper lip curled and she turned away. She couldn't stand the sight of blood.

He pulled the jacket back up. "Tori, the guy who did this is probably still after me. Him and an army of others. They're after my father too, and they're mad as hell." Maybe she wouldn't understand this part but he was going to say it anyway. "I've only seen my father a few times in my entire life. God knows he hasn't put out much of an effort to be a part of it, but I don't care. If I ever thought I'd missed a chance to get to know him because I chose to go for the money first, I'd never be able to live with myself. I know what it's like to think he's dead, and it's horrible. Now I've got a second chance. I have to find him as soon as possible." He saw the faint smile on her lips and in her eyes. "As far as I know, you're the last person to see him. And you saw him right here in this town. That puts us one step ahead of everyone else. One very small step, but that's enough for me. I have to find him. Then we can focus on the Dealey Tape."

Slowly Tori reached up and touched his cheek gently, then kissed him there. "Okay," she said softly, pulling away. She wasn't going to change his mind, that was obvious. There was no reason to argue any further. "I won't say another word about going to New York first. I'm here to help. Just tell me how to do that."

"The first thing you can do is wait here for a second."

"All right," she agreed.

Cole walked to an old phone booth outside the general store's entrance. From his shirt pocket he pulled out a long distance calling card he had Tori purchase with cash early this morning at a Billings gas station. The card was good for two hours of calls. To this point he had only made one short call, so there was plenty of time left on it. The beauty of using it, unlike Tori's cell phone, was that no one would be able to pinpoint their whereabouts because there was no record as to who was the owner of the card's PIN number.

He punched in the number for the Gilchrist trading floor reception area and the card's access code, then checked his watch. It was nine-fifteen here and eleven-fifteen in the east. Anita ought to be at the reception desk.

"Gilchrist and Company."

"Anita."

"Yes."

"It's Cole, but don't say my—"

"Hey, Co—"

"Don't say my name!" Gebauer could be out by her desk. Jesus, the paranoia was really setting in, he realized. "Just listen to me."

"Okay," she said slowly.

"When I was leaving I told you I might need your help, remember?"

"Yes."

"I need it now."

She hesitated. "All right."

"I need you to go to the following address." He reeled off the street number quickly. "There's a package waiting there for you with instructions inside. I need you to get it. This is very important. Will you do this for me, Anita?"

"Yes." She was frightened. It all sounded very strange and she didn't want to be caught up in something illicit, but Cole was a good person. He had always treated her with respect, unlike many of the other traders. "I'll do it."

"Thanks, and don't worry. Everything will be fine."

"Uh huh."

"There's one more thing."

"What is it?"

"I need you to go over to the Bloomberg terminal and check the rate on the two-year treasury note for me." Gilchrist kept a terminal in the reception area so visitors could check financial news as they waited. "The rate is in the lower left section of the main screen. You won't have to get to other screens or anything." It might be stupid to stay on the line any longer than was really necessary, but he had to know where the market was going.

"Hold on."

"Thanks."

He had to wait only a few seconds.

"Hello."

"Yes?"

"I've got the rate," Anita said.

Beautiful, he thought as he listened. The rate was down thirty basis points since he had left New York.

His portfolio had gone up twenty-five million dollars in value. "Thanks, Anita. I'll call you soon. Goodbye."

He hung up the phone and beckoned to Tori. "Ready?" he called.

"Yes."

The only person inside the general store was a checkout girl standing behind the cash register reading a magazine.

"Good morning," Cole called.

The young girl glanced up from her magazine. "Hello." She was polite, but indifferent.

Cole removed the picture of his father from his wallet and placed it on the counter. "This is my father. He has Alzheimer's disease. Two weeks ago he disappeared from my family's house up in Great Falls." Cole shook his head dejectedly. "Just flat disappeared." Cole saw sadness flicker over the young girl's face as he related the story. "We can't find him anywhere," he continued. "He used to come down to Powell a lot to fish. He loved it here. Anyway, I just wondered if maybe you had seen him."

The young girl leaned over and carefully inspected Jim Egan's photograph. Finally she straightened up and shook her head. "I'm sorry, mister. I don't recognize the man in that picture."

"Have you seen any strangers lately? People who maybe recently moved into town?"

"No. I'd notice, too. Strangers stick out like sore thumbs around here."

"Okay."

"If your father was a fisherman, maybe you should try one of the outfitter stores in town," the girl suggested. "Maybe he stopped in one of those places."

Cole smiled. "Good idea." He began walking toward the door, then stopped and turned back. "Oh, miss."

"Yes?" She had already gone back to the magazine.

"There's one more thing."

"What?" Her face brightened. She wanted to be of help now. The handsome young man had an engaging way about him.

"How long have you been working here?"

"Since the beginning of last summer."

"And you know everybody in town, right?"

"Sure. Powell's a small place," she offered cheerfully. "I knew you were a stranger the minute you walked in. Like I said, strangers stick out like sore thumbs."

"And I guess everybody living in Powell pretty much does their food shopping here."

"Oh, yeah, it's the only place within thirty miles to buy groceries."

Cole hesitated. He didn't want this question to seem too mysterious. "Has anybody been buying more groceries than normal lately?"

Tori glanced up. That was a good question. Why hadn't she thought of it?

The checkout girl put a finger to her lips and gazed at the water-stained tile ceiling for a few moments. "Mmm. I can't think of—wait a minute! The General's been buying a lot more lately."

"The who?" Cole asked.

"The General. I don't know if he was really a general or even in the army, but that's what people here call him. He moved to Powell a few years ago from someplace out east. The rumor is he was some kind of secret agent, but I think that's probably just talk. Just people around here inventing things to make the day more interesting. Not much exciting ever happens in Powell, so we have to kind of make things up sometimes to entertain ourselves. The General stays to himself pretty much. He comes into town once a week to buy groceries, but now that you mention it, it's like he's been eating for three or four people the last month or so."

"Where does the General live? My dad used to talk about an old army buddy who lived up here."

"Out in Boswell Canyon. It's north of town a few miles."

Cole smiled warmly. "Thanks. You've been real helpful. I'll come back and tell you if we find my father. I'd like you to know."

"Would you tell me? That would be so nice."

"Sure. 'Bye." He waved as he walked out the door. Seconds later he and Tori were back in the Jeep.

"Are you always this lucky?" she asked as Cole gunned the engine.

23

"Do you see any activity at all?"

"No." From his prone position beside a large boulder, Cole inspected the house one more time, staring through the powerful pair of binoculars he had purchased at one of the outfitter shops down the street from the general store in Powell. "Here. You take a look, my eyes are tired."

Tori took the binoculars from him, brought them up to her eyes and rotated the notched knob between the lenses to adjust the focus.

Cole rolled onto his back and gazed back down the side of the mountain. The Jeep was parked on a muddy road at the base of the peak but he was so high up now he could barely see it. The hunter-green Jeep was just a speck against the light brown prairie grass covering the valley floor.

It had taken them two hours to hike to the top of the slope—a thirty degree grade at its steepest, Cole judged. The mountain was covered by prairie grass, scrub pines and smooth boulders protruding from the earth. They had carefully picked their way up the side of the mountain, some of the time able to walk upright, some of the time forced to climb bent over at the waist using their hands to ascend. They kept their eyes peeled for rattlesnakes and for loose rocks that might slide out from underfoot and send them tumbling back down the slope.

Ten minutes ago they had finally reached the peak, exhausted by the arduous climb and the thin air. Their lungs were still burning from the exertion, but now they had an excellent vantage point from which to survey the General's house, which sat halfway up the other side of the mountain they had just climbed.

"See anything?" Cole asked.

"No, I don't—Hey! Wait a minute. There's a car coming out of the garage."

Cole rolled quickly onto his stomach again, grabbed the binoculars from Tori and aimed them down at the house. A white sedan had pulled out of the garage and was making its way slowly down the rutted gravel driveway.

"Can you see the driver?" Tori asked.

"No." The windows were tinted, so there was no way to discern the features of whoever was behind the wheel, or to determine if there was more than one person inside the car. Cole followed the vehicle until it disappeared behind a ridge, then aimed the binoculars back at the house sitting approximately five hundred feet below them and to the right. The house was a plain one-story ranch encased by vinyl siding, with a brick chimney at one end and a garage at the other. Like the car, the house had tinted windows.

Cole surveyed the secluded canyon once more, searching for other buildings, but from their position beside the large boulder at the mountain's crest he couldn't see any. As far as he could tell, this house was the only one in the vicinity.

"What now?" Tori asked. She sat up and pulled a small twig from her hair.

Cole placed the binoculars on the ground. "I make my way down to the house and see if my father's inside."

"You mean, break in?"

"I'm not going to knock. I've got the advantage of surprise at this point and I don't want to lose it."

"But your father might not be in there. In fact, he might not be within a thousand miles of here. The person who owns that house might have no idea who your father is, or might not even be involved with what's going on at all. There might be some poor old woman in there who's never heard of Jim Egan and you might give her a heart attack by breaking in."

"I'll apologize," Cole answered flatly.

"Or she might be a feisty old bird and fill you with buckshot."

"I'll duck."

"Or she might—"

"Or she might be Margaret Thatcher," Cole interrupted, annoyed with all the talk. "Out here to get away from it all. And if it is Maggie, we'll sit down, drink some tea and discuss world politics. But don't hold your breath."

Tori stuck out her tongue. "Maybe we just missed your father. Maybe that was him driving away."

"Maybe. And if the General is the only one in there, we'll sit down and have tea with him until my father gets back. If the house is empty, we'll have tea with ourselves and wait until whoever it was comes back so we can get some answers." Cole rose slowly to his feet, making certain he remained behind the boulder and out of sight of the house as he brushed dirt, grass and twigs from his pants. "The guy behind the counter at the outfitter shop said this was the General's place." He said the words more to himself than to Tori, as if he needed reassurance.

Cole had claimed to be an old friend of the General's. Without even questioning the story's veracity, the man behind the counter had drawn a specific map of how to get to the house. At that point Cole had not yet actually purchased the binoculars and the man wanted to make certain the sale of the high-priced item was closed. He had directed Cole and Tori to the road that would lead to the General's twisting mile-long driveway up the canyon, but Cole had decided it would be better to walk up the far side of the mountain to keep surprise on their side.

"The young girl at Miller's said the General was buying a lot more groceries lately," Cole pointed out. "And that he was military. That adds up to enough for me to investigate."

"All right." Tori groaned as she too stood up.

"Where do you think you're going?" Cole asked.

"Down there with you."

"No way."

"Oh yes I am," Tori answered firmly. "You aren't leaving me alone up here."

"I have no idea what I'm going to find down there. There might be some very unfriendly people in that house, and I don't want to have to worry about you if things get crazy. If you see that something's wrong, get back down to the Jeep and go for help. That's a better plan."

"Forget it, I'm not staying here," she said. "I didn't climb all the way up this mountain just to sit here.

Besides, if your father is in that house, I want to see him as soon as I can."

Cole didn't argue. She had made up her mind, and he had learned that once her mind was made up, nothing could change it. "Okay." He bent down and picked up the backpack holding the Dealey Tape. "Then this is the plan. We move down through the scrub pines and the rocks to that big boulder over there." He pointed to a huge stone fifty feet from the house. "Then I'm going for the door. If there's no one but a kindly old lady in the house who I'm convinced has never heard of my father, I'll apologize and we'll leave. Otherwise I'll search the place or deal with whoever is inside the best way I can. I don't want you coming in with me initially," he said firmly. "If everything is all right, I'll wave you in. If something goes wrong, try to get back to the Jeep. The keys are under the left rear bumper. I put them there in case we got separated."

"I remember." Tori heard the concern in his tone. "But why would anything go wrong?" she asked. "When I was out here a few weeks ago, your father seemed to be able to move around as he pleased. There wasn't anyone with him or watching him—as far as I could tell, anyway. He seemed fine. Once you get inside and explain who you are, or your father sees you, everything should be all right."

"Maybe, but a lot's changed since you were out here." Cole slung the backpack over his shoulders. "Come on, let's go."

This side of the mountain was less steep and they threaded their way down through the boulders and scrub pines without difficulty, at the same time remaining hidden from the house. Finally they reached the rock Cole had pointed out from their position on the mountain peak and knelt down behind it, breathing heavily even though they'd been descending instead of climbing.

Tori touched her chest. "God, I'm really out of breath," she said in a low voice.

"It's the thin air," Cole answered, peering around the rock at the house, "and the fact that we haven't had much sleep in the last two days." He studied the front door. "Okay, I'm ready. Stay here and wait for my signal."

"Okay."

Cole stood up, hesitated only a moment, then moved out from behind the rock and began making his way cautiously toward the house. He was out in the open now and completely vulnerable. Gravel crunched beneath his boots as he reached the driveway. If anyone inside decided to start shooting, he'd be an easy target.

When he was ten feet from the house, the door suddenly swung open. "Can I help you?" The male voice from within was decidedly unfriendly.

Cole stopped instantly. "Um, yes."

"What do you want?"

Cole squinted, shielding his eyes from the sun, trying to make out the figure in the darkness beyond the doorway. Finally he jerked his thumb over his shoulder. "My wife and I are out here doing some camping. We're from Georgia." He did his best southern accent, taking Bennett's advice of adding details to make his story more believable.

"I don't see anybody."

"Laura!" Cole yelled back over his shoulder, using an alias. "I'm over here."

"Okay, sweetheart," Tori called, moving casually

out from behind the boulder, looking up at the mountains as if she were sightseeing.

"It sure is beautiful out here." Cole smiled.

"Yes, it is."

The sun ducked behind the clouds and for an instant Cole caught sight of the man inside. He was short and wide, with a dark crew cut. He wore denim overalls and a gray T-shirt, and didn't appear to be carrying a weapon. "I was wondering if Laura could come in and use your bathroom. Woman stuff, you know?"

The man didn't answer right away.

"Sir?" Cole prodded.

"Yeah, yeah, come in." The door swung open further and the man disappeared.

"Come on, Laura," Cole called as he walked to the door, stepped into the dimly lit house and moved quickly away from the door in case someone was behind it. His eyes slowly became accustomed to the faint light, and he saw the man standing across the room in front of one of the windows. The room was sparsely furnished with a couch, three wooden chairs, a small television set and a cheap-looking dining room table.

Tori moved into the house. "Where is your bathroom?" she asked politely.

The man pointed down the hall. "First door on your right," he said gruffly.

"Thanks." She walked down the hall, moved inside the bathroom and closed the door behind her. Instantly the sound of running water came from within.

"Not traveling real heavy, are you?" The man eyed Cole's small backpack suspiciously.

"We're doing day trips while we're out here," Cole explained quickly, glancing around the room, then down the hall at the closed bathroom door. Past the bathroom were two more closed doors. "I really do apologize for imposing on you this way."

"No problem." The man smiled broadly, then brought the gun up from behind his back. "Cole Egan."

Cole's eyes flashed to the man's, then down at the gun.

"Now why don't you tell me what you and your wife are actually doing up here?" He laughed callously. "As if that's really your wife."

Cole shut his eyes.

"Yeah, I imagine it's—"

But the man never finished his sentence. A large rock smashed through the window and into the back of his head, and he pitched forward, collapsing to the floor as the gun flew from his grasp and came to rest against the door. Cole scrambled for the gun, rolled and aimed at the man, but he was unconscious, facedown on the cheap tile, blood dripping from a cut behind his ear.

Then Cole heard footsteps, running around the house toward the front door. He stood up quickly, back against the wall behind the door, and held the revolver in both hands, straight up so the barrel was pointing toward the ceiling. The door burst open and he brought the gun down directly into Tori's face.

"Oh, no!" She threw her hands up to her face. "It's me, Cole, it's me!"

Cole tilted his head back slowly, exhaled and let the gun fall to his side. "What the hell just happened?"

She was breathing rapidly, hands still up and eyes wide open. "I caught a glimpse of the gun in his hand as I walked past him down the hall. I turned on the water in the sink so he couldn't hear me open the bathroom window. Then I crawled outside, found a rock and threw it through the window at him. The glass is so dark I could barely see him. I had no idea if I hit him or not."

Cole shook his head. "Well, you did, and I'm glad." It seemed strange that Tori would have run *to* the door if she wasn't certain she had hit the man with the stone and was aware that he had a gun. "Quite a throw, I'll have to admit." He moved quickly across the room, knelt down and pressed two fingers to the man's neck.

"Is he hurt badly?" Tori asked.

"I don't know. But he's going to have a nice headache if he wakes up." Cole stood, held the gun ahead of him with both hands wrapped around the handle and moved quickly down the hallway toward the two closed doors. His hands were shaking as he turned the first doorknob slowly, then burst into the room, but it was empty except for an unmade bed and a dresser. Brushing past Tori, who had followed him down the hallway, he headed for the second door. He gripped the knob, turned it and slammed his shoulder against the door, bringing the gun down as he moved inside. For several moments he stood in the doorway, staring at the gagged and blindfolded figure chained to the bed.

"Jim!" Tori screamed, pushing Cole out of the way as she rushed into the room.

Cole watched, spellbound, as she pulled the gag and blindfold down and Jim Egan's eyes fluttered open, and then his father's face was obscured as Tori hugged and kissed him over and over.

Finally Jim turned his head to the side to avoid Tori's lips. "Did you get the tape, Cole?" His voice was weak and raspy.

Cole still couldn't see his father's face. "Yes," he answered loudly.

Tori glanced back over her shoulder. "What are you doing, Cole? Get over here!"

Slowly Cole walked to the bed and knelt. He gazed down at his father. Even in the dim light he could see that Jim Egan was sickeningly pale. A full gray beard covered Jim's hollow cheeks and his eyes seemed sunken in his head. Suddenly Cole noticed how gaunt he was too. Jutting bones were obvious beneath his T-shirt and jeans.

"Hello, Dad," he said softly.

"Did you sell the tape?" There were no pleasantries, and as he finished speaking Jim began coughing deeply.

The severity of the cough alarmed Cole. "We've got to get you out of here, Dad."

"Did you sell the damn tape?" Jim was still coughing, barely able to catch his breath.

"I've got it with me," Cole assured his father.

"What are you doing here, then?" Jim asked as forcefully as he could. He looked at Tori. "I told you to—make sure he sold—"

"I tried, but—"

"Dad, she did what you asked, but I wasn't going to—"

"Get the hell out of here," he groaned. "Get that thing to people who can protect it."

Cole shook his head. "First—"

"Get out!" Jim yelled. "He's going to be back here soon. He doesn't leave me for long."

"It's all right, Dad. We got the guy. He's going to be unconscious for a while."

"Are you talking about the General?"

"I guess so. He's a short, wide guy with a crew cut."

"I'm not talking about him. He's an idiot. I'm talking about—" Suddenly Jim convulsed into another terrible coughing spell.

As Cole watched his father fight the cough, an eerie feeling overtook him, and he placed a hand on his father's shoulder. "Who are you talking about, Dad?"

"A man named—Bennett Smith," Jim gasped.

"The man who delivered the envelope to me with the safe-deposit key in it?" Cole couldn't believe what he was hearing.

"Yes."

"What?" Tori was confused.

"Bennett is the man I told you about while we were driving to the Lassiter River," Cole explained. "He was my father's best friend, and the man who I suspect helped Dad fake his own death."

"That's right," Jim confirmed. The coughing fit had subsided. "Bennett arranged for me to hole-up here with the General. Bennett flew me out in a small plane the night after we made it back from our last mission, and I parachuted in. The General was ready for me. He's a retired army officer. Bennett knew him somehow." Cole's father struggled with the shackles for a moment, but it was useless. "Christ! Thirty-six years, you think you know someone. I'm here for a month and no problem, then out of nowhere the General smacks me on the back of the head while we're watching television. It was the night Bennett was supposed to have delivered the envelope to you in Manhattan. I wake up in here the next morning chained to the bed. I knew exactly what had happened. Then Bennett shows up here last night. The bastard!" he shouted as he yanked furiously at the chains once more.

"Because he was following me until yesterday," Cole murmured. It was all falling into place.

"What?"

"Bennett was the first messenger, correct?"

"Yes."

"And Tori was the second."

"Right."

"You set up two plans as insurance."

"I had to be careful."

"And you were wise to be, because Bennett turned on you. He wanted money."

"I'll rip him apart."

"I seriously doubt it," Cole said quietly. "Not in your condition."

"Did Bennett take the first tape from you?" Jim didn't want to hear about his weakened condition.

"No, others did."

"Others?"

"It was as you and Bennett thought. There was an operation buried in the DIA. Bennett explained all that to me when I thought he was my friend," Cole added.

"Jesus."

"They got the first tape before he could, so he made himself out to be protecting me. Somehow he knew about the second tape."

Jim shut his eyes tightly. "It was a mistake to tell him it existed. I should have known better."

"He figured if he kept watching me," Cole went on, "I'd lead him to it."

"And once he made the decision to go for the money, he couldn't take the chance that I'd get up and walk out of here." Cole's father was working through the scenario. "He didn't want to kill me, because if you didn't lead him to the second tape, he figured he might be able to get me to talk. So he had the General bolt me to this damn bed," Jim moaned, pulling weakly at the shackles again for a few seconds.

"Easy, Dad." Cole could hear the congestion in his father's lungs. It was thick and horrible—enough to make Tori turn her head away and put a hand to her mouth.

Jim was having a difficult time sucking in air as he gasped, "Get out of here, Cole. Now. I'm not kidding. And take Tori with you. Bennett's going to be back here soon. I heard them talking. He was just going into town to buy a few things."

"We've got to get you out of these shackles first."

"Forget me!" The cough was back. "It would take hours to cut me out of these things," he sputtered. "And unless you've got a bazooka in your vehicle, don't bother trying to break them by shooting them. That won't work. They're too thick and strong. We use these things in the DIA. You'll need keys."

"They have to be here." Cole glanced at Tori. "Search this room," he ordered as he stood up.

"Right."

Cole hurried back into the main room, knelt down beside the General, rifled through the man's pockets but found nothing. As he searched, the General began to moan. Cole sprinted to the door on the far wall, which led into the garage. He yanked it open and peered around in the dimness until he found a piece of rope lying on the garage floor next to a tire. He picked up the rope, brought it back to where the General lay and bound him tightly. Next, Cole moved into the kitchen, still searching for the keys, but he found nothing there. Finally he tried the dresser in the first bedroom. He found no keys, but in the top drawer was a revolver. He scooped it up and returned to the bedroom in which his father lay prisoner.

"Did you find the keys?" he asked Tori.

"No." She shook her head.

"Get out of here," Jim said. Veins bulged in his arms and neck as he struggled.

"I can't leave you, Dad."

"You can and you will, you son of a bitch!" he yelled.

Cole recoiled as if he'd actually been hit with something.

Tori saw the hurt in Cole's eyes. "Jim, you don't need to talk to—"

"Shut up, Tori. I told you to make sure he got money for that thing. I haven't done many good things in my life." Jim gazed steely-eyed at Cole. "I've killed people who didn't need to be killed. Your mother is dead because of me. And I've stayed away from you my whole life because I was afraid of finding out what you thought of me. I'm not the kind of man you can be proud of, Cole. That's the reality, harsh as it is." He was laboring with his breathing again, trying desperately to suck in air. "But I can begin to make amends with that tape. The public can see what really happened that day in Dealey Plaza. I can help Tori with her career. And you, Cole, I can get you a great deal of money. It doesn't come close to making up for my absence all these years, but at least it's something. That tape is my legacy. I'm ashamed of what I've become, but if the tape makes it into the right hands and I can do something for you, then at least I'll feel like my life wasn't a total waste." He coughed once more. "Now leave me. Please."

"I'm going to save you, Dad."

"No one can save me at this point, Cole. I'm going to hell. Straight to hell without passing go or collecting two hundred dollars. I'm gonna burn, Cole, and the match is already lit."

"Huh?" A chill and then a wave of heat passed through Cole's body. The match was already lit. "You mean you're dying?"

"We're all dying, Cole. I'm just dying a little sooner than the rest of the world."

Tori brought her hands to her mouth. "Oh no."

"Oh *yes*."

"Of what?" Cole asked.

"Hodgkin's disease."

"That's treatable."

"Not at this point. I found out about it six months ago. Now I've got a few months to live, tops."

"But doctors could have treated you."

"I didn't want to be treated," Jim gasped. He convulsed into another coughing fit. He had contracted pneumonia in his weakened condition. "Get out." Tiny drops of blood appeared at the corners of his mouth. "Get that tape someplace safe, *then* come back for me if you really want to."

"I—"

"Cole! We have to go! He's right. There's nothing else we can do." Tori looked up at him. "We've got to get out of here."

"Thank you," Jim said sarcastically. "If you're too stupid to figure it out for yourself, boy, listen to the woman."

Cole turned his head to the side, as if to deflect the remark.

Tori grabbed Cole by the arms. "Don't worry about what he's saying or how he's saying it. He's just trying to protect you. He doesn't mean it."

"The hell I don't."

Cole glanced at his father. "All right, Dad," he said

calmly. "The hell with you." He placed the revolver he had taken from the dresser drawer in the other room on the bed beside his father's right hand. There was enough slack in the shackle that he would be able to fire it if he needed to. Cole had checked the gun for ammunition and found that it was fully loaded. "You might need that." Cole turned to Tori. "Come on, let's go." He walked from the room without looking back.

Tori bent down and kissed Jim on the cheek. "You didn't have to be that harsh with him."

"Yes, I did," he whispered.

24

COLE AND TORI MOVED PAST THE GENERAL, NOW WIDE awake and struggling against the ropes, and into the garage. Cole had seen another vehicle as he found the ropes he would use to tie up the General. It was an aging black Bronco. Its fenders were rusted completely through and its tires were caked with mud. Cole yanked open the Bronco's door and checked the ignition. There were no keys.

"We're going to take this thing down the mountain?" Tori asked. "It doesn't look as if it could make it."

"The alternative is to climb back up the mountain, then go down the other side to the Jeep," Cole answered curtly. He was visibly upset. The meeting with his father hadn't gone as he had envisioned. "That would take a couple of hours. If we take this Bronco instead, we'll be back on the interstate in fifteen minutes."

"But what if—"

"What if Bennett Smith is coming back up the

mountain while we're heading down?" Cole finished the question for her. "That's a chance we'll have to take." Cole tossed the General's gun onto the dashboard of the Bronco. "And it hasn't been all that long since Bennett left. He probably hasn't even gotten to town yet. By the time he gets back here, we'll be halfway to Helena."

Tori hopped in the passenger seat as Cole reached beneath the steering wheel, popped the hood latch, then moved to a switch on the wall and pushed it. With a grinding noise the garage door began to rise in front of the Bronco and sunlight bathed the interior.

"Did you find the keys to this thing while you were looking for the key to your father's shackles?" she asked.

"No." Cole raised the hood, moved to the side of the Bronco and leaned over the engine.

Tori hunched down and gazed through the opening between the dashboard and the raised hood, trying to see what he was doing. Suddenly the engine roared to life and she jumped back, startled.

Cole slammed the hood closed, removed his backpack and threw it on the backseat, jumped in and thrust the Bronco into first gear.

"Hot-wired the car, huh?"

"Yes."

"You're a man of many talents, Cole Egan."

Cole had already popped the clutch and punched the accelerator. They were hurtling down the winding driveway, skidding on loose gravel as he navigated the unfamiliar road.

"Look out!" Tori yelled, clutching the handle above the door as they careened around a tight turn and the ground on her side fell steeply away toward the canyon floor several hundred feet below. She turned her head and buried her face in her shoulder. "I hate roller coasters!" she yelled.

Suddenly the white sedan they had seen leave the General's house appeared in front of them as they raced around another bend. The sedan was less than a hundred feet away.

"He must have seen the Jeep!" Cole yelled.

The sedan skidded to a stop, blocking the Bronco's path, and Bennett Smith jumped out. He knelt behind the open driver's-side door, leveled his gun at them and fired twice. The first shot smashed one of the Bronco's headlights and the second smacked the middle of the windshield and tore out the back window. The windshield didn't shatter, but it cracked so that it looked like a spiderweb and Cole had to strain to see out.

As they bore down on the white sedan, Cole jerked the steering wheel left, toward the mountain. It was his only choice. There was nothing to the right but a vertical drop and certain death. All four tires left the ground as the Bronco hurdled the deep drainage ditch paralleling the road. Then the left fender and the front left tire dug into the soft hillside, pitching Cole and Tori forward. Almost instantly, the Bronco's momentum exploded it up and out of the dirt, throwing Cole and Tori back against their seats as Cole instinctively pulled the steering wheel to the right.

Bennett rose up and fired several more times over the sedan's roof as the Bronco screamed past, but the bullets ricocheted harmlessly off the vehicle's doors.

Now the Bronco was tilting precariously to the right, at the same angle as the mountainside. Cole and Tori screamed. It seemed inevitable that they would roll. But the right front of the Bronco slammed into the bottom of the drainage ditch, tearing the bumper from the chassis, and then they were soaring skyward. Though Cole frantically pulled on the steering wheel, it was a useless effort because all four tires were off the ground and the vehicle hurtled toward the edge of the cliff. When the Bronco at last bounced onto the gravel road, it didn't turn.

Tori closed her eyes. The front of the Bronco was headed straight for the precipice. She was certain they were going down, but at the last second the front tires caught the side of the road, spinning the rear end of the Bronco crazily out over the edge of the cliff. The passenger door popped open as Tori slammed against it, and her legs were suddenly outside the vehicle. Desperately she clung to the overhead handle. For what seemed an eternity they slid forward sideways, the front of the vehicle barely hanging on, tires spewing grass and small rocks over the cliff.

Cole gunned the accelerator once more and suddenly they were back up on the road, all four tires making full contact with the ground. A few quick swerves and he was again in control of the vehicle. He reached across the passenger seat, grabbed Tori by the belt and pulled her back inside. "Close the door!" he yelled over the rush of the wind through the front seat.

But she was paralyzed, unable to move.

"Close it!" he shouted again, glancing into the rearview mirror. Bennett had already scrambled back into the white sedan and was turning it around on the narrow road. "Come on, Tori!"

Finally she responded, reaching out and yanking the door shut. "I take it that was Bennett Smith!" she screamed.

"Yes."

"Nice man."

"Uh-huh."

"I thought I was dead." She shook her head. "I thought I was going out of the car."

But Cole wasn't listening. He was analyzing their options. They could head to Powell, which was ten minutes away on the interstate, and hope to get help at the outfitter's shop where they had purchased the binoculars. But there was no telling what kind of fire-power Bennett might have in the sedan. He might have automatic weapons. If he came into the shop blazing, the General's handgun wasn't going to be much of a deterrent.

They could head out across the open meadow at the bottom of the hill across from the General's driveway entrance. The Bronco would easily negotiate the terrain, but the Missouri River was out there. The big wide bend was a quarter mile from the interstate, surrounding the meadow on three sides, and Bennett might be able to pick them off with a rifle as they tried to swim across the river.

Or they could get out onto I-15 and drive to Helena, which was only twenty minutes away at ninety miles an hour. If he could keep Bennett at bay as they raced down the interstate, they might be able to make it to a Helena police station. The DIA might have put out a bulletin, and he might lose possession of the Dealey Tape, but at least they would be afforded protection. If he could elude Bennett on the way to Helena, he might even be able to hold on to the tape.

Cole steered the Bronco down the driveway. It was straighter, wider, and less steep here. Suddenly the canyon floor seemed to rise up to meet them and they were tearing down a long straightaway toward the paved frontage road that led to the interstate. He glanced in the rearview mirror but could see nothing through the cloud of dust the Bronco was kicking up. "I'm going to head toward Helena when we reach the interstate!"

Tori nodded, still clutching the handle over the door. "Whatever."

Cole managed a smile. "Are you having fun yet?"

"Yeah, sure."

As the Bronco reached the paved road and Cole whipped the steering wheel left, he looked back down the General's long driveway. He could make out the white sedan racing through the swirling dust now. Bennett was no more than a quarter of a mile back. "This is going to be a helluva ride, Tori!"

"It couldn't get any worse than it's already been."

"You're wrong."

She shuddered. "Just don't hang me out over a cliff again. Please."

"I'll try to keep that in mind," Cole yelled as he swung the Bronco off the frontage road and up the entrance ramp to the interstate. He slammed the stick shift into fourth gear and gunned the engine, surprised at the vehicle's power. The thing was faster than he had anticipated. As he pressed the accelerator to the floor, the speedometer's needle quickly passed sixty. He glanced into the side mirror. Bennett was just reaching the bottom of the entrance ramp. Cole looked back at the speedometer. It was approaching eighty. Then he noticed the fuel gauge hovering on empty.

He slammed his fist on the dashboard and Tori jumped in her seat. "Hey, that's *my* thing. What's the matter?"

"We have hardly any gas," he yelled. "At this speed we'll burn fuel very fast."

"How far away is Helena?"

"Thirty miles, give or take a few."

"How far can we go on what we have?"

"Thirty miles, give or take a few."

As the speedometer climbed past ninety, the fuel light came on. Cole checked the white sedan in the mirror. At least Bennett wasn't gaining. "Listen to me!" he yelled to Tori over the whine of the engine. "If we run out of fuel, we're going to split up."

"No!" she screamed.

"It's the only option." Through the cracked windshield, Cole made out the shape of a truck ahead. It was the first vehicle they had encountered since entering the interstate. He glanced in the mirror once more. Bennett was slowly making up ground now that they were heading up a long incline. "He can't chase both of us. If I pull over, you take the tape. He'll probably chase me. He'll figure I have it." Cole checked the mirror again. The white sedan was less than a hundred yards back now.

A highway sign flew past. "Twenty-two miles to Helena!" Tori yelled.

"Keep your head down!" Cole shouted. "He might start shooting."

Cole suddenly noticed that the General's gun was gone. He checked the floor but couldn't see it near his feet. "Look for that gun I threw up on the dash when we were leaving the General's house!" he yelled.

"I thought you said for me to keep my head down."

"You can do two things at once!"

Bennett was only fifty yards back now. As Cole guided the Bronco abreast of the eighteen-wheeler, a bullet screamed through the Bronco and hit the windshield just over Tori's head as she leaned down, searching the floor on her side of the vehicle for the gun. Glass sprayed forward, then blew back into the front seat with the gale-force wind. Instinctively Cole raised his arms in front of his face and the Bronco lurched to the right, glancing off the back tires of the truck. He slammed on the brakes, slowing from ninety to forty in seconds.

Bennett jerked his steering wheel to the left to avoid the Bronco, and the sedan slid into the wide grass median, spinning out of control.

The truck driver leaned on his horn as Cole regained control of the Bronco and sped past.

"Why don't we try to get help from the truck driver?" Tori yelled above the wind whipping through the Bronco.

"What's he going to do for us?"

"Give us a ride."

Cole shook his head. "By the time we stop and get in his truck, Bennett would have caught up with us. On an incline like this, it would take that truck miles to get moving at any kind of speed again. We'd be sitting ducks. Obviously Bennett has weapons he isn't shy about using. Besides, if you were that guy and just saw what happened, would you stop?"

"You're right. Probably not."

A quarter mile later they crested the incline. In front of them the interstate headed down a long sweeping curve and into a narrow gorge cut by the river. Tall pines covered the rocky slopes, which rose almost straight up on either side of them.

"If we had to run out of gas, this would be the place to do it," Cole yelled above the roar of the wind. "He'd have a helluva time finding us in here."

"Then why don't we just ditch the Bronco now and head into the woods?"

Cole shook his head as he spotted the white sedan in the rearview mirror, far behind them. "No." He didn't tell her that Bennett was once again gaining on them.

The interstate moved away from the river as they climbed out of the gorge. Even as they climbed they were still exceeding ninety miles an hour. Then the double-lane highway crested a rise and suddenly Helena lay before them in the middle of a wide, treeless valley.

"We're going to make it, Cole!" Tori screamed.

Cole eyed the fuel gauge warily. It seemed as if the orange warning light was growing brighter with each passing mile.

Tori noticed him watching the gauge. "We could coast to Helena from here."

"We could if Bennett wasn't back there."

Tori turned around quickly and looked out through the smashed back window. "I thought he went off the road."

"He did, but he got the car back on the highway."

As they headed down the long, gentle descent into Helena, the Bronco picked up speed. The speedometer nudged a hundred, but still the white sedan gained. There were a few cars on the road now as they passed the first exit into the outskirts of the small city.

"Why didn't you take that exit?" Tori asked.

"It's too open out here. We've still got a good lead on him, so maybe we can get downtown, ditch the Bronco and lose him on foot, then rent another car. I don't want to go to the cops if I can help it."

"Why don't we go to the airport? I know there's one here. I flew into it a few weeks ago."

"No way. If he loses us, it'll be the first place he looks."

"If we can lose him, maybe we should hide the tape in a locker or something. There must be a bus station out here. I can call my people in New York after we stash the tape there, and they'll send some muscle out here to protect us."

Before Cole could respond, the engine went dead, suffocated by a lack of fuel. Cole pumped the accelerator, but nothing happened. He pounded the steering wheel as he checked the mirror. Bennett was racing up behind them now, just a few hundred yards back.

"Hold on!" Cole yelled. He stepped on the brake as hard as he could and the wheels locked. Instantly the smell of burning rubber rose up into the Bronco. "Follow me!" he shouted as the Bronco skidded to a stop. He reached into the backseat, grabbed the backpack, thrust open the door and bolted around the front of the Bronco and up the slope toward a large strip mall overlooking the interstate.

Tori leaped from the Bronco and scampered up the slope as the white sedan skidded to a stop behind the Bronco. "Where are we going?" she yelled.

"Just follow me!"

Suddenly he was down, his foot snagged in a hole hidden by the long grass. "Jesus!" Pain seared through his ankle—the same ankle he had injured in Manhattan while racing to the library.

"Come on!" Tori helped Cole struggle to his feet as Bennett lumbered up the slope behind them, reloading his pistol as he ran.

Pain engulfed Cole's entire leg, but he put his head down and hobbled forward. Bennett was less than fifty yards behind them as they climbed over the guardrail at the top of the hill together and took off across the parking lot.

"There!" Cole pointed at a video store in the middle of the mall. "That's where we're going."

They ran through rows of parked cars and past people pushing shopping carts. Despite the bystanders, Bennett began shooting. Bullets glanced off hoods and windshields, and people screamed and fell to the pavement for cover.

Cole limped into the video store. It was fairly small, offering only a few thousand titles. He hobbled past several puzzled shoppers to the back of the counter.

"Hey!" The manager stepped in front of Cole as he headed toward the back room where the videotapes were stored in plain black cases. "You can't go back there."

"Get out of my way!" Cole pushed the smaller man to the floor roughly and disappeared into the storage room.

"Call the police!" the manager yelled to an assistant in front of the counter as he picked himself up. Then he pointed at Tori, who stood in the middle of the store. "Your friend's in a lot of trouble, lady."

"You have no idea how much trouble." She was gasping for breath. "So are you."

"Huh?" The manager glanced toward the front door as a woman screamed and Bennett Smith charged inside, gun up and fully reloaded.

"Where's Cole?" he hissed, moving directly to Tori. He paid no attention to the customers and employees who were sprinting for the door.

"I don't know," she said defiantly.

Bennett grabbed Tori by the hair, spun her around so that her back was against his chest and leveled the gun at her head. "Does he still have the tape?"

"I don't know," she moaned.

Bennett pulled her hair hard, lifting her off her feet. "Does he have it?"

"You're hurting me!" she screamed.

"Let her go, Bennett!" Cole stood in the doorway

to the storage room. He tossed the empty backpack onto the counter. In the distance he could hear the faint sound of a siren. "The Dealey Tape is in one of the cases back there." He nodded toward the storage room behind him, then glanced at the front door. "It sounds as if the police are going to be here in about two minutes. I don't think you can find it and get out of here that fast."

For several moments Bennett stared at Cole, then slowly he relaxed his grip on Tori and dropped the barrel of the gun from her head.

"It's over, Bennett," Cole said loudly. "Over!"

But a smile spread slowly across Bennett's face. Suddenly he grabbed Tori by the hair again and hustled her forward toward Cole. "It's far from over," he snarled, pushing Tori ahead so she was directly in front of Cole. Then he brought the gun back up to her head. "Get out of the way, Cole!"

"Do something, Cole!" Tori screamed.

Before Cole could move, Bennett pointed the gun at him and fired. The bullet blew past Cole's left ear. He felt a rush of hot air like a steam pipe bursting right beside his face, and smelled gunpowder. Instinctively he tumbled over the counter and dropped to the floor. Then he heard the door slam shut.

He was back on his feet and around the counter quickly. He wrenched the doorknob to the right and pushed, but the door leading to the storage room—and the Dealey Tape—was locked from the inside.

"Hold it right there!"

Cole whipped around. Standing in the store's doorway was a lone Helena city policeman, gun drawn.

"Hands up!" the young policeman yelled. He was nervous. Cole could see it all over his face. His eyes were flashing around and his voice was strained.

"Officer, we've got a hostage situation," Cole said calmly.

"Get your hands up!" The policeman moved forward, hunched over at the waist, the revolver pointed at Cole. "Don't talk until I tell you to!"

Slowly Cole raised his hands. He could hear Bennett rifling through the tapes. Empty cases and cassettes were crashing to the floor behind the storage room door. If he somehow found the Dealey Tape, hidden in a cassette case marked *Reds,* he'd head out the back door and be gone forever.

The policeman was only a few feet away now. In the distance Cole could hear more sirens. In seconds the place would be crawling with cops, and a standoff would ensue if Bennett hadn't found the Dealey Tape by that point. The officers would surround the store and call in special forces—which would take another thirty minutes—and by the time everyone was in place, Bennett would have found the unmarked tape inside the *Reds* case. Then he'd negotiate his way out by using Tori as trade bait. Cole could see the scenario developing so clearly.

"Get down on the floor!" the policeman shouted at Cole.

As Cole began to drop to his knees, he chopped the back of the officer's wrist with his hand. The gun fell to the floor, and as the officer reached to retrieve it, Cole smashed his chin with a powerful uppercut. The policeman toppled backward, unconscious.

Cole grabbed the revolver and moved toward the storage room. As he aimed at the door, there was a loud explosion from within. Instantly Cole fired twice into the lock, blowing it apart, then slammed his shoulder into the door and fell into the room. He rolled twice, smashed against a rack of tapes and aimed in the direction of the shot.

He was unprepared for the sight that met his eyes at the end of the officer's gun. Bennett lay on the floor near the store's back door, blood pouring from a wound in his chest, the *Reds* cassette case on the floor beside him. Tori sat on the floor a few feet away, one wrist chained to a rack of tapes by a pair of handcuffs, the other holding the General's gun which she had slipped into her jacket just before she and Cole had entered the interstate.

"What the hell?" Cole rose unsteadily to his feet.

"He found the Dealey Tape!" Tori yelled. "He was going to escape out the back door. I couldn't let him do that, not after all we've been through." Her breath was coming in shallow gasps. "Get the key to the handcuffs. It's in his pants pocket. Get me out of these things. Come on, Cole! Hurry!"

Bennett moaned and pulled himself into a sitting position against the wall. Cole whipped his gun around, covering Bennett, searching for a gun in the other man's hand. But Bennett was unarmed. Cole spotted Bennett's gun lying against the far wall, where it had fallen when Tori shot him. Bennett's head was resting against the cinderblock wall and a tiny rivulet of blood was oozing down his chin.

Cole's eyes flashed back to the doorway. Policemen would be spilling through that door in a matter of seconds. They'd arrest him, and there would go any chance of getting the Dealey Tape into the proper hands and collecting the money. The DIA would hear of this incident, and the tape would be gone forever.

Cole bolted to where Bennett sat against the wall and picked up the case, checking to make certain the Dealey Tape was inside.

"Cole!" Tori screamed. "Don't leave me here!"

He gazed at her. She was pointing the General's gun in his direction. "What the hell are you doing?"

"Get the key to the handcuffs!"

He blinked. The sirens were closing in.

"She's DIA," Bennett groaned. "Don't let her out of those handcuffs."

"What?" Cole turned to face Bennett.

"Don't listen to him," Tori hissed. "He's trying to delay you until the cops get here. If he can't have that tape, he doesn't want you to have it."

"She's DIA. I recognize her, Cole," Bennett whispered. It was all he could do to speak. "She's part of the operation I told you about. She works for a man named William Seward. He runs Operation Snowfall. The one I told you about on the river."

Cole glanced back at Tori. She was still pointing the gun straight at him. She had smashed the General's head by throwing the rock through the window, then run around the house to the front door. The natural reaction should have been to run away. Now she had shot a man. Maybe she *was* DIA.

"Get the key, Cole," Tori urged, still aiming the gun at him.

"Check under the fingernail of her left index finger," Bennett said weakly, coughing. "Check for the brand."

Cole glanced at Tori's left hand, chained to the rack of tapes.

Tori shook her head as she leveled the gun at him. "If you leave here without me, you'll do the deal with someone else, Cole. Your father wanted me to get credit for finding that tape. I've been through way too much to let you walk out that door without me and sell it to someone else. Take a step for that door,

Cole, and I'll shoot you, I swear." The gun shook in her hand and tears streamed down her cheeks.

"It's all an act," Bennett spoke as loudly as he could. "She's DIA, Cole."

"Liar!" Tori screamed. "You want to see what's under my fingernail? Is that what you want, Cole? Will that convince you?" She held out the hand chained to the rack. "Is this the finger?" She made a fist except for the index finger.

"Tori, don't!" Cole yelled.

But it was too late. She shoved the finger in her mouth and jammed her lower front teeth under the nail. The nail tore neatly away from one side and she screamed in agony. Blood poured from the spot, but she sucked it away and held up the finger. There was no brand.

"You bastard, Bennett." Cole reached down and searched Bennett's pockets. It took him a few moments, but he found the key, scrambled to Tori, released her from the handcuffs, pulled her to her feet and hugged her tightly. "You're incredible."

"We've got to get out of here!" she implored.

"Right." Cole grabbed her by the hand and pulled her out the back door.

Bennett's chin dropped to his chest as he watched them disappear out the door. He could feel his lungs filling with blood, and he would die whether or not the doctors at the Helena hospital could save him. If he survived the operation, agents would find him and there would simply be another, more accurately aimed bullet.

He crawled across the floor, listening to the policemen shouting to each other as they entered the video store. As he reached the gun lying against the far wall, the first officer moved through the doorway behind the counter and into the storage room, gun drawn.

"Freeze!" the officer shouted.

But Bennett had already reached the gun. In one smooth motion he picked it up, pressed the barrel to his temple and fired.

25

TORI FOLLOWED COLE AS HE HOBBLED QUICKLY across the blacktop and into the woods behind the strip mall. It was deserted here behind the stores. There seemed to be no one milling about the Dumpsters and semi-trailers. In the cover of the woods, Cole turned right, toward the sound of cars on the interstate a quarter of a mile away.

Tori held her left index finger tightly in her right hand, trying to stop the bleeding as she stuck close to Cole. The fingertip felt as if it were on fire. She took her hand away from the finger, glanced at the nail and cringed. The nail rose slowly until it was standing straight up. It was completely torn away from the skin on one side, still attached on the other.

"Where are we going?" she asked.

"Back to the Bronco," Cole replied as he limped around trees, still clutching the Dealey Tape.

"The Bronco doesn't have any fuel. Remember, smartass?" She was furious with him. The pain in her finger was almost unbearable, and he was to blame for it.

Cole didn't answer. He just kept going.

A few seconds later they reached the edge of the interstate. Cars flashed past as Cole searched the roadway for police cruisers. It was almost five o'clock in the afternoon, and traffic had picked up as people headed home from work. A few hundred yards north of where they stood, the Bronco was still parked on the side of the road with Bennett's white sedan directly behind it. However, they saw no police cars.

"We're going down there," Cole said, pointing at the two vehicles. "You're driving because I can't. My ankle's killing me. Plus you'll be able to drive without having to worry about being recognized. That cop at the video store never got a look at you. The police won't have your description unless one of the customers in the store when we first ran inside gives it to them, and I doubt we have to worry about that. Those people were too busy trying to get out of there to remember any details. The cops will be searching for me. If we see any police, I'll get down in the seat. They won't be looking for a woman driving by herself."

"What about roadblocks?" Tori asked.

"I think the only place the police could set up any roadblocks would be on the interstates. There are too many other roads to cover. Montana is too big. And we're not going to stay on the interstate very long. We're going to travel on back roads and head south toward Bozeman, then around Bozeman and east to Livingston. After that we'll head over to Billings. From Billings we'll fly to Minneapolis. There should be a plane going to the Twin Cities in the morning.

From Minneapolis we'll go to New York and get this tape to your boss."

Tori glanced up. "What happened to me having nothing but the right of first refusal? I thought you were going to shop your piece of gold around so you could get the best offer, then come back to me to see if I could match it."

Cole shook his head and gestured at her finger, still bleeding profusely. "After your performance at the video store, you've earned yourself an exclusive on the tape. Ten million dollars is more than enough. In fact, I'm going to share some of the cash with you. If you hadn't stopped Bennett on his way out the back of that place, this tape would be long gone right now, and so would my ten million." He grimaced as he looked at her hand again. "I don't know if I could have ripped off my own fingernail. That's one of the most courageous things I've ever seen anyone do."

"One of the dumbest too."

"No, it wasn't. I couldn't trust you any more than I do right now." Cole glanced up into her eyes. Despite the hell she'd endured in the last two days, she still looked damn good. "You're something else."

"Thanks." She managed a thin smile.

Cole touched her arm gently. "Let's get down to the car. In a few minutes there'll be cops and dogs all over these woods."

Tori grabbed his arm as he started forward. "But I don't understand—the Bronco is out of gas."

He jammed a hand into his pocket and pulled out a set of keys, holding them up for her to see. "I found these when I took the key to the handcuffs out of Bennett's pocket."

She laughed despite the pain throbbing from her

finger all the way up her left arm to her shoulder. "You have an answer for everything."

"Not always." He tossed the keys to her, then limped down the slope to the interstate. A minute later they were in the white sedan and were moving out into traffic.

"What if Bennett tells the police to search for this car?" Tori asked, her eyes darting from rearview mirror to side mirror and back to the windshield in search of police cruisers. "He must have seen you take the keys out of his pocket. He could give them the license plate number of this car and a description of me."

"Bennett won't be a problem."

"Why not?"

"Did you hear a gunshot as we were running across the blacktop behind the stores?"

She nodded. Now that she thought about it, she did recall hearing a blast come from inside the video store as they were sprinting out the back. "Yes, I did."

"Bennett's not going to be giving information to anyone unless he's a very poor shot from point-blank range. Or his head is even harder than I think it is."

"What are you talking about?"

"Bennett's dead. I'm pretty sure that gunshot was him committing suicide. As I was going through his pockets looking for the key to the handcuffs, he asked me to leave his gun on the floor. He wanted to die on his own terms. I have no doubt he did that."

Tori gazed forward, as if in a trance. It was incredible what they had been through.

"Turn here." Cole pointed at an EXIT sign.

Tori guided the car down the gentle incline to the traffic light at the bottom of the hill.

"Go left," Cole directed. "South."

As she pulled the car out into the intersection, they

suddenly heard a loud siren. "Where is it?" she screamed.

"I don't know, I don't know!" Cole looked behind and to the side, searching for the police car.

Suddenly they saw the ambulance coming at them from the opposite direction. Tori eased off to the side of the road as the emergency vehicle raced past.

"I don't know about you, Cole," Tori said quietly, "but I've had enough of this. Let's pull over and I'll call my boss at NBC. He'll have bodyguards meet us. They'll fly a private jet out for us. I'm sure they could have one in Billings by the time we get there."

"Great." Cole smiled. "Now we're talking. I like the idea of a private plane and bodyguards. But first let's put some distance between the Helena police force and us. Then you can call your boss."

An hour later Tori guided the white sedan off the road and into a gas station in the tiny town of Cardwell, forty miles south of Helena. Tori used the pay phone first, calling New York with the calling card she had purchased in Billings early that morning. When she was finished, she trotted back to the car, a huge smile on her face.

"What are you so happy about?" Cole asked as he pulled himself from the car. His ankle was swollen, and he winced as he put pressure on it.

"I can't believe our luck. I tracked down Ray Burgess at his home in Greenwich, Connecticut. Ray's an executive vice president at NBC News." She was giddy. "It's after eight o'clock in the east. He was about to leave his house for some charity event. I told him the whole story. He couldn't believe it. I've never heard him so excited."

"Great."

"And I've got good news for you."

"What's that?"

"He said we'd pay you *fifteen* million dollars." She nodded at the tape in Cole's hand. "He wants to make certain that becomes the property of NBC News."

"You're kidding."

"No, I'm not." Her smile disappeared. "Although I'm a little disappointed in you."

"What do you mean?"

"You still don't trust me."

"Huh?" He didn't understand. "Oh, the tape." It had been a reflex action for him to reach in the back for the Dealey Tape as he was getting out of the car to head for the pay phone. "I'm sorry." He placed the tape on the passenger seat.

Tori handed him the calling card and watched him hobble to the pay phone. When he had entered the booth she moved back to the driver's-side door, eased behind the wheel and reached up to turn the key. But it was gone. She shook her head. Cole didn't trust anyone completely, even if he said he did. It just wasn't in him.

Cole pulled the pay phone door closed behind him. His first call was to the Helena police. He gave them detailed directions to the General's house outside of Powell, informing them that a cult suicide had just taken place in the house, knowing they would be headed out there immediately with that kind of information. Then he dialed the number of the Andersons' house in Duluth.

Tori searched the glove compartment and the backseat for tissues or a towel but found nothing. She shrugged her shoulders and began to bite the nail away as close to the skin as possible. In the end it would be less painful to tear it completely off. As she bit down, Cole opened the passenger-side door, leaned inside and picked up the Dealey Tape, then let himself slowly down onto the white sedan's passenger seat.

"Is everything all right?" she asked.

He didn't answer.

"Cole?"

"Yeah," he mumbled.

"Hey, I've got some more good news," she offered. "Ray Burgess said he could have a private jet in Billings by midnight. NBC has a plane on call in Chicago. We'll be in New York City by daybreak in the east. He said he'd send along some bodyguards, too."

"Great," Cole answered quietly.

"What's wrong?"

"That private jet is going to have to make a stop between Billings and New York."

"What do you mean?"

Cole pulled the car keys from his shirt pocket and handed them to Tori. "They've got a hostage."

"*Who* has a hostage?" She grabbed the keys from Cole.

"A covert operation inside the Defense Intelligence Agency," he said quietly. "The people Bennett accused you of being part of back at the video store."

"And?"

"And they'll release the hostage if I hand them the last copy of the Dealey Tape."

Tori gazed at him for several moments. "Who is the hostage?"

"A woman named Nicki Anderson," Cole said grimly. "A woman I care about very much."

Tori exhaled heavily. "Where does the plane have to stop?"

"Minneapolis."

"I guess we better get going." She turned the key and the engine roared to life.

Cole said almost nothing for three hours as he studied the road map he had purchased at the gas station in Cardwell. He made just muted grunts as he guided Tori over the back roads of south-central Montana. He had been so stupid. Of course they would take Nicki hostage. Bennett had known about her, why wouldn't Magee and his superiors? Cole put a hand to his head and rubbed his eyes. He needed sleep, but he couldn't get any knowing Nicki was in their hands.

For a long while Tori said nothing as Cole stared out into the darkness and the miles passed. Finally she spoke up. Maybe it would be good for him to talk. "There's something I don't understand about what happened at the video store."

"What's that?"

"When Bennett grabbed me and pushed me toward the storage room, you were standing in the way. He shot at you, but he missed. He was five feet away from you at most. How could he have missed you from that short a distance?"

"He missed me on purpose," Cole answered indifferently. "I guess down deep he didn't really want to kill me. That's why I left the gun for him. That and the fact that as I was looking for the key to the handcuffs, he whispered to me that I should take the keys to this car."

"You mean you didn't just happen on them?"

Cole shook his head. "I suppose there was still some loyalty left inside Bennett after all," he murmured as the lights of Billings appeared on the eastern horizon. "So, are you willing to help me one more time?" Cole asked. "Will you fly me to Minneapolis, or do I drop you off at the Billings airport and keep heading east by myself?"

Tori took a deep breath. "These people sound pretty serious."

"They are," Cole assured her, still silently berating himself for not anticipating their move on Nicki.

"I guess there isn't much of a chance that you'll head into a confrontation with them and come out with both Nicki and the Dealey Tape."

"Not much," Cole agreed.

She glanced at her bloodied finger in the dashboard lights. The pain had subsided somewhat over the past few hours. "What the hell. Let's go for it."

26

THE GULFSTREAM IV ROARED SOUTH OVER THE MINnesota River and touched down gently on the Minneapolis-St. Paul International Airport runway at 3:37 A.M. Central Standard Time. The plane taxied for several minutes, then coasted to a stop at the private terminal. Cole descended the steps of the plane slowly. The frosty night air was laced with the smell of jet fuel. He was refreshed after sleeping two hours during the flight from Billings, but the ankle was still killing him and he limped noticeably as he made his way into the terminal and headed for the airport's main entrance.

"I need to go to the Sofitel in Bloomington," Cole instructed the cab driver as he slid onto the seat. Through her tears, Nicki's mother had managed to give him a Washington, D.C., number when he had called from the pay phone in Cardwell. It was a number the man who had kidnapped Nicki had instructed her mother to give Cole as she lay bound to the bed. From the Gulfstream Cole had called the Washington

number and a monotone voice had directed him to the
Sofitel, a hotel located on the outskirts of Minneapolis.
There he was to wait in the lobby for further instructions. The voice had warned him to inform no one of
what had happened. If he did, Nicki would die.

Twenty minutes later the cab pulled up in front of
the Sofitel's main entrance. Cole paid the fare with
money Tori had given him, and limped inside. The
hotel lobby was pin-drop quiet and empty except for
a woman behind the registration counter who glanced
at Cole suspiciously as he eased back into a comfortable chair. Almost instantly a man Cole had never
seen before walked directly to the chair.

"Come with me," the man ordered.

Cole followed the man to the elevator bank, hesitat-
ing in front of the open doors.

"Let's go." He saw Cole's trepidation. "Nothing's
going to happen."

Cole stepped into the car and the doors closed behind him as the man pushed the button for the third
floor. The man said nothing as the car rose quickly
and the doors reopened.

"This way."

Cole followed the man down the long hallway, their
shoes padding softly over the thick carpet. After passing four doors, the man stopped in front of the fifth
and knocked. Several seconds later the door opened
a few inches and someone peered out through the
crack. The door closed quickly as the person inside
removed the chain, then opened again. Cole moved
into the suite in front of the man who had met him
in the lobby.

William Seward sat at one end of a long couch in
the suite's living room smoking a cigarette, and General Zahn, dressed in civilian clothes, sat at the other

end. Seward took a last puff from the cigarette, snuffed it out, and stood up. "I'm William Seward," he said without offering his hand.

"You're DIA, head of Operation Snowfall."

"How the—"

"Insider information," Cole interrupted. "Remember, I work on Wall Street." It was information Bennett had gasped at the video store when he accused Tori of being with the DIA.

Seward glanced to the right as the doorknob to the bedroom turned.

Cole followed Seward's glance. His eyes narrowed as the bedroom door opened and Commander Magee stepped into the living room. "Hello, Magee," Cole said calmly. "I'm surprised to see you. I thought I tied you up pretty tightly in Wisconsin. How did you escape?"

"Fuck yourself."

"That's not an easy thing to do."

"Enough." Seward held up his hand. "I assume the tape isn't on you, Mr. Egan. You've proved yourself quite a resourceful adversary. I can't imagine you'd just come up here and hand it over."

"You're right."

"Do you have the tape in your possession?"

"Let's say, under my control."

"What is the plan?" Seward asked.

"We'll make the exchange at the Minneapolis airport at six forty-five this morning." Cole checked his watch. "In a little over two hours. Nicki Anderson for the tape. We'll make the trade in front of baggage carousel number two."

"That's unacceptable." Seward reached into his suit jacket for another cigarette.

Cole pointed at Seward. "If I don't get back down

to the lobby in seven minutes and call the person I'm working with, she will take the tape to her people and President Kennedy's assassination will be playing on every television set in America within a few hours. That tape clearly shows Kennedy being shot by someone standing behind the fence on the grassy knoll in Dealey Plaza." Cole shrugged. "But why am I telling you what you already know? The point is, Mr. Seward, everyone will see what you've been trying to hide from the American public for thirty-five years. The investigation into the assassination will be reopened and everyone on the Hill will get involved. I can't wait to get my front-row seat at the Congressional hearings that will follow."

Out of the corner of his eye, Cole noticed a short figure in a dark suit moving into the doorway of the suite's kitchen.

Seward glanced at Anthony Bianco nervously. "All right, Mr. Egan, you've made your point." Seward lighted the cigarette and the match shook in his hand as he took a second look at the short man.

"That's better," Cole muttered, satisfied that Seward had capitulated to the demands so quickly. Still, he wasn't finished. "I need to see Nicki before I leave."

Seward didn't hesitate. He nodded at Magee, who moved back to the bedroom door.

Cole noticed that people seemed to be moving faster now that the short man had appeared.

Magee was back from the bedroom quickly, leading Nicki into the living room.

When she saw Cole, she bolted past Magee and ran into Cole's arms. "Please help me," she sobbed. "I'm so scared."

He held her tightly as she cried. "Everything's going to be all right, Nicki. I guarantee it."

27

UPSTAIRS, THE MORNING RUSH HAD ALREADY BEGUN AS business people hurried into the airport terminal to catch departing flights. But down in the baggage claim area, one floor below the ticket counters, things were still calm. Down here there were just a few people being dropped off in front of the arrival area to avoid the traffic jam on the upper level, a skeleton crew of car rental people behind their respective counters, and a few skycaps resting on their hand trucks.

Cole stood in front of the baggage carousel and scanned the floor once more, wondering how many of the people down here were really DIA. He caught the eye of a woman behind the Hertz counter. She seemed to be studying him too intently.

Maybe it was just his imagination working overtime again. He glanced at the monitors listing the arriving flights, then at his watch. It was almost time.

Suddenly he spotted them. Nicki was between Seward and the man who had met Cole in the Sofitel lobby. She wore jeans, a bright yellow sweatshirt with the hood pulled up over her head and sunglasses. Seward and the other man each held one of her elbows tightly.

Cole watched Nicki and the two men walk slowly through the baggage area from the other end of the terminal. He glanced up at the monitors again. Where the hell were the people? The information on the screen indicated that the flight had arrived. They should have been here by now.

Cole could see Seward's kindly face now, as he was only a few feet away. Seward was nothing but a wolf in sheep's clothing, Cole thought to himself. He glanced around again. This wasn't going to work.

Then suddenly people were streaming down from the upper level, streaming down the stairs and the escalators, enveloping Seward and Nicki and the other man like a flood. The flight from Tokyo had reached its Minneapolis destination and four hundred tired passengers were now rushing toward the carousel to retrieve their luggage. As deserted as the area had been five minutes ago, it was now a beehive of activity.

Cole smiled as he watched Seward and the other man look around nervously, straining to keep tabs on their associates stationed at different locations around the baggage area. Cole followed their eyes and quickly picked out the accomplices, obvious as they too strained to keep track of the bright yellow sweatshirt Nicki wore. He smiled to himself despite the situation. In life, timing was everything. He had studied the airport arrival information and checked with the skycaps before specifying to Seward that 6:45 would be the exchange time and carousel number two would be the location. The skycaps had confirmed that luggage from this flight always came to carousel two. But the flight could have been late. More often than not, long international flights were. Fortunately, this time it wasn't.

Then the second flight arrived, this one from Berlin, and the baggage claim area was suddenly packed.

Cole threaded his way through the mass of people until he was standing directly in front of Seward.

"Where's your trade bait?" Seward asked loudly over the buzz of several hundred conversations.

"I'll give it to you when Nicki is holding my hand."

Seward nodded, then gestured to the other man, and they moved back.

Cole stepped forward and Nicki held out her arms, sobbing uncontrollably, tears running down her cheeks from beneath the sunglasses. But he didn't take her in his arms. Instead he dropped to his knees and carefully frisked her legs, then rose up again and searched her upper body for explosive devices.

"There's nothing on her!" Seward yelled over the background noise. He and the other man stepped forward. They didn't want Cole and Nicki to drift too far away.

Cole hugged Nicki and whispered instructions into her ear, pushing back the hood of the sweatshirt with his face as he nuzzled her neck. She tapped him on the shoulder as he had instructed her to do if she understood, and slowly he extended his left arm in the air, as if he were stretching, a signal to the bodyguard standing against the wall casually reading a newspaper.

The M-80—a powerful firecracker Cole had purchased at an outlet in a small town west of Billings on the way to meet the jet NBC had sent for him and Tori—exploded with a deafening roar.

Instantly the people at the baggage claim panicked, reduced to the primal urge of survival at the sound of a blast they were certain had been made by a bomb.

They screamed, pushed others down, and climbed over strangers and friends and family members in their singleminded attempt to escape. Then another M-80 exploded and the panic turned to absolute chaos. Seward and the other man dropped to the floor at the sound of the second blast.

Cole grabbed Nicki's wrist and yanked her toward the luggage conveyor disappearing down into the basement of the airport. It was just now beginning to transport bags up from carts that had met the flight from Tokyo minutes before. As Cole and Nicki stepped onto the stainless steel carousel, it began to turn and they lost their balance.

Seward was back on his feet, shouting orders at the disguised agents, but then he was knocked off his feet as one of the bodyguards ran him down.

Cole grabbed Nicki, pushed her into the opening atop the carousel and followed her down. They plunged, tumbling over suitcases and bags moving up the conveyor belt.

Tori was waiting at the bottom in the luggage staging area, wearing a baggage handler uniform she had managed to procure. "This way!" she ordered.

"Hey! What the hell's going on?" A man unloading one of the carts dropped the suitcase he was about to place on the belt and moved toward them.

From her jacket Tori withdrew the General's gun and leveled it at the man. It had been easy to gain access to the area, so lax was airport security. "Get out of here! Now!"

"Your world, lady." The man backpedaled quickly, unwilling to confront someone with a gun.

Cole glanced up the conveyor belt, but there was still no sign of pursuers. "Come on!" he urged, taking Nicki's hand and pulling her down a long corridor.

Tori sprinted after them.

"You're safe now, sweetheart," Cole assured Nicki as he urged her forward. The door leading out of the terminal and onto the tarmac was only fifty feet away.

As they neared the door, Commander Magee stepped out of a small office to the right, gun drawn. Tori saw him first and screamed.

"Drop the gun!" Magee yelled, nodding at Tori.

But Tori ignored the order and brought the gun up to Cole's head. "Give me the tape," she said calmly.

"What the—" Magee pointed his weapon at Cole, then back at Tori, then back at Cole, uncertain of what was happening.

"You bitch," Cole whispered, turning to look at Tori.

"The tape," she said smugly. "Give it to me."

"What is . . . what is going on?" Magee stammered.

"I'm DIA," Tori said evenly. "I'm Special Agent Victoria Brown."

"DIA?" Magee asked incredulously.

"Yes." She dug into Cole's jacket, found the Dealey Tape in a large inside pocket and pulled it out. "Bingo." She moved toward Magee.

But he kept his gun pointed at her. "Stop right there."

She obeyed.

"Drop the gun," he ordered.

"I work for Seward, you moron," she hissed. "I told you, I'm DIA, Operation Snowfall."

At the mention of Seward's name and the operation, Magee dropped the barrel of the gun for a second. It was his undoing. Cole turned as if to run back down the corridor. Instantly Magee raised his gun at Cole and away from Tori, and in that second Tori aimed and fired. The bullet exploded into Magee's chest, spraying the cinderblock wall behind him with blood. He fell back, screaming and sputtering.

Cole turned and sprinted to where Magee lay and stepped on the wrist that clenched the gun in a death grip, then bent over and yanked it free.

Tori stood in the corridor, paralyzed, watching Magee die, her face contorted in horror.

"This way." Cole moved to the door to the tarmac and held it open. "Let's go," he yelled. Nicki staggered outside but Tori remained transfixed, staring down at Magee's body. Cole grabbed Tori's arm and shook her. "It was him or us. You did what you had to do." He pulled her after him out the door.

The Gulfstream IV stood on the tarmac, engines roaring. Cole, Tori and Nicki raced across the asphalt toward it as one of the bodyguards stood ready to help them up the stairs.

As Tori moved into the jet, she slipped the Dealey Tape into Cole's hand. "Here."

"Thanks." He smiled at her. "You were incredible."

The bodyguard slammed the plane's door shut and yelled an all-clear to the pilot. Immediately the plane was moving toward the end of the runway.

"I was terrified, Cole," Tori admitted, collapsing into a leather seat.

Cole smiled. "You didn't let on. I was convinced there for a second that you really were with the DIA. Dropping Seward's name was a perfect touch. Magee bought the whole thing. I'm glad Bennett mentioned Seward's name in the video store."

As Tori put her head back and closed her eyes for a moment, Cole turned back to Nicki and put his arms around her. "Are you okay?"

She nodded.

"They didn't hurt you, did they?"

"No." She shook her head and put her arms around his neck. "I love you," she whispered. "I'm sorry I treated you so badly in Duluth."

"You had every right to treat me that way."

"No, I didn't," she sobbed.

Cole glanced toward the front of the plane. "I need to go up to the cockpit for a few seconds, Nicki. The pilot might need a little urging if the tower rejects his request for takeoff. But I'll be right back."

"Okay."

Cole guided Nicki into a seat, then turned and moved up the aisle. "Beautiful morning for a flight, huh, guys?" he asked, leaning into the cockpit.

The pilot glanced up at Cole with a quizzical expression. "Yeah, sure," he responded.

There were no planes in front of the Gulfstream as it taxied toward the end of the runway, and ninety seconds later they were poised to take off.

Then the flight controller's voice came through the plane's radio. "Gulfstream N4273B, you are cleared for takeoff."

28

La Crosse, Wisconsin, would be the refuge. There they would be back on the ground in minutes, probably before Seward could scramble a jet at the Air National Guard unit based at the Minneapolis airport. Still, Cole figured, Seward might be able to track the Gulfstream on radar by using his senior DIA status to gain access to the airport control tower, then send a contingency of local police officials to meet them in La Crosse when he realized where they were headed. They might have escaped Seward for now, but they weren't safe yet. Far from it.

This early in the morning the La Crosse airport wasn't busy and they were able to land quickly. As soon as the Gulfstream had stopped rolling, they pushed open the plane's door and raced down the steps and across the tarmac, expecting to confront local officials rushing out to intercept them. But they saw nothing except a quiet airfield. Quickly they rented a car at the Avis counter and sped away. Only after they had crossed into Illinois did they begin to relax. When they reached Pennsylvania, Tori actually mentioned the word "confidence." And now that they had made it to Greenwich, Connecticut—home of Raymond Burgess, executive vice president of NBC News—they were allowing themselves to believe that they might really succeed.

"Turn here," Tori directed, studying the scrawl on the piece of paper in her hands—instructions that Burgess had given her by phone when she and Cole had stopped in Cardwell, Montana, after fleeing Helena.

Cole steered the car off the main road and onto a country lane. Through trees and morning mist he caught glimpses of huge houses standing at the end of long driveways. Greenwich was home to many wealthy senior executives who commuted to work in New York City each day via the Metro North railroad or by limousine.

"There!" Tori pointed. "That's it."

Cole whipped the steering wheel to the right and gunned the car down a driveway lined by tall oaks. He skidded to a stop beside a blue Mercedes station wagon and reached back for the Dealey Tape. "Come on, princess," he whispered to Nicki, who was dozing in the backseat. "You can't stay here."

"Okay," she said, awakening quickly.

Cole helped Nicki from the car and they followed Tori down the brick path to the mansion's main entrance. The door was already open as they reached the front step. Ray Burgess stood in the foyer, a steaming mug of coffee in one hand, and ushered them in.

"Hello, Tori." Burgess had a deep, naturally commanding voice.

"Hi, Ray." Her gravelly voice was shaking.

"Hello." Cole shook Burgess's hand. "I'm Cole Egan."

"Hi, Cole, I'm Ray Burgess. It's good to meet you." Burgess was of average height and twenty pounds overweight after years of desk work. He was polite, but direct as well, as if a huge story was breaking somewhere in the world at that exact moment and he might be forced to excuse himself from the conversation at any minute. "I'm looking forward to seeing your little tape."

Cole heard a hint of cynicism in the way Burgess accented "little." He smiled to himself. Burgess's attitude was going to change very quickly. "Ray, this is Nicki Anderson."

"Hello," Burgess said gently. Tori had told Burgess of Nicki's hostage ordeal.

"Hello."

"Perhaps Nicki could wait for us out here." Cole nodded at a sofa in the living room.

"Of course," Burgess agreed.

Cole led her to the sofa, kissed her hand, then moved back toward Tori and Burgess.

"Where's your family, Ray?" Tori asked as she and Cole walked with Burgess down the hallway to his study. "Don't you have a couple of children?"

"Yes, but everyone's away at my mother's place down in Florida for Thanksgiving. I'm flying down there tomorrow to join them."

"Oh."

"Come in." Burgess motioned for Cole and Tori to follow him into his large study. It was a wreck. Newspapers and magazines lay strewn on the rolltop desk, the leather couch and the floor. "Sorry about the mess," Burgess said as he took the cassette case from Cole and made his way through the clutter.

"I would never have guessed that you'd be such a slob at home." Tori laughed as she surveyed the room. "Your office at Rockefeller Center is so neat."

Burgess flipped on the television and the VCR sitting on the middle shelf of a huge bookcase against the wall opposite the desk. "I've got to have someplace to unwind." He took the Dealey Tape out of the *Reds* case and inserted it into the machine. "Now let's see about this piece of history," he muttered as he backpedaled through the mess to his desk chair. "Both of you, please sit down."

They obeyed, moving several magazines from the couch cushions before they could sit.

When the tape had finished playing for the fifth time, Ray Burgess put his head back and began laughing. It was all he could do. He had been cynical when Tori called from Montana, excited by what she claimed to have, but not overly so. He had learned after many years in the news business that these kinds of things often turned out to be major disappointments. But not this time. Her excitement was justified. The rifle was so obvious over the fence, the killing shot so clearly fired from that rifle. "This is incredible, Tori, really."

She couldn't hide her smile of satisfaction. "Thank you."

"It's going to make for wonderful television," Burgess said confidently. He looked at Cole. "We'll have you over to the studios the night we air it, Cole. Maybe we'll interview you."

"I don't know about that," Cole replied. The less personal publicity, the better, he thought to himself.

"Just one thing before we get to the money, Cole." Burgess's demeanor became serious.

"Yes?"

"I need to know that this is the only copy of the tape. I can't pay you all this money, then see it playing on Fox tomorrow night."

"I understand." Cole glanced at Tori, then back at Burgess. "Ray, as far as I know, this is the only copy left. But I'll make a deal with you."

"What kind of deal?"

"I know you need time to line up advertisers for the broadcast, and you need time to promote the tape so you can have the nation's attention. If you promise to air the tape within six weeks, I'll return the money if that video shows up on any other network, unless it's someone in your organization who leaks it. And as another sign of good faith, you can pay me half now and half when you air it."

Burgess nodded. "That's very fair, Cole. I think NBC can live with that arrangement."

As he finished speaking, the doorbell rang. Burgess placed the coffee mug on the desk, rose and walked to the bay window. "It's Federal Express," he said, shaking his head. "Christ, I must get more of these deliveries than anyone on earth. I'll be right back." He moved quickly across the study.

Cole glanced warily at the tape clenched tightly in Burgess's hand as he hurried from the room.

As he left Tori reached across the couch and hugged Cole tightly. "I can't believe it. We made it."

"It's not on the air yet," Cole warned.

"It will be."

Burgess was back quickly. He walked across the study and dropped the purple-and-orange-lettered FedEx package on the desk. "Let's get to it, people," Burgess said. He moved to the wall safe behind the door and tapped a combination on the keypad. "I've got a million dollars in cash here, Cole. You'll get six-point-five more this afternoon, via a wire to your bank account, and you'll get the rest when we air the tape." He pulled open the steel door, extracted a tan brief-case, inserted the tape he was holding into the safe, closed and relocked it, then moved to the desk and placed the briefcase atop the clutter. He popped open the briefcase and stepped back. "Take a look, Cole. It's all here. A million dollars. You can count it if you like."

Cole rose from the couch and moved slowly to the desk. He smiled as he saw the rows of bills neatly stacked inside the briefcase. "That won't be neces-sary, Ray."

"We'll count on you to pay your taxes, Cole." Bur-gess winked at Tori as he sat down on the couch next to her. "It's unbelievable, Tori. I've been in the news business a long time and this is going to rank as the biggest story I've ever been a part of by far."

Cole heard them starting to discuss marketing and promotion efforts—when the tape would air, who they would interview on the broadcast before airing the footage, who would make the best host. Their words faded as he stared at the money. The risks had been incredible, but the money was right here in front of him now. There was enough here to repay the people at the Blue Moon and completely pay off his mort-gage. Burgess and Tori's conversation faded back in. He shook his head. He was exhausted, almost out on his feet, but he had one more sprint to make. He snapped the briefcase closed and turned toward them. "Let's go, Tori."

"I'm going to stay," she answered, looking up from the couch. "Ray and I have so much to talk about."

A faint alarm went off in Cole's brain, but he was

too tired to pay attention. His eyelids felt like two bricks. "Okay, we'll hook up later."

"Fine."

"I'll show you out." Burgess rose from the couch and walked Cole and Nicki back down the brick path to the driveway.

Cole and Burgess shook hands, then Cole slipped behind the wheel, turned the car around and headed out the driveway toward the lane.

Burgess watched the car disappear, then hurried back into the house. As he moved into the study, he stopped suddenly. Sitting beside Tori on the couch was a short man in a dark suit whom he recognized immediately. "Oh, Christ." Burgess's voice was eerily calm.

Tori stood up from the couch slowly. "I'm sorry, Ray."

Never trust anyone. He had lived by those words his entire existence.

Cole slammed Burgess's Mercedes station wagon into fourth gear as he tore down the country lane. Tori had shown herself worthy time after time, putting herself in the line of fire over and over, even tearing her fingernail off with her teeth. But something told him she was too willing to put herself on the line. No one did the things she had done just for a career, or to impress a parent. He could have been convinced that she was doing it to help his father. Love was a strong motivator, but since they'd left the General's house yesterday, Tori hadn't mentioned Jim Egan once. Cole hadn't told her he'd sent the Helena police to the mountains overlooking Powell with the phony cult suicide story, and she hadn't asked.

Maybe he was wrong. Maybe she was as loyal as

anyone could be. But the hell with it. If he was wrong, she'd just have to understand. It was exactly the way he had felt as the cleaning woman had tried too hard to get into the Gilchrist screening room. It was better to be safe than sorry.

He glanced over his shoulder at the briefcase on the Mercedes's backseat. Inside was a million dollars and the Dealey Tape. He had placed the tape inside the briefcase as Burgess distracted Tori on the couch with talk of marketing plans and potential interviews for the television special. He had picked the tape up from where Burgess left it on the cluttered desk—typically neat as a pin—and placed it in the briefcase. The tape Burgess had placed in the safe was a phony. He and Burgess had arranged everything over the phone—including the plan to use Burgess's Mercedes in case someone had rigged the rental car with a bomb while they were inside—after Cole had met with Seward at the Sofitel. Tori had mentioned Burgess's name several times, so Cole had contacted him at NBC from a pay phone. It seemed overly cautious to Burgess—he had no reason to believe Tori was anything but honest—but if Cole had doubts, so be it.

Cole had decided to throw in with Burgess immediately. Burgess was a known quantity, a well-paid executive who had been with NBC and in the news business for years, not someone who would likely be influenced by bribes or government intimidation. But Tori was still a wild card. A woman who was trying too hard.

Never trust anyone completely. Cole had remembered hearing Malcolm X say that in an interview once. But in the final analysis you had to trust people for at least short periods of time, sometimes people you didn't even know. Indeed, sometimes that was easier. Because more often than not, the better you got to know someone, the less you trusted them.

Cole squinted as the morning sun broke through the branches hanging over the country lane as he stared at the house number on the mailbox just up ahead. It was the same number Burgess had written on the pad hidden in the Mercedes's glove compartment. The house number of a senior executive of General Electric, NBC's parent company.

Cole slammed on the Mercedes's brakes to make the turn into the GE executive's driveway, then put his hand on Nicki's knee. "Hold on, sweetheart," Cole said. "We're almost there."

Nicki put her hand on top of Cole's and smiled at him. "I love you, Cole."

"I love you, too." Nicki would be the exception to his rule. From now on, he would trust her completely.

"Ray, this is Anthony Bianco," Tori said, her eyes locked on the floor as she motioned toward the small man on the couch. "He's—"

"I know who he is," Burgess interrupted. "He's Little Tony Bianco, also known as the Chairman. He is the leader of the Bianco crime family, the most powerful Mafia family in this country." Burgess tried not to let Bianco see that his hands were shaking badly. "A friend of mine at ABC pointed you out in a Manhattan restaurant one day. You were at a small table in the back, hiding from photographers."

Bianco rose from the couch. "Get the tape from the safe," he ordered gruffly. He didn't want to waste time. "Right now."

Burgess glanced over Bianco's shoulder. At the study doorway were two very large men, so he was in no position to protest. Burgess moved to the safe, opened it, retrieved the decoy tape he had put inside the safe a few minutes before and handed it to Bianco.

Bianco gave the tape to one of the men in the door-way without taking his eyes from Burgess. "You've done a wise thing, Mr. Burgess," Bianco said in his gruff voice. "We won't harm you, and NBC will be reimbursed its million dollars."

"You're an honorable man," Burgess said sarcastically.

"I'm a businessman." The two men at the study door moved aside as Bianco turned away from Burgess. Bianco moved into the hallway, then stopped. In front of him were ten Connecticut state policemen, as well as the man Bianco had left outside Burgess's house as a lookout. The man was now in handcuffs—and fearful for his life. Bianco had no sympathy for men who failed him.

Bob Maddux, the General Electric executive who lived up the country lane from Burgess, trotted across his wide lawn as the blue Mercedes raced up his drive-way. Behind Maddux was an army of local police offi-cers, including his best friend in the world, Frank Shaw, the Greenwich chief of police. Not even an order from the president of the United States would have caused Shaw to ignore Maddux's request of abso-lute police protection for Cole Egan and the Dealey Tape. No one was going to get the tape away from Cole at this point. Especially since the state police had just radioed from Ray Burgess's house to say that they had apprehended Anthony Bianco trying to take pos-session of the decoy tape.

Maddux opened the door of the Mercedes as Cole pulled the car to a stop. He reached inside and pumped Cole's hand vigorously. "Congratulations, Mr. Egan. You're with friends now."

When the man finished pumping his hand, Cole slumped over the steering wheel. It was over, and now all he wanted to do was sleep. He turned toward Nicki. For several moments they simply stared at each other, then they hugged each other tightly.

29

"You idiot!" Jamison glared at General Zahn from behind the Oval Office desk. "How could you let this happen?"

"I'm sorry, Mr. President. I thought Seward and I had everything under control."

The veins in Jamison's forehead bulged. Finally he shook his head and closed his eyes. "Leave us, General."

Zahn rose and exited the office, glad to be out of the line of fire.

Jamison glanced at Walsh. "Tell me everything, Eric."

Walsh was far away, wondering how quickly he could get to Wall Street and insulate himself from the maelstrom bearing down on Jamison's administration.

"Eric!" Jamison roared.

Walsh snapped out of his trance. "Sorry, Mr. President."

"I want details, Eric."

"Yes, sir." Walsh could suddenly sense his multimillion-dollar compensation package slipping away. As much as the investment banks now wanted access to his long list of contacts, they would stay away from him if he became embroiled in a scandal. "Somehow Cole Egan eluded us in Minneapolis yesterday and this morning made it to Greenwich, Connecticut, where he showed up at the home of Ray Burgess, a senior executive at NBC News." Walsh lowered his voice. "Anthony Bianco was waiting at Burgess's home."

"How the hell did *Bianco* find out about Egan going to this guy's house in Greenwich?" Jamison shouted, suddenly unconcerned about using the Mafia boss's name in the Oval Office.

"A woman named Victoria Brown was the informant. Ms. Brown is a low-level producer at NBC who somehow befriended Cole Egan. She was with Egan in Wisconsin and Montana," Walsh explained. "We're still checking her out. Checking out exactly what her part was in all of this. Anyway, she was the one who tipped Bianco's people off to the fact that Egan was coming to Burgess's house in Greenwich. From what we understand, she dated someone in the Mafia when she was in her early twenties and hasn't been able to disengage herself from them since."

"That's because you *can't* disengage yourself from the Mafia once you've become involved with them. We know that, don't we, Eric?"

"I guess we do," he agreed dismally.

"All right, get a court order, Eric," Jamison barked. "We'll confiscate the tape. If that doesn't work, we'll take it from NBC citing national security concerns."

Walsh shook his head. "You'd sound like Richard Nixon firing Archibald Cox as Watergate special prosecutor. You'd sound like a man who's panicking. And when the wolves see that, they attack. You know that, Mr. President. Besides, NBC has probably made several copies of the tape by now. How would we know we'd gotten them all? The press would be all over us. Someone would tip them off that the pressure to suppress the tape was coming from inside the Oval Office. Then there'd be real trouble."

"Then what the hell are we going to do?" Jamison raged. "We've already *got* real trouble, for Christ's sake!"

Walsh folded his hands. "We'll do nothing," he said calmly as the thought struck him.

"What?"

"Bianco will be out of jail in a matter of hours, because what the hell can they really charge him with? Trespassing? Breaking and entering? Attempted kidnapping if they get creative, I guess. But nothing really serious. He'll be back in his Brooklyn compound this afternoon." Walsh's mind was working quickly now. "And we'll let NBC have their fun. We'll let them play the tape. The downside is that the American people completely lose faith in their government. They see they've been lied to for thirty-five years, but the hell with it. Most of them already believe that anyway. And we're talking about our personal survival here, so fuck the people." Walsh flicked a piece of lint off of his suit pants. "The other major problem is Anthony Bianco and our link to organized crime. If he really gets a bug up his ass, he could do us some damage."

Jamison shuddered. Bianco could explain the strange accident that had befallen his competitor in the North Carolina gubernatorial race nine years earlier. And that would be just for starters. There were many other crimes Bianco could convict him of. "He could implicate me in a murder plot."

"But what's Bianco's incentive to do that?" Walsh asked. "He screws himself in the process. If he admits he murdered someone to win you the governorship of North Carolina, he's going to go to jail for a long time. If he does nothing and the tape is aired, he's going to come under a lot of heat as the Congressional hearings get cranked up and everyone on the Hill starts grandstanding. As he so rightly believes, many people will focus on the Mafia as the guilty party. But I think ultimately he'll opt to just take the heat of the Congressional hearings and the FBI. It's certainly better than spending the rest of his life in prison."

Jamison nodded. It made sense. "But there are a few others outside of Bianco's circle who could link me to the Mafia as well," he said ominously.

"That's true," Walsh agreed hesitantly.

For several moments they stared at each other, each fully aware of what the other man was thinking.

30

IT HAD ONLY BEEN A WEEK SINCE COLE'S TWO-THOU-sand-mile sprint across the country from Powell, Montana, to Ray Burgess's home in Greenwich, Connecticut, but already the bodies were turning up everywhere.

General Avery Zahn was discovered in a motel room naked, with a bullet through his brain. No one had been arrested for the murder—and no one ever would be.

Eric Walsh was found burned beyond recognition after a violent accident on I-95 south of Washington. It took four days for the coroner to receive the dental records so that Walsh's body could be identified.

Commander John Magee was discovered floating facedown in the Potomac River, his death officially ruled an accidental drowning despite the fact that there was no water found in his lungs.

And William Seward was discovered sprawled on the couch in the study of his isolated Virginia cabin, his death officially ruled a suicide even though the two men who had killed him had also sliced off the index finger of his left hand and thrown it in a Dumpster on their way back to New York.

They were seemingly unrelated deaths. But all of the victims were killed by members of the Bianco crime family at the direction of Anthony Bianco and the president of the United States.

President Jamison sat alone in the Oval Office staring out the window. Zahn had sarcastically noted the irony in his feeble attempt at personality. How accurate and prophetic, Jamison thought to himself. Bodies were turning up all over the place, just as they had after Kennedy's death.

Jamison put his head back, closed his eyes and took a large swallow of scotch from the glass in his hand. All links between the Bianco crime family and the Oval Office had now been cut. Only he and Anthony Bianco knew what had happened. Bianco had made the decision to remain quiet, just as Eric Walsh had predicted. And now Walsh and the others were permanently quiet.

Cole met Tori in Grand Central Station at the height of rush hour. She had assured him when she called him that there was nothing to worry about, but of course that was what she would say.

"Hello, Cole," she said as they met in the middle of the main floor. Commuters rushed by them on all sides, headed toward trains.

"Hello," he said icily.

"I know you're angry with me."

"It all worked out." Cole kept glancing around, searching for any sign of enemies. He wanted to keep this meeting short.

She saw his discomfort. "I told you over the phone, there's nothing to worry about."

"And I should trust you?"

"You don't trust anyone, so I wouldn't expect that."

"Mmm." There were plainclothes policemen in the station to protect him, but he still felt vulnerable. The police had urged him not to come, but for some reason he was willing to take the risk to see her one last time.

"I came with a message," Tori said.

"What's that?" he asked.

"You're safe."

Cole gazed at her. "What?"

"You don't have to worry about being killed. Anthony Bianco has no interest in stirring up any more trouble. He realizes that if something were to happen to you, he and his people would come under even greater scrutiny. Anthony is a businessman above all else, and he realizes your demise would not be good for business."

Cole raised one eyebrow. "You and Mr. Bianco are on a first-name basis?"

"We have been for a long time. He's not the monster you think he is."

"I think you need to take a reality pill."

"There's something else," Tori said, ignoring Cole's comment. She knew she would never be able to convince Cole that Bianco had any redeeming qualities, so there was no point dwelling on the issue. "Your debt at the Blue Moon has been erased."

Despite his effort not to, Cole grinned. "Excuse me?"

"You heard me."

"So the Blue Moon was all part of what happened? All connected to the Dealey Tape?"

Tori shook her head. "No, completely unrelated,

but Anthony found out about it. He finds out about everything. He's personally picking up your tab as a show of good faith. In return, he asks that you not appear on the NBC special the night the network broadcasts the tape."

"I wasn't planning to anyway," Cole answered quickly. "And you can tell your benefactor that I will be repaying the debt at the Blue Moon myself."

"Whatever."

"Fine." Cole turned to go, then hesitated. "How long have you been involved with those people?"

"A long time," she said solemnly.

"But why?"

"It seemed exciting when I was young, and it was the last thing my mother wanted me to do."

"But you must have realized"—he paused—"I mean, at some point, why didn't you get away from them?"

She smiled sadly. "You don't do that, Cole. They arranged for several women to 'run into' your father over the years. I was one of them and ultimately the one your father wanted. I couldn't walk away from that situation. They would have killed me."

"So they were following my father all that time?" Cole asked dubiously.

"Yes. I told you that the day we met. A lot of people were."

"That's incredible." He glanced up at the domed ceiling. "Well, I've got to go."

She nodded. She wanted him to stay a little longer, but there was nothing else to say. "Goodbye, Cole."

"Goodbye." He turned and disappeared into the crowd.

She gazed after him for several moments, then retraced her steps to the black limousine waiting on

Forty-second Street in front of Grand Central. Once inside the vehicle she moved across the bench seat until she was beside Anthony Bianco. He smiled at her for a moment, then kissed her on both cheeks.

31

BARRY NELSON SORTED THROUGH THE STACK OF ENVElopes on his desk, found the appropriate one and tossed it at Cole, who sat on the other side of the desk.

Cole ripped the envelope open and pulled out the Gilchrist & Company check. It was made out for eight hundred thousand dollars, which was the after-tax proceeds of his one-and-a-half-million-dollar bonus. "Good Friday was good this year," Cole noted calmly. At Gilchrist, Good Friday was bonus day, which was the second Friday of January, not the Friday before Easter.

"Yeah." Nelson was gazing out of his office onto the trading floor. "You had a nice run there in December as interest rates kept going down. You ended the year making thirty million dollars for the firm." He pointed at Cole. "But don't get cocky," he warned.

"You don't have to worry about that," Cole assured Nelson as he stood up to go. "I'm resigning."

"What?"

"I'm going to take some time off and enjoy myself for a while."

Nelson was incensed. "You can't quit. Eight hundred thousand might sound like a lot of money, Cole, but it isn't. Your standard of living will just increase to meet your income. It always happens that way. I've seen it a million times around here. You'll burn through that check in no time. I promise you."

Cole nodded. "You're probably right." In fact, the small ranch outside of Livingston, Montana, was going to cost close to three million dollars. But the second half of the NBC money had arrived in his account this morning. After tax, he was worth almost nine million dollars now.

"Don't come back here looking for a job, Cole," Nelson blurted out. "I'm warning you. If you walk out of here, that's it."

Cole smiled as he reached the office door. No one at Gilchrist had any idea that he was the one who had recovered the tape a nation would be glued to their television sets watching in a few hours. And after the program concluded, they still wouldn't. NBC had agreed not to reveal how they had located the Dealey Tape. Cole opened the office door to leave.

"I'm not kidding!" Nelson screamed.

Cole picked up the autographed baseball from on top of the file cabinet beside the office door. "Here, Barry." He tossed it to Nelson. "Knock yourself out."

Nelson grabbed the baseball out of the air and heaved it against a picture of the 1941 Yankees he had put up on the wall to replace the one of the 1927 team.

Cole was still chuckling as he reached his chair on the government desk. He picked up a small bag filled with personal items, then leaned over the bulkhead. The two traders on the other side were staring blankly at their computer screens. "You guys still haven't heard from Gebauer, huh?" he asked.

One of the traders glanced up, pushed out his lower lip and shook his head. "Not since right after you started your vacation back at the end of November. His wife hasn't heard from him, either."

Cole knew what that meant. Lewis Gebauer was dead. He waved. "See you guys later."

"What are you doing tonight, Cole?" one of the traders yelled after him.

"I'm gonna watch that Kennedy assassination special," he called over his shoulder. "It sounds interesting."

"It does at that," the trader murmured. He would be tuned in, too.

The entire nation would.

Cole, Nicki and Jim Egan sat before the wide-screen television in the living room of the Plaza Hotel suite Cole had rented for the evening. It was ten thirty-five and the interviews were finally over. The Dealey Tape was about to roll for the first time on national television.

Jim sat in a chair while Cole and Nicki sat close to each other on the couch, their hands locked together.

Even though he had watched the tape of the assassination many times, Cole's heart was beating rapidly. Not out of anticipation, out of fear. They had come so far, but there was always the chance that somehow the DIA or the Mafia would get to the tape. But then it was there on the screen in front of them for the world to see. The now familiar sight of the rifle over the fence, and President Kennedy's head snapping back.

Nicki gasped at the sight.

Then the limousine was moving away and it was

over. NBC had agreed to cut it after that. Jim Egan's face would never be part of the tape again.

After the tape had finished the first time, Jim rose and moved to the bar on the other side of the room. Cole followed his father while Nicki remained on the couch, her eyes glued to the television screen. NBC would show the tape again several times, and she wanted to see it as many times as possible. For Cole and his father, it was enough to simply know it had made it to the airways.

"Cheers, Dad." Cole touched his glass to his father's. Cole had spent almost every day with his father over the last six weeks, making up for a lifetime of absence, and he had enjoyed every moment. Now his father didn't have much time left. "You did it."

"We did it," Jim asserted, his voice weak.

They sipped scotch in silence for several minutes.

Cole finally spoke. "All of what we've been through and what we know really points the finger squarely at the Mafia as the ones who killed Kennedy. Don't you think, Dad?" he asked quietly, so Nicki wouldn't hear.

Jim took another long swallow from the glass. "You'll never know who *really* killed John Kennedy, Cole. Be very careful of who you accuse."

"Okay." Cole heard the warning. "Hey, there's something I want to ask you."

"What's that?"

"How did William Seward know to put me under surveillance? How did he know I would be the one to get the tape?"

"Pretty logical, don't you think?"

"I suppose, but—"

"And he didn't put just you under surveillance," Jim interrupted. "He had several people followed, including Bennett Smith."

"How did Seward know when it would happen? Or have I been under surveillance all my life?"

Jim shook his head. "No. In the DIA we had to have complete physicals every six months. I'm sure he started tailing people as soon as he found out I had cancer."

Cole glanced back at the television set. The tape was playing for the fourth time and Nicki was still awestruck by the images.

"Cole?"

"Yes, Dad." Cole had been watching the television again. NBC was highlighting the rifle coming over the fence, and an expert was analyzing what make of rifle it was and who would have been likely to use that type of gun.

"I want to apologize," Jim said firmly.

"For what?"

"First, for never being around."

"It's all right. We both know—"

"Second," his father interrupted, "for your mother's death. I should have been there to protect Andrea, but I was away so much. It's been very hard for me all these years to think of her being attacked. I could have prevented that if I'd been around."

Cole glanced down at the floor. "Did you actually see her body when you got back?"

"No." His eyes narrowed as he sensed something in Cole's voice.

"Was anyone ever arrested for the crime?"

"No," Jim said. "If I had ever found out who they were . . ." His voice trailed off.

Cole took a sip of his drink, wondering whether to tell his father what he suspected. "Dad, I don't know if this will make you feel better or worse."

"What?"

"Was Mom ever sick?"

Jim hesitated. "Come to think of it, yes. A couple of times while I was away. It seemed to get worse over time. It was pretty bad right before she was attacked."

"I don't think Mom was attacked, Dad," Cole said quietly. "I think the long-haired hippie story was made up."

"What are you talking about?"

"I think Mom was poisoned. There was a massive amount of arsenic in her body when she died."

"How the hell do you know that?"

"I visited the Thomases before I went to Wisconsin, and I saw Mom's brush in her old room. It was among the things you had sent them after she died. I called Anita, my receptionist at Gilchrist, from Montana and had her take the brush to a lab. The lab analyzed the—"

"—the hair in the brush," Jim Egan finished the sentence. Ice clinked against the side of his glass as his fingers began to tremble.

"Yes. They must have put it in her food or something so they could search the house."

"For what I had taken from her in Dealey Plaza." Cole's father shut his eyes.

"Yes. I'm going to present that lab analysis to someone in Washington."

"No, you aren't," Jim said quickly.

"But, Dad—"

"Cole, leave it alone. No good can come of you opening those wounds."

Cole hesitated several moments, then nodded. "Okay."

Jim pointed at the television. "Let's go back and sit down."

But Cole caught his father by the arm. "Just one more thing, Dad."

"What, son?"

"Why did you do it?"

Jim raised an eyebrow. "Do what?"

"Why did you pass the tape on to me the way you did? Why didn't you just sell it yourself? And why did you go to so much trouble to fake your own death?" The dimple appeared in Cole's cheek. "You put me in a couple of tight spots."

"Yes, I suppose I did, but I knew you could handle it." He chuckled as he took a sip from his glass. "I knew I had to make that tape available at some point. I couldn't have lived with myself if I hadn't. I also knew that the odds of me getting to either copy were very small after the DIA knew I was sick. They were watching me closely. Even if I had managed to get to one of them and sell it, I would have been killed very soon afterward." He swallowed hard, then nodded at the television. "I never would have been able to enjoy this moment with my son."

They both looked down at the floor, neither one certain of what to say.

Finally, Jim broke the silence. "Besides, if I'd been the one to sell it, the Internal Revenue Service would have taken most of your inheritance."

Cole looked up. "Huh?"

"You sold the tape for fifteen million dollars, right?"

"Yes."

"And you probably have eight or nine million left over?"

"Yes."

"If I had sold it, the IRS would have taken their chunk of income taxes *and* a huge inheritance tax when I died, and you'd only have about four million left. This way you avoided the inheritance tax and saved five million dollars. I think five million is worth a few tight spots."

"Maybe."

His father smiled. "I can't believe you didn't think of that. I thought you were supposed to be the financial genius in the family."

Cole shook his head, and they both laughed.

"Well, I'm going to bed," Jim finally said. "I'm tired." Cole had rented his father a separate room in the hotel. "Good night, Nicki," he called.

Nicki rose from the sofa and met Jim and Cole at the door of the suite. "Good night, Mr. Egan." She kissed Jim gently on the cheek.

He smiled at her, then turned to Cole. "See you in the morning, son."

"Right."

They shook and he was gone.

As Cole closed the door, Nicki slipped her arms around his neck and kissed him deeply.

"That was nice," he murmured when their lips had parted.

"Well, there's more where—"

"So nice," Cole interrupted, "that I've decided I want it permanently."

Nicki's eyes widened and she took a step back. "Do you mean?"

Cole lifted a small jewelry box from his suit pocket, opened it, and smiled broadly. "I sure do." He glanced down at the diamond shimmering atop the gold band. "Will you marry me?"

Once again Nicki put her arms around Cole and kissed him. "Just tell me where and when."